ANIMAL'S PEOPLE

ANIMAL'S PEOPLE

INDRA SINHA

**SIMON &
SCHUSTER**

London · New York · Sydney · Toronto

A CBS COMPANY

First published in Great Britain by Simon & Schuster UK Ltd, 2007
A CBS COMPANY

Copyright © Indra Sinha, 2007

3 5 7 9 10 8 6 4

Simon & Schuster UK Ltd
Africa House
64-78 Kingsway
London WC2B 6AH

www.simonsays.co.uk

Simon & Schuster Australia
Sydney

A CIP catalogue record for this book is available from the British Library

13-digit: 978-0-7432-5920-0
10-digit: 0-7432-5920-3

Printed and bound in Great Britain by
Mackays of Chatham Ltd, Chatham Kent

For Sunil

This story was recorded in Hindi on a series of tapes by a nineteen-year-old boy in the Indian city of Khaufpur. True to the agreement between the boy and the journalist who befriended him, the story is told entirely in the boy's words as recorded on the tapes. Apart from translating to English, nothing has been changed. Difficult expressions which turned out to be French are rendered in correct spelling for ease of comprehension. Places where a recording was stopped and later recommenced on the same tape are indicated by gaps. The recordings are of various lengths, and the tapes are presented in the order of numbering. Some tapes contain long sections in which there is no speech, only sounds such as bicycle bells, birds, snatches of music and in one case several minutes of sustained and inexplicable laughter.

A glossary has been provided.

Information about the city of Khaufpur can be found at *www.khaufpur.com*

I used to be human once. So I'm told. I don't remember it myself, but people who knew me when I was small say I walked on two feet just like a human being.

'So sweet you were, a naughty little angel. You'd stand up on tiptoe, Animal my son, and hunt in the cupboard for food.' This is the sort of thing they say. Only mostly there wasn't any food plus really it isn't people just Ma Franci who says this, she doesn't even say it that way, what she says is tu étais si charmant, comme un petit ange méchant, which is how they talk in her country, plus I'm not really her son nor any kind of angel but it's true Ma's known me all my life, which is nearly twenty years. Most people round here don't know their age, I do, because I was born a few days before that night, which no one in Khaufpur wants to remember, but nobody can forget.

'Such a beautiful little boy you were, when you were three, four, years. Huge eyes you had, black like the Upper Lake at midnight plus a whop- ping head of curls. How you used to grin. Tu étais un vrai bourreau des coeurs, your smile would break a mother's heart,' thus she'd talk.

I used to walk upright, that's what Ma Franci says, why would she lie? It's not like the news is a comfort to me. Is it kind to remind a blind man that he could once see? The priests who whisper magic in the ears of corpses, they're not saying, 'Cheer up, you used to be alive.' No one leans down and tenderly reassures the turd lying in the dust, 'You still resemble the kebab you once were . . .'

How many times did I tell Ma Franci, 'I no longer want to be human,' never did it sink in to that fucked up brain of hers, or maybe she just didn't believe me, which you can understand, seeing it used to be when I caught sight of myself – mirrors I avoid but there's such a thing as casting a shadow — I'd feel raw disgust. In my mad times when the voices were shouting inside my head I'd be filled with rage against all things that go or even stand on two legs. The list of my jealousies was endless; Ma Franci, the other nuns at the orphanage, Chukku the night watchman, women carrying pots on their heads, waiters balancing four plates per arm. I hated watching my friends play hopscotch. I detested the sight of dancers, performing bears brought by those dirty buggers from Agra, stilt-walkers, the one-leg-and-crutch of Abdul Saliq the Pir Gate beggar. I envied herons, goalposts, ladders leaning on walls. I eyed Farouq's bicycle and wondered if it too deserved a place in my list of hates.

How can you understand this?

The world of humans is meant to be viewed from eye level. Your eyes. Lift my head I'm staring into someone's crotch. Whole nother world it's, below the waist. Believe me, I know which one hasn't washed his balls, I can smell pissy gussets and shitty backsides whose faint stenches don't carry to your nose, farts smell extra bad. In my mad times I'd shout at people in the street, 'Listen, however fucking miserable you are, and no one's as happy as they've a right to be, at least you stand on two feet!'

Don't worry. Everything will get explained in due course. I'm not clever like you. I can't make fancy rissoles of each word. Blue kingfishers won't suddenly fly out of my mouth. If you want my story, you'll have to put up with how I tell it.

First thing I want to say, it's to the Kakadu Jarnalis, came here from Ostrali. Salaam Jarnalis, it's me, Animal, I'm talking to the tape. Not the one you gave. That one no longer works, rain got at it, black lumps are possibly scorpion-shit. I had to hide it after you left, I put it in a hole in the wall. Long it stayed there, I never used it like I promised, now it's fucked, I guess you are thinking what a waste of shorts.

My story you wanted, said you'd put it in a book. I did not want to talk about it. I said is it a big deal, to have my story in a book? I said, I am a small person not even human, what difference will my story make? You told me that sometimes the stories of small people in this world can achieve big things, this is the way you buggers always talk.

I said, many books have been written about this place, not one has changed anything for the better, how will yours be different? You will bleat like all the rest. You'll talk of *rights, law, justice*. Those words sound the same in my mouth as in yours but they don't mean the same, Zafar says such words are like shadows the moon makes in the Kampani's factory, always changing shape. On that night it was poison, now it's words that are choking us.

Remember me, Jarnalis? I remember you, the day you came here with Chunaram. How did you make the mistake of hiring that sisterfuck as your chargé d'affaires? With him it's anything for money, didn't he charge people to watch him rip off his little finger? I guess you weren't to know that collecting foreigners is a sideline of his. Daily he goes to meet the Shatabdi, waits on platform one, exact spot where the first-class air-conditioned bogie stops. You'll have got off the train looking clueless. Well, what else is Chunaram for? 'Yes please, want a taxi? Need a hotel? Best in Khaufpur. See the city? Want a guide? Need translate? Jarnalis?' Once he knew why you'd come he'll have promised to show you everything. The really savage things, the worst cases. People like me.

'This boy,' he'll have told you, 'he lost everything on that night.'

Such a look on your face when he brought you here, as you pushed aside the plastic sheet, bent your back through the gap in the wall. With what greed you looked about this place. I could feel your hunger. You'd devour everything. I watched you taking it in, the floor of earth, rough stone walls, dry dungcakes stacked near the hearth, smoke coiling in the air like a sardarji doing his hair.

When you saw me, your eyes lit up. Of course, you tried to hide it. Instantly you became all solemn. Your namasté had that tone I've come to know, a hushed respect as if you were speaking a prayer, like you were in the presence of the lord of death.

'Jarnalis,' Chunaram informed me, giggling like he's found a bag of gold, I'd already guessed.

'Speaks no Hindi,' says Chunaram. 'Animal, there's fifty rupees for you, just keep talking till the tape stops.'

'What should I talk about?'

'Usual, what else?' He's already backing out the door.

Oh your face, when he buggered off. Such alarm. But see, Chunaram has other things to do, he has a chai shop to run. When he gave you his salaam, did you see his nine fingers?

So then, what was to do? You were sitting there gazing at me in a ghurr-ghurr kind of way, as if your eyes were buttons and mine were buttonholes.

I said, 'Don't fucking stare or I won't speak.' I said it in Hindi, I'm not supposed to let on that I know some Inglis, Chunaram gets an extra bunce for translating. You gave a thumbs-up, carried right on staring. I called you a wanker. You nodded, smiled at me. Khaamush, silent then I'm. After some time I've joined another silence to the first.

Inside your skull thoughts were scrabbling like rats. I could hear them like voices in my own head – why has this boy stopped talking, queer as a winged snake is he, leant against the wall with such a look on his face, would be handsome if he weren't so sullen, what a chest he has, deep as a wrestler's, how does it spring from those twisted haunches to which are pawled legs like hanks of rope, oh god, his ribcage is heaving as if at any moment he may vomit, maybe he is ill, boy what is your problem, alas, my wordless enquiries cause his convulsions to grow worse, I think he may be going to have a fit, what will I do if he dies, oh dear, my further anxious attempts to communicate, with twisting 'wherefore' hand motions and raising of eyebrows, seem to cause violent shudders, bugger's lips are writhing in some kind of agony, should a doctor be called, where can one find a doctor in this place, where the hell am I anyway, what the fuck am I doing here?

Actually, Jarnalis, I was trying not to show that I was laughing at you. After that, what else, I talked. Your tape crawled. Then you were happy, this is what you had come for. You were like all the others, come to suck our stories from us, so strangers in far off countries can marvel there's so much pain in the world. Like vultures are you jarnaliss. Somewhere a bad thing happens, tears like rain in the wind, and look, here you come, drawn by the smell of blood. You have turned us Khaufpuris into storytellers, but always of the same story. Ous raat, cette nuit, that night, always that fucking night.

You listened politely, pretending to follow, smiling now and again pour m'encourager, as Ma Franci would say. You were so fucking sure I was talking about that night. You were hoping the gibberish sounds coming from my mouth were the horrible stories you'd come to hear. Well, fuck that. No way was I going to tell those stories. I've repeated them so often my teeth are ground smooth by the endless passage of words.

With no Chunaram to tell you what I was saying, I could say anything. I could sing a filthy song:

I may be just a twisted runt
But I can sniff your mother's cunt

5

Hahaha, oh dear, your face, you were wondering, the song this boy is singing, with such a nasty tune, what is it, sounds like a lament, but pourquoi il rit? You scribbled something in your book. Let me guess. 'Animal chanted a poem, probably a traditional song of mourning, just now he was crazy with grief.'

Jarnalis, you were such a fool. The best thing about you was your shorts. Six pockets, I counted. Two at the side, two on the front, two on the arse. With shorts like those a person does not need a house. From one pocket you fetched out a pack of cigarettes and from another a shiny lighter, it made a grinding noise when you flipped it, and a flame sprang up. I coveted that lighter, but more than that I craved your shorts.

Thus and thus time passed, Chunaram returned reeking of apologies and strong liquor, some Inglis gitpit passed between you. He said, 'I shall listen to the tape.' The thing squeaked like a rat having its back broken and I heard my own voice earning fifty rupees.

Well, Chunaram was appalled. He started shouting, with great tappings of the brow and circlings of the temple. 'You cretin! You are not right in your head. You have not said what's wanted.'

'Did as bid.'

'You must do it again. You must tell the real stories.'

'Balls to you!' says I with wanking gestures. 'Did I ask you to go and get drunk?'

'You miserable boy,' yells Chunaram, 'Who's going to pay for this foul-mouthed shit? Why didn't you just spout the usual?'

I've thought about this. 'It is usual for me.'

'Mother's cunt? Where do you get that from, you twisted little bastard? Next time I ask you to record a tape, keep your mouth shut.'

After this, Jarnalis, I'm not expecting you back, but you show up next day with grinning Chunaram qui me dit que Jarnalis wants you to carry on telling your story.

'Don't ask me why,' says he. 'Yesterday what you said, I thought it was one of your fucking madness fits, I admit I was wrong it has done the trick now I'm thinking it's this jarnalis who's cracked.' He shrugs and gives a thook onto the floor. So smug does he look that there and then I decide to teach the fucker a lesson.

'I'm done talking to tape mashins.'

So then Chunaram's wheedling, pleading with me. 'Think of the money. Jarnalis is writing a book about Khaufpur. Last night he had your tape translated. Today he comes saying he has never found such honesty as in that filth of yours. Really I think he is mad, but listen how I buttered the shaft, I told him that you are an orphan of that night, you grew up in a crazy franci situation, you used to live on the streets like a dog, you are a unique case. Jarnalis really wants your story, this could be a big business, don't fuck it up.'

'Well,' says I, pretending to consider it. 'No.'

'Listen, you can string it out. Make ten tapes. Why ten? Twenty. I will treat you to free kebabs at my place as long as it lasts.'

Wah Jarnalis, big money you must have offered him, his kebabs are famous throughout Khaufpur, well, at least in the Nutcracker, which is our part of Khaufpur, but one more look at his greedy face convinces me.

'Salty fucks to you, I won't do it.'

So Chunaram's shouting again, I am giggling, you're meanwhile wanting to know what's going on. Chunaram does some Inglis guftagoo, then he's back to me. 'Jarnalis says it's a big chance for you. He will write what you say in his book. Thousands will read it. Maybe you will become famous. Look at him, see his eyes. He says thousands of other people are looking through his eyes. Think of that.'

I think of this awful idea. Your eyes full of eyes. Thousands staring at me through the holes in your head. Their curiosity feels like acid on my skin.

'What am I to tell these eyes?' I demand of Chunaram. 'What can I say that they will understand? Have these thousands of eyes slept even one night in a place like this? Do these eyes shit on railway tracks? When was the last time these eyes had nothing to eat? These cuntish eyes, what do they know of our lives?'

'Don't talk that way,' says Chunaram, casting a fearful glance at you. 'Think of kebabs. Plus,' he says with a nod at my rags, 'you can buy a good shirt and pant, go to the cinema every night, take the best seat, kulfi eat.'

With Chunaram everything is a question of money, I'm about to tell him to stick it up his cul when a notion occurs.

Chunaram falls into a rage. 'You idiot,' he cries. 'This deal is nestling in my palm. Why ruin it with stupid demands?'

'It's my story. If he doesn't agree, I will not tell it.'

'Have some sense,' says he, 'how can I ask such a thing?'

'Je m'en fous you nine-fingered cunt.'

I know Chunaram won't give up, he lives for money, but as he speaks to you every word is a stone in his mouth. I catch his thoughts, badmaash boy, too much cunt, fucking boy, francispeaking, got too grand, bastard. Mixed in with this is allwhat he's saying to you. I know most of the Inglis words, those I don't know spit their meanings into my ear. C'est normal. Since I was small I could hear people's thoughts even when their lips were shut, plus I'd get en passant comments from all types of things, animals, birds, trees, rocks giving the time of day. What are these voices, no good asking me. When at last I told Ma Franci about them, she got worried, soit un fléau soit une bénédiction, curse or blessing, that's what she said. Well, she should know whose own brain's full of warring angels and demons. She took me to a doctor, it's how I met the Khã-in-the-Jar, which I'll tell about later, but the voices, some are like fireworks cracking the nearby air, others are inside me, if I listen carefully I'll hear them arguing, or talking nonsense. Once I was looking at Nisha, this voice says, the hair pours off her head like history. What the fuck does that mean? I don't know. Some voices are slow like honey melting in the sun, Elli and I saw a locust spread scarlet wings in the Nutcracker, it was crooning 'I'm so gorgeous.' I said aloud, 'Yeah, till a bird sees you.' Such a look I got from Elli. She was interested in my voices, being a doctor with a mission to save, even shits like me. I will get to Elli soon, too the Khã-in-the-Jar, but right now I'm telling how Chunaram's thoughts were giving him a headache. Poor bugger was rambling like a lost soul, he did not want to put my demand to you, at one point he grew so confused he forgot to speak Inglis, whinged in Hindi, 'Don't get offended by what this idiot is asking.' Then I knew greed had him by the ear.

'Sir,' mumbles Chunaram. 'Sir, I am so sorry, this boy says that if he talks to the eyes the book must contain only his story and nothing else. Plus it must be his words only.'

Only his story? His words only?

'Sir, he is a beastly boy, but it's a good story.'

Jarnalis, your brow creases, strange figures dance on your forehead. You gitpit with Chunaram, who pleads, 'Drop this demand. It's impossible. This jarnalis already has a plan for his book. It is already agreed. Jarnalis talks of an agent, plus a type called editor.'

Makes no sense. How can foreigners at the world's other end, who've never set foot in Khaufpur, decide what's to be said about this place?

'I guess the way it works,' says Chunaram, 'is jarnalis bribes agent, agent bribes type. Business, na?' He gives a laugh, smirky bastard thinks he's won.

Well, I'm in a shining fucking rage, here and now I will cut the throat of this plan. 'Give me the address of this editor type, I'll send a letter! I'll say this Jarnalis should not be allowed to tell my story. Comes here strutting like some sisterfuck movie star. What? Does he think he's the first outsider ever to visit this fucking city? People bend to touch his feet, sir, please sir, your help sir, sir my son, sir my wife, sir my wretched life. Oh how the prick loves this! Sultan among slaves he's, listens with what lofty pity, pretends to give a fuck but the truth is he'll go away and forget them, every last one. For his sort we are not really people. We don't have names. We flit in crowds at the corner of his eye. Extras we're, in his movie. Well bollocks to that. Tell mister cunt big shot that this is my movie he's in and in my movie there is only one star and it's me.'

'I'm not saying all that,' says Chunaram, but we both know he must, it's

Animal he's dealing with, not one of his stooges, no one can get the better of me, I do what I want.

How often have I watched Chunaram make deals? After all the talking, there is always a silence as money changes hands, notes are counted, folded, put away. What is that hush? Jarnalis, I will tell you. On your side it's shame because you know you're paying shit for something priceless. Chunaram has no shame, his silence is delight, he has taken a fortune for a thing he considers worthless.

So then there's silence.

'One more thing, he must give me his shorts.'

Two days pass, comes Chunaram with a bundle. Inside is the tape mashin and many tapes, folded on top are the shorts. First thing I do is put them on, they are too big but by tying string I make them tight. There's a lump in one of the pockets. I put in my hand, out comes the shiny lighter. There's a picture of a cannon on it, plus some writing. Holding it to the light, I make out Inglis letters. PHUOC TUY so I guess that's your name, it's Phuoc Tuy. On the other side in Hindi is my name, ANIMAL, so then I know you've given me your lighter too. Chunaram reads the letter you sent. 'Animal, you think books should change things. So do I. When you speak, forget me, forget everything, talk straight to the people who'll read your words. If you tell the truth from the heart, they will listen.' There's a lot more like this, then a good bit, 'The shorts come from Kakadu where there are crocodiles.'

Such a fool you were, Jarnalis. Gave your shorts but left Khaufpur with nothing. Not a single tape did I make. Not one. Chunaram said if you are not going to use the mashin, I'll sell it, so I hid it in the wall where the scorpions live, from then till today solid time has passed, you must be wondering, why is this putain telling his story now? What's changed? What happened?

What's changed? Everything. As to what happened, well, there are many versions going round, every newspaper had a different story, not one knows the truth, but I'm not talking to this tape for truth or fifty rupees or Chunaram's fucking kebabs. I've a choice to make, let's say it's between heaven and hell, my problem is knowing which is which. Such is the condition of this world that if a creature finds peace, it's just a rest before greater anguish, I do not know what name you could give to the things I have done.

Jarnalis, I'm a hard bastard, I hide my feelings. Ask people they'll tell you I'm the same as ever, anyone in Khaufpur will point me out, 'There he is! Look! It's Animal. Goes on four feet, that one. See, that's him, bent double by his own bitterness.' People see the outside, but it's inside where the real things happen, no one looks in there, maybe they don't dare. I really think this is why people have faces, to hide their souls. Has to be, or every street in Khaufpur would be a passage through hell, which Ma Franci says it is anyway, except she sees angels suffering, I see panicked humans. One night Farouq and me, we'd drunk a lot of bhang, about enough to get you on first name terms with god, we were ogling women in Naya Bazaar, as I looked at passers by their faces vanished, just disappeared, I could see their souls. Most were ugly, some shone like green birds, but all without exception were full of fear. I told this to Farouq and said, 'Look at my soul, tell me what does it look like.'

'Your soul?' He began laughing and couldn't stop. 'Your soul, my dear, is a tomb, even god can't see inside.' This happened on the night of Holi, when he was trying to get me laid.

Jarnalis, there's a lot to tell, it wants to come out. Like rejoicing, the world's unspoken languages are rushing into my head. Unusual meanings are making themselves known to me. Secrets are shouting themselves into my ear, seems there's nothing I cannot know. Ssspsss, haaarrr, khekhekhe, mmms, this is how the voices are, often I'll babble aloud the things they tell me. 'Tu dis toujours des absurdités,' Ma says, smiling, the rest just shrug, 'Fucking boy, crazy as fishguts. Sees things, hears voices that aren't there.' Well, I do see them, I do hear. To deny what you do see and believe in things you don't, that you could call crazy. Some believe in god whom they've never seen, who never says hello. In each other's dreams we are all fucking fishguts. It's better I speak these things to the tape.

Hah! This story has been locked up in me, it's struggling to be free, I can feel it coming, words want to fly out from between my teeth like a flock of birds making a break for it. You know that sudden clap of wings when they take off in a hurry, it's that sound, listen, clap, clap, clap.

Pandit Somraj's good friend, the poet Qaif Khaufpuri, when he grew old his poetry dried up inside him, an ulcer came on his leg, an open mouth that wouldn't go, one day it began reciting such sweet verses, his poems were trying to burst their way out of him.

Same way is this, a story sung by an ulcer.

My friend Faqri gave me this mashin, batteries I stole from Ram Nekchalan's shop, he can't say anything to me. Now the tape is running. I'm remembering the eyes that hide inside your eyes, you said I should ignore you and talk straight those who'll read these words, if I speak from my heart they'll listen. So from this moment I am no longer speaking to my friend the Kakadu Jarnalis, name's Phuoc, I am talking to the eyes that are reading these words.

Now I am talking to you.

I am saying this into darkness that is filled with eyes. Whichever way I look eyes are showing up. They're floating round in the air, these fucking eyes, turning this way and that they're, looking for things to see. I don't want them to see me, I'm lying on the floor, which is of dry dust, the tape mashin is by my head.

The instant I began talking the eyes came. I tried to hide. For some time I stayed silent. The eyes remained, they were wondering where the words had gone. They watched quietly, blinking now and again, waiting for something to happen.

See, it's like this, as the words pop out of my mouth they rise up in the dark, the eyes in a flash are onto them, the words start out kind of misty, like breath on a cold day, as they lift they change colours and shapes, they become pictures of things and of people. What I say becomes a picture and the eyes settle on it like flies.

I'm looking right now at my feet, which are near the hearth, twisted they're, a little bent to one side. Inside of left foot, outer of right, where they scrape the ground the skin's thick and cracked. In gone times I've felt such hunger, I'd break off lumps of the dry skin and chew it. Want to see? Okay watch, I am reaching down to my heel, feeling for horny edges, I'm sliding the thumbnail under. There, see this lump of skin, hard as a pebble, how easily it breaks off, mmm, chewy as a nut. Nowadays there's no shortage of food, I eat my feet for pleasure.

The hearth near which my feet are resting is of clay shaped somewhat like, like what, I've never thought of this before but it's like a yoni, which is a cunt, I don't know another way to say it, there's a gap you feed in hay, twigs etc, then put bits of dungcake and sticks to get a fire, which I've one burning. Outside the sun has yet to show its face. I can hear people passing, going for dawn shits on the railway line. They'll be well wrapped up this morning, blanket or thick shawl. The poor sods who are on the street must cover themselves in what they can find. Winter nights here you can freeze. That night they say was a night of great cold. Zafar used to say that as people were breathing clouds of mist out of their mouths that night, they little knew what kind of mist they'd soon be breathing in.

The eyes are watching people breathing mist. Stupid eyes, they don't know what the mist does to the people, they don't know what happens next. They know only what I tell them.

In this crowd of eyes I am trying to recognise yours. I've been waiting for you to appear, to know you from all the others, this is how the Kakadu Jarnalis in his letter said it would be. He said, 'Animal, you must imagine that you are talking to just one person. Slowly that person will come to seem real to you. Imagine them to be a friend. You must trust them and open your heart to them, that person will not judge you badly whatever you say.'

You are reading my words, you are that person. I've no name for you so I will call you Eyes. My job is to talk, yours is to listen. So now listen.

My story has to start with that night. I don't remember anything about it, though I was there, nevertheless it's where my story has to start. When something big like that night happens, time divides into before and after, the before time breaks up into dreams, the dreams dissolve to darkness. That's how it is here. All the world knows the name of Khaufpur, but no one knows how things were before that night. As for me, I don't remember any time before my back went bad. Ma Franci would talk, proud as if she were my real mother, of how I used to enjoy swimming in the lakes behind the Kampani's factory. 'You'd dive right in, with your arms and your legs stretched out in one line.' Whenever she said this I'd feel sad also angry. I still dream of diving straight as a stick into deep water leaving my crooked shadow behind.

On that night I was found lying in a doorway, child of a few days, wrapped in a shawl. Whose was I? Nobody knew. Mother, father, neighbours, all must have died for no living soul came to claim me, who was coughing, frothing etc plus nearly blind, where my eyes had screwed themselves against the burning fog were white slits bleached on the eyeballs. I was brought to the hospital. Was I Hindu or Muslim? How did it matter? I was not expected to live. When I did, they circumcised me, if I was Muslim it was necessary, if I was Hindu what difference did it make? After this I was given to the nuns. I grew up in the orphanage. I do not know what religion I should be. Both perhaps? Neither? Or should I listen to Ma Franci, loves Isa Miyañ, he said 'forgive your enemies, turn the other cheek'. I don't fucking forgive. I'm not a Muslim, I'm not a Hindu, I'm not an Isayi, I'm an animal, I'd be lying if I said religion meant a damn thing to me. Where was god the cunt when we needed him?

I was six when the pains began, plus the burning in my neck and across the shoulders. Nothing else do I remember from that time, my first

memory is that fire. It was so bad I could not lift my head. I just could-
n't lift it. The pain gripped my neck and forced it down. I had to stare at
my feet while a devil rode my back and chafed me with red hot tongs. The
burning in the muscles became a fever, when the fevers got bad I was taken
to the hospital, they gave me an injection. It did no good. After that my
back began to twist. Nothing could be done. It was agony, I couldn't
straighten up, I was pressed forward by the pain. Before this I could run
and jump like any other kid, now I could not even stand up straight.
Further, further forward I was bent. When the smelting in my spine
stopped the bones had twisted like a hairpin, the highest part of me was
my arse. Through flowers of pain I could make out an old woman kneel-
ing by my cot, wiping my head and mumbling strange words in my ear.
Her skin was wrinkled as a dried apricot, so pale you could see clear
through it, she looked like the mother of time itself. This was Ma Franci.
She already knew me well, but this is my first memory of her. Ma stroked
my face and comforted me in words I did not understand. Tears were
falling down her face. Mine too. This feverish dream gradually faded
and became my new life.

On my hands I learned to walk, my legs grew feeble. My hands and
arms are strong, my chest is strong. The upper half of my body is like a
bodybuilder's. I walk, also run, by throwing my weight onto my hands,
hauling feet forward in a kind of hop. It took a long time to master this
new way of getting about. Maybe it was months, maybe a year. When I
could run I ran away because the teasing had begun.

The orphanage kids started calling me Animal one day during a round
of kabbadi. You'd think such a tough game I'd have difficulty playing, but
with my strong shoulders and arms I was good at catching opposing
players and wrestling them to the ground. One day I grabbed this boy, he
kneed me in the face. It hurt. I was so angry I bit him. I fastened my
teeth in his leg and bit till I could taste blood. How he yelled, he was
howling with pain, he was pleading, I wouldn't stop. I bit harder. The
other kids started shouting, 'Jaanvar, jungli Jaanvar.' Animal, wild Animal.

Another time, I'd have been about eight or nine, we'd gone to swim. Just now I mentioned lakes, really they're clay pits behind the Kampani's factory where bulldozers would dump all different coloured sludges. These pits are massive, the water in them stinks, but when the rains come they fill up and become proper lakes with reeds etc. Since rain water is clean people would wash their cows and buffalos, we kids would jump in, splash around in the water. I could no longer dive or swim, I'd wade up to my neck, but my arse stuck out of the water.

One day we were lying on the grass in hot sun, drying off. A girl about my own age, she pushed me and left the prints of her muddy fingertips on my body. The mud dried pale on my skin. She said, 'Like a leopard!' So then they all dipped their fingers in the clay and covered me with leopardy marks. 'Animal, jungli Animal!' The name, like the mud, stuck. The nuns tried to stop it but some things have a logic that can't be denied. How do you shit, when your your arse is up in the air and legs too weak to squat? Not easy. What do you look like as the turds tumble from your hindquarters? Like a donkey dropping dung, when I walk, it's

feet on tiptoe
head down below
arse en haut
thus do I go

In my street years I hated to see dogs fucking, my mates would shout, 'Hey Animal, is this how you do it?'

They'd make a fist, ram two fingers in and out with loud sucking noises, then let on the fingers were trapped, they'd yell, 'Hey Fourlegs, you get glued up like this, you and your girlfriend? You and Jara?' Never have I been able to cope with teasing. I'd lose my temper, fataak! I know how to fight. Early in life I learned to look out for myself, to put myself first, before all others and every other thing. Who else was going to stick up for me? It's a bad idea to attack an opponent who can kick shit out of you, I got a few beatings, but if they know you'll fight back, people mostly leave you alone. Plus I used to bite. Maybe they were afraid of getting rabies.

Jara's my friend. She wasn't always. We used to be enemies. In the days of living on the street we were rivals for food. We used to work the same territory, the alleys behind the eating houses in the old city. We'd get there late evening when the waiters were tired and would sling the day's scraps at, rather than in, the bins. Such delicacies we fought over, bit of naan, thrown-down banana skin, with nub of meat going gooey brown where someone had not fancied it. I might arrive to find Jara crouching over some prize, a bone to which clung a few shreds of mutton, a splash of daal. Or I'd be there first, slobbering over a choice morsel, and look up to see her eyes fastened on mine, drooling from the back corners of her mouth. I was scared of her. Of her sharp teeth, her orangey-brown eyes in which there was no friendliness. She'd lie and watch me until hunger drove her forward, crouching on her haunches, a low growl, rrrrr, starting in her throat. I came to know that snarling mouth quite well. A long curved tooth in her lower jaw had lost its tip. When she got close enough for me to see that tooth, I'd back away.

One day, I found a thing with flies sticking to it like peppercorns, fish-snout with backbone protruding behind, a fair slab of flesh, brown with masalas, lying on a bed of rice, remains of someone's dinner. I'd begun making a feast of it when I heard her growl. The fish was too good to give up. I stuck firm as she made her approach, the lips lifted over those evil yellow teeth. She started all that rrrrr business. I don't know how, but some rebellion ignited inside me. On all fours I rushed at her snapping my jaws, growling louder than she, the warning of a desperate animal that will stick at nothing. She turned and slunk back a few paces, then lay down again, giving me a reproachful look.

She was as thin as me, her hide shrunken over her ribs. A pink sore on her nose was leaking some clear mess. With my own body pumped full of victory I suddenly felt sorry for her. I fed myself then moved off,

17

gestured for her to come close. 'Eat!' She licked her lips, wagged her tail so hard her whole backside shook. Man, what a dog. A yellow dog, of no fixed abode and no traceable parents, just like me. After this we always shared. I named her Banjara, gypsy, free spirit, because she belongs nowhere and everywhere is her kingdom.

Jara and me, one day we are up to our tricks outside a cafe where I've not been before, it's not one of my usual dirty dabas. This is a smart coffee-house with a garden and a big sign saying *Coca Cola*, I can't read the sign but I know what it says. These girls are sitting at a table under a tree, drinking lassi. Three girls, college students by look. Often they'll be quite generous, so I've started my patter about how we are perishing from starvation etc, at a sign from me, Jara, canny bitch, rolls on her back and plays dead.

One of the three gets up. Comes out, stands looking at the dog and me. Some girls primp themselves up like film stars with kajal round the eyes, long sleek hair and all, this one isn't like that. Her hair looks like it hasn't been oiled for a month, kameez and scarf don't match, nose is a touch too long. She doesn't smile, doesn't offer money. She doesn't do any of the things people normally do when I pester them. She's frowning, all serious.

'Pretty clever. Did you teach her?'

'For five rupees she'll whine the national anthem.'

'Is begging fun?'

Well, this catches me, no one's ever asked such a thing before. This girl bends to pat Jara and her hair falls over her face, pretty she may not be but there's a sweetness in her which you sometimes see in people without looks.

'Is it fun to be hungry?' I reply. 'No, so then don't mock, give me five rupees.'

'Not I,' says she, chewing her lip. 'You've a look of mischief about you, I've seen you before. You roam round the city doing scams.'

18

'What scams? If you won't give five rupees at least give a smile.'

'You like winding people up. I think you enjoy being annoying.'

'It's all they deserve. People are cretins.'

'Cretins? So is that what makes it fun?'

'Fun was your idea, not mine,' I say, liking this girl. Most people who talked to me just told me to fuck off.

'Get off with you, you're up to all the tricks. I'd be surprised if you go hungry.'

'What do you know about it?'

But she was right. I was well schooled in street work. My teacher was Ali Faqri, he'd in turn been trained by the prince of scams, Abdul Saliq the Pir Gate beggar. Faqri told me to stop creeping round behind the eateries. There, if I was caught arse-up in the bins, best I could expect was disgust maybe a kicking. 'Go round the front,' Faqri said. So I began parading up and down in view of the clientele, nothing puts a person off their food more than a starving Animal watching every mouthful. The proprietors hated me but they'd give me hand-outs rather than have me upset their customers. I got the same left-overs, only this time served nicely in a bowl. In this way I learned that if you act powerless, you are powerless, the way to get what you want is to demand it.

'I'm Nisha,' says this serious girl. 'What's your name?'

'Animal. Now you have to guess why.'

'Okay Animal, you're bright, you could do something more useful than this.' Nisha told me that if I came to her father's house, which was in a part of Khaufpur known as the Chicken Claw, she would find me some work to do.

'And,' says she, 'you can meet Zafar.'

I was stupid, I should have been warned by the way she spoke his name, but already I was walking in dreams.

'Come tomorrow at noon. I'll give you a meal. You can eat it in our garden. The dog too.'

* * *

Well, Eyes, I guess you want to know what happened next, but while I've been chatting with you the sun has risen, it's dropped down through the hole in the roof, making the floating dust catch fire. The thousand eyes have begun to fade, they are melting away or else somehow merging into just one pair of eyes, which are yours. You and me, we're alone together now, but I can't keep going. I'm tired of talking, tape's nearly gone, mouth's dry, I should make chai, plus it's past time for my shit.

Aliya's calling, 'Animal, come and play.'

Her voice comes flying in from outside, plus I can hear people talking as they go past, crow craarking in the tamarind tree. Sun's well up, from far off a radio is playing the song, *Ek tu jo milaa*, meeting you I meet the whole world, one flower in my heart the world's abloom.

'Animal, come and play.' Again comes her voice.

'What, with you? I'm not a kid.'

'You are,' she calls, who's herself maybe eight years. 'Granny says you act like a kid all the time.'

'Your granny wouldn't like the kind of games I play.'

'Ho,' says she. 'Boasting of your thing again.' There's no innocence these days even in a child.

'Come on, Animal, let's play.' Her voice is suddenly faint like it's caught away by wind, or whispered on the moon, or lost in the crackling of a great fire. Eyes, I think I will go mad. I'm filled with sadness because Aliya is not really out there. Her voice is not real, it's like people say, just another voice in my head.

Shit's over, I'm back in this heap of stones with grass growing out the sides enough to feed a cow. I've just rewound the tape like Chunaram did that time, heard my own voice. Sounds so queer. Do I speak that rough-tongue way? You don't answer. I keep forgetting you do not hear me. The things I say, by the time they reach you they'll have been changed out of Hindi, made into Inglis et français pourquoi pas pareille quelques autres langues? For you they're just words written on a page. Never can you hear my voice, nor can I ever know what pictures you see. I was telling you about Nisha, how she had called me to her house in the Chicken Claw. Of course I didn't go, that's that, I thought. I was wrong. Next afternoon she comes looking for me. 'I've been going all over,' she scolds, 'asking people if they'd seen you. They told me places all over Khaufpur. Then someone said try the galla mandi vegetable market.'

Eyes, a hundred times she has narrated the story of the finding of Animal, always she tells it the same way. 'I went to the galla mandi, but you were not there. I went into the alley where the men play cards. There was a lot of wind, dust blowing, which the sun was making to glow. Out of the haze came these shapes, half a dozen starving dogs moving together with purpose. Among them was another shape, a boy walking on hands and feet. I called you and you turned and came to me.'

Fuck, what was I? Her dog? Why did I go? I had fended off a hundred attempts by the nuns, police and god knows who else to get me off the streets. What was it about Nisha that made it impossible to say no? I think it was that from the first she took me exactly as I was. When she called me Jaanvar, Animal, it was a name, nothing more. She never seemed to notice that I was crippled, nor pretend I wasn't. She was the only person I knew who treated me as completely normal. Nisha said she would find me some work, I'd even get paid. I said I did not know what work I could do. Nisha said I was clever. I'd learn new things. Zafar would know what job to give me.

Zafarrrrr. It was the way she spoke his name that at last gave me the clue as to who he was. There must be a thousand Zafars in Khaufpur, I know at least three, but there's only one who counts. This Zafar was a legend in the bastis, which is to say the bidonvilles, the slums, because he had given up everything in his life for the poor. Zafar bhai, Zafar brother, they worshipped him, who lived among them, dressed like them, shared their poverty and drank water from the same stinking wells. I had never expected to meet this hero. He was like I've said, a big shot, I was hustling and living rough. At that time I could never have imagined how tightly our lives would tangle.

*   *   *

22

First time I meet Zafar, it's at Nisha's house, where she lives with her dad. Zafar's eating a pomegranate, digging out seeds with a pen-knife, placing them on his tongue, three-four at a time. 'So you're Animal. Do you like anaar? Want some?' I would have liked to taste the pomegranate, but I'm feeling shy, I say no.

'What's your real name?' The great man is a long thin chap, curls plentiful and black has he, plus glasses that make him seem lost in clever thoughts.

'It's Animal.'

'Animal's a nickname, na? I mean your born name.'

'I don't know.'

'How come?' He gives me an interested look.

I've just shrugged. From the time before nothing do I remember. True, I had a human name, it was given to me by the orphanage, I asked a nun once what it was, she told me, but I have forgotten what she said. This I tell to Zafar, who replies that he dislikes teasing of the disabled. Says he, 'You should not think of yourself that way, but as especially abled.'

'What's especially abled?'

'It means okay you don't walk on two legs like most people, but you have skills and talents that they don't.'

'How do you know?' I'd not told him about my voices.

'Because it's true of everyone,' says Zafar. 'We just have to find out what you're good at. Plus you should not allow yourself to be called Animal. You are a human being, entitled to dignity and respect. If you haven't a name then this is a great opportunity for you. You can choose your own. Jatta for example or Jamil, go ahead pick one, whatever you like, we'll call you that henceforth.'

You're wrong, I'm thinking. Let me be as I am, like Nisha does, you would never say such things. I give Nisha a look, but she's smiling at him.

'My name is Animal,' I say. 'I'm not a fucking human being, I've no wish to be one.' This was my mantra, what I told everyone. Never did I mention my yearning to walk upright. It was the start of that long argument between Zafar and me about what was an animal and what it meant to be human.

When I say I'm not a *fucking* human, Zafar flinches. 'Brother, don't swear.'

'Sorry,' I tell Nisha and go to touch her feet but Zafar stops me. 'It's not because of Nisha, I myself hate bad words.'

'Then it's sorry to you too,' I've said without in the least meaning it. 'But my name is my name.'

Zafar sits stroking his wise bastard's beard that juts from his chin like tuesday. 'Animal it is then,' he says at last and right away begins telling me about the work he and others are doing in Khaufpur. Seems there's a group of which Zafar is the leader. He himself does not say so, but it's obvious. Zafar's group collects money to help the sick. All these years after that night, he tells me, there's still no real help for those whose eyes and lungs and wombs were fucked. Of course there are government hospitals but people won't set foot in them unless they're desperate.

'You yourself are a poison victim,' Zafar says, looking at my back. 'You know what it's like in those places. You queue all day to be seen, the doctor doesn't examine you because to touch a poor person would pollute him. Barely looks at you, then writes a chit, tells you, take this to so-and-so's shop and say I sent you. The medicines are supposed to be given free, this is how they make money out of misery.'

'All this is true, everyone knows it,' says I, wondering what sort of job he plans to offer me.

Nisha's been ear-ogling Zafar's speech. 'Animal, hardly can people afford food, how can they spend on medicines? This is why we have to help. Yesterday I had a case, a woman Lilabai needed blood for an operation, she was told she must find the blood, buy it, and take it to the hospital herself.'

Well, Eyes, I know about this. When I was starving I sold my blood to get food.

'Eight hundred rupees a bottle Lilabai had to pay!'

24

'What? That fucker Chunaram sorry for cursing gave me only eighty!'

'Who is this Chunaram?' asks Zafar kindly, removing his specs to wipe them. Freed from the prisons of the lenses his eyes appear a little watery, as if he has not been sleeping.

'Has a chai shop in the Nutcracker. Mr Ninefingers.'

'Ah,' says he, as if this explains everything.

I tell them how Chunaram once got the idea of selling blood, he could store it in his fridge. He needed a supply and I was the first one he bled.

'What happened to this plan?' asks Nisha.

'Somebody put it about that he was selling animal blood.'

'I wonder who?' She raises an eyebrow at me, but I've replied nothing.

'Part of our work,' Zafar says, returning to that matter, 'is getting money to those who need it. Cash has to be carried, it's something you can do.'

'You'd trust me?'

'Are you not trustworthy?'

'I don't know. No one has ever trusted me with anything before.'

'So we'll find out. What other work can you do?'

Work? I had no clue. I had tried a few jobs while I was on the street, scavenging for rags, tin cans, plastic and the like, I wasn't good at it because if you go on all fours you have only one hand plus mouth free to carry things. I tell this to Zafar who listens thoughtfully. He has reworn his glasses, chin's propped on his fingers, which somehow are still finding ways to irritate the beard.

'What about the scams?' It's Nisha, all grinning mischief.

'I told you, I don't do such things.'

Says Zafar, 'You know the bloodstain scam?'

'No idea what you are talking about.'

'How about the spilled channa scam? No, that one you wouldn't be able to convince.'

Well I'm impressed. The bloodstain scam is not often seen, at least in Khaufpur. As for the spilled channa, it must be played by a boy who sits in the street surrounded by roasted gram. He has to know how to cry well, and moan that his father will beat him. A bent tray must be lying there, so it looks as if he's a street-seller who's tripped up. Obviously he'd have been carrying the tray on his head, which is why I could not have done it.

'How come you know such things?'

'Lost coins you could do, broken bottle you could try but no one would believe.'

'What do you mean?' says I, who've performed that trick more times than I can remember.

'Aha,' he says, smiling. 'So you do know. Well, I'm not interested in what you have done, but in what you will do.'

'I'm an animal, I can't do much.' I say this to put an end to him feeling superior and also, if I am honest, to annoy him.

'You've the gift of the gab.'

'An animal must use its mouth, no other tool does it have.'

'How does it see?'

'Uses its eyes.'

'You can do that,' says he. 'How does it find food?'

'Smells it out.'

'We need a good sniffer. Your dog,' he says, indicating Jara who is lying in the sun asleep. 'How does she know when to play dead?'

'There's a word.'

'She hears, plus is clever enough to understand. We need someone like her. Use eyes, nose, ears, brain, this is another job.'

'Namispond! Jamispond!'

'Shabaash,' says he with a grin.

'I would like this job better than carrying cash.'

'That we'll see,' says Zafar. He shades his eyes to glance at the sun and tells Nisha he has to be going because it's nearly four o'clock.

'So! What do you think of Zafar?' Nisha asks as his motorcycle farts away through the Claw.

'Such an important fellow should at least get a watch.'

Nisha says, 'You'll understand when you get to know him.'

From her I heard Zafar's story. Seems he'd been a scholar who left his studies to take up the cause of the poor.

'I met his old professor once,' Nisha said. 'He told me Zafar was his most brilliant student. He could have been anything, but when he got news of that night, he straight away quit his college and came to Khaufpur to organise the fight against the Kampani, which he has been doing ever since. Who do you suppose has kept the case against the Kampani alive so long? So many times they have tried to stop him. He's been threatened, beaten, but Zafar is not afraid of anything or anyone. He speaks the truth and he never gives up. These are the things that make the ordinary people love him.'

You too, I thought, getting the drift.

So Eyes, this was my job, to keep my eyes and ears open and report to Zafar if anything unusual was going on in the bastis. I was to listen in the streets and chai shops, find out what the government, munsipal etc were up to, because those buggers are always up to no good. Thus within weeks I caught a plan to evict some people from near the railway and told Zafar, who put an end to it. People showed me respect because I was one of Zafar's.

Zafar's gang, how would you describe us? Saints, said the slum folk who could never take the name of Zafar without adding a spice of blessing. Subversives, said Zahreel Khan, he's Khaufpur's Minister for Poison Relief. To me, if I'm honest, we were just a bunch of fucking do-gooders. Okay, we did good, what else should do-gooders do, but I couldn't be bothered with the political shit, I hated all that talk of 'poison victims', I don't want to be pitied, I refuse to be some fucking bhonsdi-ka victim. As for Saint Zafar, don't make me laugh. I'd seen the lust in the man's eyes when he looked at Nisha, saints and angels don't feel lust, which is how I know I'm not one.

Such feelings I kept to myself. Four hundred rupees a month I earned for my work, which was easy, in this life good fortune too seldom comes along and when it does you don't want to be twisting its balls. Chunaram soon got wind of my new riches because Zafar for some reason had taken a shine to him, his chai shop in the Nutcracker became like a second headquarters. Chunaram told me that four hundred rupees was a lot of money, he offered to keep it safe for me but I wasn't falling for that. Instead, I gave it to Nisha. She said I should open a bank account.

'How can I, who can neither read nor write?'

'Then I must teach you.'

At that time she was enrolled at Iqbal Bahadur Women's College in the walled city, but I think she was not taking her studies very seriously.

'You shouldn't come home at midday,' her father said.

'Then what will you do for lunch? Papa, Zafar gets me back in time for my afternoon lectures, plus this boy needs at least one good meal a day, if he will insist on sleeping rough instead of under a roof like a human being.'

'You could leave some chappatis in a tiffin,' I said, giving a glance at her dad, of whom I was afraid. Grim, terrifying bastard he was, but with good cause, when you knew his story. 'Plus I'm not a human being.'

'Don't you like my cooking?'

'Animal's right,' said her father.

'I could get something outside,' says I, who'd newly discovered the pleasure of spending a little of my earnings on a samosa here, pau bhaji there.

'Should my dad also eat street food?'

'I can manage fine,' her father said. Both of us knew that it was not for our sakes that she came home. Zafar too came, most days. He would eat with her father, spend some time with Nisha, then take her back to college on his motorbike.

'You give so much time to Zafar's work,' I said once when we were alone. 'Is it a good idea?'

28

'Because it's important.'

'And your studies?.' To me, being a student, getting educated was not just an impossible dream, it was an impossible dream inside a dream.

'Worry about a roof over your head,' said Nisha, with a casual flip of the subject. 'How many places has Zafar found you? Why do you keep refusing?'

'I have a good place to sleep, fully private.'

'Where?'

'That's my secret.' She would be horrified if she knew.

'Where?' she demanded. 'Come on, tell.'

'Difficult to describe,' I said, which was nothing but the truth.

Ever since that night the Kampani's factory has been locked up and abandoned. No one goes there, people say it's haunted by those who died. It's a shunned place, where better for an animal to make its lair?

When jarnaliss and foreigners come to Khaufpur they always think the factory is a big building. It isn't. Its wall seems never-ending, and inside is an area equal to the whole of the Nutcracker. It takes more than an hour for me to circle the whole thing, enough steps to fill two miles. Here and there are holes in the wall as if a giant has banged his fist through, it's where people have dug out bricks for their houses, our end of the Nutcracker is made mostly of death factory. Look inside, you see something strange, a forest is growing, tall grasses, bushes, trees, creepers that shoot sprays of flowers like fireworks.

Eyes, I wish you could come with me into the factory. Step through one of these holes, you're into another world. Gone are city noises, horns of trucks and autos, voices of women in the Nutcracker, kids shouting, all erased by the high wall. Listen, how quiet it's. No bird song. No hoppers in the grass. No bee hum. Insects can't survive here. Wonderful poisons the Kampani made, so good it's impossible to get rid of them, after all these years they're still doing their work. Once inside, in the grass, it's careful hands, careful feet. Fucking place is full of cobras. Dogs too you've to watch for. See a dog, keep away. If it comes close drive it off with stones. These dogs have foaming mouths, I'm afraid for Jara but not for myself. This is my kingdom, in here I am the boss. I've been in and out of here since I was small, I'd come in to hide where no one could find me. Sometimes I'd bring other kids in to play marbles and spin tops when we didn't want the grown-ups to know where we were. To make sure they didn't come back on their own I'd tell them stories of children who had wandered into the factory and were never seen again.

the ghosts will get you, you'll never escape

I'd tell how I found their bones in the jungle, gnawed by animals with fangs of fire. How come you're still alive then, they'd ask.

the ghosts run away from my twisted shape

Eyes, imagine you're in the factory with me. See that thing rising above the trees, those rusty pipes and metal stairs going nowhere? That's the place where they made the poisons. It used to be bigger, but bits keep falling off. Each big wind pulls more iron sheets loose. We hear them banging like angry ghosts. All that's left now is its skeleton. Platforms, ladders and railings are corroding. Its belly is a tangle of pipes like rotting guts. Huge tanks have split, stuff's fallen out that looks like brown rocks. How often did Zafar warn that if the dry grasses inside the factory ever caught light, if fire reached these brown lumps, poison gases would gush out, it'd be that night all over again.

In these dry grasses that Zafar said were a danger to the city I used to make my sleeping nest. On warm nights I could dream in comfort under the stars with no insects to trouble me. During the rains and in cold weather there were rooms that the Kampani, when it fled from Khaufpur, left knee-deep in papers. The Kampani papers made a thick quilt, plus I had the dog to keep me warm. In the offices the chemical stench was less.

Inside the warehouses I never went, they were full of rotting sacks that poured out white and pink powders. Too long near them, you'd be soon be breathless, with pains in the chest. Sometimes moving through the jungle I'd get dizzy and feel a sharp metallic taste on my tongue, those were regions to avoid.

Eyes, are you with me still? Look throughout this place a silent war is being waged. Mother Nature's trying to take back the land. Wild sandalwood trees have arrived, who knows how, must be their seeds were shat by overflying birds. That herb scent, it's ajwain, you catch it drifting in gusts, at such moments the forest is beautiful, you forget it's poisoned and haunted. Under the poison-house trees are growing up through the pipework. Creepers, brown and thick as my wrist, have climbed all the way to the top, tightly they've wrapped wooden knuckles round pipes and ladders, like they want to rip down everything the Kampani made.

Here we can climb, up the ladders and up, to where the death wind blew. At the top of the highest stair, a single black pipe continues into the sky. You can rest your hand on it, it's wider than the rest. Up this pipe the poisons flew on that night. Still black and blistered it's after twenty years. Its paint was burnt off, so hot were those gases, yet that night was a freezing night of stars.

'Wah! what a view!'

It's the first thing they say when they get up here, from here you can see clear across Khaufpur, every street, every lane, gully, shabby alley. That huddle of roofs, it's Jyotinagar. Lanes in there are narrow, I don't like to think about what happened in them. My friend Faqri, he lost his mum and dad and five brothers and sisters in those lanes. See the flashes where the nala flows? It's Mira Colony, then Khabbarkhana and Salimganj. East's Phuta Maqbara, to the west Qazi Camp, killing grounds all. Those minarets far off are the big masjid in Chowk. There, see the Delhi road? On that night it was a river of people, some in their underwear, others in nothing at all, they were staggering like it was the end of some big race, falling down not getting up again, at Rani Hira Pati ka Mahal, the road was covered with dead bodies.

Eyes, there's such a thing as bhayaanak rasa, the kind of terror that makes your little hairs stand up and tremble, which is called romanchik. I feel it when I come back to this high place, I see mother Kali stalking in the forest below, her skin black as a roasted corpse. She's got these massive fangs and a red tongue hanging to her waist and a belt of chopped-off heads, each one wears a face of agony which is how they looked when they died. Eyes, you see a black pipe climbing into the sky, I see Siva dark and naked, smeared with ashes from funeral pyres. His eyes are red from hash and smoke of burning flesh, dancing he's, from all sides I can hear the screams and cries of dying people, because when Siva dances the world comes to an end. Do you suppose anyone can explain, why did the Kampani choose this city to make its factory? Why this land? Is it by chance that the old name for this place is Kali's ground? Is it by chance that Siva her husband wears cobras round his neck?

Up here with just the wind how quiet it's. Isn't always. You should hear the ghosts, the factory is full of them, when a big wind blows, their souls fly shrieking up and down the empty pipes. Some nights, there'd be nothing here, just the ghosts and me, a four-foot creature climbing in the trees and pipes. Perched like a monkey on top of this poison-khana I'd watch the moon making shadows, and the stars cutting their circles, and I would look at the lights of the city and wonder if this pipe had been mended, that wheel tightened, I might have had a mother and father, I might still be a human being.

Each morning I would creep out of the factory to do my work in the bastis. At noon I'd head to Nisha's. Her cooking was good, her company fun. I'd eat my lunch and do my best to avoid her frightening father.

Somraj is the name of Nisha's dad, pandit Somraj Tryambak Punekar. Unlike his daughter he's tall, twists my neck to look up at him, he has the same zapaat nose as hers, long and pointy, his fingers also are long, but the

32

most important thing about him is that he used to be a singer, and not just a singer but a famous one. His name was known throughout India, so many awards and honours he won, they called him *Aawaaz-e-Khaufpur*, the Voice of Khaufpur. Nisha told me that in his younger days her dad was always singing on the radio plus he gave concerts and the like, until that night took away his wife and baby son and fucked up his lungs. Nisha never knew her mother or brother, she says that when the Kampani stole away her father's breath it also stole his life, because breath is the life of a singer. From that night on he would listen to other people's records, but never his own. He became a solemn and private man. Later he started teaching music, his students won prizes, to them he was like a god but he seemed to get no pleasure from it since hardly ever would you see him smile.

Like every Khaufpuri, Somraj hated the Kampani, he ran a poison-relief committee which did what it could for the locals who were still coughing their lungs up so many years after that night. The people he helped were among the poorest in the city, which is why no politician gave a shit about them and hardly a lawyer would take up their claims for compensation. Through this work he had met Zafar, through him Zafar met Nisha. I used to wonder how Somraj felt about those two. His daughter, a Hindu girl not yet twenty, with a Muslim man twice her age, but whatever Somraj thought about it he kept to himself, he approved of her work with Zafar, where he and she differed was on the question of how the battle should be fought. The case against the Kampani had been dragging on endless years. It stood accused of causing the deaths of thousands on that night, plus it ran away from Khaufpur without cleaning its factory, over the years the poisons it left behind have found their way into the wells, everyone you meet seems to be sick. The Khaufpuris were demanding that the Kampani must pay proper compensation to those whose loved ones it killed, whose health it ruined, plus it should clean the factory and compensate the people who had been drinking its poisons. Trouble was that the Kampani bosses were far away in Amrika, they refused to come to the Khaufpuri court and no one could make them. So long had the case been running it had become part of our Khaufpuri speech such as if I blagged six rupees from Faqri he'd say, 'Be sure to pay me back before the case ends.' Or someone says something unbelievable like Chunaram is serving free kebabs, others will pipe, 'Oh sure, and the Kampani's come to court.'

One day I came as usual for lunch and found Nisha and her dad having an argument. 'Every accused must have the chance to defend himself,' Somraj was saying. 'Even the Kampani. In the end the law will reward us.'

Nisha was standing looking upset with her hands covered in white paint and her hair dishevelled. 'Papa, the Kampani has never even turned up to the court, so how can the law reward us?'

'It may take years, but its attempts to escape will not succeed.'

'What attempts? It has no need to escape, it got away scot free.'

'Justice is on our side.'

'Darling Papa,' said Nisha with a small sigh, 'You are a kind and a fair man, everyone knows it and praises you for it, but you're either being naive or you have not noticed how the world has changed. Maybe you remember such a thing as justice, but in my lifetime there's been no sign of it. If we want justice, we'll have to fight for it in the streets.'

'Violence isn't the way.'

'Who said anything about violence? It's just a march.'

'Stone-throwing? Like last time?'

'Zafar did his best to stop it, but how long must people suffer in silence?'

'To that, alas, I have no answer,' said her father, and left the room.

'What are you doing?' I've asked Nisha. She shows me this big banner she has made for the juloos, the demo, painted on the black cloth are large white letters.

'What do you think? Is it strong? Does it have power?'

'How should I know? I can't read.'

She gives a big sigh and says, 'This very day we will start your lessons.'

It was hard at first, reading. Take two letters like क and ल, they look almost the same, but the sounds they make, *ka* and *la*, are different. Slowly the letters began to make sense. ज, a shape like a begging hand, was *ja*. ह, a shape that reminded me of an elephant's head with trunk and tusks, like Ganesh on the front of a beedi packet, this was *ha* for haathi, elephant. Signs in the street gradually came to life. कोका कोला, I already knew it meant Coca Cola, which I had never tasted. I learned to spell my own name, जानवर, Jaanvar, meaning Animal. Nisha said that it was my name and I should be proud of it. Jaan means 'life'. Jaanvar means 'one who lives'.

'Life? You're full of it,' she said, casting her eye over a page of scrawled jaanvars. 'I've never known anyone with so much jaan as you.' Then spoilt it by adding, 'Except Zafar.'

When I could read and write Hindi, Nisha set me a new task. There was a group of kids to whom she was teaching Inglis. I should join them. I hadn't been to school since the orphanage, where all of us children sat together in one room and chanted our lessons. The nuns were strict, get something wrong it was a ruler cut, edge down, to the palm. Ma Franci was kind, but she did not have to teach because no one including me could understand a word she said, and she could not understand us.

'Will you beat me?' I asked Nisha, she laughed. Such a patient teacher was she, hard it's to remember she was at that time not yet nineteen. Never did she complain as we struggled to wrap our tongues round the uncouth Inglis words, mayngo, pawmgront, cushdhappel, gwaav, bunaan, which were the names of fruit trees in her garden. In truth I didn't find Inglis very difficult. Like I've told you, Eyes, I've always caught the meanings of speech even when I could not understand a word, I had not just an ear but an eye for meanings. I could read expressions and gestures, the way someone sat or stood, but being taught by Nisha really brought out my gift for tongues. Like water flooding into a field, the new language just came. Cat sat on the mat house burns down people rally to the banner, thus my Inglis progressed. Zafar too would sit and listen to me, both would praise me and marvel at my quickness to learn.

One day comes Zafar with a small book he has printed. 'It's about that night,' says he all proud, 'it shows what was wrong in the factory that caused the poison to leak. There are pictures so children can read and understand.'

Nisha hands me the book and asks me to read from it. I've given it a flick through, in it are drawings of the different buildings inside the factory, I know every one of them, but in the book they are shown as they must have been before that night, not rotting like now. Arrows show where things went wrong, here, there, there, there, all over.

'I won't read this,' says I.

'Why not?' she asks.

'I am not a child.'

'So, big man,' asks Zafar, 'what will you prefer to read instead?' He's laughing but secretly I think he is hurt that I don't want to read his book.

'I am not a man. Give me that other one that you are carrying.' Zafar used to read a great deal, never was he without a book.

'This one? I think you might find it too difficult.'

I open the book to the first page and taking great care slowly read aloud, *It is a truth virtually acknowledged, that a single man in position of good fortune, must be in want of a wife.*

Nisha starts clapping. She says I am her best pupil. Then she stoops down and gives me a hug. No girl had ever touched me till then, less hugged. It sent a thrill through me straight to my cock. This was the first time I caught myself thinking, if only things were different with me, if I could walk upright, it might be my praises she sang instead of Zafar's.

It was my clever tongue, which could curl itself to any language, that ended my days of living rough. Nisha loved to chatter, and when I was in her house having my lunch we would talk of all kind of things. One day I say, 'Nisha, after Inglis, I will learn français, then at last I'll know what Ma Franci used to yell at us kids in the orphanage.'

'Who is Ma Franci?'

'She's a nun, came from France more than forty years ago to spread the word about Isa miyañ and do good works.'

'And français?'

'The language of France, it's all she knows.'

'After forty years here she can't speak Hindi?'

So then I get to telling Nisha about Ma Franci. It's a sad sort of story, Ma's, though in another way funny.

On that night all sorts of people lost all kinds of things, lives for sure, families, friends, health, jobs, in some cases their wits. This poor woman, Ma Franci, lost all knowledge of Hindi. She'd gone to sleep knowing it as well as any Khaufpuri, but was woken in the middle of the night by a wind full of poison and prophesying angels. In that great méla of death, those rowdy, unforgettable festivities, her mind was wiped clean of Hindi, and of Inglis too, which she had also been able to speak à sa manière, she forgot all languages except her childhood speech of France. Well, this by itself was no problem, so many foreigners come to Khaufpur, how many can speak Hindi? But there was a further twist to Ma Franci's madness, when she heard people talking in Hindi or Inglis, or come to that in Urdu, Tamil, Oriya, or any other tongue used in Khaufpur, she could no longer recognise that what they were speaking was a language, she thought they were just making stupid grunts and sounds.

The orphanage was run by les réligieuses françaises, it was in Jyotinagar near the factory and on that night it was badly hit. Many of the children died, nuns too. Those who survived were sick. Afterwards Indian nuns came and the French nuns one by one were taken back home. Ma refused to leave. She said Khaufpur had felt the fist of god, the Apokalis had begun, her place was with its suffering people. So she stayed and in a loud voice prayed day and night.

None of the remaining sisters spoke français, there was no one left whose speech Ma Franci could understand, or who had any idea what she was saying. The Indian sisters did take the trouble to learn a few things such as *o*, water, *dézhoné*, meal, and *twalet*, toilet, *komoñ sava*, how's it going, etc, but this only made the old woman crazier. If they knew what proper language was, why did they keep on with their beastly gibbering?

This all was still going on when I was very small. By the time I was old enough to know who she was, my own troubles had begun and Ma Franci had already spent years with a head full of angels and a tongue sourer than a lick of tamarind.

When I've finished Ma's story Nisha asks with wet eyes, 'That poor woman, is she still here in Khaufpur?'

'She is. She lives in the convent.'

'You'll have to go back.'

'Back where?'

'Convent,' says she, snivelling into a handkerchief. 'Like you say, you will learn français no problem, you can look after that poor old lady.'

'No!'

'No? You ungrateful little wretch, what is this no?'

'It's my no, the meaning of which is no.'

'Change it to a yes.'

Eyes, I don't know how many times I told Nisha I would not go back. Ma was old. Very old. Eighty years, maybe. Perhaps a hundred. I liked her but she'd need a lot of care, plus I liked the freedom of my life, roaming with Jara, and the mind games with public and police. I was just turned seventeen, I'd been on the streets for years and was as hard-hearted a little cunt as you'll find anywhere.

'No means no.'

But Nisha too could be stubborn. She said I must learn responsibility.

'What? I'm a four-foot animal.'

'You're spoilt. It's time to grow up.' She turned her back on me. 'From now on looking after Ma Franci is part of your job, Zafar will confirm it.'

Couple of days later I arrive for work, Zafar presses a fat packet into my hand, tells me to deliver it to a family in Blue Moon Colony.

'Careful with this, it's for a family who need a new roof on their place.'

Never had I seen so much money.

'How much is here?'

'It's eleven and a half thousand rupees.'

I was amazed that Zafar, knowing I'd been a scam artist, would put so much money in my hand.

'You trust me? I could run away.'

'It's you who must learn to trust,' said he.

I replied nothing, just took the money and gave it. I despised Zafar for trusting me, and all the more because Nisha worshipped him, who was twice her age. Okay, that was none of my business but it irritated me. I denied to myself that I was beginning to have feelings for Nisha. How stupid would that be? Eyes, imagine, if a person has a rival in love, he will want that rival to be an ugly, bow-legged coward with hairs gushing from ears and nostrils, a mouth that smells like drains and skin rising up in rebellion against itself. Believe me, he will not want Zafar, who is tall, handsome, whose beard curls like a raja's and who's robed in the sweet odour of sainthood.

Not easy it's learning a language when the person who is supposed to be teaching you can't understand a dumb fucking thing you say. 'Animal, why do they make these noises?' Ma Franci would ask in her singsong voice. She asked in français, but somehow the meaning leaked into my brain.

When Ma shouted, *sallo purqwatu na parlpa lalang yumain?* I had no idea what the sounds meant, but I knew what *she* meant. It took a while, maybe two to three weeks, to get the hang of français, it helped that although Ma didn't realise it there's still quite a bit of Hindi in what she said.

'Ça va, Ma?'

'Achchha Jaanvar. Et toi?'

"Sirez quelq'chose?

'Animal, if you can learn to speak properly, why do these fools talk rubbish all the time?'

'It is not rubbish Ma Franci, it is another language.'

'Go on with you,' she says. 'I know many languages. These people are just drivelling. Why do they do it? Why won't they treat me like a human being?'

Je ne sais pas, Ma, je suis un animal.

Ma was very old and more crotchety than ever. When I had mastered français, the other nuns learned for the first time that Ma thought they were gibbering nonsense. It went down badly. Gone in the head, they said, she'll be better off in France, in a house for old nuns where everyone speaks français.

Stupidly, I told Ma about this idea of her going back to France. She grew upset. 'Non, Animal, mon travail c'est dans le royaume des pauvres.' My work's in the kingdom of the poor, it's what she called the slums of Khaufpur.

Next morning, Ma goes off to her work, which is moving from house to house attending to small sicknesses and injuries. How she manages without language no one knows except me who shares that gift, there's more said in a smile. By evening when I show up at the convent, Ma has not returned. This is unusual and the nuns are worried so I've gone out searching. Many bidonvilles has Khaufpur, where to begin? In Qazi Camp Ma had much work, but no one there has seen her. I spend an hour in this one place.

Next I've headed to Phuta Maqbara. Behind the ruined tomb that stands among the shacks of the poor, the moon's rising, and with it rises my fear. Fear plus guilt, it's me who's stirred up this trouble. In the disquiet moonlight I search alley after alley, find only shadows. It's seriously late. A loony old nun out alone, who might she meet? Where might she have fallen?

I go back to the convent, hoping she might have returned. All the

40

lights are on, they're saying prayers for her safety. I go out again right away. Towards midnight I come to the Nutcracker. Of all Khaufpur's slums this is the biggest and most desperate, but for that reason also the most interesting, I could spend all day there flying kites of gossip. Now I'm asking everyone I meet if they have seen Ma. No one has. Right in the heart of the Nutcracker, at the crossing of Paradise Alley and Seven Tailors' Gully is Chunaram's chai shop, where it's my habit to drop in each afternoon to taunt its owner and blag cups of tea. When I reach it the place is shutting down for the night, one kerosene lamp there's with the wick turned down, couple of guys playing cards in the gloom, but here finally I get word. Someone had seen an old woman of Ma's description leaving the house of Huriya Bi. Eyes, do you remember that I mentioned hearing Aliya's voice calling me to play? Her granny said I behaved like a kid? Well, Aliya's granny is Huriya Bi. The moon's lost behind clouds, in full darkness I've groped my way up Seven Tailors' towards the northern edge of the Nutcracker. By now most people are sleeping, here and there are a few flickering lights behind the sack doors of the houses and from within, soft voices and coughing. No light there's in the tiny house of Huriya Bi, it's a shack with no door just a black opening. I've gone in and shaken the sleeping forms. Huriya waking with a start, says 'Goodness, is it Friday?'

'Granny, it's me Animal.' I've whispered, so as not to wake Aliya and Hanif, her granddad. 'I'm looking for Ma. She's not returned to the convent. Everyone is worried something bad has happened.'

'What's happened?' she asks, mishearing me. 'Is it the factory?' Like all the folk living round here, she's terrified that one night the factory will rise from the dead and come striding like a blood-dripping demon to snatch them off.

'Ma's missing. I've been searching for hours.'

'Your Ma? Ma Franci?'

'Yes, yes.' I can just make out her shape, leaning up on an elbow.

'Are you hungry, son? Have you had anything to eat today?'

41

'Never mind about that,' says I, cursing the frail wits of the old. 'Have you seen Ma Franci?'

There's silence while the old lady sweeps her head clear of dreams. Then she says, 'Ma Franci was here earlier, chatting away like always about who knows what. She was laughing a lot. I do not know where she went.'

'I do,' says a little voice out of the darkness. It's my naughty friend Aliya. 'Want me to show you?' I swear she'd have jumped up and come, but by this time her grandfather Hanif Ali's also awake, even his parakeets have started squawking. The old people keep her wrapped tight in her sheet with talk of school in the morning and slaps if she doesn't obey.

'But I know where she is. Suppose Animal can't find her?'

'I'll look after Aliya,' I say, but absolutely they refuse to let her go.

She's their only grandchild, they say, all they have in the world after their daughter, her mother, died after how many years of lung-rotting illness, she's their joy, their school-going pride, the night air is full of fever, they dare not risk the child's health, all of which the child hears with heavy hearted sighs.

'Where the Nutcracker ends,' she tells me. 'Cross the tracks.'

Well at least the moon's out again. In hardly two hundred paces I've come to the gleaming rails beyond which is the factory wall enclosing its enchanted forest. Halfway across I have to stop for a train to pass, it goes by close, big wheels pumping right by my head, sparks flying, lump of coal's dropped, rolls to my feet, lies there like the fire in a dog's eye till the moonlight puts it out. When the last echoes are gone I hear the sound of old woman's quavering

Quand j'étais chez mon père,
Petite à la ti ti, la ri ti, tonton lariton

A little way off, across the tracks and near the factory wall, is a falling down tower of stone with grass growing out of its walls. Some bigwig built it hundreds of years ago, in those days the factory lands were orchards. It was maybe a tomb, no one knows its purpose, when the poison factory came and threw its wall around the orchards, this ruin was left outside. Out of this place is coming the singing, a faint light flickers inside.

That's where I find her, sitting on the floor, with a simple bundle of her possessions opened and strewn around her.

'Ah, there you are, home at last,' she says. 'Be a dear and put the kettle on.'

For long I refused to admit I had feelings for Nisha. Man, how I would argue with myself. She's not even pretty. Not my type. The voices in my head grew all excited. *Oh yeah?* growls a shnaggerfucker voice, sounds like it comes from a mouth full of blood with pigs' teeth curling from the corners.

Could you be loved? demands another.

Listen, I like those film girls with made up faces, they make an effort to look pretty.

All know what he wants! hisses a sly she hovering near my left ear.

I reply that of course I fucking want. Who doesn't? But nearest I've ever got's looking at pictures that Farouq showed me, torn from a magazine. Farouq goes to see dirty flicks in the dive underneath Laxmi Talkies, made-in-USA movies screened by the Happiness Association. He tried to take me once, but they wouldn't let me in because I wasn't a member.

Pussy pussy pussy, says a voice full of dark horrifying laughter.

Fuck off, says I, refusing to be scared. Not all of the voices are mocking or hostile. Some are friendly, they tell me not to worry, I should listen to them, they will tell me the best way to proceed. You too can fuck off, I tell them. You are all pathetic. Voices without bodies, what the fuck is the use of you? Without me you're nothing.

We've minds, blinds, lemon rinds

But no bodies. It's why you get so excited, having no bodies of your own you can only feel sexy when I do. This is why you're always putting these thoughts in my head.

44

we are voices loud and clear
in all the world there's none like we're
as for you one thing is sure
dirty little fucker you're

I don't know about where you live, Eyes, but here in Khaufpur you can see everything on the internest. Guys with money can go to this shop, they have booths with computers that show sex. The guys can see as much as they like, the owners even leave rags in the booths. Farouq, Zafar's 2iC, told me this, he claims you can even get in touch with girls, like in *Dil Hi Dil Mein* didn't Sonali Bendre meet Kunal that way? Stupid movie, with a crap song, *dub you dub you dub you love dot com*? Farouq is always singing it.

Fancy Sonali do you? sniggers blood tusks.

Could you be loved?

Definitely, I like filmi girls like Sonali who take the trouble to look good.

What's Sonali? Big nose she has.
Long as your dong. Thick as your dick. Gock as your cock.

Doesn't even make sense. Shut up, please.

Thing you want takes two. What girl'll do it with you?

Fuck off, fuck off, fuck off!

I wanted it so badly, every night the wishing would make my monster hard. In my living rough days I'd often pass through Khaufpur's street of brothels, it was close to the cafes where I liked to beg, sometimes the mamas would take girls in for their meals as they never had time to cook, one or two of the girls I got to know, they'd wave at me and smile. I thought if I could get some money together plus take a good bath, have some clean thing to wear, I could maybe visit one of those places. One girl

45

particularly I liked, young she was, her name was Anjali, she'd smuggle me bits of paratha from the restaurant and joke about what a handsome, tough fellow I was. I'd say to her, 'Don't mock, it's not kind.' 'Who's mocking?' she'd reply. She'd give a laugh, go off wiggling her backside, over her shoulder blowing me a kiss.

Maybe she was not mocking. Four parts of me that are strong and good, my face is handsome, I have powerful arms, solid muscled chest. As for the last . . . 'My god what a lund. Fucker is made like a donkey.' This was the joke of Farouq and his chums when they caught me once, splashing in the factory lake. 'Jaanvar you are hung like . . . a jaanvar.' Yes, and what joy I have found in that strong, lovely tower that oozes milk like a frangipani.

Love is different and more difficult. It has nothing to do with sex. This is what I tried to make my voices understand. Quietly does love happen. You're not even thinking about romance, then she smiles and you notice for the first time that she's not all that plain, her face is really quite sweet. You watch for her smile and notice that it pushes her cheeks up into two mango shapes, why should this shape be so pleasing, I don't know. Then one evening she puts kajal round her eyes and brushes her hair, looks quite transformed, and suddenly Sonali Bendre is not so desirable as this one who's been under your nose for so long, who's all dolled up to go somewhere you're not going, can never go.

I liked it when she smiled at me, this is how it started. So I'd do things to make her smile. Next I started noticing every time she smiled at Zafar. This is how the poison of love enters the blood. If ever their hands touched I'd feel a jab. I began making snidy remarks and did not like it when sometimes they would take themselves off to her room and I was not invited.

'So what's the big secret?' I asked the second or third time this happened, I was trying to make a joke of it. Zafar danced his eyebrows in a wouldn't-you-like-to-know style, but Nisha told me not to be foolish, they simply wanted to leave her dad to listen to his music in peace. In truth who knew what the fuck they were doing?

Of course I had no chance with Nisha. She was besotted with Zafar and my back was bent as a scorpion's tail. Over and over I'd tell myself, if only I could stand up straight, it might be a different matter, that old guy wouldn't have a chance. This made me feel better, but changed nothing. What hope was there that my back would ever unbend? I complained to Nisha that everyone else would one day get married, but no girl would ever look at me. She said, 'It's not what's outside that matters, inside you is a beautiful man.'

'I'm not a man,' I said. Even notions like these she got from Zafar. When I talked of my situation she chewed her cheek and fell into long thoughtful silences. Her hair would drift over her eyes, she'd brush it off as if it were some annoying insect. I would have liked to stroke her hair, but I didn't dare. Once, I tried in a subtle way to show her my feelings, I said, 'Nish, if you're ever unhappy, just remember, for your sake I'll do anything.'

She laughed and told me I was sweet and she was not unhappy. This did not satisfy me, I wasn't sure she had got the point. In Khaufpur we have an expression, *kya main Hindi mein samjhaun*? Should I say it in Hindi? In other words do I have to fucking spell it out? 'Sorry.' I said, 'I shouldn't presume.'

She placed a finger to my lips. 'Hush. Silence also speaks.'

'Silence is what makes sound into song.' This is what Nisha's father pandit Somraj told me one time, amazed I was that he talked to me. This was not long before Elli's arrival, which I'll come to soon. It was the rainy season and I was on the verandah peeling potatoes, admiring the large frangipani tree that grew in his garden. During the monsoon it would make flowers, white with golden hearts and such a scent, somewhat like jasmine. On this day the tree was full of flowers, rain was dripping through its leaves. Pandit Somraj came out and stood for a while beside me.

'Are you hearing it too?' he asked, solemn as ever.

'Hearing what sir?' As you know I was scared of Somraj, plus he's the kind of man you can't say a bad thing about, nothing's scarier than that.

'In Inglis,' he says, 'there is a word SILENT, which means khaamush, it has the exact same letters as the word LISTEN. So open your ears and tell me, what can you hear?'

I could hear nothing save a frog calling, crikkk-crikkk, crikkk-crikkk, happily looking for another frog to fuck.

'Just a frog.'

'*Just* a frog? Let me tell you, that frog contains more music than most pandits. This song of his is said to inspire the note of *dha*, which is the sixth note of our scale.'

'Sir,' I said, 'I think you are making me a Cha Hussain.'

'Not a bit, I am quoting the opinion of a sage called Kohala, he was the son of Bharata, who wrote *Natyashastram*, it's our earliest book on music.'

He looks so solemn, standing with his head cocked on one side listening to the randy frog that I can't help it I start laughing and he says to me be quiet and listen, music does not all have to be made with strings and bows and pipes, it can also be made by drops of rain or wind cut by a leaf.

'Sir, I don't understand.'

'Do you like music?'

'Very much, sir,' says I whose deep voice can carry a film song, oh yes it's *chai chappa chai* with full wiggling of upraised backside, wah wah darlings, where will you find better entertainment? Of course I could never speak of such things to the great *Aawaaz-e-Khaufpur*, these low performances are reserved for Chunaram's chai shop.

'Would you like to learn singing?'

'I would be no good, sir.'

'Sing a note for me please.'

'Please no sir.' Who was I to sing to him?

'Go ahead without fear,' he says kindly, which I've dared not refuse so I've opened my mouth and sung, 'Aaaaa!'

'Well, you make a pleasant sound. So then, if the frog is *dha* then you

48

have just sung *ga*, the third note. So sing again, *ga*. Now if I sing *pa*, the fifth note, then between you, me and the frog we have a tune, we can even say it's like raga Deshkar. Like this, listen, *ga pa dha ga dha, dha pa ga, ga pa dha pa ga, ga dha, ga pa dha, pa dha ga pa*.'

But these notes he does not sing, he speaks them. 'Animal, if you know how to listen you can hear music in everything.'

Then he says that according to the old writers, peacocks, goats and even the grey herons which sometimes we'd find dead beside the Kampani's lakes, these creatures too sing notes of the scale, and if you listen carefully you can hear the same notes in many other things which you wouldn't expect such as the creaking of bicycle wheels and bhutt-bhutt pigs because all things make their own kind of music. 'Listen to how the rain is dripdrop dripping into the pond, *plink PLONK plank*, it's raga Bilaval.'

Never had I heard him utter so much, nor had ever he addressed so many words to me, I sat thrilled as he spoke on, until at last he came to an end, gave me a friendly look and said, still without a smile, 'Please don't mention this conversation to anyone else, especially to Nisha, I know you are close to her, if I talk to her of such things she becomes afraid that I am losing my wits. But I understand that you too have a power of hearing, so you will understand.'

Actually what I understood was never mind bicycles, if the poor sod hears music in such things as bhutt-bhutt pigs, he must be fully fishguts. If he had not been such a forbidding man with good reason to have lost his noddle I might have made a joke of it, but on every subject other than music he was totally sane, and the fact that he was Nisha's dad, plus I had my lunch every day in his kitchen were good reasons to be civil.

On a morning of rain, cloud horses pissing in the eye of the world, Nisha says to me, 'Animal, coming to the court?' Seems there's yet another hearing in the case against the Kampani. I've no particular love of the court, who've seen more than enough of it in my scamming days, but

'Why not?' I hear myself say. 'I've nothing better to do.' Well, it's Nisha.

Normally Nisha would have gone on Zafar's motorbike, but today as there's three of us, we take Bhoora's auto. Eyes, you want to know what is an auto, it's a scooter-rickshaw with three wheels, except the way Khaufpuris drive they spend more time on two. Bhoora hangs round the Chicken Claw, if you see a guy curled up asleep in the back of his auto, spirals of orange peel on the ground nearby, you can be sure it's Bhoora. Wake him up his deep-set eyes will open and look at you as if you're part of his dream, then slowly he'll start to grin. 'Kyoñ Khã, aaj kahaañ chalogé?' So, brother, where to today?

The three of us are in the back of the auto, Zafar is looking at papers, Nisha's just gazing at the passing city and I am pressed tight between them feeling the warmth of her thigh against my hip. Things start happening in my Kakadu shorts, relief it's when Bhoora from the driver's seat turns to engage Zafar in conversation.

'So Zafar brother, will there be some progress in the case?'

'Who can tell?' says Zafar, flipping over pages. 'One day something must surely happen, why not today?'

'That's a fine philosophy,' says Bhoora. 'Me, I'd have long ago given up.'

'Giving up is not Zafar's style,' says Nisha from the danger side.

'Eighteen years, it's the lifetime of my eldest,' says Bhoora. 'Boy's just got married, his wife has a liking for chicken, daily it's Selim get me a chicken, and make sure it has no pink feathers.' Bhoora swerves to miss an onrushing bhutt-bhutt pig. 'How is the boy to afford any chicken let alone a non-pink one?' Eyes, I should explain that at Khaufpuri chicken centres they put a pink mark on yesterday's birds, which are cheaper because they've been in the cages an extra day, it makes them taste not so good.

'Bhooré miyañ,' says Nisha, 'you can't blame the girl for being used to good things. This is your fault for finding him a wife with expensive tastes.' She leans past me and gives Zafar a smile which turns my stomach.

'So what's he doing now, your son?' asks Zafar with a chuckle.

'Zafar bhai, he wants to be an engineer, but I told him, all such fancy ideas forget, learn to drive an auto, it's not such a bad life.'

'Auto driving is honest work,' says Zafar, 'but an engineer's wife could eat chicken twice a day.' I can hear the bugger's mind churning, he's thinking how he can help Bhoora's son find the money for training. No wonder people adore him.

'At least I now know what advice to give,' says Bhoora. 'Zafar bhai says tell your wife that one day she will surely have chicken, just she may have to wait eighteen years.'

The case is supposed to start in court two, Naya Adalat, at ten o'clock. Quarter to ten we are outside, half past ten we're still waiting. There's just Nisha, Zafar and me. No sign of judge, lawyers. Defendants are a whole nother joke, eighteen years late, what's a few more minutes?

'Such a faith in the law my dad has,' says Nisha, 'he should see this.' She tosses her hair, which is a thing girls learn to do from the movies to show they're annoyed, then gives a little glance at Zafar. I really hate seeing her look to him for approval, but Zafar just nods, again checks the clock.

I've tugged his trouser to get his attention. 'Why don't you wear a watch?'

'What, and handcuff myself to time?' He gives me a grin. He's thinking, I guess, that I'll ask him to explain, so I don't ask.

Nisha leans against Zafar and closes her eyes, putain strokes her hair.

'In this very court,' I say to break the fucking spell, 'I used to be a mystery defendant.' So then they want to know how, when, why etcetera, and I've done the voices.

— *Case against boy known as Animal, section chaar sau bees.*
— *Where is the accused?*
— *Your honour he is here.*
— *Where? I don't see him.*
— *Right here, your honour, in the dock.*
— *Don't be silly. I am looking at the dock, there's no one there.*
— *Your honour, accused is of unusual stature.*

51

Zafar's chuckling. Nisha pats my shoulder. 'Such a fool.'

'Not such a fool,' says Zafar. 'Empty dock's our problem too.'

Ten to eleven the judge finally turned up, arrived too are some local lawyer types in black suits. 'New judge,' sighs Nisha. 'I was four years old when this case began, now it's had thirteen judges.'

'Lucky for some.' I've climbed on the backs of the public seats, which is the only way I can catch a sight of the new m'lord, plus it brings my head close to Nisha's. She turns and smiles at me. Every bad thought about her and Zafar, they are instantly forgotten.

The judge is sat wrapped in a black robe looking serious, the legal types are gathered in front of him, talking loudly.

'I just wish . . .' says Nisha, again turning her head to me, I can smell the sweetness of her breath. 'Yes?' But she's abruptly stopped because a familiar voice is speaking. It's Zafar. He introduces himself, seems he's an intervenor in the case. Zafar's specs are flashing, beard's jutting, he says he has a petition to put, at which a couple of the local lawyers start giggling.

'My lord,' says Zafar, 'there are two sets of defendants in this case, first there are the local accused, employees of the Kampani, their personal defence lawyers are here before you. Then there are the Amrikan accused, ergo the Kampani itself plus the big bosses who took the crucial decisions. For the past eighteen years these Amrikan defendants have not shown up in this court. They have not even bothered to send lawyers. They sit in Amrika claiming this court has no jurisdiction over them, yet nothing can be achieved without them being here, thus these proceedings drag on and on, for the people of this city justice continues to be delayed and denied.'

'I have done my homework Mr Zafar,' says the judge drily. 'What is your point?'

'My point, sir, is that thousands in this city have died since that night, for them was no justice. The factory is abandoned full of chemicals which as we speak are poisoning the water of thousands more. Must all perish before these Amrikan defendants appear? Speaking plainly, with no disrespect to you, I think in no other country would the law be allowed to become such a farce, if the will existed to resolve this matter, it could have been done long ago.'

Sniggers come from the local lawyers, the judge is tapping a pencil on his desk, looking irritated. 'So have you come to lecture us?' he says. 'Or do you have something useful to say?'

'Sir,' says Zafar, 'the Kampani chooses to ignore your court, but this same Kampani has many offshoots and subsidiaries trading in India. Our prayer is for you to issue a summons to the Kampani and its named bosses in Amrika, requiring them to submit themselves for trial before this court. If still they do not appear then in accordance with the due provisions of the law, let all the Kampani's assets in India be attached.'

Well, at this, a couple of the local lawyers start giggling. 'Your lordship,' says one, 'we have lost count of how many times over the years this petition has been put by Mr Zafar to your lordship's learned predecessor in this case, before that to his learned predecessor, going further back, to his predecessor and his too, and so on beyond memory. Always it was deemed devoid of merit.'

Holy cunt, what a twisted nain rabougri is this from our own city to take the side of the Kampani? I'm glaring at this bugger with such hatred, he can surely feel me raal tapko'ing the back of his neck.

So then the judge is looking even grimmer, pencil's tapping so hard I'm thinking it will make a hole in his desk. The lawyer who spoke is looking smug, now Zafar'll get what for, here comes a right fucking coup de bec.

Says his lordship, 'Are you appearing for the Kampani, Mr Babulal?'

'No milord.'

'Mr Babulal, are you familiar with the essays of Francis Bacon?'

'No milord.'

'"Private opinion is more free, but opinion before others, is more reverent." Try to remember this, Mr Babulal.' The judge clears his throat. 'Mr Zafar, let a list of the Kampani's assets in India be drawn up and entered to the court. This case is adjourned, I will reserve my decision.'

Well, no one can believe what they have just heard. The judge leans back in his chair, like he's relishing the sensation he has created, then he turns to Babulal and says mischievously, 'I will be happy to lend you my Bacon.'

After this, great rejoicing there's on our side. On the steps of the court Zafar makes a speech. He says, 'Friends, the Kampani sitting in Amrika has everything on its side, money, powerful friends in the government and military, expensive lawyers, political masseurs, public relations men. We people have nothing, many of us haven't an untorn shirt to wear, many of us go hungry, we have no money for lawyer and PR, we have no influential friends.'

'Fuck all do we have,' shouts someone.

'Thank you,' says Zafar, all grinning, and for once does not rebuke the swearer. 'Yes, we have nothing and this makes us strong. Not just strong, but invincible. Having nothing, we can never be defeated.'

Some puzzlement there's, but Zafar rides over it. 'The Kampani and its friends seek to wear us down with a long fight, but they don't understand us, they've never come up against people like us before. However long it takes we will never give up. Whatever we had they have already taken, now we are left with nothing. Having nothing means we have nothing to lose. So you see, armed with the power of nothing we are invincible, we are bound to win.'

I've not heard this before, I guess it's Zafar's new theory, but give it ten days and it will be on everyone's lips. How happy the bugger is, he wipes his specs. Rewears them. Declares, 'Friends, today something new has happened, little enough it may be but we are going to celebrate. We'll have a picnic. We will take our whole crowd to somewhere outside the city, some spot where there's trees plus water, we'll take with us bread and chicken and sweets, we'll make tea on a fire of sticks.'

On the way home he makes Bhoora stop at a chicken centre and buys two of the biggest, juiciest fowls, not a speck of pink on their wings.

'Bhooré miyañ, here's one for your daughter-in-law, one for your wife.'

The birds are trussed and thrown, flapping, into the auto behind us.

'Just think,' marvels Bhoora when he has finished thanking Zafar. 'After eighteen long years, after all today was the day.'

'We have not won yet,' says Zafar. 'But we have to start winning one day. Why not today?'

'Why not today? Why not today?' Nisha and I start chanting. Soon Bhoora and Zafar have joined in. 'Why not today? Why not today?' To people in the street, to turbans and dhotis, shalwars and saris, to all the citizens of Khaufpur, we're calling out, 'Hey, hey, why not today?'

Soon after this I have a roundabout of madness. What happens when I go mad, the voices in my head start yelling, new voices come gupping all kinds of weird and fantastic things, words that make no sense, such as 'give us a garooli' meaning a cigarette, which I don't even smoke, or 'arelok pesalok shine from your darling arse', whether it may be some different language I don't know. Some of these voices I've already mentioned. They started when I was small, after I had the fever that bent my back, at that time most were friendly, told me stories, gave advice that saved me from quarrels etc, but they can also be nasty. They'll tell me to do bad things, or else they will say some evil thing is about to happen which often it will, during these bouts I'll be light, full of glee, I might do crazy things, I'll shout out whatever the voices say.

In this particular madness, the voices are yelling and arguing, they make so much noise I can not hear what's going on around me. It gets so bad I tell Ma. She's taken me to the big hospital where they say, joking aside, you go in with one illness come out with three. In she marches, me walking on fours at her side like a dog and demands to see the head doctor. 'Mon fils est malade, il entend des voix dans sa tête.' No one's understanding a word except me who's thinking it's nice she's called me her son. Because Ma's a foreigner and's making a grand incomprehensible fuss, they don't kick us out, but take us to the chief doctor, a high professor is he, Khaufpur's greatest expert on children born damaged by the poison.

This saala, old and fat he's, a much-writer, a whole row of pens in his shirt pocket, his head is filled with knowledge about the crazy, demented kids of Khaufpur, but never before's he met anyone like Ma, jabbering in her own tongue, pointing at me. The doctor gives me a brief look then turns to Ma and in a rough way asks, 'So what is his problem?'

'What niaiserie is this?' snaps Ma, who's no doubt thinking that such a big doctor type should make at least some effort to speak like a human being.

'Wants to know what's wrong with me.'

'J'ai déjà dit!' complains Ma. 'Il entend des voix. Il parle avec des gens qui n'existent pas.' Eyes, if you don't know français, it means, I've already said! He hears voices. He talks to people who aren't there.

'What is she saying?' asks the doctor. 'Tell her I am the director of this hospital, she can't come just like that into this office.'

'She says she has come because people say you are a great physician, the best in Khaufpur.'

At once this bastard's all smiles. 'Madam, I do my best.' He sends a self-satisfied smirk her way, totally ignoring me. 'Normally you would need an appointment, but we are not inflexible. So, dear lady what can I do for you?'

'Such guttural baliverne can you follow?' asks Ma, she has got used to the idea that I can somehow interpret the bêtises of the Khaufpuris.

'He is placing himself at your service Ma, see how he's making eyes, I think maybe he has fallen in love with you.'

'Shameless boy, tu t'en moques, soit sérieux. The people of the city are in need of care and what do they get? This baragouin.'

'What is the good lady saying?' he asks.

I was in my madness, remember, Eyes, it comes to me that I can ask him anything and there's one thing that I want more than anything in the world, yet I'm afraid to ask. A desperate business is hope, not to be encouraged if you can be content with small happiness, but the curse of human beings and this animal alike is that whatever you have, always you

56

want more. Ever since I realised my feelings for Nisha, a wish for one thing has been growing in me, day by day as I sit beside her, smell the perfume of her hair and her skin, it has become fiercer, I think unless I do something I will die, this desire will devour me and now a moment has come when I might at least ask for what I want. I cannot let it pass.

You will be disappointed, whispers a voice. *Ask!* shouts another.

Now or never. I take courage and say what's in my heart, 'Sir she wishes you to do an operation to make me stand up straight and walk on two legs.'

Now I'm down on fours looking up at this important doctor, so impatient am I for what he will say that my eyes remove from his, down his nose slide and settle on his lips, ready I'm for his reply. The lips purse and chew, he's thinking. Such a big doctor, I was right to ask, a grand professor.

Turning to Ma he says. 'Madam, I must be plain with you, whatever could have been done for this boy, the time is long past. He will have to get used to his condition. There is absolutely no hope, this boy will never walk or stand up straight again.'

Ma's asking something but I'm unable either to hear or reply. In my head a thing flees away shrieking like a bird, eee-chip-chip-chip, the sound of the world dwindles to an eerie hum. I am looking at a shelf in the professor's room. On it is a jar, a big round glass jar of liquid that flashes like it's full of sunlight.

'What did you think, it's that easy?' says a gnarly voice in my ear. 'Quit staring by the way it gives me the creeps.' Glaring at me from inside the jar is a small crooked man. An ugly little monster, his hands are stretched out, he has a wicked look on his face, as if he's just picked your pocket and is planning to piss on your shoe. Such an expression, I forget my own troubles and start laughing. There's something weird about him. Looks like someone's peering over his shoulder, a second head is growing out the side of his neck.

The doctor follows where I'm looking and turns to Ma still as if I don't exist, his lips move, I see rather than hear the words, 'Be grateful this boy's no worse, madam, that could have been him in the jar. Half of those who were expecting on that night aborted and as for the rest, well let's just say some things were seen in this town that were never seen before.'

The jar starts bubbling and shining, Ma's reply when it comes sounds like she's by a waterfall inside a huge cave, this time I don't even catch the words.

'Hey you, standing there like a fucking Sadda Miyañ ki tond, what the fuck are you looking at?' The creature's frowning through the glass of his jar.

'You, mate,' I've said still laughing. 'You are in a right fucking mess.'

'Bugger off,' says he, 'if you can't stop staring. Know what you look like to me? Come pressing your nose like a snail's foot on the glass, huge round eyes are waving, even slime do you leave from your snout's unwiped, fuckers like you have no consideration.'

'Hey hey, I too get stared at.'

'Then you know better,' he says. 'Anyway, shut up and listen. Long I've waited for a one like you. I need your help. You have to get me out of here.'

'Here's where?' I ask. 'This office, this hospital?'

'This jar, stupid. You wouldn't want to be in here, believe me, it's like being trapped in an egg.'

'Up a hen's bum?' This strikes me as so funny, hooting with laughter I'm.

'Your back is twisted,' says he with great bitterness, 'but at least you are alive. Me, I'm still fucking waiting to be born.'

'Sorry, forgive,' says I. 'Your situation is worse than mine.'

'I feel myself sinking,' says the little creature. 'I drift down into a place where it is all dark, you open your mouth but there is no air just the black stink of it filling your mouth and eyes and nose, burns too, this fucking stuff they've got me in. Cunts want to study me, but they look for the wrong things. See this second head, Animal miyañ? It's the clever one with the ideas. Such stuff it thinks, thoughts you could spin a world on. The one in front is dumb, sits swallowing liquid like a fish listening to all the shit these doctors talk. Number two knows what's what. It's stuffed with secrets they'd love to get their hands on, secrets of plants, minerals, lead to gold, mermaids, sun, moon, laughter, immortal life, all this class of thing's there, locked up in the other head, this info must never fall into their hands. You must free me.'

I'm about to ask him how I can do this when the roaring recedes, Ma's voice is buzzing in my ears, I am dropped back into this life where I find her looking questioningly at me, so I've told her I can't understand a thing the great doctor is saying, but he's sure to be talking shit as people like him always do.

'Il raconte les conneries, comme toujours.'

She gives a snort. 'As usual.' Well, I am fully back.

'What is she saying?' asks the doctor.

'She is praising your wisdom, doctor sahib and asking, what might be that creature in the jar?'

'A child of the poison,' says the mullah of medicine. 'We call it para-pagus.'

'Now what's he on about?' demands Ma.

'He says you have a voice like a nightingale.'

She simpers, 'Oh get away with you.' I can't tear my eyes away from the little bugger in the jar, I could swear he is winking at me.

'She thinks I hear voices,' I tell him.

'Should fucking hope so,' says he, 'why else do you have ears?'

This is how I met my mate the Khã-in-the-Jar, I call him that because in Khaufpur you call a friend Khã like in other places they say mate or yaar, plus he's in a jar.

59

The big thing that happened in Amrika, when it I saw it on the tele do you know what I did? I clapped! I thought, fantastic! This plane comes out of nowhere, flies badoom! into this building. Pow! Blam! Flowers of flame!

It's night, outside rain's dripping golden off the roof of Chunaram's chai house, turning Paradise Alley to glue. We're inside drinking tea, I'm going 'Fucking brilliant! Bollywallah special-effects, forget it!'

Zafar looks at me and says, 'You fucking idiot, Animal, this isn't a movie. This really happened. It's a terrible accident that just happened.'

Really upset he must be, who almost never swears.

'Wasn't an accident,' chips in someone. 'The plane didn't even try to miss.' The tele is going crazy, playing the crash over and over again. Commentators are shouting. No one knows what's happening. Nine-fingered Chunaram, our host of the chai shop, smooth-talking ex-leper, kebab-genius, doesn't care what the fuss is about, in heaven the fucker is. From all over the Nutcracker, people drawn by the commotion are coming running through the mud. Chunaram's tin shack is crammed with gawpers, some at least will buy his tea and snacks. Thrilled he's to see the tele earning its keep. Bribes must be paid to run the wire that steals electric from the munsipal. Pays to invest.

'My god, how awful! How terrible!' voices round the room are saying as the shimmering blue shape in the corner once more bursts into flame. These two women, Ashraaf and Bano, they are crying, I can make out the shine of tears. Me. I don't believe it's real. It's a hoax, clip from a movie, trailer of some coming multi-starrer. Has to be.

'In Amrika bombs, explosions, buildings falling, such things are normal. I'm telling you, yaar, see *Fight Club*.' It's Farouq, the movie expert.

60

'So what are you saying?' I ask. 'Normal it's a movie, or normal it's not a movie?'

'Arsehole, who asked you to speak?' replies Farouq. It's like that between him and me. Arsehole? I've looked at Zafar, but he's locked to the screen.

Even after the second, third, fourth, fifth and sixth planes hit and all those buildings fall, Zafar maintains it is not a movie. Zafar has to be wrong. Stuff like that doesn't happen in real life. Not in Amrika anyway. Here in Khaufpur it's different. Here in Khaufpur we had that night. Nothing like that has ever happened anywhere else.

'How can it be happening right now?' I ask. 'Look outside, it's dark, it's raining, but these buildings are in sunshine.'

'Wah, you idiot!' cries Farouq. 'Don't you know there's a time difference between Khaufpur and Amrika? When it's night here, it's day there.'

'I tell you it's a movie. Soon it will finish. Words will come, THE END.' But now I'm feeling stupid, which I hate. 'Tell me what happens,' I say. 'I have to get Ma's supper.'

I've got down from my chair to the floor. 'Let's go,' I say to Jara. She gets up and follows me out.

'C'était un film,' I tell Ma Franci when we get home. 'C'est normal.'

Says Ma, 'Pauvre Jaanvar à quatre pattes, pour toi c'est quoi le normal?' Poor four-foot Animal, for you what is normal?

'I see a star fall from heaven, the abyss opens, out pours smoke like from a great furnace, the sun and the day are gone.' Thus speaks Ma. C'est quoi le normal? Fine fucking one she is to ask this of me, ever since I told her what we witnessed she's been raving like she's fully cracked. I am trying to describe the flames, the smoke, the falling towers, she's interrupted with étoiles and abîmes, stars and abysses.

'It was a movie.'

'No Animal, it's *him*,' cries Ma in excitement or panic I can't tell. 'This is *his* work, he's up and running again, this time there'll be no stopping him.'

'What makes you so sure it's real?'

'He began the job right here in Khaufpur, now others are getting a taste.'

Ma starts gabbling on and on about *him*, what *he's* done and what *he'll* do next. She says that he is full of anger and is going to unleash his full fury on the world, all of us are going to catch it.

'Time for supper,' says I, reaching my hand into the hole in the wall where is the big purple onion I've kept aside for tonight's meal.

'Have a care!' cries Ma. Adds with a cunning look, 'Animal, dis à nos amis, soyez prêt, il vous appelera à tout moment,' it means tell our friends be ready, *he'll* be wanting you any moment.

By our friends she means the scorpions that live in our wall, press your ear to the stones you'll hear their scrapes, rustles, the clicking of tiny claws.

'What have the scorps to do with this?' I ask, removing one from the onion before extracting it from the wall.

Seems Ma has big hopes for the scorpions. 'Animal, when the time comes these little beasts who live in the walls of our house, they will come creeping out and grow huge. They'll reach the size of horses. They'll grow stiff red wings like locusts, that rustle when they move.They'll have faces like people and long hair like women, but their teeth will be like lions' teeth, which they'll gnash in the most horrifying way.'

'What will they do next, Ma?' I've somewhat crushed the onion with a stone, then buried it in the hot ashes of the hearth.

'They'll wear golden crowns, when they beat their wings, it'll sound like an army of chariots rushing to war.'

'And then?'

'Well, my little Animal, they'll still have their tails, only much much longer, ten feet at least with a sting the size of a bull's horn, what they'll do is they'll go around stabbing people, the ones who've done evil to others.'

'People like Fatlu Inspector and the Chief Minister? There's a little dough left, I'll make a chapatti'

'They'll sting them with their tails, and those people will want to die, but won't be able to, because the poison won't kill them. It will fill them with agony for five months.'

'Why five months?' Five months is not enough for Fatlu Inspector. 'Why not six months? Why not eighteen years?'

'It's what Sanjo saw,' says she out of the well of her madness.

Once Ma's eyes were bright blue, now they're milky with coming cataracts, but when she speaks of Sanjo such a look comes into them, you'd expect their milky clouds to part and light come streaming through. Ma brings out a small black book, it's the one written by Sanjo that tells about the end of the world, she holds it up close to her nose. 'Jusques à quand, Maître saint et vrai, tarderas-tu à faire justice? à tirer vengeance de notre sang?'

Eyes, in case you don't understand Ma's language, this is Sanjo talking to *him*, he's saying fuck's sake how much longer will you make us wait for justice? And if you still don't know who *he* is, well it's god. Sanjo reckons that the world is full of wickedness and is going to be wiped out, this will happen in various appalling ways and is called the Apokalis.

Sanjo's dream has a strange effect on Ma, it makes her afraid and joyful at the same time. Says she, 'Don't you see, my poor little Animal, the Apokalis has already begun? It started on that night in Khaufpur.'

Onion comes out of the embers looking like a ball of ash, break the crust it's juicy and sweet inside, smells good. Ma does not notice the food, so caught up is she. 'Listen, injustice will triumph, thousands will die in horrible ways. Well, what else happened on that night? Nous sommes le peuple de l'Apokalis.' We are the people of the Apokalis.

'Old woman,' says I giving her her share of the roti, 'listen to yourself. You ask what's normal for me, I'm mad only once in a while, you are full-time hypped.'

Ma grumbles about the insolence of the young. 'Mark my words,' she says. 'It has begun again, and will not stop. Round the world it will go. Right now it's in Amrika but it will return to Khaufpur. Terror will return to this city. It began here, here it will end.'

But Sanjo's wrong. Fucking world didn't end. It's still suffering.

In the low flicker of our oil lamp, Ma's face looks like a witch's, onion juice is dribbling from her jaw. No teeth, with a piece of roti she scoops the soft centre into her mouth. It's not much, a bit of salt plus a little chili would at least make the stomach glow, but we have neither.

Later, when we have turned out the lamp she says to me in the darkness, 'Animal, listen, can you hear it?'

'Hear what?'

'The wings of the beast, they sound just like metal shutters rattling down over the shop of Ram Nekchalan.'

Soon her snores tell me she is asleep.

I lie and think about the thing that happened in Amrika. Sleep stays far away, the rain has stopped, through holes in the roof stars are shining. During monsoon time I patch these gaps with plastic, thatch, anything, but wind must have blown it off. Through some deep abyss a star is falling, inside me wells a deep dread, such a terrible thing, who would have thought it could happen to others, to die in terror, may I never know such a death. Then it's like someone is singing softly in my ear

O my darling child let me wrap you up warm
your little nose, your flowerbud mouth, I'll hide from harm
and though my heart's breaking I must lay you down
and never shall we meet again till this world's overthrown

After a while the night is filled with silence and no more stars fall.

Out of the darkness comes a screaming that makes my hair stand on end. Instantly I'm awake. Not yet dawn. Another howl, it's the call of a train coming through from Delhi. In the gloom I hear Ma Franci whimpering. For Ma the hooting is not the 2616 GT Express rumbling through the Nutcracker, it's an angel in a sooty robe blowing the last trump. Ma's eyes are open, but she's fully asleep, how often have I heard her shriek in her bed, it's of that night she dreams, lying on her mat, so many years has she lain there the soft earth is moulded to her shape, the bumps and hollows near the hearth, they're made by a bony old bint who sees in dreams the moon turning to blood, the world curling up like a leaf in the palm of her hand.

Elli appeared the way a spider does, from nowhere. Catch a movement in the corner of your eye, it's there. We were all in Nisha's house, which is her dad Somraj's house in the Chicken Claw. Who's we? Nisha of course, Zafar, he virtually lived there. Farouq I've mentioned, he was Zafar's right hand man. As well as these there were some other cronies, plus me and Jara. We're on the verandah, talking about the thing that had happened in Amrika, and Farouq's chafing me because I'd thought it was a movie.

'It was you who talked of movies. Just love making me look stupid, I hate you second-most in the world.' I could not say who I detested the most.

'Animal, take your head out your arse, I mentioned movies because movies show how they live over there.'

All's set for one of our rows, but Zafar intervenes, 'We know zilch about their lives, they know nothing of ours, that's the problem.' How does a person become so fucking wise I don't know. I'm trying to think of some ploy that will make me look good in front of Nisha simultaneously making Farouq look bad in front of Zafar when suddenly this racket kicks up in the street, kids are shouting 'Aiwa! Aiwa!' Stopped outside in the slush of the Claw is a car, not an auto or even a taxi mark you, a full four-wheel car it's, driver in uniform, everything. This foreign woman has climbed out, she's stood with tilted hip, looking at the building opposite. Some man's with her, he's pointing at the building and talking, she's listening and nodding. Hardly have they arrived, but already she's gathered a small crowd. In addition to 'Aiwa, Aiwa!' the kids are calling out the other things they shout whenever they see a foreigner.

'Hello!' 'What's your name?' 'Baksheesh,' etc.

This foreigner is tall, taller than Nisha, plus to my mind très baisable, wah, what a sexy. Midriff's bare, she carries herself like someone who knows what she's about. Like in the song, zulfein hain jaise kandhon pe baadal jhuke hue, dark hair rests like a cloud on her shoulder, in the sun it's giving off bright flashes, like gold. The main thing I notice about her is that her blue jeans are so tight you can see everything. I half close my eyes and it's as if she has naked blue legs. She sees me watching her with my eyes screwed up and gives me a smile. I'm just about to wink back when Farouq nudges me with his foot and says, 'Look who's got his hopes up.'

'Just his hopes?' asks some other wag.

So then they're all laughing at me and Farouq says in a loud voice, 'Oy baba, must hurt going up the crack like that.'

Zafar was livid. 'Shut your filth!' None of them can stand up to Zafar, they hold him in some kind of awe because of how he's given up everything in his life for us Khaufpuris. Farouq starts mumbling that the woman won't understand, being a firangi, Zafar says, 'I was thinking of Nisha.'

The woman begins gupping with the kids, the moment she opens her mouth it's obvious she can speak Hindi. Farouq starts blushing but if she's heard what he said she's giving no sign. As soon as she and the man go into that building we're all over to the driver, it's who is she, what's going on, but he doesn't know fuck all except she is Amrikan. When she comes out we're still roaming around in the street. She stares a long time at me, I am hoping she doesn't think it was me that said that thing about her crack, although I can't deny I was thinking along the same lines.

Later Nisha's dad comes home from one of his meetings and tells us that she's bought the place.

All our lives we'd known the building across the road. It was dirty, in need of attention, none of us could think why an Amrikan woman would want it. It had once been a bicycle-repair shop, kept by a surly fucker called Ganesh. After that it became a sweet shop, rasgullas and gulab jamuns were fried there in big pans and we kids hung around hoping for treats. Next it was a carpenter's, turning out chairs and items like massage rollers. Then it was a tailor's place, where women from the bastis ruined their eyes doing gold and silver zari embroidery. I think one reel of gold thread was worth more than those women earned in a month. The tailors moved to a better part of town, a smart arcade where their saris could hang outside filling with wind like coloured sails and the arses waddling past took twice as much cloth to cover. After that the place stayed empty, until the blue-legged Amrikan.

What would bring an Amrikan woman to Khaufpur of all places? None of Zafar's contacts could tell us a thing about her. Labourers came, gutted the building, threw out its rotting wooden frames, burned them right there in the street. Next, carpenters arrived and Somraj came out of his house to listen to the music of their saws and drills, the drumming of their hammers. They were bossed by an old bugger in a lungi who chain-smoked two bundles of beedis a day.

'Health laboratory,' he told us, in a croaking voice.

Right off Zafar's suspicious. 'Why does an Amrikan come to do medical experiments in this town?'

'Son, why jump to conclusions?' says Somraj. How I hate to hear Nisha's dad calling Zafar son. 'What better place for a health laboratory than a town full of sickness?'

Zafar shakes his head. 'It's the timing that's strange.'

His frown deepens when a few days later a van arrives bringing mashins various and plural, such as are found in hospitals. 'I can just smell the Kampani,' says Zafar.

'Some keen nostrils you've,' says I because he irritates me.

'Okay so figure it yourself. Since Bhoora's chicken day barely six weeks have passed, we're awaiting the judge's decision. Let's say he finds in our favour. Then if the Kampani bosses still won't come to court, their other businesses could be seized. That they can't risk, so right now they are planning how they'll fight if they are forced to come to the court.'

'Sorry boss, still don't get it.'

'Think like the Kampani. Thousands of people say that for twenty years their health's been ruined by your poisons. How do you refute this? We say that the situation is not as bad as alleged, that not so many people are ill, that those who are ill are not so seriously ill, plus of whatever illnesses there are, most are caused by hunger and lack of hygiene, none can be traced back to that night or to your factory.'

'Zafar brother,' says Farouq. 'These "yous" and "yours" make me feel sick in the gut. Let the Kampani say what it likes, who'll believe? People here know the truth.'

'You are the Kampani,' says Zafar, showing no sympathy for Farouq's gut. 'Thousands more claim that your factory has poisoned their water and made them sick. To refute them you'll say that whatever may be in the wells, it does not come from the factory, that the chemicals in the factory don't cause those kinds of illnesses. To make such arguments you need facts and figures. You need case histories, a health survey. Now do you see? Abracadabra-funtootallamish! Out of the blue appears an Amrikan to start a health laboratory.'

Everyone's nodding, but my instinct says Zafar is wrong. Blue-legs does not fit my idea of a Kampani person and I'm not the only one who thinks this.

Says Somraj, 'There may be other explanations. We know nothing yet about this person. She may have no connection with the Kampani.'

'You are right, abba.' Zafar's polite as ever, but so deeply does he hate the very shadow of the Kampani that until the mystery's explained, for him it will remain a conspiracy. 'You are right, but before we can discover the truth the damage could be done. There's too much at stake. We need to plan.'

One morning a cycle rickshaw struggles up with a sign balanced across the back, so big that it's sticking out on both sides like an aeroplane's wings. On the sign is written KHAUFPUR FREE CLINIC, plus below in smaller letters, DOCTOR ELLI BARBER.

It isn't a health laboratory but a clinic, and not just any clinic, we soon learn, but a well-equipped modern clinic such as scumbags like us have never known. The *Khaufpur Gazette* runs an article. DOCTOR OFFERS NEW HOPE TO POISON VICTIMS. According to the paper, the Chief Minister has given his blessing, says the clinic is a great and wonderful act of charity by a good-hearted doctor, this Amrikan, Elli Barber.

'Sounds like Ali Baba,' says Nisha, Zafar laughs but not very happily.

The clinic is to be opened by Zahreel Khan, Minister for Poison Relief. That motherfucker's involvement plus the CM's blessing confirms all Zafar's worst suspicions.

'Praise from that quarter does not come free. What's happening?'

One morning there's a snarl-up in the street. A truck carrying bales of cotton has got itself jammed beneath a tree branch. Coming the opposite way is a bullock cart carrying four men and a strange curved case of polished wood, very large, that sticks out behind. Cart can't move forward, motorbikes and autos are jamming the road behind, terrific jackass-braying of horns there's.

The doors of the clinic fly open. Out steps Elli Barber, stands with hands on hips taking in the confusion. The truck driver's got down from his cab and is looking at the tree, auto-wallahs are mingling abuse and advice. Next thing this Elli's walked right into the middle of the mess.

'Okay, okay! everyone calm down! You sir, if you could jump up there, loosen the bale, driver-ji you move the truck back twenty feet.'

To the master of the bullock cart she says, 'If you just back up a few feet the autos will be able to squeeze through.'

'Madam,' says he, marvelling at this Hindi-speaking foreigner, 'Hardly is this some fancy car-shaar, a bullock cart it's.' He gives a roar of laughter and winks at the men behind him. 'It has no reverse gear.'

'So,' says she, 'it needs some help. Come on.' She's caught the bullocks by their nosebands and begun shoving. The men on the cart jump down to lend their shoulders. Bystanders are laughing, bullocks look amazed, they roll their eyes and toss their heads, slowly, slowly the wheels begin creaking backwards. This is not to the liking of the carter, who's now looking foolish. 'Just how am I supposed to steer?' So this Elli's jumped up on the cart. 'Move over,' she says and takes the ropes. Standing on the cart, gliding slowly backwards, she sees me chuckling and gives me a grin. But I can read feelings and it comes to me, my god, she's terrified.

'Bravo,' I call out. 'Brave you're.'

'Can't have them damaging my piano.' Next thing she's jumped down and's fussing round the men lifting the wooden case off the cart. It looks like a strange shaped coffin. The dammed up traffic begins pouring past. I've dodged my way across the lane through a frenzy of horns.

'Excuse me. What is a piano?'

Closer up she doesn't seem so glamorous. Her two eyes are set a little bit close to her nose, but wah! those legs! right now's their V just in front of my face. Voices in my head start making filthy comments.

'It's a musical instrument,' says Elli Barber. Seeing I'm none the wiser she explains, 'It has keys. You press them to get the notes.'

'Black and white keys?' Pandit Somraj in his house has a harmonium with such keys.

'That's right.' She steps back and's staring at me like she did the first time. 'Your back. How long's it been this way?'

'Long as I can remember.'

'Do you know what caused it?'

'Fuck should I know?' The rough words just jump out. After the grand children's doctor, I've vowed never again to talk of my back.

'Has no doctor ever explained?' she asks, unfazed by my rudeness.

'What's the point?'

'You see, if we knew why—'

I've turned and walked away on my hands and feet. Fuck and bugger why, such unanswerable questions just lead to discussions about the nature of god.

After some time I look back. The men are trying to squeeze the piano box through her doors, but she isn't watching them, she's looking at me. It's that stare, we call it ghurr ghurr. Of a sudden her eyes from across the street seem to grow larger, a voice inside my head says, *She will change your life!*

When I regain my senses, I'm in Somraj's house, with Nisha bent over me. 'What happened, darling, we were so worried about you?'

What happened? At the moment I heard the voice speak those words I turned and dived in pursuit of it. The universe with all its stars and galaxies is a pinhead compared to the space inside the mind. Into that deep abyss I went diving, chasing the voice which fled away downwards squeaking like a bat. I flew through clouds of voices, must have been millions of them, only one comment do I remember. *You got angry because when you looked at her you thought sex, when she looked at you she thought cripple.*

'Some men brought you here,' Nisha says. 'Along with that foreign woman from across the road. She said sorry for not taking you inside her place, it is not ready. She thinks you had a fit, but you don't have fits, do you darling?' Nisha's long hair as she bends over me, touches my face. Forget legs, forget sex, sweeter by far is love.

Doesn't bear a grudge, Elli doctress. Next time I see her she gives a big smile. 'Hello Animal, how's tricks?' How did she find out my name? Elli always seems to be laughing. She's a loud voice, isn't shy to call out greetings in the street. Soon the entire basti knows her to say hello. Next she's hired some staff for her clinic, we get to know them as well. There's Dayanand the manager, Suresh compounder plus an Anglo-Indian lady called Miriam Joseph, wears dresses with large flowers.

When Miriam Joseph sees me she says, 'Animal, isn't it? Y'all remember me? I'd see all of y'all when I came to mass in the convent, my, how the world's changed.' She scratches her armpit, looking sad, so I guess the convent is just not the same without Ma and me. Miriam must have told Elli my name so that small mystery is solved. Just leaves the big one.

Everyone is buzzing about the clinic. Why should such a thing be started in Khaufpur by an Amrikan woman? On whose behalf has she come? Seems Zafar's suspicions have spread for there's murmuring that Elli doctress, it's what the Khaufpuris call her, has been sent by the Kampani.

'So what if she has?' reply some to this rumour. 'The Kampani made us ill, why shouldn't it make us well again?'

'More than this,' say others. 'Why should anyone else have to pay for our treatment? It's the Kampani alone who should pay.'

'Better it's the Kampani's clinic,' yet others argue. 'Only the Kampani knows what deadly things flew from the factory on that night, who else will know the antidotes?'

People settle like mosquitoes on Elli doctress's staff and probe with sharp questions to suck out the truth.

'Elli madam is a good person,' Suresh the compounder tells a small crowd in the Chicken Claw. 'With her own money she's making this clinic. She left a big job in Amrika out of pity for the people of Khaufpur.'

Well this sounds pretty unlikely. Plenty of Amrikans are here in Khaufpur these days doing all kinds of work from teaching to planting herb gardens, all are here because they don't agree with what the Kampani did, but not one has ever opened a clinic. Not with their own money. Not by themselves.

Manager Dayanand buys his chaws in Ram Nekchalan's grocery store, it's where the people of the Claw gather to chat and get their news. We soon learn that he's partial to laal imli ka gatagat which is tamarind bits, two rupees per small piece, nicely sour, with some salt and spices, good for the digestion, but when we ask about his new boss, apart from confirming that Elli's spending her own money, he's as clueless as everyone else. Dayanand was introduced to her by an elderly doctor for whom he once worked. This doctor is retired, lives in a posh house up by the lake. Elli doctress stayed with him when she first came from Amrika, he helped her find staff for the clinic. More than this Dayanand does not know or else is not willing to say.

From where does one woman get money enough to open a clinic? This is what everyone's asking. 'Must be rich.' But Elli doesn't seem the rich type, she doesn't ride round in big cars, okay, she turned up here in a government car but since then's only used three-wheeler autos. A few times she's travelled with my mate Bhoora Khan and's haggled over each journey.

'Elli doctress, she's a real tight-fist, bloody,' says he ruefully, who like all auto-wallahs thinks foreigners should pay more than locals. This isn't only fair it's mathematical. Amrikan one dollar's forty rupees, therefore one Khaufpuri kilometer should equal forty Amrikan ones. But when Bhoora tells her this Elli doctress just laughs and asks him to calculate instead by the mathematics of free medicine.

Elli doesn't dress rich, never is she to be seen in anything but her blue jeans, plus the rich don't mix with the likes of us, but Elli likes joking with the street urchins, does not mind them shouting 'Aiwa' and 'I love you' at her, pretty soon every kid in the Chicken Claw knows her name, plus that she has come from Amrika and does not give sweets or baksheesh.

One day Elli herself goes into Nekchalan's shop. What she says to him I don't know but from that moment he's her greatest fan.

'When this clinic opens,' Nekchalan tells all who'll listen, 'any of us can walk right in off the street, we'll be examined, we'll get treatment, medicines, and how much will we pay?' He pauses for effect, fucking bada batola, so important and knowledgeable, bigshot in the street, it's a long long pause, full of Nekchalan.

'Come on then, tell us how much?'

'Nothing.' Nekchalan's smiling like he's Elli's best friend, like he'd helped her plan the clinic.

'What?' people gasp. 'Really free?' Don't forget, the government hospitals too are supposed to be free, but their kind of free no one can afford.

'Fully free,' says Nekchalan, trousering the money for their tea, matches, salt, flour, oil, whatever.

Word's soon spread from the Chicken Claw to Jyotinagar, Phuta

Maqbara, the Nutcracker where Ma and I live, plus to other areas near the factory where lots of people are still ill. Free of charge? Treatment from a foreign doctor? Sounds too good to believe, but if Ram Nekchalan says it's true. Nekchalan doesn't cheat people, never gives short measure, usually will tip in a little extra of whatever it is they are buying, rice, sugar, daal, kerosene.

Wonderful guy? I don't think so. A little generosity keeps them crowding into his shop, and friend Ram is getting fat on his own goodness.

'Now we'll get some good treatment,' this is what everyone's saying. Kampani or no Kampani, the Khaufpuris are all for the clinic.

How would Elli Barber change my life? Of unknotting the rope of my spine there was no hope, and from the day of meeting the Khã-in-the-Jar the very idea of hope had become bitter and repulsive to me. One day I said to Zafar, 'Hope is a crutch for weaklings. The strong carry on without.'

He nodded and beamed at me. 'Brother, you're right. Let go of hope and keep fighting, it's the lesson of Khaufpur.'

I was actually surprised that he agreed. I'd been thinking of my own case, plus I was trying to needle him. How could he carry on his long fight without hope? Wasn't it he who'd said, 'Why not today?'

'That's not hope.' He thought for a moment. 'You can fight without hope, if the heart finds strength in something stronger.'

'What's that?' I knew I shouldn't have asked.

'Well,' says the fool, removing and wiping his specs as he always did when he was feeling emotional. 'It is love.'

randy Animal needs a wife
how will Elli change his life?

Eyes, did I just now say 'Forget sex?' What fucking hypocrisy! Sex was the one thing I could never forget, my second impossible wish. My first

75

wish was to stand upright, but why did I want that if not because it led to the second?

talks of love, the little prick
but anywhere would plunge his dick

The thought of sex was in my head when I woke in the morning with my thing huge like a cricket bat, plus again when I lay down at night, thinking of what I couldn't have. On nights when the urge was strong, let's face it, almost every night, I'd pretend there was a woman lying beside me. She'd stroke me all over, when I was good and ready she'd show her secret place. The rest you may imagine, I certainly did, but of what use is a cunt of hay when it's a real live creature you want in your arms?

In what way would Elli change my life? Well Eyes, you can call me seven suppurating kinds of fool, but if Elli wasn't to mend my back, for me it left only one other possibility.

Animal you stupid schmuck you
really think she's going to fuck you?

One evening me, Zafar, Farouq and a couple of others from the group are in Nisha's garden, looking at Elli Barber's building. There's a light on at a second floor window. A tree's growing up right beside it.

Zafar jokes 'Maybe we should climb up and see what's going on in there.'

'I'll do it'. I don't know why I say this. Not to impress Nisha because she isn't there, maybe just to show I'm as good as them. Well, I've got strong arms, probably stronger than any of them. I can haul myself up with no need of legs.

This tree, it's a large mango, growing right by the building. We go over to it and Zafar says, 'Do you need a leg up?' I tell him to fuck off, there's enough knobbles sticking out I don't need any help. After the first branch

76

it's easier but still not that easy. I've gone up the tree best I can arm over arm, the buggers below in the dark egg me on in loud whispers. 'Higher, Animal, you bastard.' 'Come on, show us what you're made of.'

Higher up the branches spread out and nearly touch the wall, but they're starting to get bendier plus there's still a long way to climb. I've to pull myself up, get an elbow over, haul my body across, then twist and roll my arse onto the branch. Tough work it's, the legs being useless and all. I'm wearing nothing but my kakadu shorts, and getting scratched to fuck by thorns and twigs.

'Fucker climbs like a monkey.' From the darkness there's a laugh that sounds like that lout Farouq. I look down to give him a scowl, it's a long drop to where they're clustered at the foot of the tree.

The building's right across the road from Nisha's house. From where I'm perched I can see Pandit Somraj sitting in his room listening to music. Listen, listen, listen, it's all he does all day and night. If he isn't listening to records he's listening to the radio, if he isn't listening to the radio, he's listening to his students, or else to frogs and bicycle pumps and dripping taps. Nisha's inside with her father. I can see her offering him a cup of something and my heart thuds like a dholak thrashed by a monkey. Taka dum takataka dum dhoiiing dhooom! Better she stays inside. Zafar said not to tell her what we were doing. Nisha wouldn't approve. Spying on the Amrikan, she'd say it's immoral.

'Well done, keep going.' It's Our Leader, always has an encouraging word. Mr Perfect, fuck him.

'Shut up!' I hiss. 'She'll hear you!'

'Don't worry she'll think you're a baboon,' says Farouq.

I consider pulling down my kakadus and shitting on Farouq's head, but I can't see him well enough, just the glow of someone's beedi.

'Too big for a monkey,' someone else chips in.

'What does she know?' says Farouq. 'She's Amrikan.'

Eventually I get going again. I am still below the window but it is getting nearer. I can now see the ceiling, which is a bright pink, like the inside of a camel's mouth. Here's a woman's hand, holding something red. It appears in the bit I can see, then vanishes again. This happens a few times. What is she doing? The buggers down below are silent now, they sense I'm on the brink. The hand comes up again, with the red thing in it. One more branch, it dips dangerously, I struggle to keep my grip. I can see her head. It's glistening. The hand, holding a red plastic jug, appears and pours water over it. With her other hand she's rinsing her hair. Now at last I'm higher than the window. Elli Barber's in there, ten feet away. She's taking a bath and she's got nothing on.

Her legs aren't blue but as pale as milk. She reaches down and nothing is hidden from me. Next she's soaping herself all over. Every part. I'm sure you don't need me to tell you how a woman's body is made, it's the first time I've ever seen one naked.

Yes, it's the first time, except in sleep. Often I'd dream of making love with I won't say her name. I never told anyone because if people got to know, what would they do, laugh at me, pity me? 'Animal, don't have those kind of hopes', I'd see the warnings in the faces of old women who caught me looking at her. Animal mating with human female, it's unnatural, but I've no choice but to be unnatural. Many times I would dream that she and I were in love, sometimes we were married and naked together like in the movies having sex. In such dreams was my back straight? Did I stand upright? No and no. I was exactly as I am now and it did not matter. Such dreams! I woke from them shaking with hope. This frightened me, I despise hope.

'What's going on?' comes the whisper from below.

Elli turns away again. She bends, showing all she's got.

'Pssst, Animal?'

I can't answer. I can't speak. She straightens up, pours more water and hai hai hai, what is she doing? She's feeling her breasts. My heart's thudding, I'm giddy, I grab at the branch above my head, there's this great noise of leaves.

Elli Barber comes to the window. She stands there drying herself with a towel looking this way and that. Any moment now she'll look right at me.

The light goes out.

'Animal, what the fuck?'

They want me to come down now, report what I've learned. I can't move. There's a furnace in my groin. No way will I go down and let them see me in this state. I am going to be up here for some time.

Well, at least one part of me can stand upright.

Eyes, I don't know if you are a man or a woman. I'm thinking the things I am telling are not suited to a woman's ears, but if a person leaves things unsaid so as to avoid looking bad, it's a lie. I have sworn not to lie to you. If you feel embarrassed throw down the book in which these words are printed. Carry on reading it's your lookout, there's worse to come, don't go crying later 'Animal's a horrible person, full of filth,' think I don't know it already? Eyes, if you're a woman I ask you not to leave me now, in this world my best people have always been women, such as Jara, Ma Franci, Nisha. If you're a man it doesn't matter, you're a dirty fucker anyway.

So I'm stuck up the mango.

She comes to the window and looks out. There's a bright bulb behind it's outlining her shape, light is splashing the leaves in my tree. I am holding my breath hoping she can't see in the dark. Man, this thing in my pants is hot and rigid, jutting that far it's I'm thinking it'll catch in the branches.

The light goes out. A whisper comes from below. 'What can you see?'

What can I see? Are they mad? She's still there. I'm sure of it, although my eyes are playing tricks. For the first few instants after the light's doused all I can see is the ghost of the bulb, it's burning violet with a green edge. Then a black square appears, which is the window, there's a pale shape swimming about in it. She's leaning out, taking a good look left and right.

'Hey Animal, what's there?'

How come she doesn't hear them? They're not getting an answer, but what can I do? I'm stuck on the branch trying not to move. Breathing, what's that? There's a fishbone caught in my throat. I can't drag my eyes away. I'm thinking any moment she'll see two hot coals glowing in the tree. A whole dark age of the world passes before she leans back inside. Still I daren't stir. What if she is still there in the darkness? Suppose she calls the cops? Spying on a naked woman, won't the bastards be thrilled to see who they've caught? That Fatlu-Inspector, at Habibganj police station, it'll make his day to find me in this windy tree. He'll drag me down and if this pole's still sticking out the front he'll break the fucking thing off and beat me round the head with it. But Fatlu-Inspector does not come and after some time as the window stays dark I realise that she has gone. It takes me a full ten minutes to get down that tree, a dick-scraping slide every inch to the ground.

They all want to know, 'What did you find out? What did you see?'

I said, 'I'll tell you later,' because at that moment Nisha came out onto the verandah. Nisha didn't know what we'd been up to. Probably thought we were taking the night air. Enjoying the frangipani scent. It got me out of a difficult spot, didn't want to tell Zafar & Co what I'd seen.

When we get into the light, on the verandah, Nisha says, 'Animal, you've scratched yourself.'

Sure enough, there are big scratches running down my chest where I've slid down that tree.

'My god what has happened to you?'

Well, there's one thing I can't do, which is lie to Nisha, so it's, 'Je suis monté dans cet arbre la.'

She gives me a look. 'What does that mean?'

I start mumbling some shit about mangos.

'But it's not mango season,' says Nisha. She turns to Zafar, who's looking harrassed. 'What happened to Animal?'

A frown appears on that high forehead of Zafar's. He pushes back his specs like when he's about to make a speech, but before he can say anything, Farouq chips in and says, 'Oh he just slipped.'

'Slipped?' She's looking at me with concern, I swear. That girl is sweeter on me than she realises. It comes out in moments like this, you can't hide it, if you really care for someone.

'How did he slip?'

'Tripped,' says Farouq.

'How could you trip?' she asks me. 'You're four-footed.'

Then she's staring at my shorts. I nearly die. Let that damn thing not be showing. 'You need proper clothes. You're always wearing those filthy old things. I'll buy you some new ones.'

'Don't want new ones,' I mumble. 'These are my kakadu shorts came from the jarnalis, name's Phuoc, from a crocodile place. Special hero shorts, two side pockets, two gusset back pockets, two front patch pockets, useful for stashing stuff like my zippo,' this kind of thing I'm babbling.

Zafar says, 'Leave him, we have things to do.'

But Nisha takes me aside and brings some neem ointment, yellow it's plus smells bitter, to put on my scratches.

'I can't reach under there,' she says, meaning my belly, because I'm still on all fours. 'You'll have to sit. Or go on your side.'

I roll over like a big dog, like Jara does to have her belly tickled, Nisha starts rubbing the ointment on my stomach. Her fingers touching me, I'm afraid my thing is going to come to life again, maybe she's sensed, because she traces the scratches down to the belly button then gives me the tin and tells me to do the rest, plus to hurry up because they're waiting for us inside. They are about to have another of their endless meetings. Then she says she'll hang around to make sure I do it properly.

'You go. It's you they're waiting for.'

'Not just me,' says Nisha, watching me apply the stuff. Plain she might be but's looking good. Once you've seen it in someone's face it's always there, I won't say beauty, but whatever you might call the thing you love. It's the way the hair hangs across her face. She was chewing her lip, which she does when she's thinking and which is that thing of hers that gets me.

'So sweet, you're,' I say, before I can stop myself.

'Silly Animal,' says Nisha, now smiling, 'your hair's all jungli, it's matted up full of dust, there are twigs in it. Come, I'll brush it.'

So I am sitting there while she runs her fingers through, teasing out the tangles, then she starts to brush it, aaa aa aiiiee, catches here, aiiieeaaaa, tugs there. Zafar comes out to look for us, I'm looking at him, I'm smiling.

'Ça va, Animal?' he asks, who has learned it off me.

'Si heureux je vais mourir.' But this he didn't follow.

Dying of happiness, was I? Not for much longer, for after the meeting they went to her room, leaving me grinding my teeth below. I was obsessed with what they were doing together. Imagining you-know-what led to my voices having a great argument. One said it had foreseen that things would come to this. Another held that Zafar would be mad to do ghuss-pussy stuff in the same house as Pandit Somraj, who has the hearing of a bat, can strain his ear to hear an ant fart. Bollocks, said a third, a man's a man, with a thing between his legs and a man's deep urge to plant it in something moist and willing.

Of course this was no excuse for poisoning him.

Last night I dreamed of Zafar. He was heading up Paradise Alley into the heart of the Nutcracker. Nearly double he was bent, his long nose pointing sorrowfully at the ground. On his head was his favourite red turban, his beard was untrimmed, on his back he carried a shining world, blue as a flycatcher's wing, criss-crossed by tiny lines. The sun's heat was falling down on him. Heavy must the world have been, Zafar was staggering, his arms reaching up behind his back could hardly hold it, but he was taking one step at a time, like he did everything with careful patience. A small child walked ahead of him, going to school I suppose, he had a slate on which some abc and 123 were written. Nisha was in the dream too, tagging along behind Zafar, begging him to let her share his heavy burden of the world's pain, but I don't think he could hear.

My battle with Zafar was hotting up. Grim animal living without hope, that's how I saw myself. I asked nothing, expected less and was filled with anger at the world. Zafar was always giving me chances to prove what a good-hearted trustworthy guy I was. It had turned into a kind of contest. He deliberately placed more and more trust in me, I did the tasks he gave me with greater and greater contempt. Often I'd take on big tasks for which I was unsuited. One of these days, I thought, preferably when your life depends on it, I am going to let you down.

One day Nisha brought to one of our meetings a woman called Pyaré Bai. Pyaré sat on the floor with her sari draped so it was covering her face, in a sad voice she told us her story. Eyes you should hear it, because the story of this one woman contains the tale of thousands.

Pyaré Bai was married to Aftaab, he worked in the Kampani's factory, and he told her how dangerous were the chemicals in there. If by chance you got any on your hand, Aftaab said, the skin would blister. On that night he was at home off duty, when the stinging in the eyes began, the burning chillies, unlike most people he knew what to do. He covered the faces of Pyaré and their two young daughters with wet cloths then led them, walking not running, out of the wind. In this way they escaped where most of their neighbours perished. All were nevertheless damaged by the poisons, Aftaab the worst, because he'd taken less care over himself, he was coughing foam tinged with blood, his eyes were nearly shut. When they returned home all objects of metal, like cooking pots, had a green crust. Aftaab would not allow Pyaré and the children into the house. He cleaned everything, washed every corner before he let them in.

At first Aftaab seemed to recover, but his old job was gone, he was too breathless to be able to do physical work. His condition grew worse. His eyes suffered, he got rashes all over, plus fevers and pains in his joints. Pyaré bought medicines. Aftaab told her not to waste money on him, for he would die. She said, 'How can I not?' 'Think of yourself and the children,' he said. 'When I am gone, what will you live on?' She replied, '*Har ek warak mein tum hi tum ho jaan-e-mehboobi, hum apné dil mein kuch aaisi kitaab rakhté hain.*'

'Wah wah,' says Zafar. He's taken off his glasses and is wiping them. Blinking, he's. What does he think, this is some fucking poetry recital? Eyes, what she said means this, 'On every page there's you and only you, oh love of my life, it's this book I keep in my heart.'

When her husband got really ill and could no longer work, they ran out of money and had to sell their small house. They moved to a rented place with half a roof. It was the only place Pyaré could find, right by the stinking naala, in the monsoon the rain came right in. The small girls were always hungry. At night they cried. She would bind cloths round their waists and give them water to fill their empty bellies. She found a job carrying cement on a building site.

'When I started work,' said Pyaré Bai, 'my husband apologised to me for putting me through all this. How often did he tell me not to spend money on him and his illness? Don't waste your money, he said, I'm going to die anyway. And he did . . . he left me alone.'

She began to cry, Nisha sat next to her and hugged her. After this Pyaré Bai showed us pictures of her daughters. The younger one was beautiful and wild, looked much like her ma. She passed round a picture taken when she was a new bride, it showed a young smiling Aftaab Miyañ, next to him was a girl dressed in short kurta with two plaits and curls plastered round her cheeks. Nisha said, 'I saw this at your house. One of your girls said, "Ammi looks like Mala Sinha." "No," said the other one, "like Sadhna."'

Again both were in tears. I couldn't understand why Nisha was so moved by this particular story, all of us worked every day with people with awful tales to tell. The wedding picture gave the answer, the happiest moment in the love affair of a Hindu woman and a Muslim man. Like Nisha and Zafar.

After Aftaab's death the moneylender sent his goons after her. These were guys whose eyes were red from drinking, mean miserable motherfuckers, they carried Rampuri flick-knives and wouldn't hesistate to use them. They stood in the galli outside her house and called in loud voices. 'Ohé bitch, are you in there?' 'Whore, have you forgotten the money you owe?' 'Have some pity,' she told them. 'My husband has just died.' They walked into her house and took things. They took her cooking pots. They wheeled away her husband's bicycle. 'Well, he won't be needing it any more.'

At the end of this narrative all are in tears, except me who never cries and for each story as tragic as this can narrate ten that are worse.

When Pyaré has gone, Nisha says, 'We have to do something for her. We've got to get those goons off her back.'

'There is a problem,' says Zafar. 'How can we help one and not others? If we help Pyaré, where does it end? How can we say to her neighbours who also have suffered terribly, we've helped her but we can't help you?'

'Zafar,' says Nisha, 'I don't know the answer, but I know that if I do not help that poor woman and her daughters, I myself will die.'

'You shall not die,' he said. 'This is what we'll do. We will ask twenty friends to start a fund, I'll here and now put in a thousand rupees.'

'And me,' said Nisha.

'I too will give a thousand,' said Somraj.

'And I,' said Farouq. They looked at me but I looked the other way.

'Animal?' asks Zafar. See? He's determined I should have the opportunity to show the generosity of my spirit.

'Twenty,' I mumble.

'When we've paid Pyaré's debt,' said Zafar, 'we'll begin a new work, a trust to give low interest loans so people are not driven to these scum.' Thus spoke Zafar bravely, but I caught his groaning thoughts and knew that another heavy burden had just been added to the world he carried on his shoulders.

The money when it was collected was a lot more than twenty thousand rupees. It could not be given to Pyaré Bai because the moneylender might trick her. It needed to be given direct plus a receipt obtained.

'I'll take it.' This is me.

Says Zafar, 'I think better not this time.'

'What, don't you trust me?' This time I've got him.

'You're right, I don't. Not your honesty, your big mouth it's I don't trust. These are bad guys.'

'I'll take it,' I repeat. 'Trust can't be cut. You either trust or you don't.'

Zafar fiddles with his beard, ponders. 'Okay then, you take it, but Farouq will go with you.'

It was the most money I had ever carried, enough to buy a house.

The moneylender was P. N. Jeweller, shop's in Iltutmish Street, in the Chowk. Farouq and me, we've wandered up there slowly through the noise and smells, pakoras frying, crowds, money's in the bag round my neck.

'Her arse man,' says Farouq, 'it's like two sweet juicy melons, wouldn't

I love to sink my teeth into that?' Guess who he's talking about.

'You have a disgusting mind,' I tell him. 'Even a gutter born person like me doesn't talk that way.'

'Doesn't talk, but thinks,' says he, laughing. 'I've seen you looking at her, plus at Nisha too. You four-footed bastard wander the city with dick dangling, in secret you wear out your fist.'

Well, there's truth in this, Eyes, I won't deny, but don't tell me he doesn't do the same, or you for that matter, can you honestly say you've never touched yourself, so what's the big deal?

'Trouble with you, Animal,' continues Farouq, we're passing the Hanuman temple where the milkmen gather each morning, 'is you think because you've a crooked back and walk with your arse in the air no one should dare to criticise you. I'm an animal, always you're bleating, I'm an animal, I don't have to do like the rest of you, laws of society don't apply to me because I'm such a fucking animal.'

It really irritates him that I choose to be an animal not human, it's like grit in his eye. 'Wasn't me who gave myself the name of Animal,' I reply. 'Plus who was it just now called me four-foot? Oh, I do believe it was you.'

'Don't whinge,' says he. 'This is Khaufpur. In this city if a man is lame he's called Langda. If he's cross-eyed he's Look-London-Talk-Tokyo. These are just fucking words, call him Raju or Razaq, doesn't change what he is.'

Not very bright, is our Farouq. Really, he should have been a mechanic, or a goonda in a criminal gang like his two brothers. First he does not realise that everything's just fucking words, second this edge he misses, that when I say I'm an animal it's not just what I look like but what I feel. 'Your name should be Hypocrite,' I tell him, 'because in front of people like Somraj pandit you act respectable, at Muharram you'll walk across hot coals to show how pious you are, three-sixty-four other days you do not set one foot in the masjid, nor do you say daily namaaz, behind the backs of the mullahs you are up to all kinds of dirty adventures.'

I say this because of him visiting the houses near Laxmi Talkies.

87

Eyes, till now I've not told you much about Farouq, except that he's Zafar's number two. You must be wondering, what's a roughneck like him doing mixed up with Zafar and Nisha, how come he does a caring kind of work in return for next to no pay? Hardly the type he's, his uncle is Afroze Khan Yar-yilaqi, a big gangster in Khaufpur, mixed up with transport scams, smuggling, liquor, all kinds of stuff. Farouq's dad is the younger brother of this godfather but the two of them had quarrelled. Two years ago Farouq's father fell seriously ill, he could not get proper treatment, it was Zafar who fixed it, since that time Farouq worships Zafar, he came to work with him, for Zafar and Nisha he'll do anything, but me he treats like shit, he says it's what I deserve.

Farouq's people are Yar-yilaqis. They came to Khaufpur from Yar-yilaq, it's a region near Samarkand. This happened a long time ago, maybe three hundred years, Farouq told me about it once, guess I wasn't listening. There's a whole Yar-yilaqi quarter of Khaufpur, the women in that district wear high heels under their burkhas and lipstick under their veils, but if you upset one of them with some Eve-teasing type of remark she's liable to out with a knife and stick you, this too Farouq told me, in which case it's a shameful miracle that he has lived so long. Always though there's hope that one day he will burn to death. Each year at Muharram, it's tradition for Yar-yilaqi men to show their purity of heart by walking with bare feet over a bed of hot coals. Farouq does this every year, he's proud of it.

Any mention of the firewalk is bound to cause trouble between Farouq and me, in past years like others I've gone to see it, to get any kind of view I've had to shin up something, last time it was scaffolding where they had put a TV camera, my jumping about was making it shake. Farouq yelled at me, 'Animal, get down, what are you doing here anyway, little shit, don't even believe in god?'

'Since when do jungli creatures have to believe?' I yelled back.

'Get a religion and learn some respect.'

So I've informed Farouq that with us animals, our religion's eating, drinking, shitting, fucking, the basic stuff you do to survive.

'You dirty fucker,' he said, 'all this animal crap, it's just an excuse for behaving badly.'

Now, when I mention Muharram, which is drawing near, he gets hot under the collar and says that this year I had better not try any such tricks or he will personally throw me in the fire.

'Think I'm afraid of the fire? Go across fast enough it doesn't have time to burn, otherwise a filthy-souled person like you would burst into flames.'

'If it's so easy, why don't you do it?' he challenges.

'Well, maybe I will.'

'Big fucking mouth you have, you won't dare.'

'Want to bet?'

'Bet,' says he, so he bends down, we shake hands, cut, and it's done.

The jeweller's sat on a cushion, talking with a friend. We say why we've come, I remove the money from the bag and count it out before him.

'It's the debt of Pyaré Bai. Zafar brother says to tell you this is a complete end to the matter, you should now return her belongings.'

The guy's checked the money with a look on his face like he never really wanted to see it again, this is the way these moneylenders work, lend a small amount, interest of ten percent per month, who'd want the money back?

'Zafar bhai said to give a receipt.'

'Zafar bhai this, Zafar bhai that,' the man sneers. 'I know your Zafar bhai, he's a troublemaker, always sticking in his nose where it's not wanted.'

'His nose is fully wanted. Zafar bhai also says that you are to leave Pyaré Bai alone, there must be no more harrassment.'

'Listen to this sadak chhaap giving orders to his elders and betters. Who do you think you're talking to?'

'Just give me the receipt,' says I, 'names we can swap later.'

The moneylender by now is angry, he's called out behind and a couple of his goons come into the shop. 'What's up, boss?'

'This kid,' he says. 'Needs a fucking lesson in manners. Needs to learn how to show respect.'

'Give me the receipt for the money,' I repeat, beginning to feel alarmed, for if I don't get it, this guy could deny he ever received the cash.

'Sisterfuck, let me tell you, you don't talk to me that way, understood, or I'll kick your crooked arse out all the way down the street to Hazrat Mahal and from there maybe also to Ram Mandir.'

At this, Farouq who is leaning in the doorway picking his nails starts laughing. 'That I'd like to see, uncle, it's all this bugger deserves. Many's the time I've been tempted to plant a foot on his unlovely butt. I've known him since he was a snotty kid of fifteen, never had he anything but abuse for his betters, so I fully understand your problem with him. His attitude is bad, his manners are uncouth, the stupid fuck actually thinks he's an animal. This kid needs straightening out, your shoe up his back-side would probably do wonders. Trouble is,' says he, 'if you kick his arse down the road, I'll be forced to kick yours right after him.'

The moneylender looks at him in wonder. 'What's this? Another insolent time-pass man, you and he are together?'

'Unfortunately, yes,' says Farouq, still looking at his nails. 'I would not take pleasure, well not a lot of pleasure, in breaking your legs, but if you talk to me that way, don't blame me if that's what happens.'

'Saalé,' grunts one of the heavies, 'just who the fuck do you think you are?'

'I think I'm Farouq Khan Yar-yilaki. If you ever want to find me, ask for me at my uncle's house. His name is Afroze Khan. I guess you've heard of him, if not just head down to Ajmeri gate, anyone will tell you the way.'

We got our receipt, hurriedly signed by the cringing moneylender who also promised to deliver Pyaré Bai's pots and bicycle back to her without delay.

'You fucking hoodlum,' I said to Farouq, we were outside again, heading for Chunaram's, 'from where did you learn those B-movie dialogues?'

'Animal darling, don't tempt me.'

'Well,' says I, 'looks like we'll be doing quite a bit of this type of work. I too should practise dark speeches, like Shatrugan, BATTAMEEZ KUTTÉ, MAIN TUMHÉ NASHT KAR DOONGA!!!' Shameless dog, I'll destroy you!

Several passers by jump and start looking round to see where this terrible threat has come from. Farouq's killing himself laughing. 'Animal,' he says, 'you might be an okay guy, if you weren't such a cunt.'

A mystery is Elli. Zafar's tried all his sources to find out who she is and where she has come from, come up with a big fucking nul. All we know is she had a big job in Amrika, she gave it up to come to Khaufpur. Then one day Dayanand lets slip that she had worked in a hospital for veterans.

'What's the name of the hospital?' asks Zafar when I tell him this.

'Medical Centre.'

'Which medical centre?'

'Just the name's Medical Centre. Dayanand said it was a huge building that stands on a hill. Veterans are soldiers.'

'I know what veterans are,' says Zafar, 'Surely now we can trace her. Did he say which city?'

Nisha says, 'I will go tomorrow and search on the internest.'

'What? You think Elli doctress's picture will be on the internest?' I've given a loud snort of amusement.

'Why is it funny?' asks Nisha.

'I know what all kind of pictures are on the internest.'

They're staring at me like I've said something wrong so I've nodded my head at Farouq. 'He told me.'

'What did he tell you, darling?' It's Nisha. Now they're all laughing, except Farouq who looks like he's wishing he wasn't there. So here's a chance to screw that fucker.

'He said it was part of my education. What he'd show me I'd never forget.'

Farouq too's pretending to laugh. 'Fool can't take a joke,' he says, but I can hear his thoughts gritting, little bastard, my boot, your arse, so I've winked at him which makes him even madder.

'Animal, there are all kinds of things on the internest,' says Zafar, 'not just the, er, what Farouq may have mentioned.'

'Can I come with you?' I ask Nisha. 'The internest I would like to see.'

'Of course you shall,' says she, giving me a sweet smile. 'After all, it is part of your education.'

Some time after this, I'm hanging round in the Claw when Elli appears and calls out, 'Hey Animal, want to come in and hear the piano?'

'Definitely yes.' Where's the harm? I'll report to Zafar what I've seen.

Totally different is the building from when Ganesh and the others had it. More light's coming through the windows, which in the gone era used to be brown. Everything's clean. In the first room there are benches all round the walls, in the middle is a table covered with newspapers etc, in a corner's Miriam Joseph sitting behind a desk, she gives me a smile. 'Hello Animal, is madam going to look at your back?'

'She is showing me the piano.'

I'll show you something else and all, says a voice in my head, it's the rough one that sounds like pig-chunder.

What's inside those pants, go for a closer look.

Elli ahead of me, calls, 'It's upstairs, are you okay to climb up?'

Surprised she'd be, what we can climb.

Shut your trap! I don't want them spoiling things. No way'll Elli doctress do anything of that kind. All the same, her arse-pumpkins wagging up the stairs ahead of me, well it is disquieting.

She will change your life! comes that echo from before.

'How've you been anyway?' Elli calls down.

'Thank you very much, I am feeling fine. I don't have any pain.'

'Are you in pain often?' she asks, holding open a door.

'Not at all, but many people are.'

'So why did you say you don't have pain?'

'Because I'm one of those who doesn't have it. Madam.'

'Should I be confused? And don't call me madam, call me Elli.'

Good she doesn't know what I am actually thinking, which is hoo boy

I've seen you naked. Dirty little thrill is this, like I've some sort of power over her, comes joined to shame, I've not told anyone what I saw from the tree, hardly was it my fault, how could I know she was taking a bath?

The piano is in a room which I was supposing would look like Somraj's music room, but fully different it's. First off there are books everywhere, on shelves, on tables, in piles on the floor. There are fat chairs covered in cloth, plus one such-a-wide one it could seat four to five Khaufpuri backsides. She sees me looking at it. 'Stretch out on the sofa if you want, get comfortable.'

The piano I expected to be a flat instrument when it came out of that box, maybe like a santoor, but I see now that the piano is the box itself, which has been raised off the floor and is standing on three legs of polished wood. She lifts a curved flap and there are the keys. I've to stand up on the sofa chair to see them, a long row of black and white, far longer than Panditji's harmonium.

'What would you like me to play?'

Well, I don't know much proper music, fillim tunes are more my choice, but I don't want to look ignorant, plus so many times I've listened to Somraj talk and teach. 'I am quite fond of raga Bhimpalashri.'

She bursts out laughing, 'I didn't know you could play ragas on the piano.'

'Do you know *Tum Se Achchha Kaun Hai?*' It's one of my party pieces, from the film *Jaanvar*, not the *Jaanvar* movies of 1982 or 1999, but the original old one from 1965 with Shammi Kapoor plus Rajshree, the best *Jaanvar*. The name means Animal, so it's my movie, the song name means 'Oh Who Is Better Than You?' but when I sing it I change it to *Mujh Se Achchha Kaun Hai?* which means, 'Oh, Who Is Better Than Me?'

Elli says, 'I'll play something I know.' She's started tapping the keys and this rumbling music comes up out of the piano box. Deep it's, like a grumble of thunder, deeper than any instrument I've heard except maybe a drum, then she makes her hands skip to the other end, the music becomes high and sweet like bells.

'How did you learn to play so nicely?'

'Well,' she says, her fingers busy on the keys, 'we always had a piano in our house. My mother played. She was good. When I was about twelve she became ill, her hands would shake so much she could no longer play. That's when I took it up.'

'You learned so you could play for her?'

Elli drops her hands into her lap. 'It's cruel to lose a gift like that.' She looks over at me, but I am thinking of Somraj. 'Your neighbour across the way, he used to be a singer. Now he's a music teacher.'

'Tall man, always dresses in white? Has a daughter? We've hardly said hello.'

At the mention of Nisha I feel like a traitor because I can't stop having bad thoughts about Elli Barber. About Somraj I don't know what to say, the tone in Elli's voice suggests she thinks he's not very friendly, and of course I can't say why. Thinking of them across the road reminds me of what we need to find out.

'Dayanand, your manager, he says you used to work in a big hospital in Amrika.'

'That's right, I did.'

'Were there many sick in your city?'

'Sure, but not like here.'

'What is the name of your city? I have heard of New York.'

'Not New York,' says Elli Barber. 'Nor anywhere so interesting as this. This place is so fascinating. I should write to my piano teacher. Miss Girton her name was, a real old Maine crawfish, she'd be amazed if she could see me in Khaufpur.'

'We are all amazed, and I do not know what is a crawfish.' As she does not reply to this I ask again, 'So which city are you from?'

'Nowhere you've ever heard of, I grew up in Coatesville, Pennsylvania.' She says this like her mind's elsewhere.

'That's an odd sort of name.'

'What's odd about it?'

'Just sounds odd. How do you spell it?' In this way, Eyes, I've tried to make sure of the name of her city.

She's sitting at her piano looking at me. 'Animal, listen to me. The clinic will open soon. Soon's we're up and running I'd very much like to examine you.'

'Ghostville? Ghostville Pencilmania?'

'Coatesville,' she says, laughing. 'C-O-A-T-E-S . . .'

Feet first then hands, I'm down the stairs, out of that place.

Farouq says that hiring an internest booth is cheaper than a hotel room so often couples go there to have sex. No doubt this is why people stare when Nisha and I walk in together. I look for a rag but can't see one. There are two seats, I've hauled myself up onto one, Nisha's slid her neat little bum onto the other. Her fingers are tapping on a flat thing covered with rows of buttons, somewhat like those of a harmonium. First time I've seen a computer, a screen there's, like a tele except instead of movies it shows pictures plus Inglis words.

Nisha asks the internest to tell her all it knows about Elli Barber from Coatesville, Pennsylvania. She waits for an answer, but nothing at all comes. Again and again she tries, there is a Veteran's Medical Center in Coatesville but the internest knows not a single Elli Barber.

'She's using a false name,' Nisha says. 'Doctor doing an important job in a hospital, her name would surely be on record. You would expect the internest to have that kind of information.'

'How come it knows so much?'

'It just does. Look I'll show you something.'

On the screen appears a familiar building.

'Well fuck me sideways,' says I. 'It's the Pir Gate.'

'Because this is Khaufpur dot com.' She's explained that it's a part of the internest that belongs to Khaufpur. It has pictures of all our famous places.

'Bugger me backwards! It's Abdul Saliq!' Pigeons are flying up round the huge red arch. Down in the shadows, if you look hard, is the tiny figure of the Pir Gate beggar with his hand out. I had never realised that the internest would know the same people I do.

Nisha's ignored the bad words, she's caught my excitement, says she'll show me more. Next thing the screen's filled with huge golden letters of Urdu which say *Aawaaz-e-Khaufpur*, plus there's someone tall, white-clad, looking twenty years younger than I've ever seen him.

'Nisha, it's your dad!'

'So handsome he was,' says she with a sigh. Taps more. The internest has gathered dozens of pictures of Somraj. Young Somraj with his guru Sahadev Joshi, him they used to call *Lajawaab*, peerless. With various musicians. With the governor of the state. With other stars at All India Radio. Singing with hands raised in rapture. When Somraj performed he'd get into a kind of trance, he'd utter without knowing what he was singing. Meaningless sounds just for rhythm, such as *na ta da da ni odani ta re tanom da ni yayali na ta na yayalom*, even these he sang with such conviction that some swore they were poems, or else mystical Persian syllables with the power to summon djinns.

Many amazing stories about Somraj the internest knew. It told how he'd be out taking the air with his mates and would sing the stuff he saw. He'd be walking by the Upper Lake and sing fish leaping at sunset, or he'd see a V of cranes passing overhead and fire off a song at them. Once in Bombay during the monsoon he stood on Marine Drive and matched his *Miya ki Malhar* to the wildness of the sea. Waterspouts were bursting forty feet above his head but Somraj refused to move till he'd caught the swing of the waves. Forty minutes he stood on the parapet, drenched by heavy falls of saltwater, and sang, a crowd of Bombay-wallahs gathered to listen. 'Who is this guy?' they asked in their atrocious accents.

Said his spoonies, 'It's the famous *Aawaaz-e-Khaufpur*.'

'Khaufpur? Where's that?'

Says Nisha with a sigh, 'Obviously, this was before that night.'

'Does it know stuff about you, Nish?'

'Let's see, she says and taps buttons. The internest has got hold of a letter that Nisha wrote to a newspaper. Also it has taken a picture of her plus Zafar at a demo.

Of Zafar are countless reports, the internest has followed him around, taking pictures of him at a meeting in Delhi, throwing paint on the Kampani's office in Bombay, with Farouq addressing a rally in Khaufpur, no mistaking there's his unruly curls and flashing specs. Sometimes Zafar wears his old red turban, in one pic it's fallen off because he's being kicked by a policeman.

'Nisha, look me up, yaar. What does it say about me?'

'Darling it doesn't work that way,' she says, after we have examined many scenes of owls, frogs, panthers and etcetera.

'Why not? About everybody else even Farouq it has things to say. How come it knows nothing of me?'

'It will, darling, one day, I'm sure. You are going to do some great work in the world. Then everyone will know about you.'

When Zafar hears we've found no trace of Elli Barber and she's here under a false name he says he has reached wit's end. 'On the one hand, people want this clinic, on the other, it may destroy all that we've worked for. If we can get the Kampani into court, they'll have to build a dozen such clinics.'

Eyes, it amazes me that such a fellow as Zafar, who shifts his opinion daily, is considered a great leader. Each night at Nisha's house he holds discussions with different groups. Comes the turn of folk from the Nutcracker, among them's Chunaram, for like I already told you, Zafar has taken a shine to him. Zafar says Chuna's a pirate, plus it's good he has nine fingers because a pirate must always have a bit missing. 'What Chunaram's missing,' says I, 'is a fucking heart.' Zafar laughs and reminds me not to swear.

So Chuna's there among the rest, they're hacking the usual question of what should be done about Elli Barber. Says Zafar, 'No doctor of her name can be traced. No option there's, we must ask people to avoid her clinic.'

Somraj, who's a fair man, differs. 'Our people have great need of a clinic like this. Let them go and derive benefit from it, afterwards if we discover that it is a Kampani clinic up to no good, we can ask them to stop going.'

Zafar says, 'Abba, if a man is dying of thirst and you give him cool water, can you afterwards snatch it away from his lips? Better he waits a little longer.'

Somraj says, 'So you are proposing a boycott?'

Chunaram starts laughing and says that Wasim and Waqar can bowl out Inglis batsmen even with an orange. Well, everyone's amazed, until he explains he's remembering something said by an Inglis cricketer called Boycott. After this everyone starts arguing about cricket and the point of the meeting is lost.

It's now, after all this that Chunaram says, 'Animal, I forgot, Ma Franci was wandering round shouting and raving. Some women tried to take her home, she wouldn't go. They said her head was burning.'

'Forgot? You fucking idiot! Has someone shat in your brain?'

'Told you now, haven't I?' he's called after me in an aggrieved tone as I'm out of there. 'Busy man, I'm. Lot on my mind, I've.'

It's late when I get back. Place is dark, I find Ma Franci huddled in a corner. No fire there's, she's shivering.

'It wouldn't light, Animal,' she says. 'The matches are all gone. I used the last one.'

'Don't worry, Ma, I've got my zippo.'

'God bless you, you are a good boy,' says she out of the darkness,

Ma knows that I hate using the zippo because I don't want to wear it out, but this is an emergency. I fetch out the lighter, flip the lid back, grind my thumb on the wheel. Zip-zip-zippo, le bois prît feu! Shadows go jumpfrogging round the tower. I've wrapped Ma in a cloth and settled her by the fire.

99

Now there's some light to see by she's peering at me. 'What are these scratches all over you?'

'I fell in a bush,' says I who'd been up the tree again.

She sighs, 'Such a difficult child, marchais toujours au rhythme de ton propre tambour.' You've always marched to the beat of your own drum.

To change the subject I start telling her what happened earlier at Pandit Somraj's house. When I get to Zafar wanting to boycott the clinic, Ma says the Amrikan doctor is bound to have a bad time and won't be able to do anything good for the people of this town. It isn't just that the Khaufpuris refuse to talk like humans, but babble like macaques and orioles, the real reason the Amrikan will come to grief is because she has no way to reach their souls. 'People here have suffered too much. Outsiders don't understand.'

'I don't,' says I. 'And I'm an insider.'

'Such hurts can't be healed.'

'Doctors are in demand.' Somraj at the meeting had spoken of the lack of help for the poor.

'Doctors are no use. Things are getting worse. In the old days, people would talk properly to me. The Apokalis took away their speech.'

I stare at her, wondering how anyone can get it so totally wrong.

'I cope, it's not with words that you treat such wounds. The people ache, their bodies are bottles into which fresh pain is poured every day. Their flesh is melting, coming off their bones in flakes of fire, their bones are burning, they're turning into light, probably they're becoming angels.'

Dear oh dear, and here's me thinking she'd been making sense.

'Tonton lariton, that's what it is, my smallest of Animals, tonton lariton. See, people don't realise how deep is the river. The Apokalis has begun, and the whole world's full of it.'

Her old woman's voice begins to sing . . .

> Quand j'étais chez mon père,
> Quand j'étais chez mon père,

Petite à la ti ti, la ri ti, tonton lariton
Petite à la maison.
On m'envoyait à l'herbe pour cueillir du cresson.
La rivière est profonde, je suis tombée au fond.

Never have I heard her rave so. She's still shivering, despite the fire, and putting my hand on her head, I can feel the fever.

'Ma, have you eaten?'

She shakes her head.

'Rest by the fire Ma, stay wrapped up, I'm going to get food.'

I can cook two things that Ma loves, baingan bharta and chai, both are good for warming a person from within. For the first I'll need an aubergine, big and round, plus garlic plus oil, for the chai I need tea leaves, or a pinch of tea dust, too some sugar. I also need water. Some people, like Somraj, have taps that give water inside their own houses, but this is the Nutcracker. I've headed off to Aliya's house and found her holding a school book to a lantern.

'Hello Animal,' says old Huriya. 'What brings you here so late?'

'Need to fetch water,' I say. 'Ma's not well. Has a fever.'

'That good woman,' says Huriya, sucking in breath and shaping it into a prayer for Ma. 'I do hope it's not serious. Come Aliya, Animal needs our help.'

'Can I ride you to the pump?' asks the child, putting down her book.

'What, is he a horse to be ridden?' scolds her granny.

'No, a donkey,' replies cheeky Aliya, but I've said it's okay I don't mind, my shoulders are broad and strong, I've given rides to countless kids. So she's climbed atop, complete with large water pot, and it's away to the pump, her heels urging my ribs, she's shouting trrrr, hup and the like.

'Good you can read,' I tell her. 'What was the book about?'

'It's a story,' says she, 'about a girl called Anarko who won't do as she's told.'

'Like you, then.'

'Huh, aren't I coming with you? I work hard.' It's true, she does. Her granddad Hanif being blind and all, and Huriya old, Aliya does all the water fetching, cleaning and more besides, plus goes to school when she can.

'Only joking,' I tell her, 'you're a good kid.'

This compliment earns me a hard kick to the ribs.

Well, Eyes, with Aliya's help the water is no problem because although Khaufpuri pump water stinks it is free.

On the way back from the pump, Aliya's walking ahead with the big pot balanced on her head, I call to her to carry on to our place while I knock on the door of the local shopkeeper, Baju. By this time it's maybe ten at night, he's probably in bed giving his wife one but my banging gets him up again.

'Oh it's you,' says he with a surly expression. 'What is it?'

'I need an aubergine and a teaspoon of tea,' says I with my sincerest look. 'I'll give you the money tomorrow.'

'You haven't paid me for the last time yet,' says Baju.

'Listen, I wouldn't ask, but Ma Franci is ill, there isn't even a humble onion in the place, for the poor nothing is easy. '

'Hope it's not malaria,' says he, somewhat softened. 'If it's for Ma then there's no charge.'

'I'll also need some sugar.'

'Anything else?' he asks with a resigned air.

So I give him the list. Garlic and then, because he's offering, 'milk, salt, a few cardamoms, some black pepper, thumb of ginger, cinnamon stick, couple of cloves.'

'What? Is that all?'

'It's for Ma. You know what they say about proper chai, the old women say it will make a dead man warm.'

'It must be malaria,' he says. 'She has had it before. You'd better take some aspirins as well, if the fever hasn't gone by morning come back and

I'll find something better.' As I'm leaving he says, 'This lot's on me, but mind you pay me for the last time.'

Tight bastard.

News of Ma Franci's sickness must have reached the nuns because a few days later I come home to find her growling at the dog, who's curled up with her paws crossed over her nose, almost it looks like she's trying to cover up her ears. Ma isn't swearing, not exactly, she does not use the kind of bad language I do, putain con, bordel de merde etcetera, which I was taught by a jarnalis français, he and I sat on a fallen log for half a day swapping gaalis, but Ma's cursing in a way that sounds more terrible because she really means it, il vient encore, cet glos pautonnier, qu'il se morde sa langue de douleur. It means, again he's coming, that . . .

'Ma, what is glos pautonnier.'

'A bad hearted person who eats too much.'

Someone's coming who is an evil glutton, may he painfully bite his tongue.

'What is all this about?'

'Son, these wretched people can't let me be, again they're trying to send me away from here. A padre is coming, I am supposed to go with him.'

She shows me an envelope. Slowly I trace out the Inglis writing, Mère Ambrosine, St Joseph's Convent, Khaufpur, over which someone has scrawled in Hindi, Ma Franci, About-To-Fall-Tower-By-Factory-Corner, Nutcracker.

Ambrosine, so that's Ma's real name, all these years I never knew. The thought of her leaving gives a lurch to my stomach. This old woman who calls me son, she's the only mother I've known.

'I don't want to go back,' she says. 'What will I do there? It's been so long, hardly can I remember that place.'

'When will the padre come?'

'The letter does not say.'

I've right away gone to see Aliya's granny Huriya Bi, Ma's best friend in Khaufpur she's, not a word of each other's speech do they understand, yet sit cackling like a pair of old hens.

'Maybe it is best for her,' says Huriya. She's making tea, which she does whenever I, or anyone comes, to her house. Her wrinkled hands push twigs into the clay hearth, causing tiny flames to spurt under the kettle. That kettle with blackened bottom and sides, must be hundreds of cups of tea I've had from it. Let others believe in god, for goodness and a kind welcome I'll believe in that kettle.

'Dadi, Ma does not want to go to France, she wants to stay here. There she has no one, here are many who love her. We are her family now.'

'The boy is right, what will she do in some foreign country?' says Hanif Ali, Huriya's husband.

'Animal, I think in the end Ma will do what she wants to do.'

'Yes, so we must find a way to help her.'

Ever since Ma's illness I've had to avoid passing Baju, until I can pay him I'm having to dodge round behind his place through a labyrinth of huts to reach 'I'm Alive' Ajmeri's shop in Paradise.

Paris has its Champs-Elysées, in Delhi is Chandni Chowk, even Khaufpur has Nilofer Road where the rich go to shop, we people have Paradise Alley, it's that boulevard of dreams that runs from the corner of Kali Parade to the heart of the Nutcracker. Here is the shop of Uttamchand 'I'm Alive' Ajmeri. This shop, to someone like you I daresay it's not much, an open-fronted shack with packets of gutka and supari dangling from strings, twirling in the breeze, not so grand it's as Ram Nekchalan's shop in the Chicken Claw, which has a metal shutter, but it's a step up from Baju's hole in the wall. In I'm Alive's place every lad in the Nutcracker buys his first cigarette, rupee a clope. Kids come bringing coins they've scrounged for kites and tops and marbles, those who can afford buy glass marbles, others like me had to use clay ones or pellets of dough baked hard in their mothers' hearths, which, not having a mother I used to ask Huriya Bi.

On this day I'm approaching I'm Alive's from the back, when I hear kids up ahead shouting 'Aiwa! Aiwa!' So then I know there's a foreigner in the basti. From that way's come someone wobbling on his bike. I've asked him what's happening. Says he, 'Arré, nothing it's. Some jarnalis going into houses on Paradise along with a government-waali-doctress.'

Near I'm Alive's place I find a crowd of kids with the proprietor frowning at them. 'Bugger off,' he's croaking. Like all shopkeepers, he hates children. 'Fuck off, go upset your mothers.'

The kids ignore him, they are still saying 'Aiwa', but not with gusto like when a foreigner's eye is on them, they're saying it in bored voices, because it's what they do but the heart has gone out of it. A big-arsed government-waali doctress is stood outside a house, talking to the foreigner. Coming close my heart gives a jolt, no jarnalis is this, it's Elli Barber. Why is she here? Why is she with a government doctress? Well, jamisponding is my job so I've sneaked closer to ear-ogle their conversation.

'Hardly surprising they are ill,' Elli is saying quietly, I guess so the Nutcracker folk don't hear. 'Look at this filth, litter and plastic all over, open drains stinking right outside the houses. Flies. Every bit of waste ground is used as a latrine, I've seen people defecating on the railway lines.'

'Madam, it's these people, they don't know any better.'

'But you do,' says Elli. 'So teach them. Organise people into teams to pick up the litter. Bring in pipes, water taps, build proper latrines . . .'

'Of course I agree, but from where is the money to come?'

'Where did it come from for that new road near the lake, or for all the new buildings that are springing up around the city?'

'Madam, this is not my department.'

'Well it's someone's department,' says Elli doctress. 'Just look at this place. These houses look like they've been built by termites.'

At this government-waali gives an uneasy laugh.

'Seriously,' Elli says, 'this whole district looks like it was flung up by an earthquake.'

On hearing Elli speak this one word, *earthquake*, something weird and painful happens in my head. Up to that moment this was Paradise Alley, the heart of the Nutcracker, a place I'd known all my life. When Elli says *earthquake* suddenly I'm seeing it as she does. Paradise Alley is a wreckage of baked earth mounds and piles of planks on which hang gunny sacks, plastic sheets, dried palm leaves. Like drunks with arms round each others' necks, the houses of the Nutcracker lurch along this lane which, now that I look, isn't really even a road, just a long gap left by chance between the dwellings. Everywhere's covered in shit and plastic. Truly I see how poor and disgusting are our lives.

'Hello Animal,' says Elli, who's seen me staggering round on three legs with a hand over my eyes. 'How are you today?'

'Peas-potato samosa like a.'

'That good, eh?'

Government's given me a flashing specs look of disgust.

'Each one teach one,' says I to her. 'That means you. Who're you to give me the evil eye? Be off with you.'

'Are you mad?' asks government-waali.

'That I am, pudding sister,' says I, feeling seriously disturbed. Voices in my head are offering advice. Say this, do that. 'You should try washing between your legs,' I tell her, plus've gone into a kind of tail-chasing dance which brings cheers from the children.

Elli wags a finger at me, the two doctresses duck into a doorway, or what once I'd have called a doorway, now it's a termite-gobbled frame in a mud wall. What are these two up to? Well fuck it I'll follow.

Inside I am momentarily blinded. It's dark shadow, with light falling in stripes through planks of the farside wall. Elli and the other step through into a courtyard where are small papaya trees loaded with yellow fruit. I've stopped, because in the courtyard is a young woman sat on a stool in the sunlight. She has on a deep blue petticoat, but from waist up her body is bare. Her skin's very dark, black almost, her breasts are round and swollen. With slow fingers, she's pressing her breasts, sending jets of milk spurting onto the earth.

Elli is standing still like she's hoodwinked by the light. The mother, not looking up, continues to spill her milk to the dust. At last Elli says softly, 'Poor thing. How did she lose her child?'

Government-waali doctress does not reply, instead she flashes out at the woman, 'How many times have I told you not to believe rumours?'

That one says sullenly, 'My breasts are killing me.'

'Then it's your own fault,' snaps the waali.

The mother shrugs but doesn't stop what she's doing, squeezing pale milk from dark nipples. 'Why bother to come?' she says. 'You people never help.'

'I'm here to help,' Elli tells her in Hindi. 'What's the problem?'

'I won't feed my kid poison.' She's leant forward to cast the last dribbles of her milk onto the ground.

'Madam, she is deluded,' says Government. To the woman she says, 'I can cure bodies, not fairytales.'

'Canst cure nothynge,' says a very old voice. Sitting in the shadows holding a plastic bottle to a baby who's staring horrified, out of eyes heavily rimmed with kohl.

'So here after all is your baby,' says Elli. 'Why were you talking of poison?'

Says this granny, 'We have loked upon the milke and it semeth to muche thinne and watry. Plus it enclyneth to reddenesse, which is unnaturall and euill. Likewyse, it tasteth bitter, ye may well perceyue it is unwholesome.'

'Burns his gut,' says the mother.

'The infant yeaxeth incessantly,' says the granny holding up the baby. 'Out of measure he yeaxeth.'

'Yeaxeth? What's that?' asks Elli.

The laughter's dancing about in me so much it makes me want to jig, these village types, their outlandish accents and rustic way of talking.

'Hic,' says the kid, answering Elli's question.

Says the mother to Elli, 'Our wells are full of poison. It's in the soil, water, in our blood, it's in our milk. Everything here is poisoned. If you stay here long enough, you will be too.'

Of an instant, it's like the ground under my feet has turned to water. The young woman seems to be floating on a glittering ocean, the papaya trees are tall green waterspouts or else tails of monstrous plunging fish.

My brain returns from wherever it's gone missing to discover Government advancing on me with a look of fury on her face. I've sharpish scarpered from that place and run to hide in I'm Alive's shop, it's the one place that the waali won't care to follow, not if she knows anything about Nutcracker people.

'Packet of milk I need, fifty grams of flour, two candles.'

I'm Alive fastens his bulging eyes on me. Shiny they're, huge glass marbles, they give him a permanent look of horror, like a man who is watching his testicles being devoured by rats. His real name is Uttamchand, but people call him Zindabhai, Zinda for short, it means 'I'm Alive'.

'Animal, you're close to Zafar bhai,' he says, fetching out some milk. 'This foreign doctress, is it the one they say, who's opening a clinic in the Claw?'

'Yes.' I'm crouched behind a sack of rice. 'Is she coming, that Government-waali? If she heads this way I'll go out the back.'

'I don't want to know what you've done,' says he. 'I hear from Chunaram that Zafar bhai's intending to boycott this clinic. I think this is a bad idea. Zafar brother has our support in everything of course, but this is a matter which concerns people's health, it is not a question of politics.'

'Can't miss her,' I say. 'Eyes like fucking horseflies she has, plus buttocks that grind like they're cracking corn.'

'I don't see her,' says I'm Alive. 'Listen, I know what Zafar's position is. I am saying that this time, this is none of his business. He does not tell me what I should eat for my lunch, same way's this, I should be free to go if I want to this clinic.'

108

'You don't need a clinic.' I say, coming out from behind the shelter of the sacks. 'You're the man who can't die.'

'Oh but I do need,' says he, fussing around to gather my small list of wants. 'If the upstairs one hasn't called me yet, does it mean I should live in pain? My eyes are failing, chest is bad, plus I don't know how many times in the night I have to get up for the latrine, there is a numbness to the left leg, fingers also tingle, so many times I've thought, Uttam, your time is up, but always the one above has his eye on someone else. In that house opposite lived Sahara, one day blood came from her womb, it was cancer, forty-six years old she was, died right there across the road, ten years older I'm, yet I'm alive. Next door to her was Rafi, spent all he had on medicines, hardly did he spare ten rupees for food, but it did him no good. He too's gone leaving me to remember him. My neighbour on this side, Nafisa, in her neck had swelling and pain. She could not lift her arm, she used to say that it felt like someone pulling her nerves from the inside. She is no more yet I'm still here. Her cousin Safiya lived two doors along. Women's problems she had, pain like she was losing a baby, the doctor told her to drink milk and eat fruit. She came to me and said, "Zinda, you must help us. We can't even afford rotis, how will we afford fruit?" I gave her some guavas, I said, "Sister, pay me when you can." But before she could pay, she was gone, yet here I am still alive.'

Eyes, you must have guessed by now how he got his name.

'It's your goodness that prolongs your life,' says I, heading out of there.

'Wait,' he cries, 'this is two rupees short.'

'I'll be back. Don't worry, Zindabhai, you'll never outlive me.'

'Wretch!'

Not two paces have I taken when I'm brought up short, staring into a blue crotch, right next to them is a pair of stout legs in shalwars.

'So here he is,' says Elli.

'This sisterfuck owes me two rupees,' cries I'm Alive, puffing up behind me and catching me by the ear.

'Let go!' I've tried to twist free but surprisingly strong's that fucker for

109

one camped at death's door. Next thing he's thudded a foot on my back-side.

'Seems this boy is a real bad character,' says Government-waali, with a voice full of satisfaction.

'And you're a liar,' I shout. 'Elli doctress, what the woman told you about the water, it's true, everyone here knows it. Government types are lying. Zahreel Khan the minister himself came here to the Nutcracker and in front of a crowd of jarnaliss took a glass of well water and drank it to show it was safe. But Chhoté Ram, son of Mukund the tailor saw him a minute later go behind a house and stick two fingers down his throat.'

'Give me my two rupees,' says I'm Alive, landing another heavy kick.

'Stop!' says Elli. 'Here's two rupees. Let him go.'

Namispond Jamispond, I've headed round the corner to Chunaram's where I find Zafar sitting with Nisha, Farouq and all, there I've made my report, leaving out the bit about I'm Alive.

'Some crap spy are you,' said Farouq, 'this is old news.'

'We were just discussing it,' Zafar says, 'Cavorting with government.'

'Not cavorting.' See Eyes, without meaning to I'm sticking up for Elli. 'She was giving what-for to the government-waali doctress, plus you should have heard what she said when I told her about the water and Zahreel Khan.'

'What did she say?' asks Nisha.

'When government had gone Elli doctress said she'd always felt there was something not right about Zahreel Khan, seems the first time she met him he talked only to, Nisha excuse me, her lolos, which is to say her bloblos.'

'So then why is Zahreel Khan opening her clinic?' asks Zafar quickly to protect Nisha from the question of lolos plus bloblos. Adds as an after-thought, 'You and she seem to be quite friendly.'

'I keep my eyes and ears open, like we agreed.'

'Your job is to find useful information. Is this useful?'

'Zafar bhai, please tell me what you count as useful? Is it what people are thinking and saying? Or is it only what you want to hear?'

Says Farouq, 'Just listen to this street-chaff.'

'It's a fair question. Let him speak,' Zafar says.

No one will talk straight to Zafar, they daren't cross him, but I am not afraid. 'Zafar bhai, if you really want to know, people don't want to boycott the clinic. They are all crying out for treatment.'

'Nevertheless,' he replies, 'if we ask them to stay away, they will. Sometimes it's necessary to do a painful thing.'

'Zafar brother, you are always saying that the Kampani has all the money and power and rich friends etc, on our side there's nothing, you say that it is this very nothing that gives us the power to fight and maybe even win?'

'Not maybe,' he says. 'Definitely. The Kampani don't know what they're up against, people who have nothing have nothing to lose, we will never give up, out of having nothing comes a power that's impossible to resist. It may take long, but we will win.'

'So this power of nothing,' I've persisted, 'what is it? Isn't it desperation? If so won't that very power drive crowds to Elli's clinic?'

'We'll see,' says he with a frown.

'Elli doctress, she is not from the Kampani. She's on our side. I've read her thoughts, I have felt her feelings, you know I can do this.'

'Animal,' says Zafar sadly, 'you are special we all know it, but some things are just too important to trust to feelings.'

Nisha says, 'Well I think Zafar is right.' She's clasped his arm to show that whatever nasty doubting Animal says, as long as she's around he'll have the cleanest arsehole in Khaufpur.

'So what's your plan?' asks Chunaram, who's hovering on the edge of our group, where we're sat with our glasses of chai.

'Chuna brother, I guess we'll hold a democracy. Whatever it decides we'll do, but we must not allow the Kampani to gather false medical data. Anyone thinks they wouldn't stoop so low, remember the thighs-of-fate.'

Now the sighing's of a different kind, as all recall.

Thighs-of-fate, it's an Inglis name, I do not know what the Hindi might be. On that night when poisons came from the Kampani's factory, those who weren't then and there killed found themselves in a bad way with fainting, fits, pain, blood's coughed up, can't see, hardly can breathe etc. This thighs-of-fate was a medicine which was helping people get relief. News quickly spread, from all over the city people came to wait in line for injections, but suddenly the treatment was stopped. Some bigwig let slip that the Kampani bosses from Amrika had rung up their best friend the Chief Minister and told him to stop the thighs-of-fate. There was a huge row. Some doctors moved into a shack near the factory and began giving the injections. The police came, wrecked the shack, beat up the doctors. Zafar says that by giving relief this thighs-of-fate somehow also proved that the illnesses could pass to future generations. The Kampani was afraid of this knowledge getting out because it might cost them in a court case, so they had the thighs-of-fate stopped and many were lost who could have been saved.

'Why did that sisterfuck CM obey the Kampani? It had already fled.' This is what someone asks.

'Khã, so naive you're,' says a second. 'Haven't the politicians been in the Kampani's pocket from the beginning? Have you forgotten the old days, how those pompous big shots would ride in Kampani limos, never looking to right or left. My missus says Zahreel and the CM are waiting for all us victims to die, only then will their embarrassment end.'

Says Nisha, 'The CM does what the Kampani wants.'

'Zafar brother, why do they hate us people so much?' asks someone else.

'Because,' says Zafar, 'we raise our voices, we won't just lie down and die.'

'They're rich, they have everything. Why do they deny us even health?'

'You know the real reason they can't forgive us?' chirps up Gaurilal Babu, who by the way, Eyes, is one of the ugliest men you will ever see. So

112

awful is his expression that in the Nutcracker they say his glance can spoil milk.

'Tell us, Gauri,' chorus the assembled chai drinkers.

'It's because the greatest and best pleasure of life is available freely to the poor as to the rich, it's that famous thrill for which all humans are crazy. Rich and powerful people risk everything for it, yet it can equally be enjoyed by the destitute.'

Farouq who up till now hasn't said anything decides this is the moment to chip in. 'In such pleasures Animal is the expert, should see how he ogles the Amrikan doctress. Ask him yourself if it isn't true.'

Nisha picks up her bag and says, 'Okay, I have to go.'

Zafar squeezes her hand, a look passes between them, Eyes, it smashes me up inside. With a wave she's gone out into the alley.

'Shabaash Farouq,' I say, 'you got rid of Nisha.'

'Say, Zafar brother,' insists Gaurilal, 'isn't it true what I just said?'

Says Zafar, 'Not exactly, Gauri brother. For the rich sex is an indulgence, it's in the homes of the poor that it becomes an art.' Always he's trying to find new reasons to praise the poor.

'What? Are you saying that for the poor sex is better?' It's me.

'Fuck do you know about it?' sneers Farouq.

'My god, I love these philosophy discussions,' says Gaurilal, scratching his head. Other fools are grinning. They'll wag their heads and say wah wah but haven't a clue what's going on.

'Look,' says Zafar, 'suppose you're a young couple. It's spring and desire is rushing through your veins. Lying side by side, you reach out and touch one another under the sheet. But you have to be careful, ma-in-law's bundled up asleep just a few feet away. Your brother's kids are sleeping in the same room. You must wait till everyone else is asleep, and after you've lain quietly awake trying to reckon their breathing, you're obliged to proceed with minimum movement, no scrapes or rustles, uttering not the smallest sound. To be erotic in such circumstances, this is what makes it an art.'

'Might even be,' says Gaurilal, 'that these very restrictions on the poor, need for breath-control plus twisting about of the body to fit cramped and unlikely spaces, are what gave rise to yoga.'

Zafar thinks about this for a while, he's removed his glasses and polished them on his shirt-tail, then he replaces them and says, 'No, I do not think so.'

Well, the big flaw in Zafar's theory is that it's wrong. No one else will point this out, so it's up to me. 'Zafar brother, kids from the Nutcracker get used to hearing their mothers and aunts sighing, "Oh baba," plus whispers of "do it more quietly", they have to learn to keep shut and not giggle.'

So then Zafar claims his theory is not spoiled by such cynicism, on the contrary it proves that the poor have further virtues. As well as being modest, inventive and long-suffering, they are also discreet and keep a sense of humour in the face of their troubles. He speaks of how people whose lungs were ruined by the Kampani's poisons, who have difficulty just breathing, still manage to laugh. But when Zafar talks like this it's not the laughter of the poor I hear, it's the laughter of the Kampani that slaughtered them.

Later, lying alone in my bed in the ruined tower, listening to the scorpions making their tiny sounds in the walls, the question suddenly strikes me, how does Zafar know so much about tiny rustling of sheets, harsh breaths etc, plus the need to keep totally silent during sex. Then of course I remember Somraj's ability to hear the smallest sounds.

Going up the mango put the idea into my head, I swear that's where it came from, until then I had never seen the frangipani in Somraj's garden as anything but a tree. Beautiful white flowers it had, with yellow hearts full of scent, and if angels had breath their breath would be like the deep joy of those flowers, but it was still just a tree. Only after the mango adventure did I notice that this frangipani had a smooth trunk, no thorns or prickly bits, that its branches began low and would be dead easy to climb, plus a large branch was swaying only a few feet from Nisha's bedroom window.

Now as I'm looking at this tree, it occurs to me that I could climb up and just check on what she and Zafar were getting up to in there. Is this so wrong? I need to be certain that brother Zafar isn't taking advantage, I just want to be sure. If I climb this tree it's not to spy on Nisha but to guard her honour. You could even say it's a duty. I owe it to Nisha. Girl like her, from a good family, she should save her chastity for marriage. If it becomes known that she's been playing around, who'd marry her?

Who'd marry her? Well, I would. My situation has never bothered her. Nisha accepts me how I am, when she calls me four-footed it's fact, nothing more. With others there's malice, Farouq is always gibing at me, even Zafar once teased, 'Shall we photograph your gallop?' We'd just watched a show on Chunaram's tele about a chap who set up twenty-four cameras in a line and fired them so, so, so, so, as a horse raced by to see if all its feet were ever off the ground at once. I thought, even Saint Zafar forgets himself and stumbles, yet by doing so he proves himself human. 'If I galloped past those cameras,' I asked, 'what would they show, a miserable animal or a miserable boy?' So Zafar immediately said he was sorry and gave me a hug, Farouq carried on laughing. Now here's a thing, if someone says to you, you're lazy, well it's something you can change. If you say to me, Animal you are greedy, rude, stubborn, your cock is hanging out of your pants, all of these things I can change, what I can't change is being a four-foot. To be made to feel bad because of something that isn't your fault and you can do fuck all about, that's cruel. Nisha could never be cruel. I'm thinking how kind and good she is to me, I doubt if I'll ever meet another woman like her. I'm then thinking that if I was a really nasty person, I'd let gossip spread, because then no one else would marry her, but I care too much about Nisha. Morally I have no choice but to climb the tree.

First night in the frangipani, I'm terrified. The leaves of that tree don't grow thick like mango leaves, they're more in clusters at the end of each stem, but the tree is towards the back of Nisha's garden plus there are no lights in the lane, so no one can see me slipping up onto the long branch that goes past her window. It's late, after ten, the sound of a sitar is drifting up from Somraj's music room. Full of sadness it's, like Somraj's memories. Nisha's window is dark. She'll be tidying up, probably making her father a cup of tea. I know Zafar is there because his motorbike is outside. Not long now before they come up. I am petrified by the thought of what I might see. Once when I was small I caught the parents of a boy I knew, I went to their house looking for him. The house was one room which they all shared. No one was there, but noises were coming from behind a curtain pulled across a corner, I took a peek and found two brown monkeys having a wrestling bout. It took some time to realise that these were the father and mother of the boy. I said, 'Hello, where's Raju?' They jumped apart, looking round.

'What are you doing, uncle?' says I.

'Oh it's you!' says the dad crossly. 'I'm just looking for auntie's earring.'

'What, was she sitting on it?'

'Why don't you bugger off?'

Well, Eyes, I never got a proper look, that's why I told you the first naked woman I'd seen was Elli.

116

The light goes on. With no warning I'm staring into Nisha's room, a huge face is staring back at me. It's Shah Rukh Khan, the movie star. Bastard, what right have his paper eyes to see the things that go on in this place, where I've never been? Just beneath Shah Rukh's face I can see about half the bed. Now Nisha moves past it towards a shape in the corner. It's a cupboard. Of Zafar there's no sign, a few minutes later I hear the bike starting up and catch the red glow of his tail light turning and heading for Nekchalan's. I could leave. Tonight at least, her honour is safe. I should go, because she may start getting undressed, but it's too late, already Nisha is pulling off her kameez. Okay, so I won't look. I am not here for a cheap thrill. She's loosening the string of her shalwar. I'll put my hands over my eyes. Shalwar's off, hands are behind her back, then brassiere's down, what a ravishing sight. After a while I tell myself it does not really matter, because I am here to guard her honour, and the only way I can do it is this, if it means getting a view of this thing or that, well it's a price I have to pay. She stoops to remove her underwear. The things I witness now are not for you or the thousand other eyes. Try to understand, never in my life have I been with a woman yet have so badly wanted it for how I don't know long. Like a performing bear that thing of mine stands up to dance. Lights are going on all over my body, senses are drowned in the rushing of blood, a pulse is thudding in my ears, do it do it, what? what? that that, no no, yes yes, really? really? yes yes, how? how? so so, o o, oh yes, oh no, oh fuck, that pattering in the leaves, it isn't rain.

The madness is over, my body doesn't want to know me, it gets into a sulk, there's darkness now in the castle of lights. Shame comes plus terror. How will I show my face to Nisha after disgracing myself in a tree outside her window?

Well, I am sorry to say it really is not that difficult. Next day Nisha's the same as always, all I have to do is forget last night. Think it never happened. This works well. I decide I will never climb the tree again. Relief. Four full nights go by before I set foot in its branches. This time Nisha is not alone. Now, I learn three things. The first is that Nisha and Zafar are not doing anything. I can see only the tops of their two heads, they must be sitting on the floor talking to each other. The second thing is that guilt is just a feeling, you can choose not to feel it, how else do the Kampani bosses sleep? The third thing is that no matter what I might see, there is nothing can I do about it. Even if I were to see Zafar and Nisha glued together like dogs, there'd be no way to stop them except by going to Somraj, and thus proclaiming to the world that I'd been spying. I need a cleverer plan.

The idea that strikes is a good one, but involves my friend Ali Faqri who is not always easy to find, so the first step is to locate Abdul Saliq, the Pir Gate beggar. Eyes, I have mentioned this fellow before, it's said that women can't resist him, look at him you'd never know why. If you took a skeleton, chopped off one of its legs, removed half its teeth, dressed the result in rags and pissed all over it, this is the type of impression that Mr Saliq likes to give.

On a blue morning, white doves fluttering in and out the arches of the great Pir Gate, I find Abdul Saliq at his usual post, leaning on his crutch with his hand out, uttering his well-known cry, *Keep away, you faithless gits!*

'Hello Animal,' says he. 'Been a while.'

'Truly, guru. How's business?'

'God provides.'

'You're looking awful.'

'Thank, you. *Keep away, you faithless gits!* I do my best.'

Sometimes strangers to the city will give Abdul Saliq a coin just so they can ask what his cry means. Slowly, like a cricket umpire giving a batsman, he'll raise his finger, which does not stop until it is pointing at the arch far above. There, cut in the stone is a line of Inglis PROCUL HINC ABESTE PROFANI.

'It means,' says he, 'that you are entering the city of the elect, whereof the mystery is shouted from the rooftop, but none may decipher it, yea, except within their own souls.' This is the type of stuff that Abdul Saliq likes to say and do. Bit of chit, bit of chat, I've talked him into buying me a chai from the RTI shop, best in Khaufpur, nicely spiced plus frothed up with a pinch of salt, nothing like it, if you ever come here Eyes, you should definitely try it. Costs two rupees per glass but Abdul Saliq is not short of money, plus he's always generous to an ex-pupil. We get talking of the old days, I ask if he knows where I can find Faqri.

'Working,' says he, giving me a look.

'Care to tell me where?'

'Over by the bus station. What? Does he owe you money?'

'No such luck. Today I'm buying.'

'I won't ask.'

'I won't tell.'

At this he laughs. 'So it's a girl.'

'What's a girl?' It never fails to throw me, this genius of Abdul Saliq's.

'Your problem, Kuala Lumpur Police Department.'

'What makes you think I have that kind of a problem?' But of course he is right. After wishing khuda hafez to Abdul Saliq, he likes blessings almost as much as coins, I take myself off to the bus stands, pretty soon I've found what I'm looking for.

Noisy place, is Khaufpur bus station. Dirty old buses pulling in and out, smokes of diesel, crowds pushing to get on, new arrivals struggling to get off, shouting at the porters who are climbing like langurs on the roofs of the buses, tossing down bits of baggage. 'Ho you, put it down!' 'Sir, I have already carried it.' 'I never told you to.' 'You never told me not to.' 'You've taken it only ten yards.' 'Minimum fee applies.' Attach to this the coughing of rusty engines, the cries of hawkers, the blaring of filmi songs, every bus a different tune, and you will understand that it takes an expert to pinpoint within this hubbub a small upset coming from the direction of the deluxe coach stand.

A chubby, prosperous-looking gent has got down from the just-arrived a/c coach from Nagpur, he's being accosted by a beggar boy. The kid is well into his routine, he's pawing at his victim and whining, and the stout musaafir is perspiring and getting annoyed. He snaps at the beggar to leave him alone, but the fellow's whines just get louder. 'Hey master-ji, hey worship, sahib, you are my father, my life, you are my god.' 'Don't touch!' cries the mark. He's having his shirt tugged, doesn't like it. 'Take your hands off me!' Great performance by the number one, he's picked an ideal target and knows exactly how to get him seething, all set up for the switch.

So, here's Faqri now, the number two, just one more of the hundreds of faceless guys passing through that place. He stands looking on as the fat man addresses harsh words to the beggar. 'Get lost, hop it, sod off.'

Number one's backing away, gone is his whine, he is mouthing the foulest insults he can think of. The mark's furious eyes are fixed on him. Timing's perfect. Yes, here it comes, beautiful really, the loud chuckle of disgust, Faqri pointing at the man's shirt, then at the sky, I'm mouthing the next line as he speaks it, 'Oh dear, bombed by the Khaufpur air force!' A vile looking splodge has appeared on the man's shirt. Heads swivel upwards, looking for the guilty bird. I never see the number three despite I'm looking for him. The mark's still cursing the mess on his shirt, his wallet is already half a street away. Faqri stays a moment longer, then fades away into the spectators who are cracking unkind jokes at the fat man's expense. I'd clap, if I wasn't using my hands to stand on. 'Bravo, well played sir, more, more.'

There are plenty more scams, we knew them all, Faqri and me, lost coins, cigarette-stub, spilled channa, bloodstain, broken-bottle, Scotch whisky, hair-oil scam, but the most artistic was the one I'd just watched. Get some lime paste from a paan-maker, mix it up with dirt, cowdung, tobacco juice, chewed grass, anything really. The effect you're after, what you're looking for, is a big white or brown splotch with streaks of black and green that looks as if it has just exited a pigeon's arse. The rest you know. This was the bird-shit scam, we'd play it with me as the number one and Faqri like today flicking the bird-shit. Usually Abdul Saliq would find us the number three, had to be a specialist. We earned well, until I got caught. See, if you are going to con people and get away with it you have to be able to vanish in a crowd, but not many Khaufpuris go on fours, and that's how Fatlu-Inspector got his hands on me. First time I was arrested I got slapped about a bit, then ushered into His Highness's presence.

'Who's your partner?'

'Don't know what you mean.'

'Who nicks the wallet?' They hadn't twigged the bird-shit, which is funny. Mark complains he was pestered by a beggar, a boy on all fours, and next thing he knows his wallet's missing. Never mentions bird-shit. Well, it's demeaning to be shat on, quickly as possible wipe from shirt and mind.

'Which wallet?'

'Don't mess with me you miserable sonofawhore.'

His fist thuds down, it was the first of many beatings I took from Reserve Inspector Prithviraj, the street folk call him Fatlu because of his massive butt and the way his belly bulges like it's being throttled by his belt. Fatlu has hated me for years, he'd lay into me whenever he saw me on the street, didn't even have to be doing anything. Well I can take a thrashing. I'm used to sticks thudding on my back. Beat, fuckers, beat harder, maybe you'll straighten me out! If there's a god, which I person-ally don't believe, but Ma Franci says there is, he must have recorded every blow. Ma says that very soon all the bad people in the world will get what's coming to them. I am happily picturing Fatlu with his balls in a truss pulling a cart lashed by demons when here's Faqri standing beside me. 'Saw you from over there,' says he.

I congratulate him on a fine performance.

'A little rusty.' We've left the bus station, Faqri checks the mark's wallet, extracts folded notes fresh from some Nagpur bank, tucks them in his pocket. 'These days I am more in the pharmaceutical line.'

'I know. It's that I've come to talk to you about.'

'Shop's not open today, so let's go to my place.'

Just outside the galla mandi, the vegetable market, on certain days you will find Faqri sat on a stool with packages of herbs and powders spread out on newspapers by his feet. This is his shop. The packets are unwrapped to show their contents, leaves, seeds, petals, roots. He sends kids to gather these things from all over the city. Some even grow in corners of the Kampani's factory. He employs women to grind them and mix up with molasses to make pills, one rupee per pill, buy half a dozen he'll pop them in a matchbox for you. Faqri's pills can cure whatever you want and in a city like Khaufpur there's no shortage of illnesses. He has pills for coughs and breathlessness and aches and pains plus the type of problems people don't like to talk about. He tells me of the patients he's cured. Woman had white water discharge. Man couldn't get it up. Chap was worried because he has feelings for men instead of women. Faqri's now such a medical expert, he's thinking of calling himself 'doctor'.

'So you're a sex-specialist?'

'Specialist in everything,' he says proudly. It should be his motto. Look at his razor-crease pants, shirt with hoisted collar, Faqri is twenty years old, already you can see the man that's coming, prosperous, devious, can't give a straight answer, would make a perfect politician.

Subtlety is of no use, I'll have to be blunt. 'I'm after something that takes away the sex urge.'

'Takes it away? What? Your famous lund is out of control?'

'Not for me.'

'Lady friend?'

Having no choice, I tell him the story.

'Are they already doing it?' he asks.

'How would I know?'

'Jealous,' sniggers Faqri. 'Wish it was you?'

'Don't be disgusting,' I say. 'She is like my sister.'

'Some sister,' says he. 'Kuala Lumpur Police Department.'

'Fuck off.' Kuala Lumpur Police Department, it's a way of saying KLPD, which in turn is a way to say Khadé Lund Pé Dhoka, or deception of the standing cock, c'est à dire, a pricktease.

When we reach his place, Faqri sets about grinding some black seeds

122

into a powder. A litle bit later he shows me a thing that looks like a goat dropping.

'One of these, he'll feel sick as a dog, in no mood even to speak to a girl let alone get sexy with her.'

'How long do they work for?'

'One pill per day,' he says. 'If things look really bad you could give one and a half. Do not exceed prescribed dose. How many do you want?'

'Discount for quantity?'

I go away with a plastic jar containing thirty six pills.

The first pill I give Zafar on the day of the big democracy. The democracy is a meeting where everyone has their say, followed by a big fucking row, after which everyone does what Zafar wants. This one happens in Somraj's music room which he keeps sacred to goddess Saraswati and blue-throated god Siva. It's a beautiful room to my eyes, it has walls of white, hung all over with instruments that make many types of sounds. There are bolsters, cushions, plus rugs spread on the floor, one came from Afghanistan, it was brought by a Hazara who traded it for singing lessons, pictures of helicopters and guns are woven into it. Zafar despises possessions, but these carpets are the only things I've seen him take pleasure in. 'In Khorasan,' he told us, 'the weavers tie one knot of the wrong colour because only god can make something perfect.'

'Since when did you start believing in the upstairs-one?'

'Hark at Animal,' says Farouq, 'god's knot in humanity.'

Zafar was well pissed-off with Farouq, but I don't think he was sticking up for me, Zafar hates all mention of god, but even more hates being caught praising him.

So now let's tell you who all were at this durbar. The room's so full it's like a bladder bursting with important types. Zafar and his mates, they're on one side. Opposite is Somraj, with a couple of his musical chums, in between are all the rest. Ram Nekchalan the shopkeeper is there looking mighty pleased, first time he's been invited to a meeting so grand. He's sat next to a sardarji Timecheck Singh. Ask Timecheck anything, he'll look at his watch. Lawyers charge per minute. Say 'Hello,' he'll check the time, can't help it. All these are from the Chicken Claw, there are a half-dozen others from elsewhere in Khaufpur, plus two from the Nutcracker. Last of all's me, I'm hanging in the door, Zafar sees and calls me in. No room there's, but Nisha signs for me to sit between her and Zafar, so I've squeezed in. Oh joy, Nisha puts her arm round my shoulder, from the other side Zafar drops his arm round me, I'm truly among friends, chuffed to be included in the council of the great.

Zafar starts the meeting by telling how this Amrikan woman's appeared in Khaufpur and bought the building, what the *Khaufpur Gazette* wrote, she was doing a wonderful act of charity, and how Zahreel Khan, the Minister for Poison Relief, will open this so-called clinic.

'So-called?' asks a woman I don't know. 'Isn't it a real clinic?'

'I am sure it is a real clinic, Dr Misra,' Zafar replies, 'the question is, what is its real purpose?' He then reports what we've learned from Dayanand and Co about the kind of medical work that will go on across the road.

'Excuse me, Zafar bhai,' says someone else, 'but these things, they're exactly what is needed here.'

Zafar's not having it all his own way, but I'm no longer listening. Eyes, I don't give a twisted fuck about politics, I'm in Zafar's group for one reason which is to be near Nisha, and you can't get much nearer than I'm at that moment. Her thigh's pressed tight against my knee, my nostrils are full of the scent of her, she is warm and her flesh is soft. I begin thinking about certain things I've seen in the frangipani and the monster down there stirs. It shifts, gives a throb, I feel it thickening. My kakadus are changing shape. Fuck! No! Not in front of all these people. I dive a hand into my pocket to clamp the unruly beast against my leg, my fingers find Faqri's box of pills. Desperate I'm, will have to pop one, but can't slide it open without letting go of my unruly lund, which immediately starts to rear and buck, damn that fucking thing, it has no respect. Well,

124

there's nothing for it but to lean right forward and plant my other elbow on the creature, but this in turn leaves the hand twitching to no purpose, so I rest my chin on it like I'm concentrating, must look peculiar for Nisha whispers, 'Are you okay?'

'Fully. This discussion is very fascinating.'

By the time I return to what's being said, it's to hear Ram Nekchalan, the man who wants to be everyone's best friend. 'We shouldn't help the Kampani to gather its false information. We should fight.'

Hypocrite! I can't help it, I say, 'What's changed, Nekchalan? Last week you were talking as if this clinic was your idea.'

Someone laughs, it's Farouq. Ram Nekchalan looks like he wants to kill.

Now everyone is looking at me, who's crouched forward to hide the shape in his pants. Fool that I am, why did I speak? Was there ever a worse fucking time to draw attention to myself?

'Hah!' I give a shout.

Instantly there's a loud ringing in the air, people are looking round to see from where it has come. It's the instruments. Hundreds of strings singing tiny songs. Somraj whose eyes were closed as if to escape this futile discussion, now opens them and comes back from wherever he's been. He says, 'The boy is right. You people have no proof, yet you'd start fighting. This clinic is much needed, I for one will not support a boycott.'

Nisha's arm round my shoulder tightens. Oh dear, caught between her dad and her lover, this means trouble. Somraj's friends make matters no better by loudly agreeing with him. Says his student Shastri, who resembles a lizard, his jaw juts from beneath his ears like an iguana's, 'In a just society, a person is innocent until proven guilty.'

'Of women it's said, do not despise them,' chimes in Somraj's other pal, a rough and ready beardo is he, Somraj's best friend plus his tabla player from the old days, I don't remember his name, Something Khan, all tabla players in this city are something Khans. 'Why should we not despise them? Because we might be despising a thing through which god has planned much good.'

The debate goes back and forth with the three musicians ganged up anti the rest. Why are they opposed? Is it because Elli too is a musician? Somraj, who listens to all sounds, maybe he's heard her playing her piano.

On Zafar's face, I guess because of Something Khan's bringing god into it, are signs of irritation. 'Is poison presumed harmless until it kills?' he retorts. 'Isn't this the lesson of Khaufpur, that you don't wait to be harmed before you take action to protect? Friends, at long last we have a chance, however slim, of forcing the Kampani to court and winning proper compensation for our folk. We dare not put that at risk. We have to act together, so if you can't support, at least don't oppose.'

At this everyone starts talking at once. Some are grumbling, from other quarters comes loud support.

'I am not comfortable with this,' says Somraj, the only one who dares speak openly against Zafar's proposal. 'We need better evidence before we deny to people something that could help them.'

Says Zafar, 'Abba, we have failed to find any trace of this woman's history. This alone is suspicious, she's almost certainly operating under a false name. We have tried all usual channels. Nisha has searched on the internest, nothing.'

'Nothing is not evidence,' says the stubborn Voice of Khaufpur.

'Abba,' says Zafar again, I hate to hear him calling Somraj father, 'Animal is cultivating a friendship with Elli Barber. I feel confident that he'll soon extract some useful information, then we will be in a position to judge.'

'Papa, if we could win this compensation,' says Nisha to her father, 'think what a difference it will make to people.'

Still he's not looking happy. I am happy, Nisha's warm thigh is pressing against me, the demon below is thank god back to sleep.

'Just think, papa,' wheedles Nisha, 'what the Kampani has paid till now is so small, hardly does it amount to the price of one cup of daal a day.'

Somraj sighs. 'All right, I can't support, but I won't oppose.'

126

Now all can relax, what a wonderful thing is democracy. A general hubbub starts up, Timecheck looks at his watch.

Nekchalan giggles and says, 'Three rupees.'

'Three rupees, what?' asks Farouq.

'Three rupees for a cup of daal.'

'Depends which daal,' someone else says.

'Urad daal, tuwar is dearer,' says the shopkeeper. 'But it costs me more to get it in,' he adds quickly lest anyone should suspect him of profiteering.

'Pitiful it's,' says Zafar. 'What else does three rupees buy? Pir Gate tea, one glass? Yes, Animal?' This time I've raised my hand to speak.

'One tea plus one samosa at Chunaram's.'

They laugh, so things are back to normal, good even, lund's back under control, two speeches made at this important meeting.

'Talking of tea,' says Nisha, 'would everybody like some?'

I'm up onto my four feet. Thé pour tous. The gurgling and bubbling of the pan on the fire sounds like laughter. We return bearing uneven loads, Nisha carrying a tray loaded with glasses, me with a single glass.

'Zafar brother, this is for you.'

The unsuspecting bugger accepts it gratefully, pulls me down beside him.

'Sit here, Animal,' he says to me. 'You have a wise head. Let us plan how you shall interrogate Elli Barber.'

'What do you really think of her?' asks Nisha on my other side.

'What do I think?' I say, watching him drink. I can't say what I really think. Poor Elli, you're about to be betrayed by these undeserving arseholes you came to help.

'I think she has blue legs.'

The last few days before Elli doctress's clinic opens Zafar brother can be seen wandering with gleaming specs, frowning to himself, tugging at his beard. I whistle this tune whenever I see him, it's that one, you know, that goes

Strolling down the highway I'm
eating my bhel-puri I'm
if your granny's careless, what can I do?
if your heart is jealous, what can I do?

'Yaar Animal,' says Zafar, 'do me a favour, don't drive me mad.'

'Don't you like my singing?'

'It's not that,' says he, who hates saying a bad thing about anyone. 'Just that lately I'm not feeling too good. Eaten something, must've.'

In Somraj's house is an uneasy tension. Somraj won't do anything to upset Zafar's plan, but there is a tug of war and Nisha is the rope.

'A daughter should obey her father,' I've given a pull to Somraj's side.

'Fine one you are to talk of duty,' says Nisha, 'really Animal you are so transparent.' After a while she adds, 'But quite sweet.' After some more time she says, 'Zafar is upset. Some people came this afternoon from the bastis, they begged him to not boycott the clinic. Even Pyaré Bai came.'

'That day,' I said, 'when I paid off the moneylender, I was thinking that when Elli doctress starts giving free treatment, people like Pyaré Bai will no longer need to borrow.'

'Zafar's not at all well,' says Nisha. 'He feels sick, his mouth is dry, he's very hot. That's how ill this worry is making him.'

The evening of the opening ceremony we're all in Somraj's garden, watching them get ready across the road. Beside the famous mango tree is pitched a big colourful shamiana, inside Elli and her staff are hustling. Tonight her legs aren't blue, she's wearing shalwar kameez, like an Indian woman. Suresh and Dayanand are setting out rows of chairs, on a table near the door of the tent flower garlands are piled. Outside in the street Mando's band in tatty green uniforms are marching up and down, braying strange notes that scamper up and down the cracks between familiar keys. *Sa re ga* etc can't describe them, such sounds need new names entirely. I know one of the musicians, a trumpet player, an old bugger, he's from

128

the Nutcracker, he gives me a wink, folds his hands in greeting to Somraj, who's stood watching beneath his frangipani tree. All the players have an eye out for Somraj because even if he no longer sings he's still the famous *Aawaaz-e-Khaufpur*, no matter how long they live none of them will ever be a great maestro like he is. Maybe knowing he's listening makes them try harder, I mean they are playing almost in time, sometimes even in tune. Who knows what nameless things these sounds are doing to Somraj's ears? It's rarely that I speak to Somraj, mostly I don't dare, but this ruckus makes me feel so sorry for him that I blurt out my thoughts.

'Oh no,' he says, 'I find it very interesting,' and begins talking of the skills needed by a brass player such as lip stamina, range, tone, speed of fingers and breath control. 'This kind of breathing that brass players do, they take a great gulp of air and then they use their lungs, and these muscles here,' tapping his abdomen, 'and in the stomach to control how it flows to the instrument.'

'Really?' What else is to say?

'Do you know how the note can be sustained even though the performer has no breath left in his lungs?'

'No sir.'

'It's called chakra breathing, which means breathing in circles. You won't find it mentioned in any yoga sutras. Can you guess how it's done?'

I've shaken my head.

'Fill your cheeks with air and push it out slowly, at the same time breathe in through your nose.' He puffs out his cheeks like two apples. 'Try.'

I snort, puff, and make unusual noises. Nisha, who is nearby, has a fit of giggles. Just thankful I'm that Farouq's not there to mock, he and Zafar have gone off somewhere together. All day they've been mysterious, I have a feeling that they are keeping something from me.

'So you are still interested in music?' asks Panditji, his mouth seems to give a twitch, almost smiling he's, which would be a miracle.

'Sir, what happens when the cheeks are empty?'

'Let go from the lungs and quickly fill the cheeks again.' He gives a kind of a gulp, then he's coughing, he can't stop.

'Pandit Somraj sir, are you okay sir?'

Somraj pandit's doubled up retching, Nisha has gone running to fetch a glass of water, thus do the Kampani's gases rob him of his singing breath.

It's grown dark by the time Zahreel Khan arrives. Flashbulbs blossom as the *Khaufpur Gazette* gets its shots. The Minister of Poison is turned by the flashes into a ghost casting huge jumping shadows. Dayanand, Suresh and Miriam rush forward with garlands. He poses to receive them, hands folded, head bowed as if the flowers are heavy with the weight of responsibility.

Twenty minutes pass before the speeches begin. Lights inside the tent are wavering, Khaufpuri electric can't be trusted. Lurking in Somraj's garden, we see Elli on the platform, herself now loaded with flowers, listening to her chief guest making a speech into a brown gloom in which people's faces can barely be seen. Outside it's by now fully dark, she can't see us. Hardly for a minute has Zahreel Khan been speaking when from the direction of Ram Nekchalan's shop loud filmi music starts up, muffled and distorted, the minister has to raise his voice to fight against it. 'Elli Barber is an eminent consultant. We in Khaufpur are proud to have attracted a doctor of such talent.'

'How did Khaufpur attract her?' calls a familiar voice. It's Zafar. He and Farouq are standing near the entrance to the tent, behind them there seem to be many other people clustered.

'Kindly save questions for the end,' says the Minister in a testy manner, peering to see who is causing this disruption. 'You will get your chance.'

'Was she asked to come?' persists Zafar. 'Who asked her?'

These further interjections Zahreel Khan ignores. Putting aside his notes he begins to talk of that night, how he himself had been in the old city and had been caught in the panic. He speaks of the scenes in the streets and the crush of dying people in the hospitals. He tells how he like so many hundreds of others searched all night for his missing loved ones, and of the terrible scenes in the city as morning broke. The filmi music is still playing up the road, but I reckon people can no longer hear it, it has vanished into a deep silence. For those listening to Zahreel Khan, it's their own memories they're hearing. Then there's one moment, the wind catches that sound in its airy hands and brings it to the tent, one clear phrase, a grave and beautiful voice singing, *Kaun Aayaa Méré Mun Ké Dvaaré*, who's this come to the door of my mind? Pandit Somraj gives a terrible sigh, like a groan almost, and goes back into his house. Poor Nisha, standing nearby is torn, she would like to join Zafar, but the duty of a daughter prevails, she disappears after her father.

It's Zahreel Khan himself who breaks the spell he has woven. 'Since the day of disaster itself,' he intones, returning to his notes, 'Doctor Barber has yearned to come to Khaufpur to help in the relief work we are doing.'

'That *who* is doing?' This isn't Zafar, it's a voice from the crowd. 'Give one example of relief work done by your department in the past year.'

'Two years,' calls another. 'Five years,' it's a third. Scornful laughter there's, various numbers of years start flying around. I look to see how Elli is taking this, but from this distance I can't make out her expression. She's sitting on the dais with her face framed by flowers.

'Question for Doctor Barber,' calls Zafar. 'For whose benefit is this clinic?'

Elli stands up, Zahreel Khan steps aside to make room for her at the microphone. 'It's for all who were injured on that night, plus people who are ill as a result of their water being poisoned by the factory. All who come are welcome, for all who come, treatment is free.'

It's a good answer. I defy even Zafar to find anything wrong in it.

'Will you be gathering medical data? If so, who will have access to it, to what use will it be put?' This is Zafar again.

'We'll be keeping patient records,' she replies. 'But they'll be confidential. Of course if the patient requests it, we would share their medical history with another doctor.'

131

'Which institutions are funding this effort?'

'None. My clinic is funded by a person who prefers not to be named.'

'Person or Kampani?' comes a shout. At once there's hubbub, and a dozen voices start chanting, 'Kampani out! Kampani out!'

For the first time Elli looks nonplussed. Zahreel Khan steps back to the podium. 'Doctor Barber,' he says, 'These ill-mannered types shame Khaufpur. Kindly ignore them. Tomorrow, when your clinic opens, you will see how the poor of this city come in their thousands to bless your good name.'

Across the road it's shaking of hands, goodbyes, wishes for the morning. People drift off. Elli, still wreathed in flowers is wandering around the tent, picking up a thing here, shifting something there. Her staff take their leave. At last she goes into the clinic and shuts the doors.

Much later, as I'm perched in the frangipani, there comes music drifting across the road, she must be sitting at her piano. In threes her notes sound, like far bells, repeating over and over. Somraj comes out of his house and's stood listening, like a pale statue he's, on his face is an expression even I can't read. Later still, the piano's still playing, almost asleep I'm, when from much closer comes the hum of a sitar. Sounds at first like it's accompanying the piano, but soon the two musics move apart. In the small hours a glow of light moves out onto her roof, she must be sleeping up there. A light breeze stirs the leaves of the frangipani. The light goes out. I imagine Elli, thrilled and terrified by what's ahead, lying awake watching stars slide down the sky.

I wake with head's singing. Still dark it's but can't sleep. I get up, step outside. Outrageous things are going on in my skull. The morning's curled like a leaf, wind tastes like a bee's banana. With merly music springing in my brain, I climb the stones of our tower, sit on the roof slope like a monkey waiting for dawn. One by one stars fade, behind the palm trees and flags of the Siva temple, sky reddens. I call to Jara. Early, early it's, how early I do not know, hardly a soul awake, but I can't wait to be on my way. Call me a cunt if you want, I'm curious.

I see a bird circling above, wonder what it's seeing below. Up high and early, my eye dreams the start of this Khaufpuri day. I see the world and me in it. So high I'm, the earth curves away from me, the upper air's full of brilliance. I see the world spread like a map, roads from all sides coming to the city. Over Khaufpur hangs haze like stale breath round the mouth of a drunk. The tips of the minars of the Taj-ul-masjid are touching the sun, below all's dark, the lanes of Chowk are a nest of snakes.

Bird that I am sees all, white palace of gone rulers on hill, lake looks pale green from up here, eye slides along a road lined with dirty buildings, snarling away in dust and truck smoke, till it reaches a place where the city's turned to jungle, railway tracks come running up and vanish, beyond is terrain harder to interpret, mottling of brown, a pimpliness which on looking closer resolves to the innumerable roofs of the very poor. Smoke is beginning to rise among the huts as inhabitants light fires for tea and whatever meal they can grab before another day of work.

Far below, an animal is moving slowly along a lane. What kind of creature is this, arse canted steeply into the air? dromedary? centaur? Short way behind a smaller, also non-human being strolls, stopping now and again to stretch sleepy jaws. These two pass slowly through the

Nutcracker, past the jungle inside the factory walls, they are heading for a far bazaar where a lane splits in three. The middle way is a stony alley where cows with ribs like harpstrings pick at old paper bags, here's Bhoora Khan curled asleep in his auto-rickshaw, nearby is a building shaded by a mango tree, above its door a sign says CLINIC, an empty tent stands outside, last night's flowers have been thrown into the street, they are lying in a heap, a goat's picking roses off the garlands. On the roof of the building a small figure stands. She looks up, sees the bird circling. Not yet within her view, a boy is coming up the road, followed by a dog.

A little while later, in the alley recline two lolling figures, a boy who goes à quatre pattes, beside him a yellow dog.

Later still. Elli, dressed in shalwar kameez, will be giving her last-minute instructions. Downstairs she will be, fussing over magazines in her reception. 'Waste of money, madam,' the manager Dayanand had advised, 'most people round here can't read.' This is what he told the crowd at Nekchalan's. Elli sent him out anyway to buy magazines in Hindi, Urdu and Inglis, plus crayons and paper for the children.

Almost time. Elli will be going to the doors. Light will come gleaming through cracks in the wood. She'll make a joke of pressing her eye to them. Her manager, compounder and receptionist will join her.

'Madam, it is eight o'clock.'

She'll take a deep breath, throw open her doors.

Elli steps out smiling, the breath for her welcome speech already in her lungs. Man, how slowly that smile fades. Last night, didn't we all hear Zahreel Khan promising crowds? She must have expected to see people filling the street, clapping when the doors opened, but there's no crowd, no queue waiting outside, apart from me and a few onlookers, the lane is empty.

She's puzzled. She's looked up, down, checked her watch, again looked. It is taking a long time to sink in. She calls, Dayanand appears in the door beside her. He's not surprised, just scared, bloody, knew what was going to happen, didn't have the guts to warn her. Ever since the democracy word has been going round the bastis, no one is to knock on that door. That clinic, avoid. Go there you're helping the Kampani. Not everyone agrees with this, plus it's well known that Somraj and his committee think the boycotting is unfair. All over the Claw, Nutcracker and beyond people are muttering we need this clinic, hope Zafar brother knows what he is doing, only out of love for him will we stay away. Dayanand says a thing, I'm not close enough to hear what, but all of a sudden Elli's face seems to fold up, the light and happiness goes out of it.

Now, Eyes, part of me's a nasty fucker. A cruel little thrill went through me as I saw the doors open and knew what was coming, but now I'm looking at the miserable face of this woman I barely know, every bit of that pleasure turns to anger against Zafar and his mad paranoia.

Each morning at eight she appears dressed in shalwar kameez and all, opens her doors, stands staring out at the street in which no one is waiting. Three days go by, not a single person comes to the clinic. Fourth day Elli opens her doors wearing the famous blue legs like she's thought, well, what the fuck difference does it make?

On that day I've dropped by as usual, found some shade under a tree, Jara the dog's watching with me. I'm tired maybe I've closed my eyes, or perhaps I'm studying that morning's history in the dirt, which is a thing I do. From a height of eighteen inches you get to know a place pretty well, every crack in the road, every stone, every dropped, not-picked-up coin.

Blue legs appear. I look up. She says to me, 'Animal, you're here every day. The clinic's open. Do you want to come in?'

I shake my head. Angry I'm with Zafar, I like Elli doctress, but I guess as things are I should not be seen talking to her.

'You know, I want to take a good look at your back,' she says. 'I'd like to give you an examination, do some tests.'

'Please Elli doctress, leave me alone.'

She turns and walks away.

Taste of own medicine. Oh well, that's that, I'm just thinking it's time I got off to my errands when the blue legs reappear, marching towards me. She's got this doctor thing round her neck, couple of tubes with a metal disc on the end, can't recall the name. Legs stop right in front, She squats down, applies the disc to my back.

'Okay, you're my first patient.'

'Not here, god's sake.'

'Why not?' She presses the disc to my ribs. It feels cold.

'People will see.'

She fucking laughs.

'What's funny?'

'You,' she says. 'Scared of people. Deep breath take, hold.'

'I am not scared of anything.'

'Yeah, sure.' She stands, turns and heads back across the road. One moment I'm watching her walk away, then without really knowing why, I'm on my feet following her, Jara's following me. Nobody owns me, I'm no one's servant. Such thoughts pass through my head as I follow the swaying blue moons of madam Elli's backside. Fuck you, Zafar, I'll go my own way. This is how guilt infects, if you're afraid that someone will be angry with you, you immediately start feeling angry with them.

Not half the road have I crossed and I'm snarling at Zafar, ohé Zafar brother, with all your doing good plus doing without, you're a hero in these bidonvilles, no hero are you to me. You who are so fucking noble, so modest, above all, so powerful, at your one word the people of the Apokalis put aside their suffering. You say, do not go to this clinic and even though these people are full of pain, can't breathe, are burning with fevers, even though the flesh is melting from their bones in flakes of fire, still they do not go. You say to them, without any proof, this clinic is owned by the Kampani, so they spit on its shadow, curse its name. Zafar brother, you're a fool. You're making the people suffer for nothing. The Kampani is stronger and cleverer than you. Go ahead, block the clinic, march, stop the traffic, shout all the slogans you like. Nothing changes.

The people go on suffering, the Kampani does what it wants and no one can say anything to it. It's the fucking Kampani I admire.

Manager Dayanand appears in the door where Elli's blue legs and bum have vanished. 'Animals not allowed. Leave your dog, he'll be fine out here.'

'This dog is not a he but a she and unless you have forgotten I too am an animal.'

'Nevertheless.'

I whistle to Jara. 'Come, we're off.'

Elli reappears, asks what's going on.

'Madam, the dog.' It's Dayanand.

'It's okay, no problem, we're on our way.' This is me.

'Don't be silly,' says Elli, whether to me or Dayanand I am not sure. Those moments are unclear in my memory because so shocking and unexpected is what follows that even now the thought of it leaves me shaking.

Elli doctress leads me through her waiting room where are the chairs, newspapers and etcetera into an office. 'Wait here, I'll just be a moment.'

Now I'm looking round this room, at the books in shelves on the wall. On the back of one I can make out the letters KHAUFPUR, on another's written LUNG PATHOLOGY, a third says VETERANS AND AGENT ORANGE.

'Oi, Animal!'

Jara is sitting on the floor with a hind leg in the air, head's tucked into her crotch, Elli's still elsewhere.

'Over here,' says the voice.

On a table nearby is a kind of dome draped with a dark cloth. I give it a twitch, Jara's stopped licking herself and is staring at me. Bordel de merde! It's my little two-headed friend. Now, Eyes, since I first met the Khã-in-the-Jar I had seen him a few times in dreams, but this is no dream, his jar, which was in that big doctor's office, is now here in Elli's. It's the first time since that day I've seen him in the flesh, he looks the worse for wear, body seems furry, like he's starting to fall apart, but he still has that shit-eating grin.

'Kyon Khā?' he says. 'How's life treating you?'

'Okay Khā.' Far from fucking true is this, it's just what you say. 'How's it treating you?'

'Call this life?' says he with steep bitterness. 'This world for me is all angles and shadows and swimmery shapes. Of news I hear none, when I want to discuss, I must talk to myself. Anyway, good you're here, I've been waiting for you to come.'

Eyes, I don't know why, but this doesn't surprise me.

'Hospital decided to chuck us out. After twenty fucking years nothing did they learn from us except that when you poison people bad things happen. No longer wanted we're, to the incinerator we'd have gone, except your doctress heard about it, asked if she could bring us here.'

'Elli saved you?'

'Saved? You cretin, if she'd kept out of it by now we'd be free.' His two heads glug at each other, then he's back to me. 'It's up to you now, Khā. You're our only hope. Get us out of here. Break the jar, with fire destroy us.'

These are the same words he speaks to me in dreams. Now I'm confused. This little bugger is real, I can tap his glass jar and he'll curse me, but is he also real in my dreams? If so what are we to make of this world that seems so solid? Is it too nil but lights and dancing shadows?

'Who are you,' I ask, 'to order me about?'

There's gurgling in the jar, the sound of mirth bubbling through poison. 'Who am I? So tragic you have to ask. Don't you know?

> *chairman of the board I'm*
> *a rusty sword I'm*
> *by the world ignored I'm*
> *the dragon's hoard I'm*

I am the egg of nature, which ignorant and arrogant men have spoiled. I can be a friend to humans, especially the poor, for money doesn't interest me. Your Khaufpuri politician who recently celebrated his birthday with camels and elephants and dancing horses and a cake of fifty-three kilos, he does not know his gold jewellery is worthless, people like him should fear me, I'm a fire that will burn up his five senses. As for you, poor fuckwit, you think you're an animal, I am your mother and father, I was you in your childhood, I'll be you when you're old. Dead am I who never lived, wasn't buried, waits to burn. Tough I'm and tender, now you see me now you don't, I go down into the earth and leap up to the sky, I am full of the natural light, yet those who meet me think I'm worthless, nothing, less than fuck all.'

'You're an unusual fellow,' says I. 'Never before have I met a one like you.'

At this the contents of his jar churn, little gunky bits that must have come off the Khã are swept by currents of laughter into mazy dances.

'Brother Animal,' says he, 'you and I are not so different. Doublers both, we're. Two of me there's, two also of you.'

'What do you mean?' I ask, not best pleased by this comparison.

'My two heads rise from one neck. From your hips, at the point where your back bends, rises a second you who's straight, stands upright and tall. This second you's there all the time, has been there all along, thinks, speaks and acts, but it's invisible—'

Before he can finish, Elli doctress has whirled back into the room and started doing stuff with that cold metal cup. 'Nothing wrong with your heart.'

'Four parts of me are strong, head, arms, chest . . .'

'Shut,' says she, 'I know you love to yap, but the time's not now.' Her Hindi is really excellent. Way she talks, you can tell she's not from here, but her accent is better than for example a Bombaywallah's, which is said to cause pus in the ears. She's so near I can smell her scent, while she's touching me, I can't help it, bad thoughts start up again. I've seen you

139

naked, I've seen you washing your breasts, I've seen your cunt. This is shameful, for she's a good person plus I've strong reason to fear such thoughts, which are stretching my kakadus.

'Take off your pants.'

'No please.'

'Don't be shy, I've seen it all before.'

'I think not.'

'If it makes you more comfortable, Dayanand can step in.'

'No!'

'Great shorts,' she says as they come off, proceeds to examine my back, the place where the spine is welded to my hips. She's probing with her fingertips.

'What do you feel? Tell me as I press.'

'Fingers.'

'Here?'

'Fingers.'

She's at the exact place where my back twists forward, where my invisible other self is supposed to be. That one's nowhere standing tall but the same can't be said for the thing below, it has become huge and hard, reared up it's, feels like a log, with each beat of the heart it's battering my belly. If Elli's seen this lund of mine, she gives no sign, but's started questioning me about what other doctors have said, so I tell her about the great expert in the hospital, etcetera and etcetera, it's a complete waste of time, there's nothing to be done.

'Doctors aren't always right. That's why we ask a second opinion.'

'My case you need a seventh opinion.'

'Then we get it,' says she, putting away the dangly disc.

'The seventh opinion, what if it's the same as the first?'

'Well, it might be,' she says, prodding my shoulders. 'Or it might not. There's also such a thing as a ninth opinion. I can assure you that if you had been born in Amrika, you would not be running around on all fours.'

She grasps my chin and says, 'You have to trust me.'

140

It's now that the unbelievable and amazing thing happens.

I'm growling, grabbing at the dog. Elli doctress is startled. 'What are you feeling? Are you in pain?'

No reply there's except this pretend grappling with the dog, rrrrrr'ing and baring of teeth, until Jara herself gets fed up. She stands up, gives me a look as if to say, 'What the fuck are you doing?' then stalks off out of my reach, lies down again with her tongue lolling. Fuck all to do now, except go fully crazy, so I've rolled on the ground, scratched myself, screeched, grabbed stuff. Elli's run for help, I've quickly re-worn my Kakadus.

On the way out, Dayanand stops me. 'What's your game?'

'What's it look like?' I am still trembling.

He's holding a mop, for a moment I think he'll hit me, but he says, 'Take your dog outside now.'

Then he adds, casual as you like, 'I know who's stopping people coming here, you should tell Somraj pandit and all his lot that Elli madam hates that Kampani worse than they do. I have heard her say so.'

Nice try, Dayanand, but I am not going to give anything away. 'No idea what you're talking about.'

'Then why are you shaking?'

Why? Because of the unbelievable thing that has just happened, which I cannot speak about, hardly dare admit to myself. When Elli spoke of a ninth opinion, missing out the eighth, when she said I must trust her, this terrifying thought struck like a hurricane, surged up my spine like electricity, changed everything, the wild, stupid, unforgivable hope that she might cure me.

A boy's come racing on a bike, too small's he to use the seat, he rides one leg through the frame standing on the pedals, this is the way it's done.

'Animal! Animal, he's here!' This kid, he's one of those who keep their ears and eyes open for me, something useful flies in, they earn a rupee. 'Animal, the foreign priest has come!'

What? How? When?

'He arrived last night, I heard the nuns talking, this morning itself he's coming here for Ma Franci.'

When she's heard the news, Ma beckons me close, ruffles my hair, which is as usual tangled. 'Chheee, as much dust here as a donkey.'

Few people in the world I love, this old lady is one of them. Thinking of when she's gone, what a wound it will leave in my life, sky rent apart, light falling so bright you can hardly look, great sheet of light lying on an ocean. What's this got to do with Ma leaving I don't know, never have I seen the sea, it's what comes to me. Ma kisses my head, then presses her lips to my ear and whispers three things.

'Don't be rude to the padré.'

'I'm worried about Aliya's cough.'

'We'll meet in Paradise.'

When the padré shows up, wearing a long black robe, turns out he's not a français he's espagnol but he speaks la langue humaine.

'Bonjour Mère Ambrosine,' says he in that tongue, 'It is a privilege to meet you at last.'

There's respect in his face and voice, when I look inside his head at his thoughts, they are mostly made of amazement. This old lady, more lines has her face than our lord's fishing net, her whole life she has given to the poor of this city. With what tenderness he delivers greetings from the head of her order and all the sisters in France, tells her how much they are looking forward to having her back with them.

'Don't see why they want me,' says Ma. 'I'm all right here, I have my son Animal to look after me.'

So Père Bernard, that's his name, says, 'Mother Ambrosine, it's all decided. The superior wants you to go to our house near Toulouse, it's nice and warm there.' He explains that an old house it's, with a garden that touches the bank of a river. She will find it pleasant to chat with other old nuns like herself, who have spent their lives in parts of the world such as Congo, Vietnam, Brazil, plus Tuamotu which, says Père Bernard, is an island in the Pacific where the order has a leper colony.

'These Tuamotu nuns, do they have leprosy?' I ask, afraid for Ma. It starts with dry skin, before you know it you're ripping off fingers like Chunaram, although only he has the genius to do it for money.

'I don't want to leave,' says mulish Ma.

'Truly I'm sorry,' says Père Bernard, 'I know how unsettling this must be. Animal, would you like to visit Mother Ambrosine in France one day?'

'Best be soon,' retorts Ma, 'I shan't be around much longer. Who's going to look after my people? Don't you know that the Apokalis has begun? It started here and it's coming back again.'

I've tried to explain to Père Bernard that far's Ma's concerned she has to be in Khaufpur for the big event, otherwise it's fillum khatam, end of movie.

Says he, looking puzzled, 'I am sure the Apokalis will also reach Toulouse. That's near your family home, isn't it, Mother Ambrosine?'

'My home is right here,' says Ma. 'My only family is this boy. But since you won't change your mind so there's no more to say, I'll start packing.'

She opens a cloth bag. All she owns after fifty five years in Khaufpur is two sets of old clothing, one she wears while the other's washed, plus her specs, plus book of Sanjo, also a small Isa nailed on a cross. Ma hands it to me and says, 'For you my dear son. Excuse me, father, I would like a little time to pray. Animal, take father to the parlour, entertain him nicely. Make him some tea.'

So I've lit the fire, put on a pan to boil, and led Père Bernard outside to sit on the log under the tamarind tree, for so fine-leaved a tree it gives a cool shade. Ma calls it our parlour. Here I sat with the jarnalis français who taught me to swear, later also with the Kakadu jarnalis. Eyes, if you ever come to Khaufpur it's where I'll sit with you.

I think Père Bernard finds it hard to talk to me, I've asked him what sort of movies they have in France, he says he does not see many movies. Next I ask whether Ma will be able to get her favourite baingan bharta, but he does not know what this may be. I'm just explaining about bedding the aubergine into hot ashes, etcetera, when little Aliya arrives with her granny Huriya and other old women from the basti. Ma's cronies, they have come with garlands and sweets to say goodbye.

'She's inside,' I tell them. 'Please go in.'

Père Bernard is charmed that these old ladies, among whom are Muslim women in burqas plus Hindu women in saris, are so fond of the old nun. Says he, 'Such friendships are the fruit of a lifetime's work. All in France will be moved to know how much Mother Ambrosine was loved.'

After maybe ten minutes, the guests emerge and stand in the door crying, waving to Ma within. Sorrowfully, they go away. Watching the slowly retreating figures of those old hunched women, I feel desolate because in the end we are condemned to lose everyone we love.

'Well, I think she must be ready,' says Père Bernard, consulting a shiny wrist watch. Seems they are booked on the one-thirty flight to Delhi, whence another aeroplane leaves for France at six.

When after twenty minutes she has not emerged, Père Bernard goes to the hole in the wall and twitches the plastic sheet that's our door. 'Mother? Mother Ambrosine?' Receiving no reply, he bends and pokes in his head. 'Tiens! There is no one here! Where has she gone? How could she vanish like that?'

'Father,' says I, fully sobbing, 'did you hear a trumpet? Ma says when the Apokalis starts, an angel will blow a trumpet, all who love Isa miyañ will be snatched up to heaven right then and there.'

144

'Nonsense,' says he. 'Utter nonsense.'

At this very instant a train rumbling through the Nutcracker gives a loud hoot and he jumps. Eyes, that kind of joy is almost enough to make a person believe in god.

'Father, you must give me your watch.'

'What for?'

'So that if Ma Franci comes back, I can tell her what the time is. After all she has a plane to catch.'

He looks a bit surprised at this, but let's face it, his head is already well fucked. The watch I've cached in the wall. It must stay hidden for I can guess what will happen next. Sure enough, within an hour approaches a cloud of dust which contains two pandus in a jeep.

'Okay, where is she?'

'How should I know? I was here with that foreign father, when we looked inside, she had disappeared.'

'People don't disappear,' says the senior pandu. Fatlu-in-training is he, all belt and belly, standing there like a fucking Sadda miyañ ki tond.

'You're welcome to look for yourself, watch out for scorpions, don't forget to go up the ladder . . . if it will bear your weight.'

'I'll have less of your lip,' he says, giving me a filthy look, 'don't think we don't know about you, filthy little chaar sau bees.'

Now, Eyes, around us by is a crowd from the Nutcracker, among it are a few young men, none too happy to see the police. Their presence gives me courage. 'Hey fatso, threaten innocent folk round here, such a slippering you'll get, instead of chaar sau bees you'll be saying baar sau chees.'

He starts for me, of course, a couple of guys step forward, so he stops.

'We'll meet in Paradise,' Ma said. When the police have gone I have a good look to check the coast's clear, then I've hopped it to Paradise Alley and soon reached Aliya's place. Well before entering I hear laughter, a familiar voice says, 'Tout que je me souviens de mon enfance d'autrefois,

145

c'est un ciel poudré de bleu, la poussière sèche, des olives et des myrtes.'

It's Ma. She's saying that all she remembers of her long ago childhood is a sky of chalky blue, dust, plus olives and myrtes, whatever they may be.

'For those birds,' says Huriya, 'he'll go to any trouble, really he would. If he could see, be polishing the bars of that cage he'd.'

I've peered inside. There they are, two old ladies, squatting by the hearth, Ma's still got on the black burqa she escaped in. There too is heaven's kettle, a curl of steam from its spout tells me that chai has been accomplished.

'J'ai lui dit, mon travail, c'est ici, dans le royaume des pauvres de bon dieu.' I said to him, my work is here in the kingdom of god's poor. 'Besides, I don't want to leave my friends, how many years have we known each other, Huriya? Goodness, it must be fifty.'

'I tell him, husband, stop fussing over those birds, what's to become of your granddaughter when we are gone?'

'Plus he wanted me to go on an aeroplane.'

'The child's at school most days,' says her friend. 'I told her, I said, "Aliya, go to school as often as you can, learn what you can. Education is precious. Without it you're like Hanif and me, you're done for."'

'Why should I return?' demands Ma. 'When I joined the convent as a girl, they called me a bumpkin because I'd grown up on a farm. You see we had a country way of talking. Viech d'ase, we'd say which was rude, ho barro lo porta! Bits and pieces come back to me, like Jacotin's nose.'

'Have some more chai,' says Huriya and pours.

'Thank you,' says Ma, who knows 'chai'. 'Animal should be here soon, I told him where to find me.'

'Aliya's so fond of Animal,' says her granny, who has in turn caught the mention of my name. 'He's sweet to her, I was hoping he'd take her to that new clinic that's opened in the Claw, but we are not supposed to go there, I don't know why.'

Old Huriya is not the only one puzzled by the boycott of Elli's clinic. Around that time, I had to visit an old boy called Shambhu. He was a twice-victim of the Kampani. He had breathed the poisons of that night, plus the wells in his neighbourhood were full of poisons leaked from the factory.

Shambhu's body was a sack of pain, his breathing was difficult. 'Oh my life,' he told his wife, 'if I can't get a breath I'm going to die.'

'Get him oxygen,' the neighbours said.

'I don't know what is oxygen,' his wife the old woman wailed, the tears of her face making pocks in the dust,

'It is a gas, but a good gas,' they said. 'It comes in metal bottles. If you give it to him he will be able to breathe easier.'

'But from where can I get oxygen? No money for food there's, where will I find money for this?'

'Take him to the government hospital,' one said.

'Sister, what welcome do we people get at the government hospital? They won't give him this good gas, they'll send him off with a chit for aspirin. Zafar bhai and Somraj, all those big people, will they give money to buy it?'

'Let me die, wife,' said Shambhu. 'It must be god's will.'

She began caterwauling afresh. Someone said, 'What about that clinic in the Chicken Claw, the one nobody is going to? Every day you see the doctor standing outside, looking for people to come. Let Shambhu go there.'

'It is a Kampani clinic,' another person said. 'That's why people won't go there, even though it's free.'

'That Kampani is the very devil. They made it free deliberately because they knew that the poor have no money for the other hospitals.'

'If it's there why shouldn't we use it?' demanded Shambhu's wife. 'Why should he not go there?'

'It's the Kampani clinic. That doctress, the American woman, she's paid by the Kampani. This is what I've heard.'

'He is going to die, what difference does it make?' Shambhu's wife cried. 'I don't care where it gets the money from, so long as it cures him.

A cow can eat many different things, grass, leaves, but the milk she gives is always the same. It's milk. This doctress is not charging. Says all are welcome. If god has sent such a person to us, who are we to refuse?'

'Sister, we all agree, but Zafar bhai says we must not go.'

'If my Shambhu dies,' she said, 'his death will be on Zafar bhai.'

The people of the Apokalis ground their teeth against suffering and stayed away from Elli doctress's clinic. Alone among the Khaufpuris I would visit her. Zafar encouraged me. He thought I was spying on her, it's what he told people who complained, 'How come Animal's allowed to break the boycott while we all are denied free treatment?' I felt bad about this, not because of Zafar, but because by deceiving him I was also deceiving the rest.

I was there when an old man came and told Zafar, 'An ulcer weeps, it makes the skin all around putrid and this goes on day and night the pain it's unceasing, with such pain you can't think, you cannot read your prayers or work or sleep, nothing can you do but just endure it, at the end of each day you can say nothing except I've survived, and after many days and nights blur into a dream, you say, well I am still here, but so is the pain, in truth it makes you mad.'

To this Zafar replied, 'Bear it a little more, for all our sakes.'

Later, he told Nisha that he felt full of sadness for the suffering of the people, since he too was learning what pain was, just lately his stomach had been in continuous agonising cramps.

'Elli, what will you do if people don't come?' This question's pressing like a stone on my brain. It's after my second examination, she's taken blood and piss, talking we're on her roof's like a scented jungle, in big oil tins she has planted jasmine creepers, roses etcetera, scarcely three months has she been here, already they're swarming up into the mango tree, same one I climbed, it grows right by her building and hangs its branches over the roof.

148

'What can I do? Guess I'll have to pack up and go home.'

'Home to Amrika?'

'Nowhere else to go.'

'What about me?'

'My number one patient.' We are sitting on a mat spread on the ground in the shade of the mango. I'm backed to the parapet wall, legs to one side, she is cross legged in front of me, I'm having a hard time keeping my eyes off the part where the blue cloth's stretched tight.

'Don't worry,' says Elli, she smiles and reaches over to touch my shoulder. 'I don't plan to leave here without accomplishing at least one good thing.' Needs a few more tests, she says, plus x-rays, when she has enough info she'll send it to a specialist in this big hospital in Amrika.

'I don't know what he'll say. Maybe like you've been told, nothing can be done. But let's hope things work out, we may be able to get you over there for an operation. I won't make any promises save this one, that whatever happens, even if I go back to Amrika, I will do my best for you.'

I dare not think of her leaving. 'People really want to come to your clinic. They're just confused.'

They're confused?! What about me?'

'See Elli, here's the problem.' Surely she must by now know the reason for the boycott, but in case she doesn't I've tried best as I can to explain.

'Collecting data to help the Kampani? What idiot thinks this?'

'Many idiots.' Careful I'm not to mention names, but she's guessed I must mean them across the road for she says, 'Tell your friends, anyone who thinks a health study worth a damn can be done by one doctor in three months needs their head checked. It's just not possible.'

My fear of her leaving is being disturbed by risky thoughts. When you are trying very hard not to look at something, the eye keeps creeping to it, then skipping off. Quite uncomfortable I'm feeling, how can she not notice?

'The idea that I've come in response to a court decision, it's just ludicrous, I've been struggling at least eighteen months to set up this clinic, and as for conspiring with politicians I wish they knew the problems I've had. Guess how many letters I wrote to people here in Khaufpur? To Zahreel Khan? To the health ministry in Delhi? How many replies did I get? Go ahead, guess!'

'One?'

'None. Explain that! I wrote to the Chief Minister. I said, I'm baffled, so many sick needing help, in comes a genuine offer and you ignore it!'

'What did he reply?'

'He ignored it.'

'But you're here,' I point out. 'So someone must have listened.'

'Weirder still,' says she. 'One day, after months of zilch, a letter came. It said, permission is granted. Just like that. It said I should come to Khaufpur as soon as possible to . . . it had some quaint way of putting it . . . resolve all needful modalities. And this was from your Mr Zahreel Khan.'

'He is not my mister, how much investment did you make to him? . . . Investment fee,' I've explained, seeing she looks blank.

'There wasn't a fee.'

'Then there's your answer. Pays to invest.'

'God.' Elli closes her eyes, sighs. 'Why did I ever come here? I should have known right off it wasn't going to work. First the politicians, now this boycott. People in Khaufpur don't want help. I should have stayed home and raised chickens.'

'They do want help, I swear it.' I've told her about Hanif, blinded and coughing, about Aliya whose lungs are inflamed, Shambhu who hardly can breathe, the ulcer of Yusuf Omar, about I'm Alive and his dead neighbours.

'So to help these folk, who do I have to bribe?'

'Bribes are for politicians, police etcetera. This is a question of trust. Why haven't you told people of the difficulties you faced?'

'One, badmouthing politicians who could close me down, not a good idea. Two, who'd believe? Three, no one's asked.'

Elli's story just deepens the mystery of why she wanted to come here. She's saying she has nothing to hide. I'm fishing in the gaps between her words, but all I catch is darkness and unease.

'I swear I don't understand Khaufpur,' says Elli. 'At first I thought it was just the strangest place I'd ever been. Never before have I lived in a town where milk's sold by the spoonful. Where people buy cigarettes one at a time and ride three to a bicycle.'

'What three? Four, peacefully.' If we're to boast of Khaufpuri achievements then let's get it right. 'One's arsed to handlebars, two's on the crossbar, three's pedalling, four's behind on the carrier.'

'Plus bhutt-bhutt-pigs going by with ten hanging off the back . . . But you know what's the oddest thing of all? When the sun sets the city vanishes.'

'Sorry, don't understand.' Bhutt-bhutt-pig, it's a big three-wheeler, carries twenty people, front's snarled like a pig's snout, name's from the motor's going bhutt-bhutt-bhutt. But a vanishing city?

'When the sun sets the streets are gone, they're like unlit canyons with crowds moving through in darkness, at least half the traffic runs without lights, there are dozens of accidents.'

'Yes, but what's so odd?'

'That people tolerate it. This is the strangest thing of all about Khaufpur, that people put up with so much. Take a look. It's not just blacked out streets and killer traffic, people in this city tolerate open sewers, garbage everywhere, poisoned wells, poisoned babies, doctors who don't do their jobs, corrupt politicians, thousands of sick that no one seems to care about. But wait, let someone come along with an open hearted offer of help, these same citizens can't tolerate it, in fact find it so intolerable they must mount a boycott. People in this city must be either blind or mad. I don't get the way Khaufpuris think.'

'Don't be angry with the poor,' says I. 'Since when did they have power to change anything?' I am experiencing again those feelings of upheaval I'd had when she said the Nutcracker was erected by an earthquake.

She will change your life, says the voice inside. *See her bed here on the roof, draped in mosquito netting, that's where you and she will* – Shut up, shut up, shut up. I know now how she will change my life and it is not that way. Yet, as well as the tight jeans, Elli doctress is wearing a thin shirt. Being able to catch other people's thoughts it amazes me that she can't see mine, which are so blatant. However I try to conceal it I'm as bad a blo-blo c'est à dire lolo ogler as Zahreel Khan.

'Not the poor,' says innocent-of-all Elli. 'Those who should know better.' She starts telling me about this friend, a doctor who lives in a house up by the lake, must be the one Dayanand spoke of. His neighbours are a poor family who've attached to his wall a plastic sheet weighed by stones to make a kind of tent. In this they sleep, cook, do needlework, outside it they wash their pots, their naked kids play in the dirt. 'I felt worried about them, so I mentioned it to him. Can you guess what he said?'

She pauses, gives me a this-you-won't-believe look. 'He said, "Please don't concern yourself, the police will soon move them on."'

Well this in no way surprises me, but I've shaped various grimaces which satisfy her. So then she starts on about other things this friend's told her such as how Khaufpur once had a high cultural life, and a remark-able history, famous it was for poets, politically progressive, a haven for refugees including a large community of Afghans. I think her friend must have meant Farouq's lot, the Yar-yilaqis, who are really Uzbegs. He com-plained how all these things are forgotten because nowadays when the world hears the name of Khaufpur it thinks only of poison. 'I curse the day the Kampani came here because its disaster erased our past.'

'Also erased thousands of people,' said Elli.

'Forget about the disaster,' her friend said. 'Let it go! Let's talk of any-thing but that painful night. Let go, I say, it's been nearly twenty years. Let it rest. Maybe there are some people in the slums who want to keep the agitation going. Every year they burn effigies of the Kampani bosses, they daub slogans and chant. What does this achieve? Nothing. Meanwhile the rest of us, citizens, city council, chamber of commerce, everyone, we all want to move on.'

'But what about those people? The ones still waiting for justice? The ones who are suffering without help? Do you move on and leave them behind?'

'Please don't think worse of me if I tell you the truth. Those poor people never had a chance. If it had not been the factory it would have been cholera, TB, exhaustion, hunger. They would have died anyway.'

'That's such a harsh way to think.'

'I prefer to call it facing facts,' he said. 'Elli, you will eat your heart out for them, but you'll get no thanks for it.'

He's rung a bell for his servant to bring more whisky, ice etcetera. Eyes, I should say it was night, they were sitting on his terrace, which looks out over the lake. The water was black, high above all was a cold white moon. The old doctor touched Elli's shoulder and pointed. "Here's something the books don't tell you. On that night the moon was two-thirds full. It was shaped like a tear and as it appeared through the clouds of gas, it was the colour of blood."'

'You know what I should have said, Animal? I should have said, "I am a doctor, I know about blood." Instead I sat there drinking his whisky listening to him reduce the terror of dying people to a moon in a second rate poem.'

So bitterly does Elli tell her story about the old doctor, I'm scared she has come to hate Khaufpur and will surely go back to Amrika.

'Elli, there are many good people in Khaufpur.'

'Oh yes? Like who? The authorities who don't care? The rich who want to move on? The poor who kick you in the teeth when you try to help?'

'I could take you to meet them. Good people. Poor people, the ones who are sick. Like me. We people need you, please don't give up.'

'Ah, like you Animal,' she says, now softer's her voice. 'Well, I am glad I met you. Yes, you are a good person.'

Putain con! Just shows how wrong an educated person can be, but I am

153

not going to contradict her, nor tell what memories were just now in my head of her naked, bending for soap. 'Elli, everything will be okay, just you must convince people you have not come from the Kampani.'

'And how do I do that?'

'Tell them why you wanted so much to come here.'

'What? Like I heard about what's happening in Khaufpur and thought it was shocking, I hate injustice, I felt moved, I had the skills, nothing better to do with my life, plus I was stupid enough to think I'd be welcome. Which of these reasons do you think they'll believe?'

Full of sincere anger is this speech of Elli doctress, but again I'm getting that uneasy feeling, of something being held down beneath the surface.

'You need something they can check.' I'm thinking of Zafar.

'Or someone who'll believe me?'

It's now I have my brilliant idea. It can solve everything, why didn't I think of it before? 'Elli, the trouble you had making your clinic, plus these other things, there's a very decent person you could speak to, it's Somraj pandit.'

I don't know what response I'm expecting, Elli just looks surprised. 'The music teacher? I hardly think so. Dayanand says it's him and his friends behind this boycott.'

'Dayanand's a sack of pus. Somraj pandit has nothing to do with it, I swear on my life.'

'Truly? Is that so? Interesting you mention him. Such a serious man. I see him in his garden, we exchange hellos, that's it. I get the feeling he'd rather not speak to me, he avoids my eye, not once has he ever smiled.'

'He never smiles at anyone.'

'Well, I guess it's more like he's shy, sort of clenched.'

'Shy around ladies,' says I. 'Because of what happened to him. His wife.'

'I hoped it was some kind of misunderstanding,' says Elli.

I'm wondering should I tell her that Somraj spoke against the boycott of her clinic, but it would mean fingering Zafar and already there's been betrayal enough. Instead I've started on how Somraj used to be a singer but his lungs were fucked by the gases on that night. Being a doctor she's interested in this. 'Maybe if I offered to help? Could nothing be done for him?'

'You're right, nothing. Nisha, she's his daughter, says he won't even listen to his old records.'

'He must have been good, to make records.'

'The best. Somraj pandit was famous. They used to call him the Voice of Khaufpur. The internest tells how he would sing cranes and water-spouts.'

'Not sure I follow you,' she says.

'Well . . .'

Alas, what kind of integrity have I, who'd promised pandit Somraj not to repeat the things he confided to me and here's babbling to a foreign doctress? Eyes, just now I mentioned betrayal, that's what this is, but it's happened, as these things do, without planning. You go with the heart, where it leads, but the heart is blind. I've jawed on for at least an hour. Elli's full of questions about pandit Somraj, about his wife, his fame as a singer. Some things I should not have told her.

'Frogs?' she says, 'did you really say frogs?'

'Yes.'

'Bizarre. Was he joking?'

'Not he. Since the Kampani's poisons tore his lungs, and took his wife and son, Somraj pandit rarely laughs. Nor will he sing aloud. Out of his suffering he makes songs that he alone can hear.'

'That is so sad,' she says. 'I shouldn't laugh at the frogs.'

'Only one joke has pandit Somraj. *Sa, Re, Ga, Ma, Pa, Dha, Ni, Sa*, these are the notes which all recognise. Somraj says that for him the octave now runs *Sa, Re, Ga, Ma, Khā, Si, Khā, Si.*'

Eyes, this is the pandit's joke, he tells it against himself. It's not meant to be funny, it's a way of spitting in the eye of fate, of saying fuck you to the world which so carelessly mangled his life. Of course this joke is wasted on you, dear Eyes, first because no one has ever mangled you, but chiefly because you don't speak our language. *Khā* and *Si* are not really notes in the scale, if you join them they make *khaañsi*, which means 'cough'. What Somraj is saying is, every time I start to sing I begin coughing and can't stop.

No need to explain this to Elli, so good's her Hindi. 'That poor guy,' she says. 'How bitter he must be. Maybe I should go across there and take a look at that cough.'

Next day near lunchtime Nisha and I are in the kitchen, preparing food. Her dad is giving the lizard a singing lesson. We can hear him trying a phrase *sochha samajha mana meetha piyaravaa* over and over again. Comes a knock on the door. Nisha's hands are floury, so I've gone.

Outside is Elli with a serious look on her face. No greeting for me even. 'Is Pandit Somraj in?'

'Elli doctress, he's teaching.'

Says she, 'It's important.' Only then does she give a small smile and ask, 'Animal, please fetch him here.' So I've knocked on the music room door to deliver the message, in a little while pandit Somraj arrives.

'Good morning, pandit Somraj, I need to talk to you.'

'Doctor Barber, good afternoon.' Doesn't look like he wants to let her in.

'Animal tells me you're a decent person to whom I can speak openly. As you know I've opened the clinic across the road. People are staying away. Can you throw any light on this?'

My god, how devious is Elli. No wonder she showed such an interest in Somraj. Conned me, she's. Does believe he's the villain of this affair.

Somraj pandit looks taken aback. Such a brash approach to discussion, it's not the Khaufpuri way. Says he, 'I'm sorry, I know nothing of your clinic. Was there anything else? I have a student here, we are in the middle of a lesson.'

'Why are people being told not to come? Whoever's done this, they've done a bad thing.'

'I'm sorry, I can't help you,' he says, and starts to close the door.

'You must.' Elli's sounding kind of desperate. 'You must, please. At least tell me why it's happening. Why do you believe I am connected with that Kampani? I detest it as much as you do.'

'If people are not coming, that is their affair. It is not for me to tell others what to do.' He turns. The lizard Shastri's in the hall behind, staring. Somraj gives him a nod, I guess he thinks this is the end of the conversation.

'Wait,' says Elli. 'I'm sorry too, but that's not good enough. I think you know why people are staying away. I think you know exactly why. And you've misjudged me. You have treated me most unfairly. I have given up everything to come here and do this work.'

Somraj's turned back again. The look in his eyes, it seems almost like pain, but could be contempt or pity or any number of shades of annoyance. At last he sighs. 'You had better come inside.'

He leads her into the music room, where he was giving Shastri his lesson. There's a harmonium on the carpet. 'Please,' says Somraj. 'Sit. Will you have something? Tea? A glass of squash?'

'Look,' says she, 'this isn't a social call. I haven't come to pass the time of day, or ask after your health, although I have to say you don't look at all well. In fact if you have any sense you'll let me find out what's wrong with you, and you'll . . . you'll stop stopping other people . . .'

'Stop stopping?'

'You know exactly what I mean,' snaps Elli in Inglis.

All this time Shastri and I are peering in through the door. Nisha's there too by now, shooting hostile glances at Elli from her big brown eyes. 'Dad, is everything all right?'

Says Somraj to Elli. 'If you've a problem let us discuss it sensibly. Not shouting. All right, I'll be frank with you. When we heard there was a clinic to be opened by an Amrikan, an Amrikan person about whom nothing was known, people here became fearful.'

'Go ahead,' she says, 'I'm listening.'

157

'Leave us please,' says Somraj to the three of us in the doorway. Two obey, the third, whose head lower to the floor's not so easy to spot, remains.

'Is it difficult for you to understand?' asks Somraj. 'Amrikans don't have a good reputation in this town.'

'Wait one moment,' says Elli, holding up a hand. 'Whatever you're about to say, I won't have that dumped on me. I'm not ashamed to be Amrikan, there's plenty to be proud of in Amrika, there's good and bad, like everywhere else. In this world there are two kinds of people, those who help others, and those who don't. Me, I'm the first kind, I can say this because I'm here to help. Yet you, or someone you know, has told people to stay away from my clinic, and that's a wicked thing to have done. So before you start on about me being Amrikan, you better decide, which kind of person are you?'

'Mrs Barber . . .'

'Mrs nothing,' she interrupts. 'It's Doctor Barber if you must, but since we're neighbours I'd prefer it if you called me Elli.'

'Doctor Barber, the fact is people here know nothing about you, where you came from, who is funding you, whether you are working for someone. If you understood this place better, you would know why such questions matter.'

'That's the second time you've mentioned understanding, pandit Somraj. Understanding is a two-way thing. Usually it's the result of something called conversation, which takes two. If you wanted to know about me, you could have come and asked. But you did not. And as for justice, you put me on trial without informing me you were doing so, trumped up stories and played on people's fears without knowing anything at all about me, you found me guilty of what I do not know, and you passed your sentence. I have put my whole heart and everything I own into that clinic, and I'm not going to let you or any other prejudiced bastard fuck it up.'

'Now please calm down,' he says. As for me, how I am wishing that Elli was saying these things to he who deserved to hear them, not the poor pandit, who although she doesn't know it is on her side.

'No I will not fucking calm down. It's about time you heard a thing or two. I know all about your committee. What you might not know is that many of those people, the same people you claim to represent, really want to come to my clinic. Some of them as you well know, are very ill. I tell you, if there is a single death in this neighbourhood that I could have prevented, it will be on your head and your conscience.'

Why won't he tell her he opposed the boycott? But now there's an even grimmer expression on the face of that grim man. 'Since you are being blunt I will also be blunt. I will not swear at you, as you have at me, but let me tell you that if you collected every swear word in every language, every filthy term of abuse, melted them together to make one word so hateful, so utterly revolting, so devoid of goodness that its mere utterance would create horror and loathing and hatred, that word would be . . .'

'Amrikan?'

'. . . No, it would be the name of that Kampani. Have you been to the square where the court is? Yes? You must have seen, no matter what time you go there, that there are always a few people outside, with banners. If the court is in session, they may chant. You have been here long enough to have seen this.'

'I have seen it and I'll gladly join you in those protests, but what the hell has this got to do with me?'

'Everything,' says he. 'It has everything to do with you. You see, the Kampani—' One of those bad coughs begins fighting its way up from his lungs, he struggles to quell it but can't.

'You should really let me see to that,' says Elli.

'For years,' says Somraj when he's got back his breath, 'the Kampani has been saying that the damage to people's health has been exaggerated, it would like to have studies which show that things here are normal, that the last effects of the disaster are vanished.'

'Yes,' says Elli, 'I know all about this idiotic theory that I have come to do some sort of health survey, but surely you realise that a proper study can't be done in weeks, it's impossible, besides which we all know what the result would be. Things are not normal here, anyone with eyes can see that.'

'The studies need not be real. All they need's someone willing to fabricate them. A doctor, for example.'

'That's outrageous and unfair!'

'Then why did you come here? What sort of woman gives up her life in Amrika and comes to a place like this, to help people for no reward? Either you are a saint, or someone with a different purpose. So which are you?'

'I'm no saint, but how can I prove to you or anyone else what my motives are? You'll believe me or not as you choose.' Elli's turned bright red, her hands are shaking. 'This is not fair, you've already decided I am guilty!'

'It is a very unusual person who gives up so much.'

'No more unusual than one who hears music in frogs!'

After blurting this, she gives a guilty glance at me, who's already turning tail to run.

'I am so sorry,' says Somraj, 'this is not in my hands.' Without shifting his head he says, calm as you like, 'Animal, kindly tell Shastri we will resume his lesson.'

I did not dare face Somraj. I left the house while the lizard's lesson was still going on and stayed away from the Chicken Claw for two weeks. One night I dreamed that I was dragged before Somraj's friends in his music room. Somraj said, 'Now we shall hear *Raga Animal*,' and began to whack my arse with a shoe. The musicians listened enraptured to my cries then exclaimed 'Wah! Wah!' Nisha and Zafar were there too, clapping. Nisha said, 'Animal, I never knew you could sing so nicely.'

One morning Farouq comes bumping up on his bicycle. 'Kyoñ salé, where have you been hiding?'

'Not been hiding.'

'So why have we not been favoured with your presence?'

'Busy been, I've.'

'Zafar wants to see you.'

'Can't go right now.' My one regret about staying away from the Claw is that Zafar has not been getting his pills, but the thought of meeting pandit Somraj fills me with dread. 'I'm busy.'

'Oh I can see that,' he says with full sarcasm. 'What are you doing? Sitting here playing with your lund? Found a girl? Been shagging her arse off, have you?'

'Might have.'

He gives a nasty laugh. 'You've never fucked a woman in your life.'

'I have!' It's the old lie.

'I don't believe you. Go to Laxmi Talkies, get yourself laid. Thirty bucks, no problem.'

'Is that what they charge you?'

'Don't be cheeky.' Farouq gets off his bike, leans it against our wall and deliberately stands in front of me so I have to twist my neck upwards to see his face. For a moment I wonder, is he going to strike me or kick me?

Says Farouq looking down at me, 'Muharram is coming, brother Animal, have you forgotten your boast? Are you going to walk on the coals? Will you have the guts?'

Well, if one thing I learned on the streets, it's that you never back down. 'Listen, you Yar-yilaqi heap. I'll walk over your fire not just once, but twice.'

'That I would like to see,' says he.

'You shall.' I'm monitoring his shoes in case I have to leap backwards.

'I'll hold you to this promise.'

'You can.'

'I will,' says he from above. 'Come on, Zafar is waiting.'

'What does he want me for?'

'Your friend the doctress. Well, you'll see for yourself.'

Farouq has to lift me onto the carrier, then we're bumping over the rough track of Paradise Alley, the stony sludge of Seven Tailors, with Jara's running along behind. 'Seems the shopkeepers all love you,' says Farouq, hearing first Baju then I'm Alive yell as we rattle past.

'I am their favourite customer.'

Outside Somraj's house, there's a crowd gathered. On the clinic side of the street, in the shade of the mango are three tables set, sitting behind them are Dayanand, Suresh and Elli. On each table is something different.

I drop from Farouq's bike and stand gaping.

On the first table is propped a huge drawing of a human body. On it are marked all the places where the Kampani's that-night-poisons have damaged people, such as eyes, lungs, joints, womb, brain. These are marked in red. In blue are marked the places which have been harmed by drinking the poisoned water, breasts, again womb, stomach, skin. Blue and red spirals are coming from the head, which is also being banged by a hammer, above all hangs a dark grey cloud with lightning.

'For each harm,' Dayanand is saying, 'we have a good treatment, which

162

is free. So stop suffering. Come and get help for your pains. Don't listen to false rumours.'

People round the table are pointing to the things from which they suffer. Hammer is for headache. Must be. I get them badly myself, often just before I'll go mad. 'Giddiness, fainting fits,' says Dayanand to a woman who's looking at the spinning spirals.

'I thought so,' she says. 'Is this treatment truly free?'

'Fully,' replies Dayanand. 'It is excellent modern treatment. It will help you. Go, register with the lady inside, today itself the doctor will see you.'

So this woman has gone into the clinic, as she vanishes inside, so other people are coming out. I wonder what will Zafar and Co be making of this? I guess we are all learning that Elli doctress does not easily give up.

'Hurry up,' says Farouq, who has parked his bike and come to find me.

'Wait. What's the cloud?' I ask Dayanand, who looks none too pleased to see me.

'It is depression. Lightning is anxiety.'

'Oh yes? Who drew them, You, was it?'

'Don't take the piss,' he says. 'Piss off.'

'Okay,' says I, and've gone into Somraj's house to meet my fate.

First thing inside is Nisha greets me with a lund-throbbing hug. 'Animal, where have you been? You stopped coming for lunch. Is my cooking so bad?'

'Not at all, is your dad around?'

'No. Do you need to see him?'

'Not important,' says I. Hoo, relief.

Zafar is sitting in the garden, peeling a fruit with his knife, like the first time I met him. 'Animal, good you're here. We have this problem. You've seen outside, the sideshow?'

'Seen.'

'Well that's just today's fun. Yesterday Elli doctress was seen coming out of the office of Zahreel Khan.'

'Who very much admires her bloblos,' says I, myself recalling them.

163

'Leaving aside the bloblos,' he says wearily, 'That was yesterday's fun. Since you vanished we have also had the music wars.'

'Music wars?'

Says Nisha, 'Every evening. Whenever my dad plays any music, or if he's giving a lesson, there comes this loud music from across the road.'

'Elli doctress has a thing called piano,' says I. 'I have seen it. She learned it because her mother was ill.'

'Well it's making my father ill,' says Nisha. 'I have never seen him in such a state. Walking up and down he's, like a fishguts, holding his head.'

'Oh that's terrible!' says I, certain now of an arsewhacking by the angry pandit and his mates.

'Papa says that his brain is being chewed by this Elli doctress.'

Says Zafar. 'I think that not until the moon starts spinning backwards will we understand what's going on in Elli doctress's head. Until then, Animal, there's you.'

'Me? What can I do? I know, I'll make you a cup of tea.'

'Namispond,' says he.

'Jamispond,' says his adoring echo. 'You are friendly with her, find out why she went to see Zahreel Khan.'

I've managed to slip one of the black golis into Zafar's tea, then gone back outside, where are sat Elli doctress and her staff trying to convince the Khaufpuris. On the second table are picture leaflets about tuberculosis and how to stop it spreading. Here's Suresh explaining that TB is contagious, yes, but with a few precautions you can easily protect yourself, plus you can help those who are suffering. 'We will teach you. All treatments and medicines are free. Just go inside and register.'

'How can this be a bad thing?' someone asks.

Others agree, 'So many will benefit.' 'It's just what's needed.'

By now there's a regular stream of folk coming and going from the door of the clinic. At this rate the boycott will soon be over.

On the third table are many sheets of paper, Elli doctress is waving a pen at people. 'Come and sign!'

'What is this?' a man asks.

'It's a petition,' says Elli in a loud clear voice. 'It is addressed to Pandit Somraj and his committee. It says, please do not stop the people from getting the good free treatment they need. Support this clinic. Encourage people to make good use of it.'

'What should I do?'

'Just sign your name, write a comment, if you have one.'

The man makes a mumble, he jabs at the paper then moves off.

'Doesn't know how to write.' Hidden as I am by the edge of the table, it takes her some time to see me.

'Animal! Thank goodness, I've been wanting to talk to you. Wait right there, don't go anywhere.' She looks over to Suresh. 'At least one hundred have signed. How many registered inside?'

'Madam, seventy, more than.'

'Good.' She's turned back to me. 'Animal, can you spare me a few minutes?'

'Elli doctress, what are you doing?'

'I am telling these people that pandit Somraj is unfair. He should not be stopping them from getting treatment.'

'Good morning, Dr Barber,' says a voice like death. Somraj is standing right there beside us.

People around kind of hold their breath. All heads turn to Elli doctress, she is looking like what old folks call a duck on thunder. So the heads turn back to Somraj, stood there grim as ever.

'Pandit Somraj,' says Elli, collecting her wits. 'Since you are here I would like to present you with this petition.' She's gathered up all the sheets of paper and thrust them at him.

'I will be happy to receive it,' he says politely, not taking the sheets. 'Before that, there is something I would like to do.'

A crowd of Khaufpuris presses close. What a rabble of turbans, dhotis, burqas, saris, a wave of Khaufpuri breath, perfumed with betel and supari.

'Get back you scum,' I'm shouting, 'you will step on my fucking fingers.'

165

Says Somraj, 'I would like to sign it.'

Then people are goggling, because for the first time anyone can remember, pandit Somraj is smiling.

'What do you mean, you would like to sign it?' asks Elli, who's gone like a cut beetroot.

'Like this,' he says. He picks up a pen and signs. 'Collect more signatures. When you have finished, please bring them to me.'

Then he's gone into his house, still smiling, leaving behind a babble of voices plus one astonished doctress sat holding her papers.

'Elli doctress?'

She says at last, 'That horrible man, he's just making mockery. How dare he? Suresh, did you see what he just did?'

'Madam, Somraj pandit has signed the petition.'

'I know he has signed the damn petition.' Her voice has gone high. 'Can you believe it? The petition is aimed against him, and he has signed it himself.'

'Madam, pandit Somraj has a reputation for fairness, maybe he feels he is being unfair.'

'But if he feels he is being unfair, why doesn't he just be fair? I give up with this town, I don't think I will ever understand it.'

Next she's ghurr-ghurred me. 'Animal, will you sign?'

'Not I.'

'Why not? If even pandit Somraj can sign it, why can't you? Come on, sign your name.'

'It's not a proper name,' says I. Somraj can do whatever he likes, never will Zafar say anything to the man he calls 'abba'. But me?

'Sign!'

'When all's said, what kind of a name is Animal?'

'Have some guts.' It's like she's read my thoughts. 'You're a free human.'

'I am not a human.'

'You're always saying that. You don't really believe it.'

'Of course I believe it, because it's true.'

166

'So then, what else is true?'

I've thought about this for a moment, then said, 'Give me the pen.' Under all the signatures and crosses, I write:

Je ne suis pas un homme, mais un animal
dans cet hôpital je ne trouve rien de mal

'There, Elli, I've made you a poem.'
Growls the blood-tuskery voice before I can stop it:

Mere muñh se nikli insaan ki zubaan,
qurbaani ke jaanvar ki aakhri qurbaan

My lips have uttered human speech, the last sacrifice of the slaughtered beast.

'I am so sorry,' she says later, when we are inside her clinic. 'I should never have said that about frogs. It was stupid.'

To this I've replied nothing. I may be pissed off with Elli, but I'll never criticise in case she gets angry and stops my treatment. If your mission in life is to look after number one, sometimes it means biting your tongue, but there's usually another way to get at a person.

'Elli, how do you expect people round here to trust you, if you go visiting people like Zahreel Khan?'

'How do you know about that?'

'Namispond Jamispond.'

'Well, I got nowhere with the gentleman across the road. He's got quite a nerve, hasn't he? Listen to this.'

She sits at her piano opens the lid and thumps her hands down. There's a sound like rumbling thunder. Jara lifts her head and yips. Elli makes more great crashing sounds.

'What are you doing?'

167

'Ever since that day I had the row with him, whenever I play the piano a loud music starts up from inside that house.'

'I know nothing about it,' says I, with perfect truth.

'Wait and see.' She begins to play her favourite, that piece that sounds like bells. Sure enough, after hardly a minute, comes the full throat of someone singing a raga.

'How long has this been going on?'

'A couple of weeks. I don't mind, I just play even louder. The piano can easily drown him out.'

So, both sides of the road it's the same complaint.

'Animal, your friends.' Her fingers are still jumping around the keys. 'They are not much liked in high places.'

'Really?'

'The minister said they were "professional activists"'.

'Ha ha, is that all?' 'Agitator', 'trouble-maker', 'ring-leader' etc, these are the words the politicians usually use to describe Zafar.

'Worse.' So then she stops playing and tells me what happened.

Eyes, I don't have difficulty recalling her words. Even after all this time, I've only to think of Elli, imagine her standing in front of me with her slightly too-close-together eyes plus too-tight blue jeans, it gives a throb to my zabri plus I can hear her voice speaking in my head.

Elli goes to the government building where Zahreel Khan and the other Khaufpur politicians have their offices. It's in the posh part of town, by the shore of the lake. It looks clean from outside, but inside it's filthy. She says, 'At first I thought the reddish criss-cross streaks up and down the stairs were some sort of decoration, but then I realised that they were made by clerks letting fly betel-spit.' They send her to an office filled with steel cupboards, on top of them are toppling stacks of brown paper folders. Hundreds more folders are stuffed in sacks on the floor. Everything wears a thick shawl of dust.

Zahreel Khan's secretary does not seem pleased to see her. 'The minister is rather busy. It's not possible to see him today.'

From inside Zahreel Khan's office she can hear a murmur of voices.

'But he's expecting me. I rang to say I was coming.'

'Nevertheless.'

'Then when can I see him?'

'Tomorrow he has a cabinet meeting, then he is gone to Delhi for three days. After this . . .'

'It can't wait that long,' Elli says. 'There are sick people who need my help, they're being stopped from coming to my clinic. Some might die.'

The official points at the heaped up files. 'Madam, we are dealing with claims that go back twenty years, what difference will a few days make?'

'I am sure the minister must have a few minutes free soon. I will wait here until he is able to see me.'

'Madam, you are wasting your time.'

'I'll be the judge of that,' says she. 'What are all these files?'

'Each one is the claim of a person who was injured on that night. What you see here is just a few. We also have a godown full of dossiers, we have processed more than half a million.'

'May I look at one or two?'

'They are confidential.'

'They are public health records, I am a doctor, your minister personally assured me I'd have access to whatever information I wanted.'

'Madam, go ahead,' says the harrassed secretary. Fed up he's with this pushy foreigner, but dares not be rude for his minister had opened her clinic. An hour passes. Elli is deep in the depressing records of Khaufpur's tragedy, when from behind Zahreel Khan's door comes a loud yell, plus a kind of a roar. It then strikes Elli that for quite some time she's been hearing strange tok tok sounds. In a flash she's up and at the door.

'Wait!' shouts the secretary, 'you can't go in!'

Too late, she's in. First thing she sees is a tele screen on which are white figures of celebrating cricketers. A guy with some kind of bat, says Elli, who knows nothing of cricket, is walking off the field. Zahreel Khan is dozing in an armchair, a newspaper is spread on his lap. He wakes to find Elli smiling down at him.

'So sorry to disturb your meeting minister,' says she. 'I need a quick word.' Before he can protest, she's pouring out her problem.

'Arré, why are you still there?' says Zahreel Khan to his secretary, who's wringing his hands in the doorway. 'Can't you see I have a guest? Send tea plus cake for two. At once.'

Then Zahreel Khan tells Elli she should not worry, in Khaufpur things move slowly, people are cautious, they stick to what they know. 'Give it time and they will come crowding, you'll see.'

'It's not caution,' says Elli. 'People have been told to stay away. The only reason I can get is that they are afraid I have come from the Kampani. You know that's not true. Can't you tell them not to worry?'

At this the minister looks miserable and even as she asks, Elli realises it is pointless. No one will believe a word he says.

'The people behind this so-called boycott, who are they?'

Hearing Somraj's name he scowls. 'That bunch, they are troublemakers. Professional activists. Dear lady you should realise that they have an interest in promoting Khaufpur as a tragedy. Ask yourself, if the problems are solved, what will happen to their funding? It will dry up because there is no further need for it. For this reason, they are bound to oppose any and all efforts to improve the situation.'

'And my clinic is one of those efforts?'

'What else?' says he. 'Why else are you here?'

Tea comes on a tray of silver, brought by a bearer in a fancy uniform. Elli who does not like tea with milk in, watches as Zahreel Khan sips his tea and eats cake. He has dainty fingers, for so large a man.

'Mr Khan, why am I here?'

'My dear, who should know better than you?' Zahreel Khan's eyes have by now zigzagged their way to her blos.

'How was it that I wrote so many letters, for months I had no reply, then suddenly it was all go?'

170

'Permission in such cases takes time to arrange, obviously,' says he sounding aggrieved. 'After all, it's a virtually unheard of thing, a foreign woman coming on her own, in a strange country.'

'What about Mother Teresa?'

'Idealism doesn't work in Khaufpur,' he says. 'I think you are beginning to find this out.'

Elli tells me she could see his mind calculating how long it would take before she's worn down and broken by the heat, dirt and despair of Khaufpur.

'So are you saying there's nothing you can do?'

'I've already done all I was asked,' says Zahreel Khan, looking at his watch.

'Animal, I just don't know what he meant by this,' Elli says.

But listening to her words, I've felt a strong alarm, because again in her mind there's that uneasy darkness.

Elli's finished her tale of Zahreel Khan, now from across the road comes the sound of someone singing, it's *Dil Hi To Hai Na Sang-o-Khisht*, a ghazal of Ghalib's, I'm hoping Elli won't start pounding her piano and spoil it.

'Animal, the piano. Would you like to play?'

Okay, Ghalib I can hear any time, when will I ever again get a chance to play a piano?

'Come and sit here, on this stool.'

So I've climbed and faced the piano. 'Now spread out your hands like this and place them on the notes. Play, one at a time, like this, *do re mi fa so la ti do*. That's what the notes are called.'

'This is the same as our *sa re ga*. So this one is *sa*,' I've pressed a key.

'Your *sa* is our *do*,' she says.

'And this is *re*.' Ding goes the next key.

'Your *re* is our *re*. Same name, some note, they're exactly the same in both our musics.'

'Now listen.' Elli takes over and plays wonderful clusters of notes, different from anything I have heard before. Somraj will play one note

171

after another, very fast and graceful, but these notes combine to chime, they sing together, sometimes three, four, even five of them, each with a different voice, the effect is very beautiful.

'Okay, now you know the notes, let's make a tune.'

'How?'

'Just use one finger, like this.' She plays one or two notes, but then two together. So I've done the same.

'Think of some words we can fit to your tune.'

So I've thought of some words, and she's helped me make a song of them.

> *I am an animal fierce and free*
> *in all the world is none like me*
> *crooked I'm, a nightmare child*
> *fed on hunger, running wild*
> *no love and cuddles for this boy*
> *live without hope, laugh without joy*
> *but if you dare to pity me*
> *i'll shit in your shoe and piss in your tea*

'That is so sad,' says she, laughing.

'If it is sad, why are you laughing?'

'I don't know,' she says, wiping at her eyes. 'Maybe because otherwise I would cry. The idea of living without hope, it's terrifying.'

'Elli, it's just a song. This is how it is, in the kingdom of the poor.'

'I guess,' she says, 'I was thinking of my mother too. In her bad times she didn't know what was going on, but she had sane moments too. She must have known her case was hopeless.'

'You learned to play the piano for her.'

'That's right. I learned all her favourite pieces, they're still all I know, really. The other night I was sitting here, trying to think what my own favourites were, I couldn't think of one.'

172

'Elli, I think you are very lonely.'

She says nothing, but nods.

'Pandit Somraj, it's a pity you didn't get on, he is a decent man, plus he is fascinated by music. You should try to get to know him.'

'How can I, when he is boycotting me?' Now she's dabbing her eyes with a handkerchief.

I should have taken that moment to tell her that it is not Somraj who is doing the boycotting, that he has in fact all along spoken out against it, but for some reason my lying mouth stays shut.

'Now, how have you been?' she asks, and the chance has gone. Long I spent, that day, talking to Elli doctress. Down below her staff closed up the clinic and left. All kinds of things she told me, about her town, her family, her parents. Eyes, you shall hear this from her own mouth soon, so I'll not spoil it. Plus she said that the very next day she would take an x-ray of my back. It's dark by the time we finish talking.

As I step out of the clinic, ready to head home to Ma Franci, there arrives the moment I've been dreading. Pandit Somraj is standing outside his door. 'Animal, please spare me a minute.'

No escape, now I am fucking for it.

'Yes, sir?'

'Were you there to hear her playing?' he asks.

'I was. Plus I played myself. I made a song.'

'Very good. How did you do it?'

'Elli doctress taught me. Sir, she showed me how to put my hands on the piano, and press the keys to make *sa re ga* etc. Also, in her music *re* is called *re*, which is the same as in ours, she was very pleased by this.'

'Was she now?' The way he says this, I'm thinking now he'll get furious, but instead of shouting at me, catching my ear or landing a kick to the arse, he just puts his hand on my shoulder and says in a friendly tone, 'Son, we have all missed you.'

'Me, sir?'

'You sir. My daughter was worried.'

'Sir, no need for worry.' Oh happy, happy. Pandit Somraj has forgiven me, plus called me son plus Nisha cares about me.

'You had other business to attend, no doubt.'

'Yes, sir.'

'Nothing to do with frogs, I suppose?' His face is stern as ever, but his shoulders give a twitch, on this day of surprises not only have I seen pandit Somraj smile, but now I realise that he is doing his best not to laugh.

'Fully not frogs, sir.'

'Goodnight, Animal.'

'Sir, goodnight.'

'The kingdom of the poor, I want you to take me there.'

It's the day after the petition. Despite promises, not one of those who signed yesterday have turned up to the clinic. I've come for my x-ray, expecting to find quite a few others, but apart from me and Jara the place is empty.

Elli says she has decided to take matters into her own hands. 'If the poor won't come to me then I will go to them. I will confront them in their own houses, I'll rouse out the sick and ask them straight, "Will you die listening to rubbish, or will you let me help you?"'

'Well, I don't know,' says I, thrilled by this tirade. 'Seems nothing's changed. People still think they must avoid.'

'You're here, aren't you?'

'I do as I please. Maybe I'm jamisponding on you.'

'Jamisponding?' When she realises what this means Elli starts laughing, after she has finished laughing she says, 'Come on, let's get these x-rays done, then can we go?'

'Of course, we can go.' Must be that I hesitated for she's sensed something is wrong. 'What's up? Don't care to be seen with me?'

'It's not that.' I get on well with Elli doctress, plus because of my back I don't want to upset her, but a principle is a principle.

174

'First there's something we must agree.'

This principle, it's one of Chunaram's, in fact his only principle, since no others does he have. Elli seems not very sharp on the uptake so I've to explain.

'There's a question of the fee.'

'What?!'

'For this type of work I always get a fee.'

'A fee?' she says again, as if she has not heard me right.

'Fifty rupees. Nothing it's, to an auto-riding superstar like you.'

'Animal, you're amazing, you really are.' Shaking her head, she's. 'Do you actually have a conscience?'

Well, conscience I don't believe in, if I was given one I'd hand the fucking thing straight back. 'Elli, this is my business. For showing foreigners round I always get a fee.'

'I thought we were friends,' she says, looking kind of hurt.

'What has that got to do with it?'

'Friends don't charge each other for favours.'

'We are friends,' says I, 'but not equal friends.'

'Crap. Of course we're equal.'

'No, we're not. You are rich and I am poor.'

'What has that to do with friendship?' She's led me through to the room where's the x-ray mashin. 'Come on, you're joking.'

'Ellie, someone like you needs a lot of money. How could I go about with you? I can't even afford to stand you a Coca Cola. You know how much I spend in one day? Guess.'

She thinks then says, 'Forty rupees.'

'Forty?' I've laughed till I've choked, held up some fingers.

'Four?'

'Yes, four.'

'That's ten cents US. No one can live on that, not even in Khaufpur. Move a little to your left.' While talking she's positioning me against the x-ray mashin. A little this way, a bit that.

'You're right. No one can, but I do. Know how? I walk everywhere, four legs, leff-rye-leff-rye, no autos for me. All morning I'm roaming around doing my work. Two rupees I'll spend on chai. Lunch I eat at pandit Somraj's place, no cost. Every afternoon I'll show up at Chunaram's. One rupee's for a samosa, one more for a chai.'

'How about we make a deal? You do this for me just as I am doing this', she waves at the x-ray mashin, 'for you.'

'Elli, you may choose to work for nothing, but why does that also have to be my choice?'

She's thought about this. 'You said our friendship was not equal, well I am giving you something, you can give me something, each of us gives freely, not because we have to, but because we want to. This makes us equal.'

'Elli, this equality leaves me broke.' Got to stop her cheapskatery, so I jerk my chin at Jara, who's lying near Elli's feet, panting, with a dog smile on her face. 'Why's the dog allowed in, Elli? So desperate you're for patients, you even took me.'

'Goddamn!' she shouts. 'Hold still. Take a deep breath and shut the fuck up! One . . . two . . . three . . .'

When the x-ray is done she says to me, 'Now you listen to me. I'll do what I can for you because I want to. I'm a doctor, that's what I do. But I'm damned if I'll pay you to take me around. So make up your mind. Will you do it, or won't you?'

So I've thought about this, then called to the dog. 'Come on, let's go.'

We get to the door of the room. Elli's still standing by the x-ray mashin, looking really sad.

'Well, madam doctress? What are you waiting for?'

This big smile appears on her face. She runs up and gives me a hug, for which she's got to get down on her knees, she kisses me on both cheeks, I'm thinking how I love being hugged by women, also I'm thinking stop, stop, stop, because I've got Monsieur Méchant living in my pants.

*　　*　　*

'Forget your doctress's bag, forget you know Hindi, people will be shy to speak if they know you can understand. Make out you're some dumb fucking jarnalis. Look around with big eyes. Sigh a lot, ask stupid questions in Inglis. Then you can see for yourself how things are.'

'Do we need an auto?' she asks, 'your friend is probably outside.'

'No more autos for you, Elli. You cannot enter the Kingdom of the Poor except on foot. Come on, I'll show you. Full tour. Everything. Follow me.'

I've run à quatre pattes into the Claw up past Nekchalan's shop, where his spoony mates are gathered. She's following some way behind. 'Good morning' she says, polite as a pot of ghee, hypocrite bastards, they don't reply. The lane's crowded, hard for her to keep me in sight so I lig on slowly, Jara the dog keeps stopping and looking round as if to say, come on Elli, hurry up. Once or twice I check back that she's there. She's not happy. Quite a few low-lifes there are in the Claw, their eyes glued to those bluesy melons, sweet-sweet noises they're making like you'd tempt a dog. At last she's followed me out of the Claw through a gully to the main road. At the city end this same road is smarter, there's more money, big shops there are, families with fat children licking ice creams, in our part it's a filthy chute with truck exhaust for air.

Across the big road we come to the corner of Kali Parade and take the road that runs past the Kampani's factory. On our left now is the wall, high as a man, covered with writing, some of it's by Zafar and friends, who paint at night when the police are asleep. Zafar's lot never write what they really feel which is FUCK YOU WICKED CUNTS I HOPE YOU DIE PAINFULLY FOR THE HORRIBLE THINGS YOU DID TO US AND THE ARROGANT FUCKING CRUELTY YOU'VE DISPLAYED EVER SINCE. They write high-sounding shit like JUSTICE FOR KHAUFPUR and KAMPANI MEET YOUR LIABILITIES but in a few places freer spirits have been at work. HANG PETERSON and DEATH TO AMRIKA. These are the bits the munsipal scrubs out which need repainting more often than any other.

'Aiwa! Aiwa! Aiwa!' No sooner do we enter the Nutcracker, that place assembled by an earthquake, than there's a gang of kids on our trail.

'Animal, Animal,' comes a little voice I know well. Someone's running along behind us. 'Animal, who's this? Where are you going?'

'Hi Aliya, this is a very important jarnalis. Don't make her cross because she eats small children. It's what they do in her country. They roast them with yogurt and mint leaves.'

'Don't be silly,' says the child. 'Can I come too?'

'Where do you think we're going?'

'How should I know? But you always do interesting things.'

'What do you think we're doing today?'

'Going fishing?' she asks hopefully.

'I'm taking her to meet your granny and grandpa.'

'Then I won't come,' she says, making a face, and runs off.

Low are the doorways we come to now, perfect for a four-foot animal. I know a lot of people here, so I'm in and out, calling greetings to those inside. People come stooping to their thresholds. Some stare. Others beckon us in but I tell them we can't stop

It's old Huriya's house I'm heading for, an earthquake-erected room with a floor of bare earth. The air is made delicious by the smell of wood burning in the hearth. I love the scent, plus these people, Aliya's grand-parents, Hanif and Huriya, she's squatting kneading dough on a board.

'Hello Dadi, what's cooking?'

'Hello Animal, I'm making rotis for his lordship's meal.'

Hanif's bent in front of the cage in which are his two green and purple parakeets. His fingers feel for gaps between the wires, when he finds one he feeds in a seed, one seed at a time. He's looking not at the beautiful birds, but up into a corner. Hanif hasn't seen a thing since that night.

'Who's this you've brought with you?' the old lady asks.

'Oh no one, just a jarnalis.'

'Another one?'

'Well you know, Chunaram collects them.'

'Will she have tea?'

'She's Amrikan, there's no way to ask her.'

'Well, if she can't talk, she can't refuse,' says Huriya, reaching for the pot in which they store water.

'Don't waste it, Dadi.' Huriya's old, the pump's a long way off. 'We're not stopping long. We've just come from the Chicken Claw.'

'A guest in the house and you talk of waste!' She starts unscrewing a paper containing some black tea leaves. 'I'll send the child for more later. So what's the latest from the Claw?'

'Haven't you heard? Yesterday the foreign-waali doctress was trying to entice people into her clinic. But still no one's going.'

'Yes, we know about that,' comes the gruff voice of the old man, Hanif Ali. 'I don't agree with it.'

'As if that Kampani has not done enough wickedness,' Huriya says. 'Make your friend comfortable. Ask her to sit.'

'She's not my friend, she's a jarnalis.' Elli pulls a face, useless jamispond she'd make. 'So why don't you agree with the clinic, baba?'

'You're hearing me wrong,' says the old boy, giving a harsh cough. 'I don't agree with what's going on. A clinic is a clinic. So what if it's paid for by the sisterfuck Kampani? Don't they owe us for the harm they've done? Isn't our own granddaughter sick and needing good treatment?'

Elli says to me in Inglis, 'Call the child. I'll look at her.'

'Not a word of Hindi does this fool jarnalis speak,' I'm shaking my head sadly. 'Aliya's out there somewhere. Let me call her.'

'Leave the child be, we have a guest. Will she take something with her tea?' Huriya gives Elli an encouraging smile. 'These rotis are nice and hot.'

Elli's looking as if she wants to say something, but she mimes no thank you, and returns the smile.

'She seems almost to understand,' says Huriya. 'Her eyes are a little close set, but she's quite pretty really, isn't she? In that bizarre way that foreigners are. It's a pity her clothes are so indecent.'

'Hah! Fine thing is this,' says the old bugger. 'An indecent woman in my

179

own house and I haven't the eyes to see her. What a cruel fate. Her voice is sweet, does she have good tarboozas?'

Ouf! Shot, sir! I'm creased up laughing. Elli is impassive, which makes it even funnier.

'You be quiet,' says his wife. 'Don't go embarrassing yourself.'

'Baba, you were saying about this clinic?' Good idea to turn the talk away from Elli's melons.

'Well, I want to talk to Zafar about it,' Hanif grumbles. 'If it is a good clinic why shouldn't we take Aliya there, poor child? Animal, when will Zafar brother come?'

'I don't know, Baba. Zafar brother is an important guy. Everyone wants him. I guess he'll come soon.'

'Inshallah. Where are you taking the foreigner?'

'Round and about. To hear people's stories. You could tell her yours.'

'Mine? Who'd want to hear my story?' But you can see the idea tickles him, I guess he's never been asked before. Then he remembers. 'What's the good? She doesn't speak our language.'

'Never mind, did you ever read anything good a jarnalis wrote?'

'Me read?' He points at his eyes. 'What, like you ride a bike?'

'I can ride a bike bloody,' says I, 'Arse to handlebars, hands on pedals, look between legs to see where you're going. Easy. One day I'll show you.'

'What nonsense,' chuckles the old man. 'Such a prize idiot as you I think there's never been. How is Ma Franci, recovered yet from her adventure?'

'Day by day going madder.'

'It was a sweet time she spent with us,' says Huriya, reaching for heaven's kettle. 'Like a schoolgirl she was, all naughtiness plus pranks.'

'She's talking a great deal about her childhood. Plus also angels.'

'I pray for that good woman. At the end of time when God judges us humans, I just hope He remembers to judge Himself as well.'

'Tauba tauba tauba,' says Hanif, touching his cheeks. 'Don't talk that way, old woman. Animal, when you see Zafar be sure to tell him that the child needs more medicine, her coughing is worse.'

180

'Well, you can tell me,' Elli suddenly says in Hindi.

Such a silence there's. Even old Hanif turns and sends his sightless eyes searching for her. 'Animal, she speaks. Why didn't you tell us?'

I shrug, open my mouth, out's come nothing but a giggle.

'I'm the doctor you were talking about,' says Elli. 'I'm the one who opened the clinic that everyone's afraid of. I'm not a monster, I'm not from the moon and I hate the Kampani as much as you do.'

'Tauba tauba tauba,' says Hanif again. 'For shame, Animal. Madam, great apologies, don't think us rude.'

'Wasn't me talking about tarboozas,' I've said.

Says Huriya, placing a glass of tea and a plate with a roti in front of Elli. 'This beastly boy deserves a good slapping.'

'What is wrong with your granddaughter?' asks Elli, but first she must taste the tea, also the roti, which Huriya has sprinkled with sugar plus a little coriander leaf. When she's pronounced both to be delicious the old folk begin to tell how Aliya has been ill for almost a year with a cough and fevers.

'Where is she?' says Elli. 'May I look at her?'

The old man lifts his head and calls, 'Aliya!'

'Aliya! Aliya!' shout the kids in the doorway.

Presently the child appears, steps shyly forward. One reason I'm so fond of Aliya is she's cheeky. Cheeky in kids is good. It's a real shame for a kid to be non-cheeky.

'Hi Animal.'

'Hi again Aliya.'

Elli asks in a soft voice, like she's cooing to a pigeon, 'Aliya, how long have you been coughing?'

'Forever,' says Aliya. 'I've not been well for ages.'

Elli's produced her doctor's dangling thing which she must have hidden in a pocket, she listens to Aliya's chest. 'Aliya has an infection. I need to find out what it is. I'll do a throat swab, then I will give you medicines, there will be nothing to pay. Everything is free. Bring her to the clinic.'

181

Elli has that smile on her face, same as when she flung open her doors. It has again to fade because Huriya's looking worried, shaking her head she's.

'Doctress madam, I'm so embarrassed, we can't bring the child. We are not supposed to come.'

'Who says you're not to come,' asks Elli. 'I suppose it's pandit Somraj.'

'Not Somraj. Zafar brother. He says we must be careful.'

'Oh, how I'd love to slap Zafar brother,' cries Elli. 'Come on people, this is your granddaughter we're talking about.'

Now everyone is silent. Aliya stands there looking from one to another of her grandparents. 'Hey Aliya,' I tell her, 'go and play.'

Hanif gives a sigh. 'This is stupid,' he says. 'It's cruel, by my life. Heaven knows how much we love that child. Nevertheless we must do as Zafar asks. We will come when he says we can come. Let's hope it's soon.'

'What?' I ask, 'does he hold you in his power like slaves?'

'If you bring her, what will Zafar do?' Elli asks.

'It's not like that, madam,' says the old man. 'Animal knows this. All of us here respect Zafar bhai, plus Somraj, that whole family. They are good people, they do a lot to help us poor. If we do what Zafar asks, it's because we trust him, and we do it out of love.'

'Strange kind of love,' says Elli. 'It's not them I blame, it's this Zafar. He is one of Somraj's gang. They're all one family.'

'Not one family,' I say sharply, this kind of talk I find upsetting. It's like a dark cloud spreading in my mind, that first Hanif, then Elli, talks of Zafar as part of Somraj's family.

There's a gaggle of folk now, following us from house to house. The kids are still there of course, but also plenty of grown-ups, who soon put a stop to the endless Aiwas. 'Stop eating the doctress's head, such a dhaap you'll catch!'

Word has spread that a foreign doctress has come to give free treatment, people are appearing from their houses, calling, 'This way, come to my mine.' 'No, mine first.' 'There's someone sick in here who needs help.'

Well, someone's sick in every house in the Nutcracker, in many houses everyone is sick. Elli's quickly into and out of a dozen houses. All want treatment, but not one is willing to come to the clinic. Time after time there is the polite, embarrassed refusal. Elli's disbelieving. 'These people have nothing. Why do they turn down a genuine and good offer of help? I just don't get it.'

Seeing how unhappy she is, I try to find something to say that will make her feel better. 'Elli doctress, no surprise or shame. I understand because these are my people.'

'So what the hell do I have to do to get through to these people of yours?' She cups her hands to her mouth and shouts, 'HEY, ANIMAL'S PEOPLE! I DON'T FUCKING UNDERSTAND YOU!'

Oh what glee among our young rabble. Forgotten is Aiwa, as we leave the Nutcracker we can hear the chorus of small voices gradually falling behind, 'Hey hey, Animal's People! Hey ho, Animal's people! Hee ha, Animal's people! Ha ha, Animal's people! Don't fucking, fucking, don't fucking understand! I don't fucking understand you!'

Up Paradise Alley out of that place I've led her, across the railway tracks. Remembering that she understood français I'm thinking I will take her to meet Ma Franci, but when we get there of Ma there is no sign.

'You live *here*?'

Eyes, wherever a person lives is normal to them, but in Elli's eyes is the same look that I have seen in Kakadu's, Père Bernard's and so many others.

'Please, Elli doctress, will you take tea?'

I've placed my hand into the hole in the wall where we keep our food, it is a somewhat nicer hole than the one in which Kakadu's tape mashin is quietly rotting. Ellie shrieks.

'What is it now?' I've brushed a couple of scorps off the paper screw of tea leaves. Still angry I'm, that the world in its ignorance considers Zafar to be Somraj's son-in-law.

'Those things!' says she, pointing, as the creatures scuttle back to the wall. When their tails have safely vanished into a crack between the stones she turns to me and pigeon-coos, 'Oh poor Animal, what a life!'

'Look Elli,' I say, feeling like I want to explode, 'I'll tell you what disgusts me about this place, which isn't what disgusts you, such as scorpions, filth, lack of hygiene, etc. It's not that if I want a shit, I must visit the railway line . . .'

'Hardly your fault,' says she, misunderstanding.

'Not a question of fault. You foreigners talk as if the sight of a bum is the worst thing in the world, doesn't everyone crap?'

'Not in public, they don't.'

'There's a lot to be said for communal shitting. For a start the camaraderie. Jokes and insults. A chance to discuss things. It's about the only opportunity you get to unload a piece of your mind. You can bitch and moan about the unfairness of the world. You can spout philosophies. Then there's the medical benefit. Your stools can be examined by all. You can have many opinions about the state of your bowels, believe me our people are experts at disease. The rich are condemned to shit alone . . .'

'Please! No more!'

'Okay. How did I get started about shitting?'

'You said that it wasn't that which disgusted you.'

'Right. What really disgusts me is that we people seem so wretched to you outsiders that you look at us with that so-soft expression, speak to us with that so-pious tone in your voice.'

She asks very seriously, 'Don't people here deserve respect?'

'It's not respect, is it? I can read feelings. People like you are fascinated by places like this. It's written all over you, all you folk from Amrika and Vilayat, jarnaliss, filmwallass, photographass, anthrapologiss.'

'I'm not a jarnalis, I'm a doctress. And I did mean respect. If I don't give it, how will I get it? It's clear to me how these people love Zafar, plus I do understand why, he treats them as equals with respect.'

'Bollocks!' I don't have such an idealistic view of people, who are shits.

184

'These people love Zafar because he's all they have. He's the only ally they know. And he's always there for them. That's why they'll turn out on demos with him, block roads, shout slogans.'

'I too am there for them, they will get to know me,' says Elli, as if just wishing a thing can make it true.

I'm in no mood to be nice. 'You haven't a hope. You are a good-hearted doctress but nothing do you fucking understand. Tell me please, what is that?' I've pointed at her wrist.

'My watch?'

'Yes, your watch. What do you need it for?'

'To tell the time of course. Why do you ask?' Maybe she thinks I'm going to ask for her watch as a fee.

'Elli, I don't need a watch because I know what time it is. It's now-o'clock. Look, over there are the roofs of the Nutcracker. Know what time it's in there? Now o'clock, always now o'clock. In the Kingdom of the Poor, time doesn't exist.'

'You're right,' says she, 'I don't understand.'

'Elli, if you had no watch, your stomach will churn and growl and say, hey Elli, it's food time, hey it's still food time, hey don't you hear me, it's food time. What happens if you can't afford food? When you can't remember the last time you ate something? I'll tell you. When it's light there's binding a cloth tight round your belly to squeeze out the pain, when it turns dark you've to drink plenty of water to fill your miserable gut. Hope dies in places like this, because hope lives in the future and there's no future here, how can you think about tomorrow when all your strength is used up trying to get through today? Zafar says this is why the people don't rise up and rebel.'

Thus in my lousy mood do I rattle off the ideas of our leader, his vision of a people for whom there is no night and day, only a vast hunger through which suns wheel, and moons wane and wax and have no meaning.

'Animal, I don't know what such suffering is like, but it doesn't mean we've nothing in common. There's simple humanity? Isn't there?'

Cheap lying bastard, I'm. 'No good asking me,' I tell her. 'I long ago gave up trying to be human.'

On the way back I've turned instead to follow the factory wall as it runs beside the railway. I've brought her here because if you want to understand Khaufpur and Khaufpuris, plus particularly how they feel about Amrika, this is where you have to start.

'Elli, see inside there, it's the factory. In there everything is just as it was on that night. Since then, hardly anyone has been in. Except me.'

I start to tell her about what's in the factory, Eyes, the very same things that I have already told you.

She grips my shoulder. 'Let's go in!'

Well this is not in my plan. 'You can't. Not allowed.'

'But you do.'

'That's different. I'm an animal. I come and go.' If she gets in trouble with the powers-that-be, thrown out of Khaufpur maybe, what will become of my back? But Elli, like everyone, thinks only of what she wants.

'Elli, you can't go inside. People like you must get a permit from the Dippety Collector, Poison Affairs.'

'FUCK THE DIPPETY COLLECTOR, POISON AFFAIRS!'

Two fat tears are running a race down her cheeks. She turns away like she doesn't want me to see. All the way back to the Claw we've walked in silence. My mood grows worse. Zafar married to Nisha, this thought grips my brain with red hot tongs. It's me who should marry Nisha, no other ambition is greater than this, and walking upright on two legs is the way I'll achieve it.

I must repair Elli's mood, I must show her that I am her friend. I was a fool to ask for a fee, nothing more must I do to upset Elli doctress. This very morning she took my x-ray, tomorrow she will send it to Amrika. Soon a reply will arrive. It will say come for an operation. This fucking hope grows wilder every day. When I return to Khaufpur after my operation, I will walk up and down the Claw. Nisha will not recognise me. She will see a young stranger, upright and handsome, there and then she'll fall in love. She'll forget Zafar, phhht, he's gone. She will be besotted with her new love, desperate to marry him. Only one regret, in some part of her mind she will be wondering, what happened to my dear and faithful Animal, where has he gone? She will mourn for Animal who's vanished no one knows where, but he will never return.

Eyes, I'm not a complete cunt, I know these dreams are so much crap, but with fluff like this, once it's there it's there, and you see stranger things in the movies.

'Zafar bhai, may today be a chicken day!'

It's Bhoora, grinning like a fool. A small crowd is gathered outside Somraj's house. Today the judge will give his opinion. Everyone's excited, ready to leave for the court.

I've suggested that for luck me, Nisha and Zafar should travel with Bhoora like last time, so Farouq is taking Zafar's motorbike. Another auto will bring Pandit Somraj with a couple of his music chums.

Quite a noise we're making, chatter and laughing, the clinic doors open, Elli comes out, surprised to find all these people outside. Seeing me she says, 'Hello Animal, what's happening?'

'Elli doctress, we are going to the court.'

'Good morning Pandit Somraj,' she says coldly.

'Good morning Doctor Barber,' replies Somraj. No smile today, he keeps his feelings locked in an icebox, but Something Khan's staring at her as if he has never seen legs before.

We're just passing the big Hanuman temple when I spot Farouq, weaving through the traffic ahead. 'Quick Bhoora,' I say, 'speed up.' Bhoora obliges, I've reached out, caught Farouq such a slap on the back of his head, fucker's all but toppled from the bike, cursing, vowing all kinds of bitter revenge.

'Animal, that was dangerous,' says Nisha reprimands me, but with her thigh pressed against me I'm just laughing, ha ha plus hee hee plus ho ho. 'Why not today?' I'm shouting. 'Why not today?'

When we arrive at the court there's a big crowd, with jarnaliss plus a tele crew. The *Khaufpur Gazette* wants to interview Zafar. Our great leader has no time, says he will do it later, so I've bounded round the bugger, 'Interview me, I'll give a story that will shoot steam from your ears. Je te raconterai l'histoire de Jacotin et son nàs superbe.'

Nisha says, 'Darling, you are out of control.'

'I am, I am!' It happens sometimes, just filled full of excitement and yap and don't know what, some big thing is going to happen. Well, the *Khaufpur Gazette* is in no way interested in my interview so I head for the tele-wallahs and've jugged around making faces at them, Eyes, I wish you could see . . . I am pulling those faces now, tongue out eyes glaring, cheeks bulging eyes fully crossed . . . a hefty kick lands on my arse, it's Farouq, 'Little bastard, you could have killed me.'

'You have to die one day,' I yell. 'Why not today?'

The court is fully crowded, hardly space to stand. I've tried to climb on the bench backs, this time all kinds of dirty looks I've got, but Nisha's with me, she's found me room.

At last the judge enters, he's wearing a black robe over his suit. The local lawyers are right up at the front, Zafar too is there. Milord sits, shuffles some papers on his desk, a court-wallah announces that this is criminal case number RT 8460/96.

'Look who's here,' says Nisha in my ear. I've followed her eyes, there at the back of the court is a foreign woman wearing a head scarf and dark glasses.

'Why has she come?' Nisha demands, but how should I know. I'm still in that mad grinning mood, I give Elli a wave, she sees and waves back.

Now the judge is talking, 'With regard to the petition laid before the court by Mr Zafar, the aforesaid petition is hereby . . .' here, just to be a cunt, he pauses and looks at all of us over the tops of his glasses . . .

'. . . granted. The necessary summons plus letter rogatory . . .'

But the rest of what he is saying is lost in cheers.

'We've won! We've won!' shrieks Nisha, she's jumped and run to Zafar, who has a huge grin on his face. Even Somraj, for the second time in a few days is smiling. People are stamping their feet.

Calls a familiar voice from the back of the court, 'Sir, a great decision!'

'And who might you be?' asks the judge.

'Sir, I am Doctor Elli Barber, I have opened a free clinic here in Khaufpur for the victims of this heartless Kampani.'

'Good work, Dr Barber, very good work. We wish you every success.'
I'm thinking that Elli will not start complaining to the judge about
pandit Somraj, thank god she keeps her mouth shut.

'Now things are different,' Zafar tells the *Khaufpur Gazette*. 'The
Kampani bosses must come. If they don't, the Kampani's Indian assets
may be attached.'

The big hearing, when the bosses must show up, is set for some
months ahead, it will fall around the middle of June, just before the rains
come to Khaufpur, the hottest time of year.

Bhoora sings all the way back, it's another chicken day.

On my way to Nisha's next morning, I meet Farouq on his bicycle's flapping from side to side like a dog's ear, laughing so much he's.

'Animal,' he says, 'Animal, you crazy fuck, lord of dogshit, pawnbroker
to flies, you will love this. Do you know what your Elli doctress is doing?'

'So? Say.'

'She's only staging a demo outside Somraj's house,' says he, hardly can
he squeeze out the words for mirth. 'Not just a demo, but a picket, everything. Says it is a gherao. It is just hysterical.'

'What is Somraj doing?'

'When we told him, he just stood calmly, then he says, I see, and turns
to Shastri, this morning we'll practise the alaap of *Yavanapuri*. I think the
poor fellow is in shock. Who's ever seen anything like this woman?'

'And Zafar? Nisha?'

'Well, what do you expect? Zafar is worrying about what is the right
response, Nisha is just getting upset.'

'She's been upset a lot since Elli showed up.'

'Ha ha, yes,' says he, giving me a wink. 'Dirty little shit, you notice such
things.' He's wobbled away, still chortling, then turned and yelled over his
shoulder, 'Muharram is nearly here!'

When I get near Somraj's place, I begin to hear hooting and cheers.
There's a sizeable crowd of ne'er-do-wells and time-pass tapori types

hanging around, shouting encouragement to her who's provided them with this free spectacle.

Elli blue legs is walking up and down outside Somraj's, carrying a sign mounted on a stick. SOMRAJ IS UNFAIR, it says. Following behind her are Dayanand, Suresh and Miriam Joseph. The two guys look like they wish they could be anywhere else in this world, only Miriam Joseph is smiling. All three carry placards, on which are written, SOMRAJ LET THE SICK BE HELPED, STOP THE BOYCOTT and SOMRAJ HAVE A HEART.

Much wondering there's at this unusual sight, doubly unusual because although many foreigners come to march in our demos, none has ever started their own. Not in their maddest dreams can Zafar and Co suppose they'd get such a taste of their own medicine.

I stop to admire these four circling outside Somraj's house, they're vowed to do this every day until he lifts the boycott.

There's a stir in the crowd. The door is opening. Out steps pandit-ji, stony faced as ever, immaculate in his white kurta pyjama.

People start jabbering, now we'll see some real drama, fireworks there are bound to be. 'Somraj is an important guy,' says someone behind me. 'He will know what to say to this arrogant foreigneress.'

Somraj is holding a cup of tea, balanced on a saucer.

'See how cool he is,' says the same voice. 'He has come outside to drink his tea, to show us people that he is no way bothered by this nonsense.'

'Now he'll give the doctress what for,' opines another.

Somraj goes up to Elli, who stops marching. Instead of giving her what for, he holds out the cup of tea. 'It is a hot day,' says he in that beautiful voice of his, every word carries clear across the street. 'You must be thirsty. Please, take this. More is coming for your companions.'

I'm getting Elli's thoughts, they are rushing round like a flock of chickens scattered by a dog. Then she pulls herself together.

'Thank you,' she says. 'But as you see, I am busy.' She shrugs show that her hands are full carrying the placard.

'So please,' says Somraj. 'Allow me.' With one hand he removes the placard from the astonished doctress, with the other gives her the tea.

'So clever,' says the idiot behind. 'See, he has the sign, how he's looking at it. Now he will smash it down on the ground, it will fly to bits.'

Elli standing there, takes a sip of her tea, fixes hostile eyes on Somraj and says, 'Well, what are you waiting for? You signed the petition against yourself, will you now join our demo against you?'

For one moment Somraj stands there expressionless. Then he's turned to Dayanand and the others, who have come to a nervous halt and are looking on. 'So then,' he says, 'while Doctor Barber drinks her tea, I must take her place.'

Thus is the crowd treated to the amazing sight of Somraj picketing his own house, calling upon himself to stop being unfair.

Eyes, Khaufpuris aren't the brightest lot, I guess it takes a minute for the message to sink in, then in the crowd someone cheers. A few more join in, but most people are puzzled. Is pandit Somraj making a mockery of the doctress, or has he turned against his own? By the time tea arrives for the others, the watching crowd has dissolved into knots of people. Some are drifting away, others are clustered around Dayanand and Suresh and Miriam Joseph, slapping them on the back, saying that it takes those who have courage to speak. Elli and Somraj are stood together. I, who have the ability to read thoughts, watch their lips and I swear that Elli doctress says to him, 'I do believe you really are against this boycott.' To which he replies, 'You may draw your own conclusion.'

A while later I've passed Ram Nekchalan's shop. 'Kyon, Animal?' he says to me. 'What's Zafar doing about this? People are saying that the foreign doctress has put pandit Somraj under a spell.'

'Count your money, shut your trap. Hypocrite cunt, you're just wondering which way to jump.'

'Come here, I'll give you such a thrashing,' says he, enraged. But I've just laughed and gone away.

*　*　*

192

Some way outside Khaufpur is a greenish river called Bewardi, there's a place on the edge of the forest, some cattle-herders have made a small hut there, to watch over the animals as they drink, no more it's than a thatched roof hoisted on four bamboo poles, but it has a smooth floor of clay, there's a small hearth where tea can be made.

Our bhutt-bhutt-pig has farted its way through the city and out to this peaceful place. This is after Elli's demo by one or two days, as day by day my tale unfolds, it's the weekend, we're at last having the picnic promised by Zafar after our court victories against the Kampani. The original plan got postponed because of last year's rains, then everyone forgot about it, but after the recent hearing someone said we should now definitely have the picnic, so Zafar told Farouq to organise it.

On the day there's about twenty people, we've hired the bhutt-bhutt to carry us. Somraj is coming later in Bhoora's auto. He's bringing the wind-up, it's a wooden gramophone mashin with a handle, he's had it since he was a kid, belonged to his dad, it does not need electric, so it comes to places like this and performs very old songs, songs older than anyone here alive.

On the way people start singing. Everyone must teach a song to the rest.

'Ma Franci, Ma to teach one.'

So I've put this to her. 'Something that's easy to learn.' Shyly she starts singing:

> Dormez, dormez, mon petit pigeon
> Dormez, dormez, mon petit agneau
> Ferme tes yeux mon petit mignon
> Et laisse toi faire des rêves si beaux

Soon all are doing their best with this, after which Ma sings *Tonton Lariton* and Zafar gives *Hillélé Jhakjor Duniya*. Add to such songs a big pot of chicken biryani, kebabs by Chunaram who's here to brown them, plates, cups etc, in this way we've come to the Bewardi. Now smoke is rising from the hearth, food's heating in the big pot, kebabs are dripping on twig spits, games we play, mostly kids' games such as seven tiles, gulli danda, bird fly-up, cards, etc.

Nisha says, 'Animal, can we talk? I've something to ask.'

When we're sat by the river, she comes straight out that she and Zafar know I've been spending a lot of time in Elli's clinic, plus recently I've been seen with her in the Nutcracker.

'When have I tried to hide it?' I've been expecting this. 'Hardly a secret, it's right across the road. Plus she wanted to see the Nutcracker.'

'Yes, but she was trying to get people for her clinic.'

'Which of course she'll do. Wouldn't you?'

'Have you told her anything about us, how we work, our plans, etc?'

'Aren't you forgetting,' I reply to deflect this question for I hate lying to Nisha, 'I am your Jamispond, jeera-jeera-seven?'

Nisha bursts out laughing. 'Animal, so desperate is your Inglis accent, you know what you just said, *cumin-cumin*-seven. So what have you found out?'

'She's harmless.' None too pleased I'm that Nisha's making fun of me. 'She's sincere. We shouldn't be troubling her.'

'Leave those decisions to people who know more.'

Soon the person who knows more's come to join us, Nisha tells him what I've said, he sits cupping his chin, serious as ever. 'Animal, you are a free human being, you are free to make your own decisions. Nobody will stop you or say you shouldn't.'

'So?' I don't say what's in my mind, which is I'm not a human being, plus I don't need anyone's permission to be free.

'Nothing more, that's it.'

'First of all, Zafar, Elli doctress is not from the Kampani, at least I don't believe so, but like I said I am keeping an eye open.'

'This Elli,' says Zafar, 'she's pretty, has a nice smile.' Nisha shoots such a look, it's aimed at him but pierces me. 'What do you suppose

194

Kampani-wallahs look like? Blood-dripping teeth, red eyes, claws?'

Well, I've never thought about this, of course I've no idea.

'They look ordinary,' says he. 'You know why? Because they *are* ordinary. They are not especially evil or cruel, most of them, this is what makes them so terrifying. They don't even realise the harm they are doing.'

After lecturing some more on how some people who think they're leading normal lives are in fact creating hell on earth he goes away, leaving Nisha curled up in a little ball of misery.

'Nish, it's like you hate Elli doctress. But why?'

'I don't hate,' she says, throwing a pebble into the river.

'You're too sweet and kind a person to dislike without reason, what is it?'

'It's nothing.' But there are tears in her eyes.

'Nish, this is your own Animal you're talking to, whom you plucked from the gutter, to whom you taught writing plus Inglis, who owes everything to you, who adores you, who never wants to see you sad. So tell me, darling, what is it?'

So gradually it comes. At first it seems, Nisha disapproved of Elli's blue legs, she disliked the way men's eyes used to be drawn to them. At last out slips the real reason. 'It's so embarrassing to see your own father looking at a woman. To think such things go on in his mind.'

'What things? Things such as . . . ?'

'You know what I mean,' she says. 'The way he looks at her.'

'How looks? He just looks. He's a fair man, darling. Besides, what if he finds her attractive? Don't you find anyone attractive?'

She blushes and won't say another thing. This tears me up. Not that I myself was hoping for a compliment but I feel certain she's thinking of Zafar. The merest hint of sex, she thinks of Zafar! I feel sure they're shagging. How have I missed it, so many nights in the tree, never once have I caught them. To be on the safe side I decide to double Zafar's dose.

'Living this way is hard,' says Nisha at last, her pebbles plop in the river louder than mine. 'To have a dream, yet not dare to believe in it.'

'Yes,' says I, who's about to confess a terrible hope. 'What is it, your dream?'

'For this struggle to end. For us to win. As things are going, maybe it can even happen.'

'You really believe that?' I'm looking over to where Ma's sat at the centre of a group of young men and women, holding forth. They're giving it their best nods and grins, though no word of hers do they understand.

'Do I believe it?' says Nisha. 'Not really, that's why it's a dream.'

'Is this all you dream of, Khaufpur, the struggle?'

'You don't understand,' she says, 'I want it to end. I don't want to spend my whole life fighting against the Kampani.'

'Suppose it ends, what will you do?'

Nisha sighs and says, 'I'd like to have kids, but I told Zafar, I don't want our children growing up here. The poison in Khaufpur's not only in the soil and water, it's in people's hearts. Zafar and me, we've promised each other that the day we win, when there's justice and no more need for us, we'll leave this city. Animal, have you ever seen the coast near Ratnagiri? Zafar says it's a really peaceful place. We would live in a little house by the sea, we'd grow vegetables and have lots of children.'

'Name one after me.' It's the first I've heard of this plan of theirs, with what jealousy it fills me.

'Whoever heard of a kid called Animal?' she teases.

'There's only one Animal.'

'That there is. There's no one like you, you are such a dear friend. You would come too, to Ratnagiri. We'd be a group of friends. We'd get some land and build four or five houses. Zafar will write his poetry, and books too, he wants to write books. I will teach all our children, and yours, and local kids too. And what will you do?' she asks me.

O my crazy heart.

'I've a yen to go fishing. In one of those black canoes with an outrigger. All day long I will float and fish on a silvery river, at night I will drink toddy and sleep under the palms and wake to watch the sun rise over the sea.'

'Idiot, on that sea the sun does not rise, it sets.' She throws more pebbles into the non-silvery Bewardi. 'Okay, your turn, what's your dream?'

'Elli thinks she can maybe cure me.'

'Ah, I see,' she says. 'Yes, of course. I should have guessed.' She puts her arm round my shoulders, hugs my head to her. 'I hope she can cure you, darling.'

My heart, O my heart, I think it will explode.

'My god how could he? Has he gone mad?' exclaims Nisha. My head is still hugged tight to her, beyond the blurry swell of her bosom something extraordinary comes into view.

Bhoora Khan's just pulled up in a cloud of dust. There's his auto standing by the bhutt-bhutt-pig. Out gets Bhoora, reaches in the back, he's carrying the gramophone mashin. Out gets pandit Somraj, holding the black records older than anyone here alive. But what's this? I catch a flash of blue now emerging. From the hubbub where the group is gathered, they too can't believe their eyes. Merde à la puissance treize, it's Elli. Stranger still, she's walking alongside pandit Somraj. More bizarre's that he's introducing her to people, 'Please meet my neighbour Doctor Barber.'

'Oh god,' groans Nisha, 'my father has gone mad.'

No one knows why this is happening but it's Somraj who's brought her, and he's a man to be respected so they're all greeting her with polite smiles, neatly folded hands, while their minds are gabbling like geese.

'How could he invite that woman to our picnic? After all those dramatics?' says Nisha into my still-clamped, much-enjoying ear. Thudding, her heart's.

'Maybe he felt sorry for her.' But it's not that, I know. I'm remembering pandit Somraj's embarrassment when Elli challenged him in his own music room. He hates unfairness, he hated having to lie. Or maybe this is his way of showing Zafar who's really boss. That too, Nisha would not like.

Well, Eyes, you can imagine that after Pandit Somraj plays this stroke there isn't much carefree chat at the picnic, everyone's watching what they say. All are pretending things are normal, all know they are not. Zafar has gone over to talk to Somraj and Elli, the three of them are together. I wish I could hear what's being said, but it doesn't look like anyone's getting upset, except Nisha. 'I guess it's brave of him to ask her,' she says, making no move to join that group.

'Plus brave of her to come,' says I.

After a short time Elli spots me with Nisha and comes over, smiling, but Nisha gets up and walks past her without a word.

'How come?' I ask, when lund-pasanda number two takes the place of lund-pasanda the first beside me on the river bank.

Says Elli doctress, 'He is a most unusual man, is your Pandit Somraj. This morning he came over the road. Said the neighbours were having a picnic, I should come. I apologised for yelling at him that time in his house, but for the other things I would not apologise. He said he perfectly understood, in my position he would have done the same. Then he said that the picnic was just a social thing, it would be helpful for me to get to know people.'

'And Zafar, what was he talking to you about?'

'Wait, I haven't finished. Then Somraj says, "We are on opposite sides, but does it mean we should be enemies? We are both musicians. I have often heard you play your piano." "Yes," I said, "And every time you tried to drown it out." He protested that it wasn't so, that he and everyone else thought it was the other way round, I had been trying to drown his music.'

'Surely not!' says I, who'd realised this but said nothing to either side.

'I said I certainly had not been trying to do any such thing to which he made the weirdest reply. He said, "In any case it did not bother me, there was a certain beauty in the clashing of our musics." All this time he was totally solemn, then that grim face of his broke apart in a grin, he said, "As you know, I am that unusual person who finds music in the croaking of frogs."'

'Oh baba, what a fun!' says I, unable to guess what's coming next from either of these two.

'So then, if you please, he asks if I will play the piano for him . . .'

'Animal!' there's a shout. 'Come here and translate what Ma's saying.' The old lady is surrounded by a group of young Khaufpuris. Flapping her hands, she's, and rattling away in français about angels and abîmes.

'Is this Ma Franci?' asks Elli. 'I'd like to meet her.'

The group around Ma, seeing us approach, falls silent, but at least there are polite nods and smiles. For Somraj's benefit everyone is acting.

'Ma, ici Elli doctress,' I tell her in français. 'She speaks human.'

'So you're the famous doctress,' says Ma. 'How nice that you don't babble like an imbecile. I hope you can do something for this stony hearted lot. Not that there's much point, seeing there's no time left.'

'Time left for what?' asks Elli in français.

'For the world and all in it,' says Ma, gazing at Elli with milky blue eyes. 'That's why I wouldn't let them take me away, they keep trying you know.'

Elli looks mystified, so I've told the story of how she escaped Père Bernard dressed in a burqa.

'Clever,' says Elli, 'That's a trick I'll have to remember.'

Ma gives a witch-like cackle. 'Just wish I'd been there to see his face.'

Later, after all have well-kebabed and biryani'd themselves, chai drunk, sweets eaten, Zafar says we will sit in a circle on the grass and each shall tell a story, which must be about their own life. Some good yarns are then floated, a man who believes in alchemy, he's wasted a lot of money trying to make gold, describes how a chap he knows will go to the burning ghat and by tantra mantra hocus pokery plus some flour scattered cause a spirit to rise up from a corpse, it will do whatever he says, if he wants it to kill someone it will do that.

When comes Chunaram's turn, people begin demanding his well known stories, such as Motiyari the seed-sucking cobra, or else Maggot Man, which in addition to Ninefingers he's called because he knows the use of maggots to clean wounds, others demand the tale of how he tore off his little finger.

Says Zafar, 'Since we are not able to agree, plus we've heard these stories before, let the next tale be narrated by Elli doctress.'

So Elli stands up. 'I know that many people are wondering where I came from and why I came here,' she says. 'I will tell why I became a doctor.'

Eyes, near as I can recall, plus taking full help of my voices, here is Elli's story. Some of it I do not understand, I will just say what I hear in my head.

'The world is made of promises,' my father said. I was fourteen years old and didn't understand. He said, 'Think of everyday things. Mail gets delivered. Farmers grow crops. The stores take our dollars, each bill says "This note is legal tender for all debts, public and private," which means, you've done a good thing for someone, I promise you something equally good in return.'

I said, 'But that's people. The world's also rock and water and trees.'

'Rocks keep their promises. They behave like rocks. Water boils at one hundred degrees. The sea rises and falls, that's the sea and the moon keeping their own kind of promises. To have the world work for you, you've got to make your own promises right back.'

'People break promises,' I said bitterly. A boy I liked had asked me to a school dance then at the last minute decided he'd rather take another girl.

'This isn't about other people, Elli. There's a satisfaction in keeping your word that no one and nothing can take away from you.'

We were living in the town of Coatesville, Pennsylvania. It was a steel town and my father worked at the mill. I had no idea about the actual job he did until years later when I was a junior doctor at the local veterans' hospital. I was talking to a man who'd quit his job at the steel mill. He couldn't stand the din. 'Not noise. Particular noises.' He described explosions of water heewhacking to steam as it hit red metal at two thousand degrees, a crane that sang like a helicopter turbine, a deep-thumping compressor that reminded him of the whup-whup-whup of Hueys coming in low over jungle. 'I don't want those memories in my head every day.' Well, I was a child when the Vietnam war ended, I found it hard to imagine an ordeal so bad that twenty years couldn't heal it, but this man's hands were shaking as he spoke. He was my dad's age, I wondered if they knew each other.

'Harry Barber? Sure I do.'

Which is how I learned what my father's job was. Forty feet below the main control floor, among furnaces that roared like volcanoes, was a tin shack on whose door someone had chalked HELL HOLE.

'Down there,' said my dad's friend, 'it's so hot it can burn the hairs right out of your nose. There's steel plates, glowing red as the devil's eye, going by on a roller belt. Water's spraying on them but it bangs off, boom! boom! boom! like a stick of bombs. Your dad's job is to step outside of the hell hole and check the plate. Is it good and flat or does it need more rolling? He's got on fireproof gear and a face guard and he's holding four-foot long calipers, even so he has only four seconds per sheet. Thirty seconds out there and protection or no, your skin is going to start blistering. One slip, you're history.'

It was a job for a skilled man with plenty of guts and a steady hand and my father was proud of it. 'We built Amrika,' he used to tell me. 'We made the steel for the Walt Whitman Bridge and the World Trade Center.'

Elli pauses and looks around as if expecting a question or a comment, but all are silent, waiting for her next words.

'The world is made of promises.' It's all very well to say such things, but noble ideas don't dull pain, not when you're a teenager and people snigger and make jokes behind your back. When my mother Martha was found wandering the town in her night-clothes, my dad had to be called away from his work at the steel mill, I got home to find him sitting with

201

his head in his hands, for the first time ever I saw him cry. My mother was ill with a sickness that affected her mind. There'd be times when she wouldn't know who she was, who we were. One day, on my mother's arm I found red marks, they could only have been made by a man's strong fingers. My father's. The realisation that he'd been momentarily cruel filled me with anger, but not against him. I was angry with my poor mother, whose illness had caused him to lose self-control, also I was angry with myself because I could do nothing to help either of them. In my shame I remembered reading about a doctor who had gone to Africa, he worked among pygmy women who gave birth to the planet's tiniest babies, two small discs of coconut outlined in milk, for some reason that's how I thought of them, I decided I would become a doctor. 'To be able to help. To have the power to help.' I became a doctor to save not my mother, but my father.

Before Martha became ill we rented a small house with a view across the railroad tracks to the grey steel mill where my father worked. When he realised that my mother's health would not improve, this was after she'd gone running round town in her underwear, my father decided that she needed a change. He'd take her away to somewhere with trees and fields, where a person could breathe. He could not afford to buy a house, so he built one. I helped him. It was a timber frame house in a small development a few miles out of town. It stood in an acre of land and was constructed in what was locally called 'ranch style', all on one floor, spread out. More prosperous people built 'colonial style', which was two stories, one above the other. My father began the house during the winter, working weekends. When days grew longer he'd return from his job to the little house in C'ville, as we locals called it, and we'd drive in his beat-up old car out to the property. The neighbours came over and helped us raise the frames. My dad climbed a ladder, he sawed and hammered. I climbed nearly to the top and held the nails and handed up tools as needed. He worked late, those summer nights, nine, ten, till the last light was gone from the west. Often he'd carry on by lamplight. When the house was done he landscaped the yard and planted trees. He put in rhododendrons and azaleas, a willow, a mimosa near the house, evergreen trees round the lawn. He was tireless. Whatever the difficulty, he never gave up.

'You're a hero,' I thought, loving my dad, 'you made our house.'

The day it was finished, we took Martha out to see the new house. She clapped her hands at the sight of its neat white boards, blue-painted windows. Her illness seemed to fade away, as if the demons feeding on her brain could not survive out of sight and sound and smell of the steel mill. 'How I do love this place,' Martha said.

This house of my childhood stood on land that once had been fields. The backyard was ridged by generations of ploughs. Two homes away was a small farm that raised horses and if the wind was right it brought sweet, rich gusts of manure. Of the old forest there still remained patches of woodland, mainly maples and oaks. Honeysuckle, wild raspberries and blackberries climbed on the fences. At night, the stars were brilliant, you could hear frogs and crickets, and the wind running like a river in the trees.

'Oh my, just look at all the little birds!' What Martha loved best about the new place was the wilderness all round, but one day I found her distraught because one of the songbirds was dead. 'A hawk got it. I hate them, they are so cruel.' A pair of red-tailed hawks were soaring overhead. Two days later Martha said, 'I love the hawks, they are so beautiful.'

I still recall the dismay I felt that my mother's illness could not be cured either by prayer, or by my own force of will and sincerity of purpose. After this I fell out with god, we went our separate ways, he to demonstrate his strange way of loving human beings, while for me began the long process of learning how to heal their broken bodies and minds.

After hearing this story many people go up to Elli doctress to say how sorry they are to hear of her mother's illness, they hope she has recovered, what a truly wonderful thing to be a doctor, etc.

It's Chunaram, he's come up and asked about promises, how come they're so important. Elli says, 'I mean that things work when we keep our promises to each other and to ourselves, when we don't keep our promises, things fall apart.' Some folk, including Zafar, are nodding, as for me, I'm thinking that things couldn't be better for Chunaram who's hardly kept a promise in his life.

Last of all's come Pandit Somraj. Says he, 'We come from different worlds. Yours is made of promises, mine of music. I wonder if the two are as far apart as they seem.'

'You know what,' Elli says to me afterwards, 'I think this is pandit Somraj's way of making peace. Now at last people will come.'

But next morning, when she opens the doors, the street is still empty.

I have nine days to live, for tonight there's no moon in the sky, it's the first night of Muharram. The ninth night is Ashara Mubarak, the night of the fire walk, the night I will surely die.

Never have I been more scared, I've been dreaming of those cruel coals, the fire pit's no fake. In past years I've watched men with leather bellows blow air onto the fire until the coals glow white. In my dreams I walk onto them and my hands burst into flames, I fall and I'm all burned up.

The fire is part of Muharram here in Khaufpur and will always be, because it's the heat of the desert where the Prophet's grandson, Hazrat Imam Hussein was martyred.

Everyone in Khaufpur knows the story of Iman Hussein. How many times have I heard it from the mouth of old Hanif Ali, he'll rock back on his heels and close his eyes, the cataracts that stop him seeing dissolve away, he's seeing the world of a thousand years ago. 'What are these red tulips that bloom in the desert? In Karbala that dreadful place, I see Hussein, grandson of the Prophet, upon whom be peace. Tired he is and thirsty, and all around his companions lie fallen. Alone he defies Yazid the tyrant and his thirty-three thousand men, better it is to die with dignity than to live a humiliating life.'

A great hero, was Hussein, to defy such odds, to stick up for what he believed in, that kind of courage I admire, but do not share.

Even Zafar, who refuses to believe in god, says we must all be like Hussein who never gave up and refused to be cowed by the evil powers that rule this world. When he says this I know he is thinking of the Kampani and its friends who rule countries and cities, who have guns and soldiers and bombs and all the money in all the banks of the world, and that pitted against them he sees us, the people of the abyss, Ma Franci's

205

people of the Apokalis, he tells us that we will win, because we are armed with the invincible power of nothing.

Nine more days. I'll never walk upright. I'll never again hear Nisha sing, for in Somraj's house out of respect for the neighbours the singing and sounds have stopped, for the rest of my life there'll be silence. I'll never marry Nisha. I'll never marry anyone. I'll never know what it is like to fuck.

Nine days to do everything I want to do in my life. I've caught Zafar aside, 'Zafar brother, there's something I must do before I die, will you help me?'

'Say, brother. What is it?' he asks kindly.

'I would like to ride on a motorbike at one hundred miles per hour.'

He strokes his beard. 'Hmm, on roads like ours, could be deadly.'

'In nine days I will be dead anyway.'

'Why will you die, you fool?' he asks, laughing.

'Because of my bet with Farouq. I have to cross that fire, I swear in my mind it burns like the pit of hell itself.'

'First, there's no such place as hell,' says he. 'Second, you won't walk.'

'That I will. I'm not backing down.'

Farouq is also counting, he comes to Chunaram's looking for me, I'm sitting with Zafar and others.

'Eight more days, Animal, until the fire.'

'I'm ready,' says I, meaning I am ready to die.

'Better get a religion quick,' says Farouq. He says that if I reform, become a Muslim, and lead a good life, I'll get to paradise. So I look at him and ask does his religion not forbid him to smoke and drink, plus what of his visits to those houses in the old city?

'You're just jealous,' he says, 'because no girl wants to do it with you.' But he's scowling, so I know I've scored a hit.

I tell him that Ma Franci also talks of heaven to me. 'Isa-miyañ loves you as you are, your soul is as precious to him as anyone's. Take him to

206

your heart and you'll be saved from hell.' I replied that I deserve to be more precious than anyone else because I've already been to hell.

'Wah, wah,' says Zafar. 'Sixer.'

'Heaven and hell forget, we're stuck on this earth,' says Chunaram, who also believes in life after death, but of a different kind. Chunaram says I should be a Hindu because of all I've suffered in this life, I'm sure to get a better deal next time round, more than likely be a prince or politician or something. Trouble with that way of looking at things is by the same logic my situation is the result of evil things I did in my past lives, some people do look at me as if they're wondering how many children I murdered last time round.

Whoever I talk to, seems the main reason for having a religion is to cheat death and live again, here or in heaven, wherever. Well, I don't want another life, thanks, not if it's anything like this one.

'You wouldn't be crooked in paradise,' says Farouq. 'You'd be whole and upright.'

Well, this is also what Ma says about heaven but I don't believe a word. If religions were true there wouldn't be so many of them, there'd be just one for everyone. Of course all say theirs is the only real one, fools can't see this makes even less sense. Suppose people talked of beauty in the same way, how foolish would they sound? Times like this I feel sorry for god's being torn to pieces like meat fought over by dogs. I, me, mine, that's what religions are, where's room in them for god?

I hate to praise Zafar but he is the only one who has a sensible view because not only doesn't he believe in god, he thinks religion is a bad thing. The idea of heaven was invented by the rich and powerful to keep the poor from rebelling. Zafar will dip in his pocket for a beggar but never gives to those who ask in the name of god. He says if he believes in anything it's humanity, that deep down all people are good. I don't know where he gets that idea, because there's no evidence for it in the world.

Zafar and Farouq have this in common, I should cease thinking of myself as an animal and become human again. Well, maybe if I'm cured, otherwise I'll never do it and here's why, if I agree to be a human being, I'll also have to agree that I'm wrong-shaped and abnormal. But let me be a quatre pattes animal, four-footed and free, then I am whole, my own proper shape, just a different kind of animal from say Jara, or a cow, or a camel.

Farouq says if I want to end up in paradise I'll have to turn human.

'Why so, moosh?'

'Paradise is for humans, not for animals.'

'What harm do animals do?'

'Not a question of harm. Do you expect that every ant that gets crushed under a villager's horny heel goes to paradise?'

'Don't see why not. If they have flowers and birds in paradise why not ants? Isn't there room?'

'There are no insects in paradise,' says Farouq.

Zafar hearing this remarks that in that case the Kampani's dead factory must be a kind of paradise because it too has no insects.

'Wait!' I say. 'Didn't you tell me that in paradise people will have fine couches surrounded by precious silks and carpets?'

'Surely,' says Farouq.

'And fountains and rivers will come gushing forth and there will be fruit orchards as far as the eye can see?'

Farouq nods, I have got him now.

'And wine, milk and honey will flow?'

'They will.'

'How can there be honey without bees?'

So Zafar starts laughing and says Farouq must admit I have a point.

'Leave bees out of it,' says Farouq, aggrieved as if his mother had been a bee and was being insulted here. 'Animal is not a bee. What kind of animal are you, anyway?' he demands. 'You've never said what sort you are.'

Well, Farouq thinks he has turned the tables here, because like I just said I am not a cat, or a dog like Jara, nor camel, goat, leopard, bear etc.

'I'm the only one there is of this type.'

208

'You look a lot like a human being to me,' Farouq says.

'Of course he's a human being,' says Zafar.

'You pretend to be an animal so you can escape the responsibility of being human,' Farouq carries on. 'No joke, yaar. You run wild, do crazy things and get away with it because you're always whining, I'm an animal, I'm an animal.'

'And I'm an animal, why?' I retorted. 'By my choice or because others named me Animal and treated me like one?'

'You're well enough looked after now,' says Farouq. 'We are your friends. Don't we care about you? All this bitterness, it's in your own mind. To be accepted as a human being, you must behave like one. The more human you act, the more human you'll be.' He spoils the effect of this decent speech by adding with a smirk, 'Four-foot cunt.'

At this Zafar looks down in the mouth because he's not in favour of making a mockery of those who are otherwise. He says this discussion has gone far enough and that Farouq is a bad loser and also that we are both wrong, because there is a heaven, but in the words of the poet,

Agar firdaus bar roo-e zameen ast,
Hameen ast-o hameen ast-o hameen ast.

'If there is a paradise on earth, it is this, it is this, it is this!'

I daren't tell Ma of my problem, first because she will fret, second she is already mad as a leper's thumbnail.

Six nights to go, she leans towards me with a crafty smile and whispers, 'The angels, they're already here. They're here among us in the Kingdom of the Poor.'

'What kind of angels?'

She gives me a look, like it's me who's crazy. 'The usual sort, of course.'

Well, it is no good arguing, plus I don't want to. There is little enough pleasure to be had from life, if someone is getting a kick from seeing angels, then good for them.

'These angels, you say they're here in the Nutcracker?'

209

'Of course. I heard a trumpet this morning, before it was light.'

'Would be the Pushpak Express.'

'Always some facile explanation,' says she. 'There was another blast not ten minutes later.'

'Hooter at Khaufpur Heavy Electricals factory.'

'Faith is evidence of the unseen.'

'No doubt, no doubt.'

'Listen Animal, I have seen the angels burning inside people's bodies. I'll look at someone and suddenly I'll see the outlines of this other bright being locked inside. Angels I call them, although some may be demons, but they're all alike trapped in this flesh, which for spirits is like being buried in mud. Only their eyes look out and they are so pitiful.'

'Is there an angel trapped inside me?'

She takes a look. 'Can't see one, but it might be sleeping, or doing some other business.'

'Very true.' At such times there is nothing to do but humour her.

'We live in hell. You realise that? This is hell.'

'Yes Ma.'

'When you look at the smoky flames that pass for lamps around here, you can understand why I say we're living in hell.'

'Yup.'

'But that's not why I'm saying it,' she cackles. 'To be trapped in a human body, that is hell, if you happen to be an angel.'

I can sympathise with these angels. To be trapped in an animal body is hell, if you dream of being human.

I don't want to die. Farouq says the fire can be crossed safely only by those whose hearts are true, which mine certainly isn't, but if I back down he'll never let me forget it. In my dreams I find amazing ways to survive the fire. I leap across in one bound. A downpour comes and puts out the flames. An angelic hand plucks the back of my kakadus and hoicks me clear.

210

So scared am I, next day I ask Elli doctress what can be done to protect hands against the touch of red hot things. My hands are hard and horny because they're also feet, but I feel they will not survive pressing on coals.

'What on earth's going on?' she demands. I end up telling her about Farouq, how we have a bet.

'Of course you are not to do it,' says she, same as everyone else. I tell her I've never yet seen anyone fall in the fire, or burn, plus Somraj told us that he had once done it as a young man.

'How can that be, Somraj is a Hindu?'

'And I'm an animal. So?' See, Eyes, in Khaufpur it's the custom for people of all faiths to go to this famous Yar-yilaki fire walk and many have also walked across the coals. 'Somraj pandit said he didn't feel the fire, it was like walking on cool water.'

'Think I'll have a word with that Somraj,' says Elli with a grim set to her face, and I feel sorry for the poor pandit, he has already had it in the ear from Nisha, who went cross-eyed fishguts when I told her the same thing.

Elli looks at me, 'My dad risked his life near red hot metal, but he was doing it for his family, what are you doing it for?'

'I am doing it for my honour.'

But this is nonsense, because if I cared for nothing but honour, which is a kind of heart's truth, I wouldn't be afraid.

Eyes, the real reason's Nisha, so jealous have I been since learning of her and Zafar's Ratnagiri plus children plans. I want to impress her, also I want her to keep worrying about me and realise what she will miss if I am roasted.

'Animal, you are a total fool, will a doctor be there?' Seeing I don't know the answer, she says that if I insist on going ahead, then she herself will come and wait by the fire, in case I, or anyone else, should need her.

'Elli, you can't go, it's impossible.' She's a foreigner plus she's Amrikan, how should she go to a masjid at this holy time, when her country is bombing Afghanistan which is right next door to the Yar-yilaqi homeland, plus many relatives of our own Yar-yilaqis are living there? She says nothing, but knowing Elli by now I should have realised, she's like me, no one can stop her doing what she wants.

This conversation happens in her office where's sitting the Khã-in-the-Jar, but today he keeps his mouths shut, just floats regarding me with a pissed-off expression.

'What? You, parapagus sahib. Have you nothing to say?'

'What can I say?' replies the Khã, crossly. 'You are not going to do this. You know it, you're just a posturing wanker. Bloody, it's your friend the Khã who needs to burn, but do you think of him? You don't. With you Animal, it's all me, me, me.'

'Zafar brother, what speed is it now?'

'Sixty-seven.'

'Now, Zafar bhai? What speed?'

'Eighty-nine,' comes the reply torn away by wind.

It's three in the morning, we are roaring from the lake up towards the CM's house, this is the widest road in Khaufpur and the smoothest.

'What speed?'

'One hundred and two.'

The world is speeding by so fast, only time is flying faster, it is the eighth night of Muharram, tomorrow I meet the fire.

The house blurs past, already we're at the big hotel Jehannum. On the way back down, Zafar chuckles to see lights have come on in the CM's windows.

'What speed, Zafar brother?'

'Thirty-two,' says he. 'Staying that way.'

Zafar brother, I didn't say this, if I did not hate you I would love you, you are an unusual human being.

The night of Ashara Mubarak, I've gone to Somraj's house to meet Bhoora, he's going to take me to the masjid in the Chowk.

Out of her clinic steps Elli. She's wearing a scarf on her head and a long-sleeved shirt, long to the knees over loose pyjamas. The outfit is dark blue, beads all over are sparkling, it sets off her dark hair. Except for her blue eyes, 'like holes through which you see the sky', this is what an old woman in the Nutcracker had told her, except for these eyes which could be hidden behind a veil, almost she looks like an Indian woman, her skin is browned by the sun almost as dark as Nisha's, but it won't be disguise enough.

'Elli, you cannot come.'

'Oh, I am not going with you,' she says. A figure dressed in immaculate white is exiting Somraj's house. 'Someone else has kindly offered to take me.'

When I reach Chowk, it's thronged with every kind of Khaufpuri. The Yar-yilaqis are out in force, Muslims of other communities, also Hindus and Sikhs, have come to watch the firewalk, some to join in. Of Elli and Somraj no sign there's, but near where the pots-and-pans street joins the cloth bazaar I see Nisha with Zafar, they are talking quietly. I creep up until I am right behind them, they don't notice so absorbed're they. Nisha's saying, '. . . left her husband in Amrika.' This much I catch, but not Zafar's reply. Nisha then says, 'He's not himself,' after which there's silence until Zafar puts his arm round her waist. Some kind of growl I must have given for Nisha whirls round and starts gabbling, 'You wretched boy, so there you are, don't you realise you're driving everyone crazy with worry? No way are you doing this stupid thing, Zafar has already told Farouq, now they will not let you. No, don't speak, don't say a thing. I am so angry with you. Why are you spying on us? Don't you realise what you've done, with all your antics? If you want to spy, go find my dad and the Amrikan, then let's all go home.'

How I hate that 'us, us, us.' Nisha can have no idea how painful are such words or she'd never say them. I've given every hint I can to Nisha that I love her and would like her to be with me. What more's to do? You tell me. Give up the battle? What chance had I against Zafar? I know what you're thinking, Eyes, that I should have accepted defeat gracefully and wished Nisha joy, but I just couldn't do it. I never said I was a good person. How can I explain the rush of feelings whenever I saw her, how my heart seemed to jump when she entered a room? All I know is that I loved to be near her. I wanted to touch her. I wanted to stroke her hair and press my lips on her closed eyelids and tell her that I would always be there to take care of her.

Eyes, I know that such talk is the sorriest kind of bullshit. What to do? A creature in love, its brain is fully fucked.

The lanes of Chowk are so narrow, in most places you'll hardly get two fat buggers past one another, it's a total jostle from the alley of the tin-smiths to the gulab-baadi where strings of white jasmine buds hang down and the stalls are heaped with marigolds and roses. Near the masjid, all kinds of rugs and carpets are hung up for sale, plus saris and cloths. Here I've at last spotted Somraj and Elli and commenced navigating towards them through groves of legs, trying not to get my hands trodden on.

'Bastard,' says a loud voice, 'You're saved, you know that? Zafar has said you are not allowed to do it.'

It's Farouq, wearing a black headband, barefoot, ready for the fire-walk.

'I can still watch you make a fool of yourself.'

'If you misbehave I'll throw you on the fire myself.'

'Fuck off. You love me.' With any luck Farouq will fall on the coals and burn to death like a big black moth. I am not going to tell Farouq that Zafar or no, nothing is going to stop me keeping my word.

We've exchanged a few more insults but his hearts's not really in it, he moves off and I've slunk closer to Somraj and Elli, who are slowly strolling towards the masjid. She's looking around with a kind of eager-ness, like a child, I'm hanging a few paces behind, struggling to hear.

'. . . never been outside Amrika,' it's Elli speaking. 'He would not believe this place. These rugs, they look like if you sat on one it might fly away with you.'

214

'They are of a good quality.'

'Oh really!' she says laughing. 'If I said I wanted a magic rug, I do believe you'd take me looking for one.'

'But of course, it's my duty.'

'Your duty?'

'You are a stranger in my city. I am your host.'

'Is it just duty?'

'Also my pleasure.' Said without the smallest smile.

'That's a bit more friendly,' says she and her next words are lost, but she's laughing. The mela intervenes, next thing I hear is, 'After we were married I came here with my wife, she chose a rug for the house.'

Elli asks, 'You miss her?'

I didn't hear his reply, if he made one. Probably he didn't speak because after a bit she says, 'Sorry, I didn't mean to pry.'

Now he turns and gives her a smile. One of those rare smiles of his. 'No, no, not at all. I was listening to the music.'

'You sure? I haven't upset you?'

'No, no,' says he. 'Definitely you have not upset me. Listen, how so many musics are running together.'

From all sides are blaring chants and laments for Imam Hussein. Every doorway seems to pour out a different song, it's like walking through dense clouds of music. Marsiyas, these laments called, there are dozens of them. Some are in Hindi, others in Arabic and Persian, but whichever language they are in you catch the same meaning, At least I do. It's like every good thing in the world is dying and the people of the world, they see but do not care. The mourners are defiant, never will they give in to evil powers. For me, who am neither Muslim, nor Hindu, nor Isayi, this is a music that could also comfort Isa miyañ dying on the cross or go with Sri Rama into exile from Ayodhya. It's all one to me, what I like is the defiance, I like it a lot. Somraj does too, but for different reasons, his head is turning this way and that, as if the sounds are butterflies and his ears are nets.

We are near the big masjid and the marsiya from inside is coming out full blast through big speakers.

Standing alone on the field of battle,
O Hussein, never shall I forget Hussein!
showing no fear, the zibh-e-Azeem of Abu Abdillah
Ya Hussein! Ya Hussein! Ya Hussein!

'You're listening always,' says Elli. 'How do you distinguish the sounds?'

'I don't distinguish,' replies Somraj. 'I try to hear it all together, all at once. When songs clash, as you called it, sometimes out of that comes a new music, something completely fresh.'

'Like with lives,' she says.

The fire is burning in a big courtyard outside the masjid. Tele screens all around show those like me who cannot see directly. The coals are laid in a large square pit raised a few feet, surrounded by a platform on which are the guys with big leather bellows making it hotter still. Every time the men heave the bellows, sparks fly sideways, the coals glow with anger. Already fierce red they're, and must get hotter still. The bellows groan, jets of air turn the coals white with fury. Long ago I've lost track of Somraj and Elli. Now I have to be devious, I am going to do this fire walk and no one shall forbid me. It is to my advantage that I am low to the ground, people are not used to talking at knee level. The crowd is thick with young men wearing black headbands, they are forming into lines which move slowly forward converging, joining, like streams becoming a river, heading for the platform where the steps lead up to the fire.

On the ground I find a black scarf where someone has dropped it and with some difficulty tie it one-handed around my head. I have no black shirt to wear, nothing else in fact except my kakadus. I've joined a line of guys who have begun moving towards the inferno. Their legs are like trees before and behind me, their feet are wet where they have dipped them in

216

water, they leave damp footprints on the paving, I did not know to do this so I place my hands and feet in patches of moisture, hoping to pick up some. The others are singing loudly the words of the lament.

now comes night to roof the dark horizon,
the black standard of the People of the Cloak
slides from the shoulder of ever-revolving time,
pitiless heart, let your sigh of sorrow scorch the sky!
tongue, it is time to mourn, eye, it is time to weep!

We are coming near the steps and men around me are flinching as they feel gusts of heat from the fire, still they move steadily forward, me with them, we are going up the steps. No one has stopped me, nor said a thing.

It's like my mind is detached and floating above, I see myself mounting the stair on fours, my hands on the wooden planks, splashes of heat catch my face, beyond the topmost step is a ledge of wood, then the brick wall of the pit, from then on it's fire. I can now hear the the fire, it does not crackle or roar, it's hissing like some giant cobra stirred up and enraged, if had anyone to say prayers to, I would say them, but I haven't, so I've started under my breath singing a different song.

I am an animal fierce and free
pure in heart I'll never be
but not this way shall my life end
this fire itself shall be my friend

The man ahead of me steps off into the fire. Little clouds of smoke squirt from under his feet as he runs, where he has stepped the coals are dark for an instant. A voice in my head says 'You shall cross,' and then my fear is gone, I'm filled with a certainty that I will do this and live, I will run across like that man did, quicker than he, I will live.

'Hey, who's this?' A burly Yar-yilaqi guy is looking down at me. A black band is round his head, his black shirt's unbuttoned, something of gold is gleaming in the hairs of his chest.

217

'I'm doing the fire,' I mumble.

'No you are not, get him out of here.' So I'm bundled back down the stairs and into the crowd.

Two feet appear under my nose, toes pointing right at me. It's Farouq. 'Ha ha, enjoying yourself, Animal? What can you see?'

'Nothing. I would have done the firewalk. They stopped me.'

'Yes, I know,' he sniggers. 'Want to watch me do it?'

'Would give me a laugh if you catch fire.' I retort. Bitter disappointed I'm that I was stopped. I could have done it.

Without a word the bugger beckons to one of his chums and suddenly I'm hoisted off the ground and into the air.

'If I burn, you burn,' he says with a weird laugh, like he's high, next thing I'm arsed to his shoulders which is exactly the last place I expect to be.

'Pray I don't drop you,' says he from below.

It's crossed my mind that Farouq's not joking, he plans for me a terrible end. Or maybe he'll trip and, oh, Animal le pauvre's short, awful life ends in a public cremation. Now again I'm terrified.

Way above the heads of the crowd, the fire's heat is fierce on my face. A little way off I spot Somraj and Elli. A couple of guys are looking at her in a not too comfortable way, but Zafar's there beside them with Nisha and the surliness turns to smiles flashing. Nisha looks round, our eyes meet. Fully amazed she's, to see me looking at her from a firewalker's shoulders. She tugs at her dad and points, so I've given a wave.

All wave back, except Elli. Elli's eyes are fixed on the pit of cokes being quickened by the bellows-men, strange eddies are playing under the red glow of the fire, her father in his hell hole, he had quietly faced such danger every day out for love of her.

Somraj is speaking in her ear, I think he's telling her the story of Hussein, but such is the hubbub in the place, the sound of the fire itself and above all the waves of chanting *Ya Hussein! Ya Hussein! Ya Hussein!* that she cannot hear much. Then Eyes, it comes into my head with perfect certainty what she is thinking. It's of a different kind of fire, that Somraj had breathed, which had scoured his lungs and taken away his singer's breath. What must it have been like, that inferno? *O who will speak now for the orphans?* She has heard so many stories of that night, so many accounts of that vast slaughter of innocents. *Who now will speak for the poor?* What must have been the terror of waking in the dead of night, blinded by acrid gas *who will protect these wretched ones* running out into the night gulping fumes that tore and burned your insides *where now will they find refuge* causing you to drown on dry land because your lungs have wept themselves full of fluid. *Ya Hussein! Ya Hussein! Ya Hussein!* That night had been cold, a night of bright stars *hear what harm the heavens have wrought* and all over the city, weddings were taking place for the astrologers had decreed it an auspicious time *a strange wedding for Hussein, the son of Ali* somehow they did not see the knot that fate had twisted *for they have dressed the bride and the groom* the threads of thousands of lives gathered together not in wedding clothes, but shrouds and severed, all at the same moment. *Ya Hussein! Ya Hussein! Ya Hussein!* Elli feels horror, also the failure of her imagination. *What music was played at this wedding?* She's unable to imagine the cries of the dying, of those who lost their families in the stampede of panicking people *the thirst tormented cries of men and women* whose children's hands had been ripped from theirs. One woman there was who, knowing that she was dying *instead of festive lamps, the house itself was torched* wrapped her newborn son in her shawl and laid him in a doorway hoping he'd be found *the colours used at this wedding were bloodstains* by someone who would love him. *Ya Hussein! Ya Hussein! Ya Hussein!* Elli's thinking that this woman was perhaps lucky not to have seen the furnace that melted her son's spine, the hammer-blows that beat his humanity out of him. She wants to give that boy back the gift of walking upright *the bride's gift was the groom's severed head* but as she thinks this she looks at Somraj and realises there is something she wants just as much *in which country may a bride expect such a gift* a gift for the sad, gentle man standing beside her *by God I swear, never will I wish to marry another* she would reach out and take his hand did she not fear he would be embarrassed, perhaps offended no, *not until I am covered and in the grave* how she yearns to give back Somraj the gift of his voice *Ya Hussein! Ya Hussein! Ya Hussein!*

The marble balconies that surround the courtyard of the fire are lined with women in dark robes. On this night most of them have pushed back their veils, their faces are lit from below, the glow softly rouges their cheeks *watching with unblindfolded eyes.* As I sway towards the fire on my strange two-legged steed, the men just ahead of us are placing their feet on the wooden steps *as the seventy-one rode off to die.* A thrill of excitement or dread goes through my body, the pitch of the chant rises.

Ya Hussein! Ya Hussein! Ya Hussein!

The black-robed Yar-yilaqi women raise their arms and bring them down hard on their chests *pierced by the spears of his enemies.* There are old women up there, and young pretty ones *trampled by the hooves of horses* I try to imagine Ma Franci in her black nun's dress among them, she would fit, lamenting Sanjo and the death of the world, with a grief as pure as these women mourning for their lost Imam *O Hussein! Never shall I forget Hussein!* How their arms all rise at the same instant, and all fall, thump! *Ya Hussein!* thump! *Ya Hussein!* thump! *Ya Hussein!*

We are so near the fire that my forehead is burning. Only a few paces more to where the steps lead up onto the platform. I'm perched high on Farouq's shoulders. *Swords drank, busy with slaughter.* Ahead of us men, and boys too, those with black headbands and some without, are climbing to the burning edge of the fire. *Corpses were scattered in the desert.* There are men on the sides, keeping well back from the edge of the pit, ready to help those who are going across. *Savage birds hovered overhead night and day.* A little ahead a man steps on to the coals, which are dancing with a bright heat. In four long strides he walks across. *Ya Hussein! Ya Hussein! Ya Hussein!* The second goes, and the third, and the next. *Paradise is theirs, they have gone to Paradise.* Helping hands pull them to safety on the far side. No one is left ahead of us. *They have become burned up in God.* I feel Farouq take a deep breath and tighten his grip of my legs. *Ya Hussein! Ya Hussein! Ya Hussein!*

As he steps out I open my mouth to warn him not to drop me but instead I'm bellowing with the rest

> now Shimr Maloon do what you do
> the blessed head kissed by Al Mustafa
> tormented by thirst as if the desert was in it,
> now lies there on the desert sand
> Ya Hussein! Ya Hussein! Ya Hussein!

The strangest thing happens to me. As the heat roars up around us I feel that I am floating above the sand of a baking desert which is shimmering with heat *he who was a shining light is murdered* my mouth is on fire with a burning thirst and my eyes are burning and the passages of my nose are burning where the fiery heat rushes in *murdered in Karbala and lies unburied* and all around there are crowds and commotion, people falling dead, and somewhere in the distance are the banners of the enemy, shaking with hatred for all that's good and I'm helpless and unable to prevent the terrible thing that's happened which is the murder of goodness and innocence and the victory of evil and in some part of my head there is a roaring noise like a great wind, fanning the flames, a voice in my head is saying l'injustice ramportera la victoire and I realise that we have gone across and that I have been dreaming Ma Franci's or rather Sanjo's dream of the end of the world.

Ya Hussein! Ya Hussein! Ya Hussein!

We are turning around. We are going back around. We will go over again. I begin to feel dizzy *I, Muhtasham, the beggar at your door.* Again it comes, the heat, the crimson wound, the fire is flowing, such colours are shifting in the coals. My head is doing spirals. I feel myself begin to slip from Farouq's back, sliding I'm *standing, empty, empty-handed, at the door of helplessness* falling and there is nothing now between me and the fire.

Let me die I'm thinking as I fall, I'll be happy. Everything in my life is swallowed up in that wish for oblivion. The fire itself as it jumps towards me has lost its ferocity, seems like a mild sunshine. Next thing I know I'm lying on a carpet inside the masjid, Farouq and others are bending over me.

'He's come to,' says one.

'Little idiot,' Farouq says. 'Picked your moment, didn't you? I'm halfway across and you let go from round my neck.'

'What happened? Did you drop me?'

'You fainted,' says this other Yar-yilaqi guy. 'You were lucky, if he hadn't danced and caught you, you'd have burned.'

'You caught me? You danced?'

'Thank me some other time,' says Farouq.

'Did you burn your feet?'

'No.'

'Fucking shame.'

'I should have let you die,' says he.

A big book of animals from the library Nisha borrowed once and she showed it to me, this book had pictures in of all the animals of India, bears and apes, wolves, deer of all kinds, rhino, tiger, lion, buffalo, you name it. There was cobra, king cobra, python, bloodsucker lizard, hoopoo, fish eagle, kite and crow, there was gharial crocodile, mahseer fish, hyena and jackal and dhole, which is a wild dog with round ears, but in all the book, in all of its hundreds of pages and pictures, there was no animal like me. Nisha said, 'That's because you are unique. Be proud of it.' But I just felt sad.

Why mention this now? Because two nights after the fire walk I'm up in the mango tree, higher than Elli's roof. Above the Little Bear's swinging by his tail, a few shapes are flitting that might be bats. No problem now is this tree, which had so fought me the first time I climbed it. By now I know its ways as if they were stairs, this knot that stumpy branch, twist here, pull up there, leaves above me black, the moon tonight's not yet risen. See, I have found a name for the animal I am, I'm the bat-eared ape that climbs only in the dark of night.

Elli and Somraj are sitting on the terrace, their faces are lit from the glow of an oil lamp. My bat ears are flapped forward to hear what's being said. She's telling him about her marriage. It seems she met her husband when she was studying medicine and he was learning law. They met many times before they fell in love, at friends' houses, at demonstrations against the war in Iraq which the Amrikans called desert storm. Much of her talk, which is Hindi-Inglis mixed, I don't follow. There are some things even a don for language can't explain. What does it mean 'students at pen state came out to support gay rights'? Appears these two were both idealistic idiots who thought that with law and medicine hand in hand they could change the world.

'He seemed so exciting,' says she. 'He'd been to Colombia and eaten fried ants and drank stuff which he said was like a cannon blasting the skull into fragments.'

'We have daru like that,' says Somraj, 'but I don't advise you to try it.'

'I was naive,' she says, 'I didn't realise people change easier than worlds.'

The shadows on his face change, so he must be smiling. What? More smiles? And here he is drinking whisky with Elli and not even disapproving. I cannot imagine him behaving like this with any other woman. Maybe it's because she's a foreigner. But Somraj really seems to like her. You can see it in the way he leans forward when she talks, you can tell he wants to hear. He wants to know everything about her.

After getting married, she says, she was working long days in a hospital, the husband was struggling to make it as a lawyer. They'd come home tired and flop in front of the tele. Forgotten their lofty schemes, they were becoming the sort of people they once despised. 'I mean,' she says, growing more passionate, 'the sort of people for whom the world's nothing more than a box of dancing illusions, whose ideas of what's important stop at the edges of their own self-interest.' Somraj nods. Well, there are plenty like that in Khaufpur.

'We were drifting to a place I did not want to be. I could foresee golfing weekends and evenings out with company wives, the whole hateful middle-class flapdoodle. I wanted nothing to do with it. I felt I was losing my life. If the marriage had been better in other ways I might have tried harder to save it. I'm ashamed to say I didn't.'

Moths are whirring round the lamp that sits between them. He is silent, thoughtful, bent forward like a statue. What did he know of marriage, whose own had lasted only three years before it was terminated by that night?

'This is when I thought of coming to Khaufpur. I would open a clinic. I would touch the real world. It was a completely unreasonable idea and I was sure he'd hate it. Instead he praised me for being noble. When I began taking Hindi lessons, he said it was a beautiful dream to have.'

'I am glad you had that dream.'

Oh please, Mr Somraj sir, let's not have you descending into slush. Any moment now they'll be holding hands and after that, who knows what? Of course it's why I am here, I'm waiting to see what they'll do, jamisponding has become my career. Will they kiss? Maybe even do *it?*

'I wish you'd let me treat you,' says Elli, after they have been silent a while. 'I hear you coughing at night.'

'You know I can't do that,' he says. 'How can I take your help for myself while others are still denied it?'

'Then make them come, reason with Zafar.'

'Be patient with us, Elli,' says Somraj. 'One day the patients will come.'

'That's what Zahreel Khan said,' she replies. 'Him I didn't believe, but somehow I believe it when I hear it from you.'

Once again the moment comes close for which I am waiting. Night has plunged Khaufpur into its peculiar blackout, beyond the small cloud of lamp light is a deep sky of stars. Somraj in his white garments looks like a headless ghost, his dark face and hair have vanished.

'Can you smell the flowers?' he asks, ending this new silence.

'The jasmine?' It's like both of them are relieved to change the subject.

'They are not simply jasmine,' says Somraj, 'they are raat-ki-rani, which means queen-of-the-night, the most powerful of all the jasmines.'

'Well, they certainly grow fast. They've climbed right up into the mango.' They glance up towards me, I nearly die of fright.

'I love the scent,' says Elli. 'It reminds me of the jasmines my mother grew in our house near the forest. The scent is shining white, just as patchouli is a deep red note. Do you ever think of scents that way?'

'It's intoxicating,' says Somraj. 'Like a woman's voice singing both high and sweet. A pure voice, yet the notes are grainy, diffused, glowing.'

Again a silence, seems to me they are gabbling just in order to reach these wordless moments when perhaps are thought things the tongue dares not utter.

'I am determined you shall sing again,' she says. Well, now she's blown it, touching that forbidden subject which never must be mentioned.

'Alas, I think not.' To my surprise Somraj's voice is gentle as before. 'The breath of a singer is not ordinary breath. My father could take a breath and hold it for two minutes and then exhale it smoothly for one minute more. At first I could not do that, I learned slowly. I'd draw a deep breath and then recite a verse without inhaling. I had to speak clearly and slowly. When I could do this, I was given a longer poem, and a longer one. It came slowly, my father would get impatient and say it was a pity that breath could not be dissolved in water and given to me in a glass.'

'Who knows what can be done?' cries Elli. 'I won't let you give up.'

'Breath is everything,' says Somraj. 'Sa can be sung in as many ways as there are ways of breathing. For a singer, breath is not just the life of the body but of the soul.'

This is the moment! She leans towards him, the lamp outlines her face in golden light, in her thoughts I hear a kind of confusion, all now depends on Somraj, does he see the effect he is having on this woman, has he recognised the effect she has on him? Surely now that dark gap between their heads will diminish, they will come so close that no longer will they have a choice. After that, anything could happen, a kiss, strokes, more, clothes off, him on her in the bed, oh I can just imagine her pale arms on his dark skin, but the gap does not diminish, Somraj is still as a statue, she settles back in her chair, and me, who've been imagining all kinds of things, it's my nerves which are jangling, aiiee, que j'ai vachement envie de tringler, as they say in the human tongue.

It's late when they stop talking. Somraj gets up to leave, she accompanies him down. After a few minutes she returns in her nightclothes. She's climbed into her bed, carefully tucked in the mosquito net all around, but looks like she's having difficulty getting to sleep. She tosses and turns and can't settle.

Now is the time for my aching creature to have its freedom. I peer at it in the dark, what a relentless monster, no peace does it give me, always it's demanding, demanding, in my hand it feels hot and stupid, swollen like a jackfruit. My beastly lund wants to be pointed at Elli, brute thinks it's a kind of magic to mark her as prey, who's in control here? I aim the fucking thing away. Big moths are flying in the tree, I'm thinking maybe I'll accidentally shoot down one of them, what a dismal way to die.

That very night Zafar fell ill. I'd taken a big risk increasing his medication. His risk, not mine. The poor guy has had an appalling time. Nisha tells me that while her father was over at Elli's, Zafar's mouth became dry, he complained that insects were crawling over him. After this his heart started blurring like a tabla player's fingers doing a fast solo. No way could he drive his motorbike. When Somraj got home from Elli's, he found Zafar burning up and babbling. Somraj wanted to call Elli, but Nisha said no. Zafar's heart had slowed to normal. They put him to bed, she sat with him most of the night.

All next day Zafar sleeps, by evening is feeling a little better, tells us of a dream he had in which he's flying above Khaufpur sitting on a plant stalk, and while he is high over the clouds a crow comes along and flies by his side and asks if he has the time. 'I am afraid not,' says Zafar, all polite, how irritating that he should display such perfect manners even to a worthless bird like a crow. 'You seem a decent sort,' comments the beady-eyed shit-eater, 'I will grant you three wishes.' Quick as a flash Zafar pours out his heart's deepest desires, 'The Kampani must return to Khaufpur, remove the poisons from its factory plus clean the soil and the water it has contaminated, it must pay for good medical treatment for the thousands of people whose health it has ruined, it must give better than one-cup-chai-per-day compensation, plus the Kampani bosses must come to Khaufpur and face the charges from which they have been running for so long and the court case against them should conclude.'

'Whoa,' says the crow, 'I make that at least seven wishes.'

Says Zafar, 'All these proceed from one wish, which is that simple natural justice should prevail.'

So the crow starts cawing with laughter. 'What a fool,' it chortles, 'to think that such a thing as justice is simple or natural. Why do you expect that the lawyers up at the Collector's office wear silly little wigs and funny collars? If justice were simple what need for fancy dress? Why do they charge so much? If there were such a thing as natural justice, wouldn't you be entitled to it, whether or not you could pay?'

'Undoubtedly you are right,' says Zafar, 'but a wish however foolish is still a wish, and that is my first one.'

Says the crow. 'Granting an impossible wish is even more foolish than wishing it. What is your second wish?'

Zafar without hesitation replies, 'My people are the poorest on the planet, those we fight against are the richest. We have nothing, they have it all. On our side there is hunger, on theirs greed with no purpose but to become greedier. Our people are so poor that thirty three thousand of them together could not afford one Amrikan lawyer, the Kampani can afford thirty-three thousand lawyers. So my second wish is that you go back to my first wish and make the impossible possible.'

'Impossible possible?,' caws the crow. 'This is more foolish than the first. And your third?'

Zafar thinks about this for a long time then he says, 'I would like to see the face of my enemy.'

'Look then,' says the bird.

As the crow says this, Zafar looks down and sees himself, a small figure standing alone on the shores of a sea that stretches up and away to the edge of the world, which begins to flash like a neon sign. Over the horizon appears a city of tall buildings. It grows taller, pushing above the ocean. It sprouts huge buildings like tusks in a pig's jaw. One building towers above them all, bleak, windowless, formed of grey concrete. The air around Zafar now starts to throb with pulses of purple and green light, a fierce fire howls in his bowels. The fire begins to consume him, his sight blurs, he has trouble focusing on the huge building.

The crow says, 'Behold, the Kampani. On its roof are soldiers with guns. Tanks patrol its foot. Jets fly over leaving criss-cross trails and its basements contain bunkers full of atomic bombs. From this building the Kampani controls its factories all over the world. It's stuffed with banknotes, it is the counting house for the Kampani's wealth. One floor of the building is reserved for the Kampani's three-and-thirty thousand lawyers. Another is for doctors doing research to prove that the Kampani's many accidents have caused no harm to anyone. On yet another engineers design plants that are cheap to make and run. Chemists on a higher floor are experimenting with poisons, mixing them up to see which most efficiently kill. One floor is devoted to living things waiting in cages to be killed. Above the chemists is a floor of those who sell the Kampani's poisons with slogans like SHAKE HANDS WITH THE FUTURE and NOBODY CARES MORE, above these are a thousand public relations consultants, whose job is dealing with protesters like Zafar who are blind to the Kampani's virtues and put out carping leaflets saying NOBODY CARES LESS. It is the job of the PR people to tell the world how good and caring and responsible the Kampani is. In the directors' floor at the top of the building the Kampani is throwing a party for all its friends. There you'll find generals and judges, senators, presidents and prime ministers, oil sheikhs, newspaper owners, movie stars, police chiefs, mafia dons, members of obscure royal families etcetera etcetera.'

The crow pauses to draw breath after this lengthy speech. Its wings brush close to Zafar's face and blot out the light. Zafar, seeing himself down there alone, begins to despair, no matter how long and hard he works, how can he win against such a foe?

Says he, 'This is not my wish. I asked to see my enemy's face.'

'Third time impossible,' says the crow. 'The Kampani has no face.'

It wheels away and vanishes and Zafar begins to fall from the sky. As he falls he sees the land of India spread out beneath him with all its forests and fields and hears his own voice crying *agar firdaus bar roo-e zameen ast, hameen ast-o hameen ast-o hameen ast* and he remembers that he is not helpless, that he possesses the invincible, undefeatable power of zero. Against that que dalle, zilch, nil, rien de tout, the Kampani's everything stands no chance. Instantly, the patterns of the land dissolve to designs such as are woven into carpets by the Yar-yilaqis and others from Kabul to Kurdistan. Zafar, marvelling at the ravishing colours and shapes, thinks, 'By god, in whom I don't believe, if I could remember these I'd be a champion carpet weaver.'

Finally he sleeps, a deep sleep that lasts most of one day. He wakes free of pain but with his mind in turmoil and this thought chasing itself round his head: 'I'm blind as a bat, mad as a hatter, red as a beet, hot as a hare, dry as a bone, my bowel and bladder have turned to stone, my heart runs alone.'

'Faqri you cunt, what did you put in those pills?'

After Zafar's dream which everyone receives with awe, but which was really every old mantra he'd been regurgitating for years jumbled into one big druggy nasha, I've no choice but to stop the medication.

'Trade secret,' Faqri informs me.

'Don't give me that.' Trade secret is a big joke in Khaufpur. It's what the Kampani said after that night, when the doctors asked for medical info about the poisons that were wreaking havoc in the city. 'What's in those pills?'

He's thinking about telling me, but taking his time, so to encourage him I lean forward and sink my teeth into his calf.

'Fuck!' he says, leaping back. 'You're a fucking savage, you are.'

'What's in 'em?'

He's rubbing his leg, looking aggrieved.

'Do I have to do it again?'

'Fuck off, no.'

'So what did you put in them?'

'Datura.'

'Datura?' I am not sure I've heard right.

'Yup,' he says. 'I had a bit lying spare. I use it in my medicines, you know what a place Khaufpur is for asthma . . .' he hesitates, seeing my expression. 'World capital of fucked lungs.'

'You stupid git.'

'Working, aren't they?' says Faqri.

'Working? You idiot, I said to make him feel sick, not kill him.'

'Depends on the dose,' said Faqri stubbornly. 'But I have a suggestion. Stop giving the pills to Zafar, take them yourself because it seems to me the real problem is your famous lund.'

Fuck Faqri, the bastard's right, all this day I've thought of nothing but sex, it's all I want. I want to fuck. Everyone's at it, why not me? The whole world fucks away day and night, why am I the only one left out? Why shouldn't I too have the pleasure, my thing aches with need of it, I mean need of the real thing, spit on your palm it's not the same. It hurts when people hint, never do they say it to my face, that I should face facts, no woman will want me. Eyes, admit it, even you have thought this. Why shouldn't I be wanted, even loved? Nisha loves me, okay not how I'd like, but she will when my back's straight. It's why even in his sickness I hate Zafar, he could have any woman, but he'll take the only girl who treats me like normal, which by god I am, one day I'll prove it by plunging this thing of mine into a living woman. I'll pierce her and open her up until my cock is stroking her heart and she's crying my name, 'Animal! Animal! Animal!' and I will suck the sweetness of life from her lips.

Ever since he saved my life Farouq's been acting like he's my best mate. At his suggestion I must eat with him, drink chai with him, roam around the city with him. We should forget past quarrels and be chums, what a horrible thought. On the festival day of Holi, hardly a week after the fire walk, I'm in his flat near Ajmeri Gate, where most of the Yar-yilaqis live, it's the one place in Khaufpur where you'll always find camels parked in the street. Farouq says to me, 'Animal, Kha, today is your birthday.'

Well, that it isn't. I don't know on which day I was born, but it must fall close before the anniversary of that night. When I was smaller, and cared about such things as birthdays, there was no one to wish me happiness, so I'd pretend that the torchlight processions and the chants were in my honour, plus the burning of the Kampani big boss's effigy was my party, because he was the monster who killed my parents.

'Nonetheless it's your birthday,' Farouq insists when I've uttered all this. He gives a strange grin. 'Must be, friend Animal, because I've a gift for you.'

'Such as?' I'm amazed, but also intrigued, usually the only gifts I get are those that I myself have stolen.

'It's a surprise. Something you will like very much.'

Of course I am suspicious. I don't think there is anything Farouq could give that I would like very much.

He's looking me up and down. 'Have you nothing to wear besides those disgusting shorts?'

'What's it to you?'

Says he, 'I've a mind to take you somewhere special.'

'Where?'

'For a special treat. Very special. Trust me.' The weird smile stretches itself like a mask across his face.

'Trust you? What am I, fishguts?' I'm trying to sound like I couldn't give a damn, but the truth is he's got me wondering. 'What treat?'

'If I tell you, it won't be a surprise,' says he. 'It's supposed to be a surprise. That's the whole point.'

'When you tell me, won't that be a surprise?'

'No, no,' says Farouq. 'That would spoil everything. Let's forget it.'

'Okay.' No way am I going show my disappointment.

'Pity. You'd have liked it,' says the salaud. 'It's a thing you've always wanted. When you know what it was, you'll be kicking yourself.'

To this I make no reply, so we sit in silence, listening to the cries of those who are playing Holi in the streets. After some time Farouq says, 'Remember when you nearly died, and I saved you from the fire?'

'I'll never forget it, because you'll never let me.'

'Don't be that way. I got to thinking about you, you having a bad time and all, no chance of getting a girl, no chance of darling-mischief.'

232

'Worry about yourself,' I tell him, but he just shrugs.

'Don't pretend you're not always thinking about it.'

Fucker's got a point there. It's spring, when the balls grow heavy and the todger leaps to attention like a drunken soldier saluting every woman he sees. At this season, when every male thing wants to ghuss into the nearest puss, Somraj is giving Elli the glad eye, Zafar pills or no is probably having his way, and I'm the only one getting no satisfaction.

'I see lots of girls, can pound puss whenever I want.' Such shameful lies. I've been seeing a lot of Elli and Nisha, albeit without them knowing, I want to do it with Nisha but I'd do it with Elli, to be honest I'd do it with anyone.

'What rubbish,' says Farouq. 'You've never fucked.'

'Course I have. Done it loads. More than you, probably.'

'Well, well,' he says, 'and there's me thinking you were a flute soloist.' He sits staring at me. The stupid grin is back. Then he says, 'Animal, yaar, let's drink some bhang.'

'Well now,' I say, relieved to change the subject, 'at last a good idea.'

Farouq's fetched his bike, I've climbed on the carrier, and we've bumped away to the government shop in New Market, where they sell hemp balls ten rupees for four. It's Holi and the streets are lost in clouds of colour. Every stall in the bazaar has put out baskets of yellow, pink, orange, blue pigments. Flings of powder come at us from all directions. We're hit by rainbow squirts.

Farouq calls over his shoulder, 'Hey Animal, later, we can go girl dousing.'

I should explain, Eyes, that Holi is a time when men claim they're allowed to do whatever they want, get fresh, drench a girl till her blouse clings, give a little grope to her she-bits, she can't say anything back. This is one reason why a lot of girls stay inside at Holi with their doors locked, at least that's how it is here in Khaufpur. I can't speak for the way it's done in Bombay or New York.

We wobble back to his place, completely streaked in blue and purple and green. The hemp balls are like small round cow cuds, we've stirred them into milk, added sugar, plus, because it's Khaufpur, a flick of salt. Pretty soon I am floating about sixty feet above my own head. Oh how I'm flying. The bhang is roaring ahead, so powerful it's, must have been grown from seeds spat on by a snake. Eyes, if you ever drink this stuff be careful it can knot your liver round your eyebrows and weld your toes into your eye-sockets. Maybe erotic feelings come with bhang, because I can't stop thinking about sex, recalling things I've witnessed from trees, frangipani and mango, my monster is beginning to stir, swelling it's, lifting its blunt snout to sniff the air, blame the season, whatever, this troublesome phallus of mine is beginning to be solidly aroused.

Out of the forgotten past comes a voice. 'Ouf! Baap re! Don't point that thing at me.' It's Farouq, staring goggle-eyed at my kakadus.

Brother, this nasha leaves no room for embarrassment. 'You're just jealous,' I say, convulsed with giggles. 'You'd die for one like mine.'

'How should I be jealous of someone who's never had a girl?'

'Course I have.' My voice sounds like it's arriving from a far off country.

'Kampani style lie,' says he, meaning that an untruth endlessly repeated does not become true. After a time, which may have been long or short, there being no way of knowing, he asks, 'So which house do you prefer?'

'House?' In this nasha, each word buzzes with a hundred meanings.

'That kind.' Each meaning has a hundred nuances. 'Laxmi Talkies.'

'Ah!' He means les sordides maisons de passe of which there are quite a few near that cinema.

'You've never been. You lying, fucking toerag,' says Farouq. 'Come on, let's go there. To Laxmi Talkies. Right now. We'll get you laid by some sultry bitch with tits like jars of honey.'

'You wouldn't be talking like this if Zafar was here.'

'Well Zafar isn't here,' says Farouq. 'Come on, I'll pay for you.'

'Why?'

'Fun of it. Come on, this is your big chance to do that.'

'Can do that any time.'

'Kampani style lie.' He laughs. 'Come on. Your first time. You're feeling good. Let's go.'

'What will you get from it?'

'Pleasure of making a friend happy.' Then he announces that this is the grand surprise he's been planning all along. Tonight, this very night, I am to get my heart's desire, I will get laid.

After this things are a bit hazy. At some point Farouq and I go on a long bicycle trek through the chunter-munter of Holi, the jets of coloured water and powder squalls. Him pedalling me balancing on the carrier, we circle the walls of the old city, we dart back and forth through the Pir Gate, on which is written the message that Abdul Saliq shouts, telling people with dirty souls to fuck off and die. We drink chai at the RTI shop and watch the world go by.

It's evening, people are out in crowds, on the fruit barrows and cloth stalls bright lamps are burning. The bazaar is aswim with lights and colours and half overheard scraps of conversation which, put together, add up to revelations of great truths. But the real truth is that the nasha has deepened. This nasha is not drunkenness, it opens things up, shows their inner natures. Just by looking at people walking by I know their souls. Here's one whose face is a history of selfish acts, money he has gorged, and squeezed lives, no mercy or pity is here, but a trap-jowled self-righteousness which is the way the wicked cloak their crimes. Here's a woman who drowns men in her eyes, and when she looks in the mirror they're all still there, looking out at her. This walking ditch believes no one loves him, so he in turn neglects the woman who droops at his side. And who's this tusked swaggerer, sneering lordly down at me over his belly's swell, fuck him, his dick's no bigger than a rotten carrot. Kind faces there are too, in the crowd, but so many have that look common among Khaufpuris, tiredness, sickness, futility, their faces drift and dissolve like pools of cloud. Into view floats a girl whose hair falls across one eye, the other delicious as a tray of sweets. 'Wah wah,' comes the voice of my

235

forgotten companion, 'her I wouldn't mind.' I look round in amazement. What spoke?

Farouq is sitting nearby with a leer the size of Pir Gate smeared over his face. Examining his insides I find something I don't expect, it's fear. What? My playful tormentor, afraid? My usual hatred for Farouq is replaced by a tender contempt. What a cunt. Exposed by his own bhang-drinking bravado. We begin playing a dirty game of eyeing up and appraising every woman who comes near, regardless of age or respectability. A waddling matron who must use at least two saris to gird her massive hips? 'No way, yaar.'

Demure housewife with small child? 'She'll do.'

So it goes on. 'No good.' 'Definitely.' 'Nothing doing.'

I sort of recall Farouq pressing into my hand another bhangy glass, plus drinking as if all the thirst in the world's in my mouth. I spit in the mother's milk of time, which, I suppose, passes. How can you tell?

Hearing a knocking in my brain I open a door that leads into a room in which is a long table of dark wood polished like glass. On this the Khã's jar stands balanced on its own upside-down reflection.

'I've been waiting for a good moment,' says he, 'to remind you of your promise to us. Ladies and gentlemen, say hello to our good friend Animal.'

Further along the table are other jars in which are small forms floating in fluid, I can't make out their features.

'Evening, evening,' they chorus, in little voices that sound like bells.

'Animal, meet the other directors of the board.'

'Board of what?' The children in the flasks all have terrible injuries. One has a single huge staring eye in the middle of the forehead, another has three arms, a third lacks nose and mouth.

'The Kampani of course,' says my friend, as if I'm a fool to ask.

Well, this is shocking news. 'So you are the evil-minded, greedy—'

'No, you idiot,' cries my two-headed mate. 'Everyone on this earth has in their body a share of the Kampani's poisons. But of all the Kampani's victims, we are the youngest. We unborn paid the highest price. Never mind dying, we never even got a fucking shot at life. This is why, Animal miyañ, we are the Board of Directors of the poisonwallah shares.'

I am thinking that this is a very strange turn of events which nobody could have predicted and how life is stranger than stories and these little creatures in their round long-necked flasks, even they have found some purpose in the web of things.

'Not only have we never lived, but so long as we are stuck in this situation, we will never die. You see our problem. After some time we realised that the Kampani also never dies, so we formed the Board.'

'And what is your work, exactly?'

'To undo everything the Kampani does. Instead of breaking ground for new factories to grow grass and trees over the old ones, instead of inventing new poisons, to make medicines to heal the hurts done by those poisons, to remove them from the earth and water and air . . .'

At this I start laughing. I say, 'You are fooling yourselves if you think you can ever change the Kampani. It is too big and powerful, it cannot die, it will go on for all eternity.'

In the jars some transformation is taking place. Around the small forms of these youngest of the Kampani's victims the soft light of moons and stars begins to shine and symbols of justice appear. As I watch they grow tall and change into shining beings of such terrifying beauty that I want to fall on my face for surely they must be angels.

'Release us,' says my friend, 'and then Animal, you may rest your troubled mind, for even eternity does not last forever.'

Back to this life in a small room, sunlight creeping under my eyelids. I'm lying on a narrow cot. Curled to me is a girl, naked as the day she emptied from her mother's womb. The dark skin of her back and arse is a shocking sight, it appears to be split, as if she's been whipped, or some beast has raked her with its claws, but then I see it's thick streaks of colour. Her body bears amazing markings, stripes of orange hug the

237

curves of her ribs. Who is she? I've no idea. Checking myself reveals more mysteries. First of all, I too am naked. Stained I'm with the colours of Holi, my kakadus are gone, plus my lund-of-lunds, lying thick and floppy between me and the girl, is fully covered with bright powder-blue dots. What the hell has been going on?

Failing to remember, I crawl to the window. Outside, dawn is breaking over Khaufpur. It's a morning of bright, cool air. The tops of the houses are just catching the sun and in the distance pigeons are circling the minarets of the Taj-ul-masjid. At the corner of the lane below, I can make out a sign,

J
A
X
M
I

T
A
L
K
I
E
S

My god, so Farouq kept his word. It's a bordello.

'So,' says a sleepy voice. 'His lordship is awake.'

The girl's eyes are open. Slanting they're in a face daubed with green leaf shapes, looks like she's peering through a jungle.

'Say good morning, Animal. How is your head? Remember last night?'

Full of consternation, I'm. Often I've thought of coming to such places, but never dared. The girl's staring at me.

'How do you know my name?'

'Pretending you don't know me? Ogled often enough, you've.'

So then it comes to me that this is Anjali, the friendly girl who used to tease me in my street days. Hard it's to recognise her under all the colours've changed the way she looks, completely different she's.

'What? Lost your memory? You don't remember coming in shouting to make way for the lord of beasts, you'd show us something we'd never seen before?'

'No.'

'You'd have every girl in the house. You do remember saying that, after your friend left?'

'Where's my friend? You say he left?' The two of us are naked, covered in colour, this is a very bizarre situation.

'Right after he dropped you off. Don't blame him. I've never seen anyone as out of it as you were. Can you remember what you were wearing?'

Ah, it's coming back to me now, that deep nasha, the world breaking up into points of light connected by coloured shapes, in the alley of tinsmiths that winds down from the Pir Gate, I am with Farouq. Despite the fact that it's night and Holi night too, the smiths are doing their stuff, working the metal, pouring it into their moulds white hot flaring so bright it hurts the eye. Farouq for some reason is wearing shades and asks if I would like to borrow them. Good idea, now the furnaces are easier to look at, so many colours there are in flame, it's like they too are playing Holi. Next thing Farouq has draped a cobra round my neck. Well I know he's a desperate man, but this is too much. I leap back screaming in terror, the bastard just laughs. 'You moron, it's a tie.' Well, never have I seen one loose before, how was I to know they were so long and shaped like that, like a snake with a fanned out hood, like the cobra that garlands Siva? Farouq, giggling, knots it round my neck. 'Wah, a fillum star you look,' says he, standing back to admire. 'Shah Rukh Khan, step aside, here's Animal Khan.'

No more than this do I recall.

'You came roaring in,' says Anjali, 'some of the girls were terrified, others were laughing at you. You demanded drink, when it came you spilled it on the floor and said you would not touch such vile daru. Some were for throwing you out, but madam said no, you'd paid, or at least your friend had. Then they ask which girl you like, you've said "My old and

239

dear friend Anjali". Difficult bastard, you. Madam asks your name, you say "Animal!" in a fierce voice. So I said, "Always boasting, men. What are you going do, Mr Animal, bite me?" "Talk to me like that, I will," you said, so I grabbed you by the tie and led you up here like a dog, the rest of them were falling about hooting. Do you really remember none of this?'

I don't but a big question is burning in my mind. 'Excuse me asking, Anjali, but after we came up here, what exactly happened?'

'What happened? That too you've forgotten?'

'Please tell me.' Surely it can't be. What vile and malicious fate would give me my first fuck then completely erase the memory?

'Did we . . . do anything?'

'Last night,' she says, 'you wouldn't stop talking. You talked of old times, when we knew each other before, all your friends. Oh don't look worried, it was interesting, I enjoyed it, we had a laugh. Then you got all dowly, said you were the only animal that never would find a mate because there's only one of you, no female like you there's. I said, not surprising have you seen how you look, well, you resembled a wild rainbow, so then I got this idea, I found some Holi colours, we painted each other.' Leaning there in bed she seems quite happy to chatter, I become aware of her bare breasts, hanging near my face.

'So we didn't do anything?'

'Darling, don't look at me like it's my fault.'

'Well, did we or didn't we?'

'You fell asleep.'

Seeing my dejected expression, she says. 'Aha, so you'd have liked it? I did wonder whether your friend was taking the piss.'

What can I say? Of course I wanted that thing for which I've been lusting so long, plus I used to be fond of this girl. Almost pretty she's, her face is fully pocked, what in Khaufpur we call naqshin katora, an engraved bowl, but her smile is certainly friendly, plus of course she's naked, never have I been so close to a naked woman.

I think maybe she has guessed what's going through my mind, for a look of mischief comes to her face, she says, 'O ho, so now after all you'd like to do it? Today is a new fee, let's see your money. Give.'

'I haven't any.'

She bursts out laughing, 'I am teasing you. Your friend paid, you're still owed. I guess I could throw you out if I wanted, but you know what, Animal, I always liked you, I used wonder what it would be like to do it with you. And that was even before I saw this thing you're toting around.'

'Please, I am so embarrassed,' I've mumbled. This sets her off in fresh peals of laughter. 'Wah, hark at this gentleman. Comes to a place like this and wants to show off his Lukhnawi manners. Come on, do you want it or not?'

'Of course I do.'

'Well, what are you waiting for? Oh my!' Suddenly she's got it. 'You haven't done it before. Your first time.' She's laughing at me.

'Never mind,' says I, whose head is full of pain. Naked, covered in colours as I am, let's try to recover whatever dignity a person like me can have.

'Don't be that way,' she says. 'I'll show you what to do. Look, you could touch me if you want. Here, like this. And I could touch you, so. See, if we lie like this, if I'm like this and you are there . . .'

Well, I would like to touch her. I reach out a hand but at the last moment hesitate. She takes my hand and presses it on the breast which is warm and full, the nipple's tickling my palm.

'Take more.' She offers the other one. 'Do you want to kiss them? Or lick? Do you like to suck them? You can bite too, if you're gentle.'

'I just wanted to touch. To see what it's like.'

At last I take away my hand from her breast. I've made no further move, after a while she begins stroking my back. 'So strong, beautiful the top half of you, such a fine chest, strong shoulders. So good-looking a face. And this thing of yours . . .' She's reached out and taken my heavy monster in her hand, 'If only the rest of you matched, you could marry a princess.'

So then she begins doing stuff which, Eyes, I don't want to tell, nor is there a reason why I should. Let it be enough that at this moment, when at last I could have my desire, enjoy that pleasure of which I've so long dreamed, you know what, my big, boastful, out-of-control lund won't wake up. Deep asleep, it's, or else cringing in fear.

'Don't worry,' the girl says. 'You and me, sweetheart, our life is tragedy. Come here.' She gives me a cuddle, this I like a lot. We two rainbow-coloured animals lie curled together in the dawn light of that small room.

'Anjali, did you really like me? Before?'

'Yes I did.'

'But why?'

The cot's narrow, our bodies are touching. My hand is on her side, I let it slide to where her waist narrows and on over the high curve of her hip.

'We were both in the shit,' says Anjali, 'but you were always laughing. So I laughed too.' She looks so sad, it comes to me that she's hardly older than I am.

'Anjali, how did you come to this life?'

Her story's the same as so many you hear. She had gone to the fields near her village to cut grass. A woman came, accompanied by two men. They took her to Lucknow and put her in a kotha. 'That's where I learned the trade. From there I was brought here. I can't escape, it's my life now.'

'Sounds like you hate it.'

'What's to hate? Automatic it's as namasté. Undress, close your eyes, after that, what can I say, time passes.'

'You want to leave? Walk out of here. Come, we'll go together.'

'It's not that easy. I have no money.'

'You don't need money,' I told her. 'I can show you how to live without it.'

'Dreaming, you're,' she says with a bitter sigh. 'Madam paid money for me. Think she'll let me go just like that? A girl tried to run away, the pimps caught her, they beat her, then they threw acid in her face.'

'Don't worry. I have friends who can deal with those bastards,' says I.

'You're crazy. Better not even to think of such things.'

We lie in silence a while, each with our own thoughts. At last she says, 'Sorry I couldn't do anything for you.'

'There is one thing I would like.' I whisper and she looks amazed.

'Just that?'

'I swear, nothing else.'

So she lies back and obliges. Now this is the third naked woman I've seen, this one has a figure like a Coca Cola bottle, and plump brown legs. When I spied on Elli and Nisha all I saw really were dark shadows, never did I get a good look. Now at last I'm seeing from close up, just a few inches, in all its detail, this mysterious thing, this alluring grace of which I have dreamed, for which I've lusted, over which I've disgraced myself and behaved like an idiot.

Dark it's, the outer parts look like the swelled lips of a large cowrie, within it's more like a canna lily, two whorled petals whose edges are almost black, tinged with purple like the bloom on a grape. These edges are also somewhat frilly, do not join below, at the top they collide in a small peak that resembles a woman with her head veiled. This is it, the most powerful thing in the world because all men go crazy for it, more precious than gold since for its sake rich men lose fortunes, sweeter than power because craving for it makes leaders of countries risk their jobs, more powerful than honour because it makes fools of respectable men. What is this thing? It feels wrong to call it a thing, from nowhere the word grace jumps into my head.

'You can touch if you want,' she says, but I don't want to, I just want to look. So her fingers open the petals to let me see, a glistening rosy cavern is revealed. How delicate the skin is, of such softness, threaded with tiny veins, like you find in leaves or petals, really it is most like a flower and reminds me of the hibiscus at the base of whose petals is a tube filled with liquid, you pick a flower and suck, it's joyous as honey. She shows me how the rose cave leads to a tunnel whose mouth at first was hidden, this is the way that leads to the womb, where life begins, where I began, where we all began. I try to imagine the womb and realise that it's an empty space, which means there's nothingness at the very source of creation. No wonder by some this grace is worshipped with incense and flowers and prayers. I said it was the most powerful thing in all the world, I was wrong, it's more powerful than all the world for it contains the whole world plus heaven and hell beside, in its depths is the whole of the past plus all that will be. I'm thinking of le pouvoir et la gloire that Ma Franci's always talking about, the power of this grace makes nuclear bombs look like firecrackers, the glory is that it makes its home between the thighs of this child whose thighs are bruised by the hips of drunken men, not one of whom, I'm willing to bet, has ever understood what he is defiling.

'I have seen now, thanks.' With that I've looked for my kakadus and begun preparing to leave.

Says Anjali, 'You are a very weird person, Animal. Give me a little money,' but I say no and she says, 'Animal, you are a hard-hearted bastard.'

Oh the homecoming from that day and night of bhang, the city is full of coloured winds, scents sing in my nostril, my four feet press lightly on the earth. As I near our place Jara comes running, and there's Ma. 'Where have you been, we were worrying, the dog and me.' 'Never fear,' I say cheerfully, 'See, I've brought food.' I'd found money in my pocket and bought ishtoo and kulcha from a cafe. 'Today we'll have a feast.'

What joy, I'm telling myself that it's a good thing my zob didn't get hard like it normally does, must mean I didn't want it to. I've conquered, mastered that unruly thing, it cowered like a sulky dog all the while I was with the girl, no longer am I ruled by a fucking quéquette, this is how I'm celebrating. This foolish state of affairs lasts until night, when the last of the bhang has worn off. Listening to the scorpions, unable to sleep, I imagine the girl beside me. No longer does my monster wish to abstain. The curse of lust is back worse than ever. No peace the bastard lund now gives, constantly it begs for the fist, sends you blind they say in which case I've no right to be seeing the light of this world, oh it fills me with shame to remember, Eyes, don't tell me you've never touched yourself, if you felt shame, imagine it a thousand times worse.

From joy runs a straight road to despair. Cursing silently on my bed of grasses, why do I allow myself to be dominated by the thing between my legs? Is it my master? Have I sworn to obey it? Will it kill me if I tell it no? Hatred of the self, deep and harsh I feel, loathing for all the dreadful things I've done. Claim to love Nisha yet spy on her and go to bed with a prostitute. Elli's my friend yet secretly I gloat that I have seen her grace? I dream of tumbling down endless stairs until I am at the bottom of a deep well with the opening far above me and out of reach. Days and nights are the same down there, but one night the moon shines in, a crow flies down to dip its beak in my guts.

Next day, when I meet people I fancy they are looking at me strangely, as if they know my dirty secrets. I become convinced that Farouq has spilled the beans. Nisha seems offhand, as if she has no time for me. I hate myself and my wretched life. Plus, Farouq is even more of a pain. He's on at me to say what happened in the house of putains. Nothing, I say, or if something, then definitely not what you think. So Farouq's frustrated with me and even more of a lousy bugger than before. One amusing thing, he makes me swear, 'Animal yaar, never mention to Zafar or god forbid Nisha where you were. It would look bad for you.'

And you, you hypocritical bastard, and you.

Next time in the clinic, Elli grinning, asks if I am looking forward to seeing Amrika.

'This came today!' She holds up an envelope. Inside is a letter from the hospital in Amrika. She reads it out. They believe they can probably help.

Hoo! hoo! I guess you can hear me all over Khaufpur.

'Wait, don't get too excited,' she says. 'Probably is the word. We are still a long way off actual surgery, we don't know exactly what will be involved, how many procedures, nor how long they will take, nor how long you might have to stay over there, plus we still have to find the money.' All smiles she's. 'It's a good start.'

Good start? Already my brain is racing with all the things I will do when I can go on twos. 'How much money?'

'Better you don't know.'

'I would like to see.' She hands me the letter, Inglis numbers are the same as Khaufpuri ones. There's a lot of zeros. So then I am discouraged, because no one in Khaufpur has that kind of money, Elli doctress herself hasn't.

'Look, money can be found,' she says. 'There are many ways. Soon I

246

will go back to Amrika, and you'll come with me. Stay hopeful.'

I ask when will we go to Amrika, she says it depends on a lot of things like whether this cursed boycott ever ends. 'Don't worry about the difficulties, just think how much better your life will be.' She says that after the operation my back will be straight, I will be upright, but it'll take time to become strong, I'll need support to walk, a pair of crutches, or sticks. 'It's easy,' she says, 'you can swing along at a great rate.' She knows this because in her town there was a hospital for people wounded in the Vietnam war, and many of them had crutches. Then she asks what I would like to see in Amrika and I say I don't know because I have no idea what's there. Well, she says, if we make a tour we could visit New York where there's a lot to see, near where she lives there's a museum with a lot of dinosaur bones, do I know about dinosaurs? Course I fucking know, what else for does Chunaram steal his tele signal? I have watched many programmes about them, they are huge animals that lived in the times before there were humans, the weirdest of all was the one whose head was stuck out on a long neck so far away from the rest of it that it had to have two brains, one of which was above its arse. Then Elli smiles and says I've a good brain, if I had been born in Amrika I could have gone to college. 'Maybe even Harvard,' she says. 'I think you could turn out to be an intellectual.' So I've asked what's one of them, appears it's someone who thinks a lot about things they don't need to. We folk in the Nutcracker may regard ourselves as nothing, but we are as clever as anyone else. We're as clever as the Amrikans, says Elli, but they have all the money so they have good lives and ours are little more than shit. If I had been born in Amrika, Elli says, I'd never have had to walk on all fours all these years. Yes, soon I shall walk like a human being, I will think clever thoughts, amaze people, and no longer will I do things that shame me.

'Fuck off,' says the Chairman of the Poisonwallah Board from his jar in the corner. 'Upright or not you'll still be playing with that thing day and night, after all, what other pleasure do you have in life?'

*　*　*

'Of what is the world made, music or promises?'

This is the question I've put to the assembled company at Chunaram's.

'What kind of fucking question is that?' asks the owner, who well knows the world is made of one thing only, which he ripped off his finger to prove.

'Listen, for Pandit Somraj it's made of music, Elli doctress says it is made of promises. Can these worlds fit together?'

'O ho! See where this is going.'

'Zafar bhai, what do you say?'

Zafar, who is not best pleased by my bringing up this subject, replies that likening music to promises is as absurd as comparing a vulture and a potato, potatoes don't have feathers and vultures don't grow under the earth. Says he, 'You are making an equation of two things which have nothing in common.'

'Zafar brother, what is an equation?'

'A way of showing how two different things can be the same.'

'So then I accept this vulture-potato challenge. It's easy. A vulture's egg is the same size as a potato.'

Zafar laughs and says my answer is ingenious, but how do I know?

This I can't admit. Up until a few years ago there were plenty of vultures around Khaufpur, they used to fly down and settle on the garbage dumps where I also foraged, one day I found an egg which at first I thought was a potato, till I picked it up. Washed and boiled, it tasted good. Nowadays there are no vultures left and whether it's because hungry fuckers like me ate all their eggs I don't know.

'Saalé,' says Farouq, still well pissed off with me, 'don't get ideas above your station, which is low in life.'

'So say, Zafar brother,' it's Chunaram. 'People are puzzled. Elli doctress, Pandit Somraj. We all see these days they are quite friendly. So why continue this boycott? Shouldn't we all benefit from her friendship?'

'Pandit Somraj is just being kind to a neighbour, that's all,' says Zafar who's well aware that people suspect that Somraj has been quietly receiving treatment from Elli doctress.

'Forgive me, Zafar bhai, even this idiot boy has noticed that whatever's going on, it's something more than kindness.'

'You fucking turd's apostle,' I yell. 'Here I'm trying to have a philosophical discussion, all you can do is gossip!'

They're all in stitches, so I've left that place of wankers.

'Zafar brother, tell me.' I've caught him a while later. 'The first secret of music, many times I've heard Panditji say this, is that the notes themselves are nothing, their only meaning is when they're compared to the boss note of *sa*. "Don't listen to the notes," Panditji says, "listen to their fluctuations away from *sa*. This is what gives rise to rasa, or emotion. If you grasp this you have got the music."'

'Yes, so?'

'So I got thinking about this fluctuation business. Stuff can't fluctuate without moving. Further, nearer, it's a question of measure. So the notes of music are measures. Plus, see, you can't know what a thing is if you don't know what it isn't. What makes a thing itself is it always keeps its difference from other things. The note of *dha* always stays the same distance from *sa*, isn't that a kind of promise?'

Zafar groans, 'Go away Animal, I wish Elli had never said you were an intellectual.'

I pluck up courage to ask Somraj about my idea that the musical notes are promises. He listens gravely, then says there's a thing I've forgotten. The nature of a promise is that it comes without guarantee. Then he says he will tell me the deepest secret of music. Says Somraj, 'The notes of the scale are all really one note, which is *sa*. The singer's job is to sing *sa*, nothing else only *sa*, but *sa* is bent and twisted by this world and what's in it, by grief or love or longing, these things come in and introduce desires into *sa*, bending and deforming it, sending it higher or lower, and the result is what we call music. The singer's job is to express the emotion yet remain true to *sa* which itself is eternal and changeless. And since in our music there is no difference between the singer and the song, the promise is made by the singer not the notes. Ragas are journeys through the human condition, scales that express certain feelings, and the singer's promise is to deliver that emotion. But it can happen that the singer departs from the scale, making the audience cringe, then the promise is broken.' Then he says that it's because of all music being one thing that there's music in all things.

'Zafar bhai, listen to one more idea.'

'What is it now? I am really busy.'

'You will like this one, it solves everything.'

So I've explained that if Somraj is right, then it's obvious how a world made of such music is also a world of promises made by auto-rickshaws and blacksmiths, bees, rain and railway engines, for the squeaky bicycle of Gangu who pedals round the Nutcracker selling milk would not be heard if he did not keep his promise to be a milkman, there'd be no rattle of truck exhausts if the drivers and their assistants who perch in the cabins with their feet out the windows weren't all keeping their promises and doing their jobs, maybe there's even some kind of music to be had from potatoes and vultures, if so Somraj is sure to have thought of it, and all these sounds are fluctuating around some great Sa that hums constantly in Somraj's head, by which he tunes the universe.

'Zafar, why are you crying?'

'Something in my eye,' says Zafar, down whose cheeks tears are running. 'Animal, do me a favour, don't spout these theories to Nisha, I don't think she would understand. She's not so happy about her dad being friendly with Elli.'

But it's thinking about rain that solves my mystery, for there would be no music of falling drops if the clouds each year did not keep their promise to burst overhead, and I remember Elli saying that the tides are the moon and sea keeping their own promises, and that's that. A promise involves a thing that can't be measured, which is trust and I can't speak for rain and the sea and moon, but I can ask why people keep their promises, and maybe the answer in the end is love.

One midnight Elli's woken by her doorbell, someone's out there with their finger jammed on the button. She grabs a shawl around her, runs downstairs. Of all the people she doesn't expect to see, it's Nisha in her night clothes, looking frightened. 'Please come. My father, he's very ill.'

'I thought you were boycotting me.'

Says Nisha, who's terrified, 'There's no one else. He often has nightmares, he'll shout, he gets breathless, but never have I seen him this bad.'

'Go back to him,' says the doctress. 'I'll fetch my bag.'

A minute later, she is beside the bed where Somraj is lying. He's propped on a pillow, his body bare from the waist up, covered in sweat, his breathing's shallow, kind of whistling, a pinkish froth's crept out the corners of his mouth. She listens to his chest, takes his pulse, plus his temperature.

'I am so sorry,' says Nisha, who by now is in tears. 'I've no right. I didn't call you even when Zafar was ill. So many people could have been helped by you, we have stopped them. This is selfish, I feel totally ashamed.'

Somraj opens his eyes, wants to speak, but the doctress puts a finger on his lips. 'Be quiet,' she tells him. To Nisha she says, 'You are not to worry. Let's just see to your father.' Somraj closes his eyes but Nisha keeps hers fixed on Elli, who's preparing a syringe. As the needle slides from his arm, Somraj gives a deep sigh.

'Now he is relaxed,' says his daughter, but Elli knows he'd begun to relax even before she gave the injection.

'I thought he was going to die, Elli,' which is the first time Nisha's called Elli by her name. Somraj is burning up, sweat's brimming his forehead. Nisha fetches a cloth, wipes his face. He opens his eyes again and says to Elli, 'You are a good person. I've tried to make my daughter a fine person.'

'She is a fine person,' says Elli, who has no reason at all to believe it.

251

'Shhh father,' says Nisha, fully embarrassed. She's bent over and kissed his forehead.

After a while he sleeps, but then begins to cry out in a voice filled with fear. 'He has such nightmares,' says Nisha. 'Always the same thing. He will not talk about them, but I think they must be very horrible.'

'How do you know they are always the same?' Elli asks.

'Because he shouts out loud. And it's the same things each time.'

'What sort of things?'

'Wait,' says Nisha, 'you can hear for yourself.'

The two women sat by his bed and watched. Nisha brought some tea. It was not the way Elli usually took it, this tea was milky, a frothy affair in which she could taste ginger and cardamom.

'God knows what you must think of me,' Nisha said.

'I think you are a kind girl, who loves her father and cares about people in this city. Animal has told me a lot about the good work you do. For example how you pulled him out of the street. So don't worry.'

'What will I say to Zafar, and others? We've stopped people going to you.'

'You will say that this boycott must end.'

Nisha just nods. After some time, she asks shyly, 'Elli, will you tell me something about your life? About Amrika?'

'What can I tell you? What would you like to know?'

'What it's like to grow up there? To be young there. Here I think we don't have so much freedom.'

'I am not sure freedom is the right word.'

'I mean,' said the girl, 'freedom to fall in love with whoever you choose. Not to worry about what people think, what they will say if he is the wrong caste, or the wrong religion.'

Of course, Elli thought, Zafar's Muslim and she is Hindu. But if anyone disapproved of their romance it was certainly not Somraj. Really he was a most amazing man. She said, 'My first great love was when I was in High School. I'd have been about fifteen. He was an Italian boy named Paulo, but we all called him Paul.'

'Tell me about Paulo.'

'Well,' she said, 'I got to know him because both he and I would get to school quite early. I'd help him put down the chairs in the lunchroom before school started. At first it was just for something to do.'

'But you discovered you liked him? I can't imagine what he was like.'

'He was a nice boy, not bad looking. We were friends for pretty much the whole year. The strange thing was he wasn't in any of my classes, so I only saw him before school.'

'So how did he become your great love?'

'We had a school dance, just before Valentine's Day, and he asked me to dance with him. It was the last dance of the evening, he probably took the entire night to get the courage up to ask me.' The memory made her want to giggle, but Nisha's face was serious. 'It was a slow dance. You have to put your arms round each other. I don't think he dared at first. But slowly slowly we got closer, closer, until at the end of the dance, wow, we were touching chest to chest. I remember being really attracted to him and I think he was to me, because his heart was pounding like a big drum.'

'Did he try to kiss you?'

Elli laughed. 'No, he never did, but you know what? On Valentine's Day I made a card for him, saying inside "I like you." I left it in his locker, and of course I didn't say who it was from. Later that day I found a note tucked inside one of my books that said, "I like you too." So that was that. Official.'

'But if you made a card, why didn't you sign it?'

So Elli found herself explaining that Valentine's Day was a day wholly devoted to romance, when people if they were lucky received cards telling them that they were loved, or, if the sender was playing it cool, 'liked', but the cards had to be sent anonymously.

'But then how does the person know who loves them?'

'They don't know. They guess. It's kind of delicious trying to work it out.'

'And if they guess wrong?'

'Well, not many girls would be lucky enough to have lots of admirers. I certainly wasn't. So you have an idea who sent it. But if you started dropping hints to the wrong person, then I guess you could end up a little embarrassed.'

'It seems an odd system to me,' said Nisha. 'Here we have something a bit similar, called rakhee, when a girl ties a token around a boy's wrist. It's made of coloured thread and glittery stuff, sort of like a flower.'

'Did you tie one round Zafar's wrist?'

'Oh no!' she said, with a small frown. 'If you like someone in that way, you would never tie a rakhee on him, because it's like saying "You're my brother". A sister ties rakhees on the wrists of her brothers to remind them of their duty to protect her and the whole family from harm.'

'Isn't that also what a husband would also promise?'

'Of course,' said Nisha. 'But if a woman has no one to look after her then she can tie a rakhee on a man's wrist, and it makes him her brother.'

'Who do you tie rakhees on?'

'Nobody,' said Nisha. 'First of all I can look after myself. Second, there isn't anyone. I tried to tie one on Animal's wrist once but he ran away.'

Oh really, thought Elli, amused, I wonder why. With her long hair loose and falling down her back, Nisha looked very charming. Elli relating this whole episode to me later, said she could see why my heart was torn.

Not very many hours later when Elli opens her doors, the lane is full of people. Coughing, lame, ill people in a queue stretching almost as far as the eye can see. At their front stands Zafar. When he sees her, he comes forward, shyly says, 'We have done you an injustice. I am sorry. I apologise. These people,' with a sweep of the hand he indicates the crowd, 'they would like your help.'

Now comes a time of peace, it's the golden age of my story. Everyone is happy. All our quarrels are resolved. People are coming day and night to Elli's clinic, so busy is she these days we hardly see her, except Pandit

Somraj will go over some evenings and then we hear piano music. Used to be me who sat with her, nowadays I find myself at a loose end. Sometimes I will sit with Nisha and Zafar, until they go upstairs. Still I am crumbling Zafar's medicine into his food, sometimes into his tea, but since the dream of the crow I've been giving smaller doses. Zafar still complains of stomach pains but not so much as before and these days I've little heart to go up the trees. Already my life has changed. To tell the truth, I am not so happy about it, plus I am not the only one who's unhappy.

'Animal, am I a bad person?'

'Depends,' I reply, not very clearly because my mouth's full of mango.

'Depends, does it?' says Nisha. 'On what does it depend, Animal sahib, down whose chin juice is dribbling?'

'Want to lick it off?' So fickle are the emotions, you'd never know this is the same Animal who was so recently engulfed in despair about the tyranny of the lund. My visit to Anjali seems like ancient history, it no longer has power to shame. Besides, I did nothing, what's to regret?

'Get lost.'

'You and me, sweetheart, it's a matter of time,' I tell her, gnawing at the stone. Just lately I've started this light-hearted banter, it's to make sure she realises I am a candidate, one of these days I will be walking upright. Just to show how casual I am, I've thrown the tooth-scraped seed into the garden, sucked my fingers slowly, one by one, with a little pop at the end of each.

'I feel like a bad person,' says she, ignoring my attempts to flirt.

'The only bad thing about you is you're besotted with Zafar and cannot see the virtues of your humble servant meaning myself who's ready to die for you, so think again please, it's me you should marry.'

'Animal, do you ever listen to anyone else? Talk talk talk, is all you do. How you chunter. Honestly, if talking's what makes people human, no one is more human than you.'

Well this is a dirty dig, but I adore Nisha, and content myself with giving her a reproachful look like one of Jara's, all big eyes. This does the needful, never is she cross with me for long. She sighs, 'You idiot, I'm trying to tell you something important. I've just been to Ghanshyam's to have my photo taken.'

Eyes, this Ghanshyam has a shop in Iltutmish Street with pictures in the windows of people with hairstyles from twenty years ago. They've gone yellow, these pictures, and there is flyshit on the corners, but people go to him to have their babies photographed and, oh my god, for wedding pictures.

'You are not getting married?'

She bursts out laughing. 'No, fool, I am getting a passport.'

'Passport?' In times of surprise, Eyes, maybe you do it too, I transform to a parrot. 'A passport? What for do you need a passport?'

'Going to Amrika,' she says, no longer laughing.

'Amrika? Why are you going to Amrika?'

'Elli is going, she is going with my dad. They are taking me to meet Elli's family.'

'Elli and your dad? But why?' Hardly am I able to breathe, it's like a heavy stone is crushing my chest.

'My dad and Elli, they're going to be married.'

'Animal, won't you speak? Please say something. You were the first to suspect this. Why are you looking so upset?'

Upset? Eyes, I'm gutted. How can I tell Nisha that it was me that was supposed to go to Amrika with Elli? She was taking me for my back, somehow we would find money for the operation. She was going to show me New York, dinosaur museum etcetera. Now she will go with Somraj and Nisha and what's to become of me?

'Nisha, this is very fine news.'

'Is it?' she asks. 'I wish I did not feel so miserable.'

'Why miserable? You are going too.'

'I never expected him to fall in love.' She utters the word 'love' as if it tastes of dung. 'He's told me since I was small that he would never marry again.'

256

'Twenty years is a long time to be alone.'

'I know, I know,' says Nisha, with her head in her hands. 'It is wrong of me to feel this way. I should be happy for them.'

So the story comes out. After Somraj and Elli discovered they were in love, Elli asked him and Nisha to go with her to meet her family. Tickets she has bought for the three of them to travel by plane to Amrika.

'When is this happening?'

Nisha told me they would wait until the big hearing when the Kampani would have to show up in court, then for a month they'd be gone.

'The hearing, it's when?' I'll be counting the days.

'It's about three weeks away. Elli has arranged for some old doctor she knows to stand in for her while we're gone.'

'What does Zafar say?' Strange it's, although I'm jealous of Zafar, plus I've nearly killed him with Faqri's pills, in a crisis I feel it's him we must turn to. Zafar will see what's right, he will tell us what's best to do.

'Oh Zafar's thrilled,' says Nisha bitterly. 'He says our case against the Kampani will be strengthened because Elli will report the truth about people's illnesses, it will help us when we get them into court.'

So Zafar has gauged this, as he measures everything, by how much good it will do for the cause. What a selfless man, such singlemindedness is rare, and Zafar shines with it.

'Are you looking forward to seeing Amrika?'

'I don't want to go. Know why they're taking me? My dad's feeling guilty, plus Elli wants me to like her. She says her father will take me fishing.'

This raises a pang, when Elli talked about taking me to Amrika, she had said the same thing about fishing to me. 'You should go, Nish. No one can see the future. It might be the best thing.'

'I asked her if she really loved my father. You know what she said?'

'Well, how should I?'

'She said, "He has the purest soul of anyone I have ever met."'

'So that's good. Why does it upset you?'

257

'I don't know. I'm selfish. It means my childhood is over.' Poor Nisha's dabbing her eyes with a kitchen cloth. 'Ever since I can remember, it's been me and my dad, and I've looked after him and the house. Now those days are over.'

'A new time is beginning, darling, it'll bring a new kind of happiness.'

An odd look she gives me. 'Animal, you should not go around wearing just shorts. Times've I told you? Let me buy you some proper clothes.'

'I won't be parted from my kakadus.'

She sighs. 'This news is still secret. Don't tell anyone. Not a soul.'

'On my life.'

Well, I am feeling sick and betrayed, but I keep my promise to Nisha. Only two people do I tell, Ma and the Chairman of the Board, alias my little two-headed friend. His advice proves that he too is a selfish cunt and that everyone in this world is out for number one. 'This is good,' says he, 'when Elli doctress is in Amrika, it will give you a chance to get us out of here.' Some days later he informs me he has told the other members of the Board, they've passed a resolution welcoming the merger between Somraj and Elli.

Somraj and Elli, Elli and Somraj. What else does this news mean? Eyes, I'll gulp down old remembered bitterness, be a ringmaster of the imagination. When it is announced, the news means celebrations. A party. Not just a party, a grand party. It means a big tent in the street under the mango tree, yes, a coloured shamiana just like the one Elli's opening ceremony was held in. It means drinks, snacks, barfis in silver paper, supplied by Ram Nekchalan who claims to have hired a sweet maker-from Agra. It means a feast of biryani and kheer with plenty of cream and raisins. Everyone is there. Musicians come from far away to celebrate the engagement of their great hero. Elli has asked me to make sure Ma Franci is there, so the party is enlivened by her ton ton lariton and crazy etceteras.

'Je connais tes oeuvres, ton amour,' she tells Zafar, smiling blessings on him, taking his face in her hands. 'Ta foi, ton fidèle service, ta constance,'

'Ma, it is Somraj who is getting married. Not Zafar.' How I hope this

258

remains true. The music and reciting of poetry continues deep into the night, each of the city's poets trying to outdo the next.

'Chalo dildar chalo, chand ke paar chalo. Somraj-ji, let's all go to the lake. Right now, yaar. You must take a boat. Look, there is a moon, it's a night made for love.'

Love, what a charade. Too much of it in the world. Everyone is in love. Elli with Somraj, Somraj with Elli. Nisha with Zafar, Zafar with Nisha. Everyone except me. This world no longer pretends to be made of such things as music and promises but announces its true nature, which is love.

The happiness wished on all sides is endless and ever deepening. Thus do we spin and spin, trying to turn a moment's pleasure into forever, but why not, let's make the most of it, because it never lasts long. Always, there's something along to spoil it.

The Kampani lawyers arrive in Khaufpur with no warning.

Timecheck sees them first. Four Amrikans, leaving the Collector's office, getting into a car. 'They met senior persons,' Timecheck tells us, 'their leader is a big fellow dressed peculiar.' Well, no one knows what this might mean but alarming information is soon flying in thick and fast. This very afternoon the Amrikans will meet Zahreel Khan, tomorrow the CM.

Says Zafar to the gang assembled at Chunaram's, 'The big hearing, it's less than two weeks off. They have come to Khaufpur to strike a deal. Has to be.'

'What kind of deal, Zafar bhai?' someone asks.

'What kind? With politicians there's only one kind. Out of court, into pocket. What else?'

'But they can't stop the case, can they?'

'Charges could be dropped, if a settlement is reached.'

Well, people are horrified. 'No! How can they do this to us?' 'After we've waited so long, they should let justice take its course.' 'What can we do?'

As ever, all eyes are on Zafar. Gone are all doubt and indecision, this is Zafar the Great, war leader and legend. 'The politicians are going to betray us, but we will wreck their plans. We'll bring thousands to protest, right there at the CM's house.' These few words are the entire plan for what Khaufpuris would come to call the CM demo.

Next day the *Khaufpur Gazette* runs a big headline DEAL IN THE WIND? The Amrikan lawyers, says the paper, are to meet the CM and the Minister for Poison Relief. The writer speculates that a deal may be struck between the Kampani and the government. Its timing is just before the long-awaited and crucial hearing, as a result the charges against the Kampani and its directors are likely to be dropped. 'There is something rotten in the wind,' the *Gazette* writes. 'Not just the smell from the factory. This is the stench of a deeper evil. To drop charges relating to the deaths of thousands of our fellow citizens, with no attempt to establish who was responsible, without applying to the law for a just remedy, is contrary to democracy and people's rights. If this deal goes ahead it will prove that the odour in our nostrils is justice rotting in Khaufpur.'

The city's anger blazes up like a huge fire. On the same day as the *Gazette* article is published, small presses in the Claw and Jyotinagar are working overtime printing posters, WE WON'T LET YOU BURY JUSTICE, plus LIFE POISONED IS LIVING DEATH, plus NO SELL OUT. Nisha wants one to say LAW DIES, HELL IS BORN, but Zafar says that the court case is still alive, to say that law is dead is to accept in advance that the Kampani has won.

'And if they do?' demands Nisha. 'Then it will be too late. We must show the politicians what the consequences will be.'

'What do you think, Elli?' asks Zafar. Elli's been quiet, grieving almost, since the lawyers arrived, as the joy of her plans is suddenly submerged in the old and endlessly foul stream of Khaufpuri politics.

'I do not know what to think,' she replies.

The smell of ink clings to us as we rush from place to place pasting the posters wherever we can find space, on the Pir Gate, on the courthouse. Next morning walls all over the city blare their messages.

On the night before the demo, new slogans appear alongside the old ones. They've been painted by other groups, but Nisha must have talked to them. In tall red-dripping letters the wall shouts, IF LAW DIES, HELL WILL REIGN.

There are four lawyers. Bhoora sees them next morning leaving their hotel, which is a white palace on the hill above the lake. Jehan-nabz, this place is called, meaning the pulse of the world but we Khaufpuris always refer to it as Jehannum. This has been its nickname for a hundred years or more, since the time of Ghaalizali Khan, the Little Nawab as he was known for two reasons, one, he was short, two, he was fond of sodomy which he performed with equal zest on both sexes, including the wives of his friends who were summoned to the palace and given the royal four inches up the bum. Thus it earned the name of Jehannum, or Hell. Jehannum is not far from the Chief Minister's house. Sure enough that's exactly where these four lawyers fetch up. Their chief, reports Bhoora, is a white-haired man built like a buffalo.

Says Zafar, 'Someone must follow wherever they go.' Of course everyone wants to get a look at them, but in the end Farouq goes on Zafar's motorbike to the CM's house, while I'm sent to watch the hotel.

I ride up to Jehannum with Bhoora, who's in a good mood and gives me a beedi. He stops where all the autos wait, by the big gate of the hotel. A loudspeaker booms 'Auto!' when one is wanted, who's first in line chugs up to the entrance which is of marble with fountains and glass doors. Everyone in the city has heard of Jehannum, but hardly any have been inside. To stay there costs more in one night than someone in the Nutcracker earns in a hundred days of work. Bhoora knows the duty doorman, he vanishes for a while, comes back to say that the lawyers' rooms are on the garden side, near the swimming pool.

'Do you know how much such rooms cost. One night, six and a half thou! Baba, what a waste! Two weeks in there you could buy a brand new auto!'

'What should they do with autos?'

'Not just any auto,' says obsessed Bhoora. 'GL-400 diesel, air cooled, four-stroke, electric start, compression of 18 to 1, what fools these lawyers are.' With this he falls asleep.

It's late afternoon when the Amrikans return, driving past us without a glance. The doorman, who's wearing a fancy turban like you'll see nowhere else in Khaufpur, rushes to open the door of their car. Bhoora's neighbour he's, lives in Jyotinagar, where the water is poisoned and many are ill, how can he show such respect to Kampani-wallahs? Of the first two that get out of the car there's not much to say, old they're, with short grey hair. The third is young and tall, a handsome saalaa with wavy blond hair. I'm staring at them with full fascination. You can't tell they are evil bastards, these servants of the Kampani. Last of all out gets the buffalo, ouf, has trouble exiting the car, so heavy he's. Now I can see why Timecheck said he dressed peculiar. His black coat discloses a red shiny lining, but it's his boots that mesmerise. Of snakeskin they're, like his legs are being swallowed by two pythons.

'Such boots,' says prodded-awake Bhoora. 'I'd die happy in such boots.'

He's gone back to dozing, leaving me contemplating how it is that in the same world there are people like the lawyers and creatures like me.

There's music coming up the hill, voices and people laughing. I'm itching to be there. After no sign's been of the lawyers for a couple of hours, I reckon they'll not go out again. What harm in creeping down to have a look?

I prod Bhoora, poor fellow wakes with a snort. 'Eh, what's up? Are they leaving?'

'Errand for Zafar-bhai. I'm going down the road for a few minutes. If they move you are to follow them, then come and get me, I'll be under the big tamarind tree near the lakeside gate.'

Three gates has the CM's house, two grand entrances where soldiers with white gloves stand holding guns. The third is on the side overlooking the lake. Near this is an area with trees and grass where people are gathered, the place is buzzing like a fairground. Sun's just slipped behind the hills, the sky is a lake of fires reflected in the watery lake below. This is our famous inland sea of which they say, *taal to Khaufpur taal, aur sub talaiyya,* beside Khaufpur Lake everything else is just a pond. On the grass under the trees lamps like fireflies are flickering. This is where the women are, hundreds of them, their placards laid down for now, the buzz of their voices I heard up at Jehannum. Among the crowd, hawkers are moving, selling watermelon, nuts, pastries. I've a couple of rupees in my pocket, I'll find some kachambar, oh yes, cucumber sprinkled with pepper and lime juice, makes your tongue sit up on its hind legs and beg for more. Tea arrives in huge urns, pushed up the hill on bicycle-wheel carts which look like buckling under the weight. It's a Chunaram enterprise. The nine-fingered saalaa was proposing to charge one rupee a cup, but complains to me that Zafar has ordered him to serve it free.

'Good, I'll take two,' says I, who's not supposed to be there.

Next thing, a loud music starts up. Eyes, it's *Hillélé Jhakjor Duniya*, which is always sung at our Khaufpuri demos, kids in the bidonvilles learn it in their mother's arms. The music's coming from a loudspeaker van, so loud it hurts my ears, plus never have I liked this song because it's about marching, upright and tall, towards freedom. I will give you a verse or two so you can see the sort of thing which brings tears to Zafar's eyes.

> *janata ké chalé paltaniya, hillélé jhakjor duniya*
> *the people's platoons are on the march*
> *the earth trembles, mountains quake,*
> *the motion ripples rivers and lakes*
> *huge waves rush across the ocean*
> *the whole world shakes, when the people march*

Outside the main gate of the CM's house stands General Zafar, hemmed in by his henchies, Brigadier Nisha and Lance-Corporal Farouq. In his strength is our hero, leading the chant, bellowing through a loud-hailer, causing the earth to tremble by the power of nothing.

> *ASIA, AFRIKA, AMRIKA SHAKE,*
> *THRONES AND KINGS FALL DOWN, QUEENS' CROWNS*
> *SET WITH JEWEL STONES GO ROLLING IN THE DUST*
> *WHEN THE PEOPLE WAKE*

Police are arriving, wearing metal helmets and carrying staves, they line up outside the gates of the CM's house. Someone shouts 'CM's car is coming!' Under the trees people stir, the crowd's getting to its feet, it surges forward under a forest of waving placards.

POLITICIANS QUIVER, KAMPANI TREMBLES
RIP-OFF LAWS BEGIN TO TOTTER
AND THE CM, DIRTY ROTTER, SHIVERS WHEN THE PEOPLE WAKE

A couple of cops standing near me, their lips are moving silently. Like the rest of us they are murmuring the familiar words, one's even tapping time with his staff. 'See these fuckers, how they've made their fucking bellies,' says a man in the crowd, but so amused am I that the police are singing, that I call, 'Let them be, cunts that they are, they're also sons of ordinary folk.'

A new shout tells that the CM's car is arriving. As usual I can't get a view, so I've climbed onto the roof of the loudspeaker van, song's rumbling out from the speaker right by my head. As the CM's car passes, its flag is the only thing waving, occupant is wearing a fuck-you look. I know that look, I used to know the CM quite well. Faqri and I took to going to his house after we heard that he gave free meals to people from his home town, Sitapur. We did not know where Sitapur was, but nobody questioned us when we said we were from there. Mutton curry we'd get and roast chicken hot from the tandoor. The CM would sometimes come and question us about life back home, so we would invent whatever it would please him to hear. This happy state of affairs lasted until the CM went back to Sitapur where some idiot accused him of breaking a promise to his brother. The CM took the speaker by the arm, dragged him to the village temple and called on the gods to witness that this allegation was untrue, plus on the spot he swore to give up alcohol and never again touch meat, so after that Faqri and me stopped going.

265

The pandus have formed two lines, a kind of tunnel through which the car moves. At the last minute the big gates swing open, CM's in, cops re-form in front of the rapidly closing gate. A second line of police forms in front of the first.

'Come out,' Zafar shouts, and the crowd chants, 'Out! Out! Out!'

The CM has not the slightest intention of coming out. He's in and that's that. Lights go on all over. Master's home. The servants will be running round, there's dinner to be served. So what's he be doing now? Accepting a cup of tea from his loving wife, patting his kids on the head, asking how the homework's going, or if there's anything worth watching on the tele tonight?

With a blip and a twang the loudhailer hurls Zafar's voice across the crowd, the music from the loudspeaker van is meanwhile blaring, so Zafar's comments are clashing with the song.

'COME OUT, CHIEF MINISTER. WE WANT A WORD.'

'COME OUT, DON'T SELL OUT!' yells the crowd.

Zafar walks forward, stands right in front of the line of police.

'COME OUT CHIEF MINISTER, TALK TO YOUR PEOPLE!'

The crowd's mood has changed, no longer's festive, full purple darkness is upon us, only a few lights glitter on the black waters of the lake. Abruptly the song cuts out and there's only Zafar's voice repeating his call over and over.

'COME OUT CHIEF MINISTER, WE ARE WAITING FOR YOU!'

Cries of fear go up from the crowd, great bats are swooping out of the dark and flitting in circles and complex figures above our heads, the ghosts of that night are with us, that's what people are saying.

'WE WILL STAY HERE UNTIL YOU COME OUT!'

Dark vans are drawing up, police are jumping out, wicker shields they carry, and rifles. Among them, I swear, is my old enemy Fatlu Inspector. These new cops right away begin to force their way towards where Zafar stands. The crowd, sensing their intent, presses more closely about him.

At that moment a man comes from inside, speaks urgently through the gate to the senior cop who's standing with arms stretched gripping the gates as if he alone is preventing the crowd ripping them down. The message is relayed to Zafar.

'CHIEF MINISTER, YOU CANNOT MEET JUST OUR LEADERS, YOU MUST FACE US ALL.'

The emissary goes back inside.

'CHIEF MINISTER, IF YOU WON'T COME TO MEET US, WE'LL COME IN TO MEET YOU.'

The cops begin a new push for Zafar & Co. They grab a man and drag him off struggling, the enraged crowd grabs him back. Now the mood is nasty. Stones and half bricks start flying through the air, the police are forced to lift their shields against this hard rain. The small victory is greeted by ironic cheers. Without warning the loudspeaker van begins to move. I have to scramble off as best as I can, the driver leans out to curse me as I slide down his front glass.

At that same moment I've spotted Fatlu Inspector with a group of cops trying to sneak round the back of the crowd. A devil of mischief enters me, badly I want revenge for all the blows and insults Fatlu has heaped on me. I grope on the ground for a good-sized stone. Here's one the size of a guava, hard it's, with sharp edges. Sitting to free my shoulders, I've hurled it with all my strength at Fatlu's back, it catches the cunt square, spins him down, he's on the ground yelling in pain. Shot sir! His men are looking to see whence the stone came, but I've dodged behind a tree. Three of them start towards me, dogmeat I'd have been for sure, but at that moment a new commotion kicks up. The CM has come out on a balcony with a loudhailer of his own. People now begin calling for quiet to hear what he has to say.

'I WILL NOT YIELD TO THREATS,' booms the CM, the loudhailer makes him sound like his mouth is full of razor blades. A huge shout of anger greets these words. 'NO DECISION WILL BE TAKEN THAT IS NOT IN YOUR BEST INTERESTS.'

'WHO DECIDES WHAT ARE OUR BEST INTERESTS?' replies the metallic voice of Zafar.

'YOU HAVE NO CAUSE TO WORRY. THIS I PROMISE.'

'HA HA HA!' goes Zafar's loudhailer. 'PEOPLE, TELL THE CM WHAT WE THINK OF HIS PROMISE.'

'Yes, of what use are your promises?' people call. 'Was it three or four years ago you promised us clean water?' 'What do you make from the pollution board, 50 lakhs a month is it?' 'Have fun shagging your friend's wife?' 'Your father was as bad who got his servant pregnant.' More join in, and more. 'How much has the Kampani paid you?' 'Won any lotteries recently?' 'How's the transport business?' which is a dig at a scam which involves Farouq's gangster uncle. Thus do the enraged Khaufpuris dredge up twenty years of grievances and gossip and scandals to hurl in the face of the CM and the anger of the crowd is turned to mocking laughter. Truly in the scam game the politicians make us street performers seem like amateurs.

'THAT'S ALL I HAVE TO SAY. GO BACK TO YOUR HOMES.'

Taking his own advice, the CM vanishes. Immediately the police charge forward, there are screams from the crowd, the thud of heavy staves on thin backs, but people are in a bitter mood. They retreat to open a space and the cops are soon being pelted with stones. I see one clutch his eye and collapse.

BANG! FATAAK! BANG! It's the sound of firing.

Amazing how quickly thousands of people just vanish. The grass beneath the tree is empty, but the fireflies are still twinkling, lamps left by the crowd have been kicked over in the confusion, they lie burning here and there on the grass. A breeze blowing up from the lake catches these flames and makes them dance. A small group of protesters surrounded by cops is moving away from the CM's house. Among them I make out Zafar and Nisha. There's a scuffle. The police have got hold of Zafar and are laying into him with their sticks.

'Nisha!' I'm shouting, galloping that way, because she's in there, clawing at the cops, trying to pull them off Zafar. A motorbike roars into the melee. Our friends drag Zafar free of the cops, he's mounting the bike, with Nisha behind him.

'Nisha!'

'Animal,' yells Zafar, 'fuck off back to your job, stay there till I call you.'

No Bhoora at Jehannum gate, half an hour it's before he chugs in with news that there's big trouble in the city, rioting in Jyotinagar and the Nutcracker. I'm filled with fear for Ma. Often people bring her home and report that she had been found wandering. Who or what might she encounter in those dark alleys, if she gets lost with a head full of visions and cauchemars on such a night? I tell Bhoora, 'Brother, go, make sure Ma is okay. See that she has the dog with her and ask the neighbours to watch. I have to stay here.'

With Bhoora gone there's no auto to curl up in. I can't stay at the gate, so I decide I will creep into the hotel garden and look for a spideyhole. Must be careful, things are quietening down but there are still people about, doormen stay on duty all night plus there's sure to be a chowkidar prowling.

Rich and delicious scents rise up from Jehannum's damp earth. What? Has it been raining? The monsoon is still some weeks away, it's the dryest season of the year. Fool! In the haunts of the rich, rain falls daily via a hosepipe. Darkness, trees. What spirits haunt here, what emotions still charge the air, the rage of those dishonoured by the Chhoté Nawab? After creeping for some time through bushes, admiring the passing scents of roses, jasmines and other flowers whose names I do not know, I find myself in a shrubbery looking at the swimming pool which is lit from under the water, making a blue shining shape in the grass. Beyond are verandahs, which must belong to the suites of the Amrikan lawyers. It's as good a place as any to hide, I can still see the hotel entrance and will be able to note cars coming and going. I lie in the bushes, thinking about the demo and what's happening in the city.

269

Some yards away is a tree with coloured lights looped in its branches, very pretty it's, underneath it are long tables covered with white cloths and on the cloths are dishes of food. These dishes have not yet been cleared away because further away are still one or two guests in basket chairs, with waiters coming and going bringing drinks. The aroma is very distracting. I swear I can smell kebabs. The demo and all of that fades into the background. So hungry I'm, my mouth is watering. Try to think of something else. From inside the hotel's coming the sound of a piano like Elli's. Oh baba, it's kebabs, plus chicken from a tandoor. Well there are not that many people about, plus plenty of shadows, too the brightness of the pool makes everything around it look dark. I'll have to make a dash for the food. Must be done. No other choice, there's. I wait my moment then creep out, low to the ground. My dark bare skin is blended into the Jehannum night, my kakadu shorts are dark because filthy. No one sees. People see what they are looking for, no one is looking for me, but what I'm looking for is there in abundance, crisp samosas with spicy sauce, bhajias and kebabs of all kinds. I settle under the table, pull down a corner of the cloth till I am pretty well hidden. In no time at all I'm gobbling like a dog.

The piano has stopped. Of a sudden I hear voices near, crouch further under the table. Next moment the hairs on my neck are lifting.

One of those voices is familiar. Carefully, oh so carefully, I lift the corner of the cloth. I peer out and oh god, what I see fills me with fear. A few yards away is the youngest of the Amrikan lawyers, the handsome one. Walking beside him is Elli. They are deeply into a talk, like two people who know each other well. Not just well, very well. The lawyer guy reaches out and touches her arm, it's a thing you can only do to someone you know intimately. She does not protest or prevent him. It's horrible. Somraj you poor fucker. This man is a Kampani-wallah, he works for the Kampani, yet she lets him touch her. What does it mean? A sick feeling's throughout my body. All her stuff about hating the Kampani is lies. She did come from the Kampani. Zafar was right.

I'm crouched under the table as they walk past. Elli's taken this lawyer's arm in her two hands and's looking up at him. They're talking in Inglis but I recognise the familiar tone of her voice. In reply he's leant and kissed her cheek. Then he puts his hands on her shoulders and says, 'You have done a great job Elli, you can come home now.'

O you foolish people, with your karnails and jarnails and paltaniyas, you naive trusting ignorant twats, deaf you are and blind to your fate, the earth is trembling all right, yes, it's the abyss opening under your feet. You've been betrayed. I have been betrayed. When I hear the lawyer say that thing and see him kiss Elli whom I'd trusted, I start shaking, I'm trembling so hard that I think the cloth must surely slide off the table. It's not anger I am feeling but terror. I knew the world was evil but never did I realise how fucking evil. Now it shows its true face of horror. I want to howl. She never meant any of it. All that talk of me walking again, all just lies.

I beg a ride from an auto and head for Somraj's house. No money have I, but the auto-wallah doesn't argue, without me saying anything he can tell it's important. My news is so big, I should go there right away, if they're asleep I should bang on the door and throw stones at the windows. With what grief do I enter the garden gate and the frangipani scent? The house has lights on, so they are awake. But now something weird happens, I find that I cannot go in, I don't want to and I can't exactly work out why. There's a rowing of voices in my head, which seems to have split into two heads, each shouting at the other. Fool! yells the first. If you tell what you've seen it's the end of Elli, she'll have to leave Khaufpur, what then of two-legged walking? Stop your bakwaas, says the other head, you have lost nothing, she never meant it so it was never there. You can't keep quiet about this, you cannot side with her. She is a stranger, she'll soon be gone and your life is here in Khaufpur with the people you know. Wait, screams the first voice, you too have sordid secrets, you should keep hers. Your secrets can no way be compared to hers, retorts the other, spying on naked women is one thing, betraying a whole city is another. Look, says the first head, just say nothing and no one's hurt. Everyone is happy. Show me the problem with that. The problem, says the second voice, is that you have to live with yourself. Exactly, cries the first, it's a question of self-interest. Don't you have troubles enough? If life's taught you one lesson, it's look after number one.

Endless the way home is, there's moonlight on the ground, splashed all over, making familiar ways strange, it's glittering in the gutters, washing over small unlovely things, transforming them into precious objects. At the corner of the Chicken Claw where the gulli goes to the main road a piece of shiny foil from a tobacco sachet has been lying for at least five days, on the main road itself, as you cross to Kali Parade, that heap of bottles is diamonds, on the wall the letters HELL WILL REIGN look black in the light of the moon, close by is a blown-apart rubber ring, a dead truck tyre in which weeds have rooted. How well I know this city's zameen, its ground, from an altitude of two feet, this is my home earth, discarded things are my city's treasures, this wall is its history plus also where its history finished without warning when no one was expecting it, on a night of moon alchemy just like this. Past the rusty gates I go, past KILLER KAMPANI and skull, the moon is shining on my arms and hands as they pace forward before my face, I am a silvery beast casting a four-footed shadow on the factory wall.

I'm heading home and normally I would go across the railway into the nearer end of the Nutcracker and thus to Paradise Alley but there is a shorter way. On this night perhaps because I am thinking of Elli I turn north by the tracks and make my way along the wall to the hole where I took her into the factory. Looking through I see leaves caught by the moon. In, then, the smell of chemicals rises to meet me, softly I move through the long dry grasses, thumping my fist on the ground every few paces to warn the snakes that I am about. Of snakes there's no sign, but after ploughing a hundred yards through thick grass I come to one of the dead zones. Suddenly there's rough growling, one of the guardians it's, maddened by the moon and glaring, but I know how to deal with dogs, I take a step towards it and say 'Brother dog or bitch sister I can't make out which, quit your tamaasha I am in shit just like you are, so fuck off and find someone else to annoy.' The creature turns and disappears into the bushes. Nearby is the poison-khana with its pile of poison rocks and its stairs to nowhere. Seized by an impulse, I don't know why, I find a ladder and start climbing. Instantly the whole structure vanishes, it takes a second to realise that a cloud has blotted out the moon.

Up on the highest platform, where the death pipe starts its solo climb into the sky, I'm sitting with my arm round its blackened stack, the city is mapped out below in a million pricks of light. Join the brightest dots, you get the lines of the main roads. High above the lake is a cluster of lights, it's Jehannum, a little way below some lesser lights where a few hours ago the demo was held. Around me the factory is a region of darkness, a black shape outlined by the low glimmer of slums. Now a strange thing happens. In one instant all the lights of the city go out, between them appear pale shining shapes, triangles, squares, oblongs, in Chowk the minars and dome of the mosque are shining, it's like my eyes are playing tricks, then I realise that the moon is out again.

There's a battle going on between earth and sky, war is being waged between the light of human beings and the light of the moon, I am thinking of Somraj, because his name means lord of soma and soma is the moon and also the golden sun. Somraj, what will become of you? This animal, with his inner eye, sees you crushed beneath heavy blows. My news will wreck you. I think you will die, Somraj, because death has been in your mind a long time. That dream of yours, the one which keeps coming back, which won't leave you, Nisha told me, it's your memories of that night, but in the dream all the things of then are happening over and over again. You are in a street where lights are reduced to pinpricks by a thick cloud of gas. In this dim kerosene light dying figures are stumbling past. Nafisubi Ali's child is standing at the corner, crying for his mother.

273

The boy's crying grows louder until in your mind it becomes a raga, one so awful that no instrument except the human throat can sing it. This raga fills you with fear and despair. Your mouth opens and emits no sound. The dead in their hundreds are sprawled in the roads, they are leaning half upright in doorways, their mouths are open and they are singing, out of their throats the death raga pours in green gusts, it swirls round them and flies in your face, in that green burning fog your world is lost.

My arms are round the pipe, now cold, up which the poisons flew to kill a city. The pipe is moaning. A hundred feet above my head wind is blowing across its mouth, the death pipe's wailing like a giant flute. I put my ear to its rough surface and listen. Inside are voices and it's like they are screaming. It's the dead of night, in my head is this howling that makes the hairs of my neck stand on end. I have the power to understand these things, I know right away what this is, it's the dead beneath the earth, it's their bones and ashes crying out in rage against their murderers. The dead are shrieking at me that the good earth has been defiled with blood. In thick clots the blood lies, won't be washed away by rain. The blood cries out for justice. Once the earth has tasted blood it craves more, now the killers must be killed. This is the old and the real law, it's the price that must be paid for murder, the price demanded by the furious spirits beneath the earth. Give us justice, screams the blood. It promises years of disaster, years of illness, if I do not take revenge. It warns me that ulcers will eat my flesh with white and weeping sores. Things will come to haunt me, nightmares from hell, sent by my murdered parents, hideous night demons, unnameable horrors of the night. If I do not take revenge they will come for me. Whips, like scorpion stings, will flay my body and drive me out of human society. Never again will I share food or drink with human beings. I'll be an outcast. For me there'll be no sanctuary, no relief, no end to suffering. No one will shelter me. I will end up friendless, despised by all, and then, worn away by endless pain, I'll die. This is the song of the blood. The dead are rising up in the factory grounds, they are coming, looking as they did on that

274

night, with eyes dripping blood they are coming, they're coming for me.

There are times to be afraid and there are times when you can be pushed just so far. This day's had too much of everything, of mayhem and excitement and betrayal and emotion and confusion, I too have fucking had enough. I say to the dead, who the fuck do you think you are, to threaten me with your reedy fucking complaints? If you had power you would have long ago taken your revenge, you are as powerless as us living, all you can do is wail in empty pipes, nothing can you do to the people who took your lives, they will grow fat and we will die and they will build factories above our graves and use our ashes for cement. Another thing, I yell, descending. You can hurl what curses you like, but I've already lost my place in the human world, plenty of people already despise me, but you are dead and I am alive.

'Here's a filament of fluff, spun on a farting breeze. So it crows, so it crows.' Long before I reach home I hear Ma's thin voice scraping at the sky. It's past midnight. I'm afraid, the shouting in my head's getting louder. I slide in under the plastic sheet to find Ma sitting on the floor crooning to herself. 'Hear it all-hallowing out of the sea, one, three, look there's four, how many more, how many more? Hello, Animal.'

'Ma,' I say, 'I am in a mess.'

'Off its scales see the sea pouring, hear it roaring, just like snoring, shut the door shut the door, ha ha there's no door.'

It's not a good time to be hearing this strange crap. 'Ma, come back from wherever you are. It's important.'

She listens carefully as I pour out my story.

'Ma, what should I do?'

'Be a dear and fetch my name. I had it just a moment ago, I must have put it down somewhere.'

'Your name?'

'Yes, dear, I seem to have lost it.'

'Where did you have it last?'

275

'Well, I was reading, by the lamp there.'

'I shall have a look for it.' I make a show of hunting round, lifting things, looking in corners. 'Oh look, here it is, it's in your book. You must have used it to mark the place.'

'Are you sure?' she says, peering at me with milky eyes. 'I don't see it.'

'It's here.' I've picked up a leaf from the floor and blown it towards her. 'Your name is Ma Franci.'

'That's not my name, that's a leaf,' she says, getting cross, 'What have you done with my name? Have you taken it?'

'What would I do with your name?'

'Well, you need a name, don't you?'

'My name is Animal.'

'Oh look, it's all right,' cries Ma. 'Here it is. It was keeping my place in Sanjo's book.'

Sleep is impossible. talking to Ma solves nothing. She informs me that there are a lot of angels operating in the Nutcracker, they seem to be planning something big. 'All's arranged,' she says. 'Isa's on his way.' What kind of world is it where you have to ask advice of the insane?

The dog, as if sensing my turmoil, comes to the foot of the ladder and whines, but she can't climb up. Out of the darkness comes Ma's voice singing.

> Qui vient là frappant de la sorte
> Qui vient là frappant comme ça.
> Ouvrez donc j'ai posé sur un plat
> De bons gâteaux qu'ici j'apporte.
> Toc! Toc! Ouvrez-nous la porte
> Toc! Toc! Faisons grand gala

After some time she says, 'Animal, are you awake? Aliya is not well. I told Huriya to take her to the doctress, but of course the mad old fool didn't understand a word, you must make sure she goes tomorrow.'

276

Tomorrow, tomorrow, I want to cancel tomorrow.

Above my head there are holes in the roof, through them I see the moon a silver ball and I think of all the people in this world who are also looking at the moon and I wonder what they are thinking.

I wake to earth's shivering. It's vibrating like when a train goes by a mile away and you can feel it under your hands and feet but you're not really sure what's happening. If you put your ear to the earth you can hear it as well, a kind of growling. Only today it's not a train and it's not the platoons of the poor on the march and it isn't me, if you are crazy enough to put your ear to the earth today you will regret it because the earth is shivering not with fear but with fiery, blistering heat. The Nautapa has begun.

Eyes, Nautapa is nine days of heat so fierce it fries any part of you that touches the ground. You know how air shimmers over hot ground, well during the nine days, the air dances so violently you can't see straight, it's like looking through rippling water, but water is the one thing there isn't. Bang, it's gone. Being out in the Nautapa is like breathing inside a clay oven. They say that when these nine days arrive the rains are just around the corner, which is just as well because suffering this bad can't last long. Things crack, wilt, start to give up. The air is sucked from the sky and out of people's lungs.

On this first morning of the Nautapa I get to Huriya's and Hanif's place to find that Ma was right. Aliya is coughing, her forehead is virtually glowing.

'Could Elli doctress come?' the anxious old people want to know.

What can I say? Can't tell them I don't want to face Elli the Betrayess, besides she'll be busy. Nobody but me knows the truth about her so things will be going on as normal, the clinic will be full of people waiting to be seen.

'Aliya will have to go there,' I say. 'I'll take her.' I can't see how I am going to do this. Autos, which need paying customers, don't bother

278

coming to this part of the Nutcracker, anyway, there's no money to pay for one. I could go to the Chicken Claw and look for Bhoora but he might not be there plus it would take a long time. Neighbours who could have taken Aliya on a bicycle are not at home. There's a rusting bike a few doors away but even if it works it will be no use to Huriya, and Hanif's blind. As for me, despite my boasting this Animal can neither ride nor push a bicycle.

'I can walk,' says Aliya, but outside is wicked, the best part of a mile to the railway crossing and the road past the factory, however there is no other plan, so we set off.

As we step outside the heat hits. 'Lean on me,' I tell her, 'we'll stop if you get tired.'

'I can't hold your hand,' she says. 'You'd fall over.'

'True. So hold just here.'

Yip! The ground burns like hot metal. I'm wanting to dance, skip from shade to shade, but the poor kid is gasping, her mouth is wide open and her hand on my neck is a flame, hot and angry like when my back began to twist.

'Listen Aliya, and I'll tell you a story I heard from Ma. Once there was a man called Jacotin, who had a massive nose. He was a lonely fellow and lived all by himself.'

'Wasn't he married?' asks Aliya, brave she is.

'No, he never found a wife. He was a bit simple, you see.'

'Like you.' She's limping. The earth is biting our feet with fiery teeth.

'Me? What crap. There's nothing simple about me. The older this Jacotin got the lonelier he became.'

'Granny says you're a bit touched.'

'Does she now? He could hear music, could Jacotin, that no one else could hear. He called it the music of angels.'

'Yes, she does. Because you talk to people who aren't there.'

'It was a sweet music beside which human music seemed dull.'

'Animal, I'm all dizzy.'

279

'Aliya, listen.' I'm very afraid for her. 'I am going to be a horse and you shall ride on my back.'

We stop in the shade of a wall and look for a foothold from which she can scramble onto my shoulders. 'Aliya, wrap your arms round my neck, hold tight to my hair.' Thus, with her small burning body on my back I've started again, thinking it won't be long before we meet someone who'll help.

It gets to be a question of counting steps. When you are a human you can count left right left right, but with four feet left hop right hop, it's not so straightforward. For the next hundred paces I'll think of water. There's no water. A hundred is too many, do twenty at a time, think of soft grass. The grass in the factory is by now long and dry, the grass at Jehannum last night smelt of earth, the kind of rain that comes from rich men's hosepipes. Last night, how I wished last night had never happened. How will I break the news? I don't have the guts to face Somraj, so I should tell Nisha, but I don't want to upset her, so I must tell Zafar, because he will know what to do.

By god how each step hurts. Aliya is whimpering, I'm afraid she'll slip and fall off. Still the track is empty. I can't really lift my head to see how far away the road is, her fingers are wound in my hair, I might send her tumbling. She's pressed so close, I can feel her heart thudding. It's racing. Farouq told me once that the heart is made to beat a certain number of times, the number for each is different, but the heart keeps count, when it has done its stint, it stops, not one extra beat will it give. He said it was best to make the heart beat slow, that way a lifetime can be stretched and I said some might ask why anyone would wish to stretch a life like mine? Meanwhile Aliya's small heart is rushing her life away and never will I reach the road.

How much time passed I do not know, but there comes a moment when I hear voices and start calling for help, people come running. Some men lift Aliya off my back and carry her while I fetch along behind on my blisters.

When we reach the clinic I'm all done in. Miriam Joseph takes one look at Aliya and runs for Elli, who's furious with me. 'You should have phoned, she could have died,' says angry Elli.

I cannot look at her, who must at this moment be play-acting, for how else could she so badly betray us? I say nothing. I have nothing to say. What use to say there is no phone in the Nutcracker? Without a word I turn and go across the road to Nisha's house where I can bathe my hands and feet in cool water.

It's evening before Somraj brings news. Aliya was so bad that Elli said she must go to hospital. This of course terrified Aliya. Like all Khaufpuris she believes that if she goes into the hospital she will never come out again, so Elli kept her in her own bedroom all day with ice and fans and medicine to take away the fever. By evening Aliya's temperature was down. Elli took her home in Bhoora's auto and ordered him to bring her and her granny Huriya to the clinic each morning without fail for the next seven days. She's sent word for me to go over and have my hands and feet looked at.

'It's too late.' No fucking way am I going there.

'Elli's waiting,' says Somraj.

'Sir, I have to get home or Ma won't eat tonight.'

'Don't be silly,' Nisha says, 'how will you get home like that?'

I tell her I am feeling much better. My hands and feet are pretty tough, any time other than Nautapa it would have been no problem.

Nisha says. 'No, you must go to Elli. After our meeting Zafar will take you home. I'll send food for Ma.'

Well, is there ever saying no to Nisha? To keep her sweet, I promise to go to Elli's, but what I actually do is sit outside Somraj's house and listen to the voices inside.

'No violence,' Zafar says. 'This I insist, there must be no violence.'

I'm sitting eavesdropping outside Somraj's house, plus at the same time worrying that a whole day has gone since I caught Elli kissing the lawyer. It's more difficult to speak now because I'll have to explain why I didn't pipe up straight away. Maybe I will tell Zafar when he takes me home. Right now he's busy talking. I can hear his voice. He's telling them what he has found out from his spies.

'Only blanks in the air, sir,' this is what the police chief told the CM, who was livid, the firing was a big embarrassment. Already he'd issued a statement, regrets, response to provocation, glad no injuries, restraint needed all round, enquiry, appropriate action. Zafar says that he and others only escaped arrest because with the Amrikans in the city and a deal to hatch, last thing the CM wants is further protests plus jarnaliss asking questions. Trouble he cannot avoid. A stone-throwing crowd had stormed the Narayan Ganj police station. Somraj and the committee had sent people out into the bidonvilles to calm things down.

'When it starts,' repeats Zafar, 'there must be no violence.'

'Can't guarantee,' says someone else. 'There's fury out there.'

A woman's voice. It's Nisha. 'Why won't people be furious? Twenty years they've waited. For what? This betrayal?'

Zafar says, 'Friends, it's like this. If we allow anger to rule us, if we break the law, we place ourselves in the same situation as the Kampani. Listen, it's we who have suffered injustice, and the Kampani which has committed it. We are the ones who are asking for justice, let's not ourselves break the law. Friends, the Khaufpur media, or some of them, may be sympathetic to us, but in the world the Kampani is powerful. The Kampani has armies of lobbyists, PR agencies, hired editorialists. We must be impeccable, or else we make it easy for them to say, "these people are extremists," from there it's a short step to "these Khaufpuris are terrorists" . . .'

He then relates how the Kampani in Amrika had staged a mock-attack on one of its own factories. 'It was a drill. Police, FBI, fire service, all were involved. The Kampani invited the newspapers to watch and said, look, this is how we'll deal with terrorists. Can you guess who these "terrorists" were? In the story given out by the Kampani they were Khaufpuri protesters. In the Kampani's fantasy the Khaufpuris took hostages and demanded coffee, then executed one of the hostages because the coffee was not to their liking.'

'What was wrong with it?' someone asks.

'Not enough cardamom, probably,' says someone else.

In typical Khaufpuri fashion a debate starts about how much cardamom or clove should be used in coffee, and whether adding a few grains of salt improves the flavour.

'It was not hot enough,' says Zafar.

Silence, a moment's incredulity, then a rose of laughter blossoms in the room. Says Zafar, 'Friends, for a moment think what's really going on here. What is terror? The dictionary says it's extreme fear, violent dread, plus what causes it. On that night our people knew terror beyond what a dictionary can define. Who caused it? Our people continue to feel extreme fear, violent dread, because they don't know what horrors might yet emerge in their bodies. Who refuses to share medical information? Our people want justice in a court of law. Who sneers at justice by refusing to appear in court? Terrorists are those who cause terror, who endanger innocent lives, who don't respect law. The only terrorists in this case are those who run the Kampani.'

'It's a strange world,' says one, 'where a Kampani does acts of terror and then calls us, its victims, terrorists.'

'Bastards should be executed,' says another. More voices pour out anger.

'No violence,' says Zafar. 'Not now, not ever. Listen, it might be that we'll never win against the Kampani. Maybe we won't ever get justice. But even if those evil ones escape punishment, they will still be just as blood-stained, just as wicked, in their hearts they themselves know it. Whatever happens they are ruined beings, their souls are already dead.'

Hail, Saint Zafar. What a fucking hero. Champion of the good and true, he'd even spare our enemy. No way do I buy it. Eyes, I've said I admire the Kampani but thinking of what those people have done, how they hideously took my parents' lives and left me in this world alone, I'm filled with such hatred, I think my skin will burst. Wicked are they beyond all limits, didn't I see the proof myself last night in the gardens of Jehannum? An animal isn't subject to the laws of men, I will slit their eyeballs, I will rip out their tongues with red hot pliers, I will shit in their mouths. Blood's shaking my heart, I'm giddy with rage. Then it's just as quickly gone, leaving me limp, body's like a goatskin filled with grief.

Nisha is speaking. 'Zafar my love, when grief and pain turn into anger, when rage is as useless as our tears, when those in power become blind, deaf and dumb in our presence and the world's forgotten us, what then should we do? You tell us to put away anger, choke back our bitterness, and be patient, in the hope that justice will one day win? We have already been waiting twenty years. And when the government that is supposed to protect us manipulates the law against us, of what use then is the law? Must we still obey it, while our opponents twist it to whatever they please? It's no longer anger, Zafar, but despair that whispers, if the law is useless, does it matter if we go outside it? What else is left?'

After this there is a long silence. No one is saying anything. No one can speak. At last comes Zafar's voice, sounding weary.

'Nothing is left.'

'And then?'

'What else? We fight. We carry on. We don't give up.'

'People do give up,' says Nisha. 'They give up when they've nothing left to give.' A private battle's still going on between them, something that must have started long before this day.

'There is always something left to give,' says Zafar.

'Zafar, my love, there's nothing left.'

Then Zafar says something beautiful. *Jahaañ jaan hai, jahaan hai.* While we have life, we have the world. These words send thrills up and down my crooked back, they make me want to weep. 'Wah wah,' I say, before I can stop myself.

'Who's there? Who's out there?'

So I am brought into the room.

The music room is full of people. Nisha, standing, is staring down at Zafar who is seated beside her father, looking at his own toes.

'Are you asking people to give their lives?' Nisha demands. 'Say it here, openly, in public. Zafar, would you give your life?'

There's an eerie silence every bit as long as the earlier one, then the fool says quietly, 'You already know the answer. Yes, I would.'

When Zafar says this, Nisha walks out of the room. Nobody else moves or says a word. I'll go after her, I tell them. She's in the kitchen, where she and I usually eat. Nisha has her back to me, she's got a knife and is chopping down into an onion, slicing it into rings.

'Nisha?'

'Oh, it's you.' She seems disappointed, like she'd been hoping it would be someone else.

'What's going on? What was all that about? Nisha, don't cry.'

'It's the onion.'

It rips my heart to see her in tears. 'Some good will come of this.'

'Like what?' Her mouth's filled with the dust of their hopes.

Faced with the bleakness of her despair, I suddenly understand what Zafar meant, back there in the music room. 'Nisha, is revenge a reason to ruin your life? What about Ratnagiri, children, that little house by the sea?'

She's turned round to me. 'Animal, do you think I like being a Khaufpuri? Well, I don't. I'm not heroic enough to fight other people's causes. I'm not like Elli, came here from her own free choice. I'm caught in it because I was born here. This struggle, it's going to go on and on and on. It will outlast all of us. If our children grow up here, it will blight their lives too.'

'Then let's leave Khaufpur. All of us. Why must we stay, just because we were born here? Let's go to Ratnagiri. Let's go and forget this horrible place.'

'Now it's you who's dreaming.'

'Why? The Kampani has everything on its side, even our own

285

politicians. We Khaufpuris have fuck all. Why give our whole lives to a lost cause?'

Again Nisha's weeping, this time's no onion to blame.

'I'm lost,' I say. 'Please tell me why you are so unhappy.'

She lifts her shirt hem to dab her eyes. 'For me there'll be no Ratnagiri, nor children either.'

'Stop it. Why are you saying such things?'

'Animal, if I tell you, you must not tell anyone, nobody outside this house knows yet, do you promise?'

'I swear.'

'Zafar is going on hunger strike. A fast unto death.'

'Hunger strike?' Hearing this I've started laughing. 'Hunger strike! Darling, dry your tears. He's bluffing, it's a sham, every corrupt rotten politician fasts unto death at least once during his career, it's compulsory, somehow the noble bastard is always persuaded to stop in time. Don't worry, Nisha. Zafar is not mad. He'll stop after a few days, when he has made his point.'

'You know Zafar is not like that,' she says. 'He has given his word. He is pledged not to stop, not until we win.'

Now I understand her terror. Zafar doesn't lie and when did we, le peuple de l'abîme, ever win anything? Worm meat he'll be, if this is really his plan.

'You can stop him,' I tell her. 'You're probably the only one who can.'

'He says I mustn't try, yet how can I not? He is not even well. All those stomach pains he's been having. Such bad cramps, and nightmares. He gets no better and the politicians will not give in. The Kampani will offer too much money for them to resist. Animal, I'm afraid I am going to lose him.'

My darling covers her face with her hands, she really believes the bugger is crazy enough to do it, and as for the stomach pains, I've cloaked myself in guilty silence. What can I say? Never before have I realised how many secrets I have from her. She wipes her eyes. 'Thank god Elli will be with him.'

'Yes, thank god.' In my head a vicious voice whispers, speak out now and you will deprive Zafar of his doctor. Zafar himself would want you to speak, says another voice, if he wants to kill himself why should you worry? Says a third, if you don't tell, you are doing Zafar a good turn, plus it may benefit your back. Shut it, I tell myself, for I can't in truth blame these thoughts on my voices, as soon as I've figured out what's best for me I'll do what I will do.

'I am so sorry,' I say aloud. 'I am such a bad bastard.'

'What are you sorry about, Animal dear?' asks Nisha, smiling at me through her tears, 'you have done nothing wrong.'

The fast begins in a small gaggle of jarnaliss and photographass on the pavement opposite the Khaufpur court where in a few days' time the hearing's to happen. Zafar makes a speech for the cameras. Blah justice blah. He'll be joined on this fast unto death by two women from the slums near the factory. One of them I know, Devika, used to give me sweets when I was younger. The other's from a place called Blue Moon Colony, her kid is sick from drinking the poison water. To my amazement a fourth hunger striker steps forward. It's Farouq. For once my arch-enemy is looking serious, even respectable. He's all in white kurta pyjamas, around his head is a strip of black cloth like the one he wore for the fire-walk. Zafar's dressed the same except his turban cloth is red.

The court house is in the old city behind the Chowk, near the lake. It's a big building of yellow stone, on its black iron railings they've hung a banner which says fast unto death for justice. Opposite's a small dusty square. Under the shifting shade of four tamarind trees a tent has been pitched, it's where Zafar and his crew will do their starving. Camped around the tent in a mass of bright saris and black burkhas are hundreds of women, always it's women who support, from places like the Nutcracker and Jyotinagar, same women were at the CM demo. NO DEAL, their placards say.

When the jarnaliss get bored and fuck off, the four hunger strikers dodge across the road through the don't-give-a-shit trucks and crazy speeding autos, and take their seats like four sages inside the tent. Elli the betrayess is waiting there with Nisha, whose face is a cupboard full of woes.

'I urge you not to do this,' Elli is telling the four, who listen politely but without expression. 'If you insist on going ahead then you must drink plenty of water, at least two litres each day, plus electrolytes. You're going to need it in this heat.'

'Electro-whats?' asks Devika.

'Uh, just a fancy name for a little sugar and a pinch of salt. Plus a squeeze of lime juice won't hurt. I'll be coming here regularly and every few hours I will take urine samples and check your blood pressure.'

Nisha chips in, 'If the doctress sahiba finds danger signs she will tell you to stop and you have to listen to her.' Normally she'd say Elli, now it's doctress sahiba. Who is Nisha trying to convince, so desperate must she be?

'Okay, let me explain what will happen to you,' says Elli betrayess. 'In the first few days your body will raid your muscles and liver for their stores of easy energy. It's called glycogen. You'll lose weight fast. With the glycogen gone the body starts feeding on muscle. That includes heart muscle. When the muscles are exhausted, the body burns ketones produced by cracking fats. This also makes a lot of toxins. When the fat is used up the body goes into meltdown. It has nothing left to feed on but vital organs, but serious damage begins well before that. In this heat I reckon you can do at most twenty days before things start getting really dangerous.'

'We have five days until the hearing.' This is Zafar, he's saying this because our enemies will have to sign their deal before the hearing, which falls on the morning of the sixth day.

'Five days you'll manage,' says Elli, everyone can hear the relief in her voice. 'It will be uncomfortable, but drink plenty of water and you'll be fine.'

The four of them look at each other, then Zafar beckons to me. I shuffle over and he whispers to me, 'Animal, take Nisha away somewhere.'

'Where?' I whisper back, bemused by the secrecy.

'Anywhere,' he says. 'Just get her out of here for a few moments.'

So I four-foot over to where Nisha is watching us, suspicion settling like a swarm of flies on her face.

'Nish, come with me for a moment.'

'What? Why?'

'I have to show you something.'

'What?'

'Well, not show, exactly,' says I trying to think of something she might believe. 'Zafar wants us to do this errand.'

'What errand?' she demands, twisting her brows.

'He needs socks.'

'Socks? Are you mad?'

'He is worried about his feet swelling, so he needs us to buy some socks.'

She eyes me as if I have gone crazy. 'Then we'll go later.'

I give Zafar a shrug which he's received with a look of resignation.

'Okay, then I guess it's time to tell you all.' He waves at the water bottles stored at the back of the tent. 'We won't need these. There's little time, we must put the maximum pressure, we've decided to fast without water.'

'No!' Nisha's on her knees beside Zafar, she has her arms around him and she's saying, 'No! You will not do this.'

He catches her hands, whispers something in her ear and suddenly she wilts. So strange, to see this. It's she who's the tough one, who keeps him strong when he suffers that black despair, but now she's on her knees, begging, and not one of us knows what to do.

Zafar says, 'We have to do it this way because there's no time.'

Among the friends and well-wishers there's silence, then Elli voices what all are thinking. 'Zafar, in this heat, it's suicide. Without water you'll last maybe three days.'

'Five days is all we need,' says Saint Zafar.

'I beg you,' she says, 'don't do this.'

Oh, Betrayess, what hypocrisy! What do you care what happens to him? I should speak up right here and now and tell all these people the truth about you and that Amrikan lawyer. I keep silent. For two days I've been struggling with my conscience, can't decide what to do. If such self-ishness you find hard to understand, consider if you were four-foot and had a chance to be human? With Elli gone, so's my chance, but right now this same two-timing Elli looks like she's about to start blubbering, mouth's twisted, too close eyes flutter like moths' wings. She says, 'Zafar, please give me a chance,' which is weird, like she herself can somehow solve his problem.

It's Nisha who recovers a flash of her old self. 'You stupid man,' she says. 'Do you want to die?' With that she's walked out of the tent, leaving us who are to keep the hunger strikers company.

Welcome to the hell hole. The sun on that first day of the fast is like the mouth of a furnace, pouring molten misery onto the city. The heat of the Nautapa is paralysing. By noon it's 114 degrees. Everywhere there are only two topics of conversation. One is the heat, the second is the hunger strike. At five in the afternoon, Elli returns to check on the hunger strikers. After only a few hours their eyes are like sandpaper, blinking for moisture that has already fled their bodies.

No reasoning there's with Zafar, sits cross-legged and reads papers brought to him, peers over the tops of his specs when he talks to people, makes calls on a mobile, carrying on his daily work.

'You're so thirsty now that you don't notice hunger,' Elli tells the four, 'but soon you may lose all feelings of hunger and even thirst. This is not a good thing.' She tells them what she knows about hunger strikes, the slow wasting of the body. 'In Ireland prisoners lasted sixty days on water before they died, but blindness plus other irreversible damage occurred long before that point. Fasts by Turkish prisoners confirmed these grim statistics. These were with water. There's hardly any data on fasting without water, but in this extreme heat, the body will dry out and begin its collapse within two or three days.' Again and again Elli tries to make the four see how suicidal is their decision. 'You're now in the same situation as people who get lost in a desert without food or water, except that you've put yourself there, you are making your own desert.'

'What is Khaufpur but a desert?' replies one of the women, someone says 'wah wah'. All inside the tent nod. I can see Elli's expression, I know what's in her mind, which is that they'll soon learn how hard it is to survive on rhetoric. Despite living among us and speaking our language, she knows next to nothing about us Khaufpuris.

Everyone in Khaufpur is talking about Zafar. What a hero, bloody. It's not as if he was unknown before, but now every bugger is his best friend. Zafar bhai, who gives everything for the poor. This old cry now has a new ring because if someone doesn't stop him the mad bastard is going to give his life. Farouq, Devika and Bluemoon are new saints and their pictures are pasted on walls all over the city alongside Zafar's. Four martyrs in the making.

Suddenly every fucker's an expert at fasting. Well, many are of course, though not by choice. 'It's the moon's full,' says Ramprasad the fruit seller. 'It pulls fluid up to the brain and disturbs the thoughts. That's why people go mad. The best way to deal with the moon is to fast without water. See this lessens the fluid in the whole body and the liquid from the brain flows down into the body, thus the maddening effect of the moon is removed.'

'Poor cretin, you know nothing.'

'What, Animal? Are you an expert in medicine?'

I am not but it's time to reveal an unexpected and appalling discovery, which is that I seem to be infected with this disease called conscience. Seeing Nisha's misery I find that I am not keen for Zafar to perish, plus I hate to admit it, there is a part of me that admires the git. He's always been kind to me and the place would just not be the same without him.

Zafar's three days into the fast and Elli Betrayess keeps on saying that if he doesn't stop soon he will die. His body has started to devour itself and the blood is thumping in his head. He is having severe attacks of cramp, which Faqri says might be after-effects of datura. Since yesterday these have been fading which means that Faqri is probably right. Farouq is turning out to be a tough one, 'Today better than yesterday' he tells me with a grin when I go to see them, his lips are cracked and his breathing is like wind in a thorn tree. He and the other hunger-strikers are telling each other jokes and indulging in the old Khaufpuri pastime of abuse. A crowd of Khaufpuris is with them singing *Hillélé* and suchlike and keeping up their spirits with jokes. It's Friday, fourth day of Nautapa, 120 degrees. In the afternoon Devika, the one from the Nutcracker, collapses and is rushed to the big hospital. The Blue Moon woman is persuaded by her family to stop. Zafar and Farouq carry on. They are exhausted and by the end of that afternoon both are asleep. Nisha, who is afraid and agitated, takes her chance. While these two are sleeping she brings a wet cloth and wipes their faces, then lets a few drops of water fall on their lips. What Farouq did, I do not know, but Zafar wakes immediately. He's very angry, he's opened his mouth to shout at Nisha, but only a kind of croaking comes out. What does she think she is doing? Nisha, near to tears, replies that he and Farouq should end their ordeal.

'You are behaving like a child,' he says. His lips are so cracked, his tongue is swollen up in his mouth. He sounds like he's been drinking daru, looks that way too, red eyed and hair standing on end. Even his glasses are dusty and he no longer has the will to wipe them on his shirt like he usually does. No longer is he reading papers. 'What has happened to you?' he demands of Nisha. 'They used to joke that Zafar's backbone was named Nisha. Now this?'

'I am strong,' says she, 'and with all my strength I am begging you, give this up. You can't fight if you are dead.'

'Why talk of death?' asks Zafar. 'Talk of winning.'

'You think you are being strong,' she says, 'but you are not. Giving up your life is just that, giving up. It's surrendering. These Kampani wallahs, they're not impressed. They're laughing at you. You are making them a gift of your life.'

When she says this, I am watching Zafar's face and it seems to me that a great weariness appears in it. He knows she is right. It comes to me then that he is doing this because he is tired of fighting and that this is the only way he can stop with honour. We have not supported him well, we've not appreciated his years of struggle for our sakes, now he is tired, wants it all to end, ending this way will not be without honour. But I've underestimated Zafar. The man is, after all, a saint, already he's apologising for losing his temper with Nisha, but now it's her turn to go mad. She shouts at him, 'Don't expect me to stay here and watch you die! I won't! I refuse!'

'Then you must go,' says the hero, but I swear if there had been a drop of moisture left in his body it would have been rolling from his eye. 'Please do not come here again until it is over.'

'Until it is over? What does that mean?' says Nisha, shaken by this.

'It means that you are my life,' says Zafar, which, being the dismal sod he is, is the nearest he will ever come to saying I love you. Women sitting near go ooh and ah, but many are weeping.

'If I am your life,' says she, 'then you are killing both of us.'

'You shake my resolve,' says Zafar. 'Please go now.' On his face is a look like he is being tortured. Nisha gets up and walks away, like her heart and guts are trailing on the ground behind her.

Saturday, fifth day of Nautapa, 118f. No more singing around the tent. Zafar and Farouq are lying on their mattresses, for long periods now they do not speak. Their fourth day without food or water. People are whispering that they are sinking. The crisis can't be far away. When the doctress sahiba orders them to quit what will they do? The wisdom is that they are going to carry on to the dreadful end. People really believe this, a sure sign is that many folk, Hindu and Muslim alike, come hesitantly to the tent to ask for their blessings. To be in the presence of saints, this is something. A delegation of elders from the Nutcracker arrives and pleads with them to stop. Through their destroyed lips, they refuse. Fire of thirst, burning of hunger, these two are cremating themselves on the pyre of their dead cause.

At lunchtime I am at Somraj's house eating my lunch, and packing some chapattis and pickle to take home for Ma. Since this drama began I have not been spending time with Ma, which I should because every day she is getting madder. Two, three times now the neighbours have found her shouting in the lanes and brought her home. They do not know what she's yelling, but I do, because she tells me at night. 'Animal, I am trying to warn people, but they don't listen. Hell is coming, it will open underneath our feet, you can feel the heat already. Le camp des saints et la ville bien-aimée. Un feu descendera du ciel, et les dévorera.' The camp of the saints and the well-loved city, a fire will come from the sky and devour them. Then she's confirmed that angels have moved in all around, they're taking over the city, preparing some big showdown. Soon there will be no people left.

Nisha comes to me with eyes red from crying, she kneels in front of me so she can look me in the eye. 'Animal, you have to take a message to Zafar from me. Will you?'

'Of course.' Nothing I'd like less, but how to say this?

'I've been thinking a lot about what I should say. But in the end what else is there? I love you. With all my heart and soul.'

Oh wicked to say so but the fire that burns Zafar is nothing to the flames which now engulf me. 'Yes, yes,' I say. 'Of course I will tell him.'

'Say that I respect him and admire him and support him and wish to be his strongest ally,' she babbles. 'How can I stay here alone? Look.' She shows me a cap, carefully embroidered in blue and scarlet silks. 'I have made this for him, for our wedding.'

'It is beautiful.' God, how this hurts.

'Tell him that if he goes, he's taking me with him.'

'I will tell him,' I mumble.

'The thought of him gone,' she says, now talking more to herself than to me, 'it makes me desperate. The Kampani is not worth spitting on, it's not worth dying for. If there was one good person in that Kampani, even one who might be moved by such a sacrifice, then it might be worth it. But they'll be cheering when the news comes.'

'Stop this talk Nish,' I tell her. 'No one's fucking going. No one's going.' This talk of her going with him is spooking me. 'Not in a million years will he do this. Think about it, not even Zafar could be such a dork as to suppose that dying would be a better option.' But I am not sure of this, not at all, because Zafar is a hero, a saint, and his death would cause such mayhem that no politician could ignore it. The way Nisha is talking, I want him alive now, very much so. A rival who's alive can make mistakes, who knows, she might grow tired of saintliness, but one who's dead and eternal, no way.

'Animal, next to Zafar, you are my best friend. Give him my message.'

Zafar says the hunger has stopped and he has been feeling a kind of peace, but he doesn't seem very peaceful because when I have said the message he starts flapping his swollen tongue at me.

'Animal you are always saying you don't have to think, you are fucking lucky mate, because thinking is doing my head in I think my head will bust with all the fucking thoughts bulging in it.' It's not usual for him to swear so I am a bit amazed. 'What a place is this Khaufpur,' he says, 'where even the sky is broken and when rain comes it's just a loan against long overdue debts.'

He rambles on in this way, well you know what they say, the tongue has no bone so it can twist and turn to all kinds of things.

'Is Khaufpur the only poisoned city? It is not. There are others and each one of has its own Zafar. There'll be a Zafar in Mexico City and others in Hanoi and Manila and Halabja and there are the Zafars of Minamata and Seveso, of Sao Paolo and Toulouse and I wonder if all those weary bastards are as fucked as I am.'

'What should I tell Nisha?'

'Nisha?' he croaks, as if he's having trouble remembering who she is.

'Your girlfriend.'

'So where is she?' He starts looking around. His eyes are sunk in his head. So dry and inflamed are they that as they swivel I'm expecting them to creak.

'She is at home crying because you told her not to come here.'

'Why would I do that?' he demands, glaring at me as if I am lying. No, worse, as if I am to blame for all this.

'She tried to put some water on your mouth.'

'Water? Please . . .' His voice dries up, for a moment I think he's asking for water, but probably he was begging me not to mention it because in a moment he starts again, following some thoughtway of his own. 'I never walked in fire because I refuse to bow to god. Refusing to bow is not the same thing as not believing. Look at the world's misery and you have to believe that something very malevolent is at work here. I can't honour this vile thing.'

He looks at Farouq who is lying asleep nearby with a sheet draped over him, pretty much like a corpse in its shroud. 'Farouq can walk through fire because his mind is calm,' Zafar whispers. 'But right now the fire is inside me and I tell you Animal it's fucking burning me up.'

I think Zafar doesn't hear these words that are crawling out of his mouth. It's like he is this parched old corpse, uttering thoughts which have chewed him up from the inside starting with his muscles and bones and ending with his soul. Now they are like beetles, dropping from his mouth onto the ground. Never would I have expected it, but it pains me to see my old rival in this state. It fucking hurts, for a moment I even feel proud of the man. He's talking like a weakling, but he's not weak. If he was weak, he'd take a drink and he'd live. It's his strength that's killing him. Once inside the factory I found a parcel of furry skin stretched over bones, it was a dead dog, so old it no longer stank. I prodded it with a stick and a lizard ran out of a gap in its ribs. Its insides were full of white peas, which must have been lizard eggs, and it was crawling with black beetles. This will be Zafar in another day or two.

I am just thinking what news I can carry to Nisha when, of a sudden, there comes cheering outside the tent. People are applauding. Then Elli's here, she's telling Zafar and Farouq that they can stop their hunger strike, they can drink water, they can eat an orange, they can chew a date, they can rejoice, get up and dance because the deal has been delayed. She's just had a call from someone she knows. The deal is not going to happen. There's no way it can be signed before Monday, which is the day of the hearing. We have won.

Khaufpuri style celebration is a no-holds-barred affair, every festival it's, all rolled into one. Folk have so little good news in their lives, when they get some they go apeshit. Some one has brought gulal, coloured powder, the stuff that's thrown at Holi, others are lighting firecrackers, little bundles of red fatakas, they're flipping about in the dust like exploding fish. Happy people are jigging round the square, everyone's saying 'We have won, we've done it, the Kampani's on its knees'. All around us Khaufpuris are dancing and yelling. Some are hugging each other. The tent is full of people grinning and giving victory signs and there's a long queue to shake Zafar's and Farouq's hands. In the midst of all this rejoicing I am wondering, who has really won? How come Elli, who is in cahoots with the lawyers, has brought such news at such a time?

Through the excited crowd I catch sight of Elli's pale face, she is the only person other than me who isn't smiling.

The scorpions have gone barmy, or perhaps it's Ma. I'm woken by the madwoman chuckling to herself and've gone down the ladder to find Ma with a pissed-off looking scorpion crouched on the palm of her hand. Seems to be giving it instructions. I freeze so's not to alarm the creature. These red ones, they're the dangerous kind. One bite from one of these you are history. This is not what's needed right now. I've hardly slept. All night I have been fighting with my newly discovered conscience, I have decided that I must warn Zafar, brother don't be fooled by Elli's news, Elli is a fake.

'Can you feel the heat?' Ma asks, giving me a sweet smile. 'Hell is opening under this city. The stones in the wall are burning, it's driving the scorpions out, poor little things, their time has come, soon the earth will burn, plus trees and all green things, the abyss is opening, smoke will hide the sun and moon, like a scorpion it'll sting, with such pain that men will beg to die.'

'Yes yes,' I tell her, 'please put that creature down.'

'Honestly Animal, don't you hear a word I say? The night is coming when this city will be full of angels and dead people, don't say I didn't warn you.' She holds out her hand to me, the scorpion still crouched there flexing its tail. 'Here, mind you don't hurt him, isn't he lovely? His name is François.'

Carefully, carefully, I take François and lower him to the earth. A score of heartbeats shake my body before his little legs start moving and he grants me the gift of my life. It's only seven in the morning, already the heat's climbing a spiral to the unbearable.

Sunday, sixth day of the Nautapa. 124F. I call at Somraj's place expecting to find Zafar there, now there's no more reason for his hunger strike. Somraj looks ill. There are dark marks under his eyes as if he has not slept. Zafar and Farouq are still in the tent, he informs me, the fast goes on.

'But what about Elli's news? Last night, people were dancing.'

Somraj says there's been no confirmation of her news. The politicians are terrified that Zafar or Farouq will die, the story might have been a trick to get them to stop their fast. Tomorrow morning is the hearing, Somraj says. One way or another, by then we'll know.

The crowd outside the tent has grown, it fills the small park and it is quiet. Word has got about, our heroes must endure one more day. Everyone knows that if tomorrow comes and if Zafar and Farouq do not call a halt, by day's end they will surely die. Eerie is the silence of so many people, almost, you can hear them breathe. Farouq and Zafar are lying on rugs with their eyes closed, a few people are sitting silently by. One of those in the tent is a man called Ramlal who knows me, he's the husband of Devika, one of the original hungerstrikers, so I ask if anything's been heard.

'What? You don't know? It's all over Khaufpur.'

'I've just come from home.'

Ramlal is about to speak when Zafar stirs and mumbles, 'Who has come?'

'Zafar? Zafar-bhai, it's me, Animal. I've something to tell you.'

'Animal? Good you've come,' he says out of lips so puffed, blackish they are, falling apart, they hardly can speak. 'I also have something to tell you.'

'What is it, mate?'

'Come near, I can't talk so well.'

Yesterday he was bad, today he's worse. His eyes are red storms. His breath rattles like dice.

'How are you feeling?'

'I've stopped sweating. Can't take a piss. I'm burning up.'

'It's Nautapa.'

'No. I'm burning from inside. Like a furnace.' Poor fellow's trying to lick his lips but they don't get moist. 'Let that be. Come nearer, I don't want anyone to hear.'

So I crouch down right by him and he takes my hand. Almost I jump back, his skin is so hot. It's like when I was carrying Aliya.

He says, 'You are fond of Nisha, I know.'

'Of course. We all are.'

'Yes, but with you . . . for you it's special, na?'

'What do you mean?'

'No time to argue,' he says. 'Can hardly talk, so just listen.' I nod, and he says, 'What we are doing, it could go wrong. If anything happens, look after her. Make sure she's okay.'

This request and his pessimism catch me off guard. 'Zafar, you silly sod, stop this right now, you don't need to do it any more.' Even as I say this I realise that my news is bound to make him even more determined.

300

'She trusts you,' he says, ignoring my remark. 'She has a real soft spot for you. You must look after her.'

'Me? How can I look after anyone?'

'Because you care for her.' Once again his arid tongue fails to moisten his mouth. To watch it is painful. 'That is the main thing, Animal, that you care, but there's this too, you're clever, you're gifted. You're the brightest guy I know.'

'Come on, don't try to sweet talk me,' says I. Never did I guess he thought such things about me.

'If some untoward thing happens,' says he, closing his eyes, 'if it happens, she'll need someone she can trust, who can lift her spirits. You've such a wicked sense of humour. You must get her through.'

I cannot believe he's talking like this. 'She loves you, arsehole. If you die, what will I do? Crack jokes to lighten her mood?'

'I envy you,' he says. 'Seriousness is a curse. I wish I'd laughed more. Been more like you.'

'Stop!' I say sharply, seeing him beginning to slide to some dark place. 'Never did I think to hear you say such things. You are our hero, you are our leader, we need you. Now come back and fight.'

He says affectionately, 'Fucker, you pretend you're an animal, and in this much you resemble one, you keep your nose to the ground and your tail up.'

'Fucking fishguts. Who says I'm pretending?'

His eyes open, a slow smile tears at his mouth. 'See? Such an ironist. You have understood something worthwhile, my friend, in the end the only way to deal with tragedy is to laugh at it.' His dry tongue scrapes the smile away. 'How I wish I had some water. I've had to tell them, don't drink in front of me. It makes me crazy.'

'Who drank in front of you?'

'A friend. Yesterday. I saw her drinking out of a bottle. She didn't know I was watching. The bottle was frosty.' He closes his eyes, swallows, you can almost hear his throat cracking. Poor bastard, every word is costing him. 'I was imagining, no, I was longing for, the sensation of cold water going down the throat. The image of that bottle would not leave me, it just got worse. Last night all my dreams were about water, I woke with such a thirst.' He falls back, the long speech has exhausted him.

All of a sudden I am ashamed to my depths of what I have done to Zafar. 'Zafar-brother, forgive me. I came to tell you one thing, but first I must tell you something else.'

'Go ahead.'

'I have been jealous of you.'

'I know.'

'How can you know?'

'Nisha told me,' he says.

'You don't know. Not how bad it was. It was like your fire, burning me up from inside. You know what, I thought of every way to split you up. Hindu girl, Muslim boy? I even considered fomenting communal troubles so your marriage would be impossible.'

'So what happened?' he asks, something like a gleam returning to his eye.

'Pointless, this is Khaufpur, na?' So many times the politicians have tried to stir trouble between the communities in Khaufpur. Always the Khaufpuris say, we have suffered together, we will not be divided.

'Fucker.' He's still holding my hand and gives it a squeeze.

'Zafar brother, I have something else to tell you. It's bad. Very bad.'

'Tell me, my brother.'

'Zafar bhai, I am afraid that I have poisoned you.'

Confession is like puking, you can't stop till you're empty. So I tell him about the pills, how Faqri had assured me they were for one purpose, which was the derogation of his sexual urge, Nisha vis-à-vis. Plus I wasn't to know they contained datura.

'Datura?' he says. 'Fucking datura. No wonder I felt so bad.'

Then I confess to climbing the tree, once, to spy on him and Nisha. He doesn't need to know about the other times, only once can you be exe-

302

cuted no matter how murders you commit. I am expecting he'll be livid, but he lies on his rug looking at me out of his reddened eyes.

'Aren't you going to get angry?'

He sighs. 'Animal, brother, I'm too tired to be angry.' Then he reaches out and taps my head. 'So all this turmoil, chaos, this churning rage against the world, has been going on in here?'

'Anyway, no need to be cross,' says I, 'For I did not see anything. You did nothing of that sort.'

An odd snort escapes him, and his chest is palpitating. I'm thinking oh shit the shock of this is killing him, but turns out he's laughing. It's a dried up kind of laugh, somewhere between coughing, sobbing and snotting.

'Animal, you are too much. By god in whom I refuse to believe there are limits, but you exceed them all.

'Nothing that I saw, anyway.'

'Yes, I know that. Such things can wait till marriage.'

'What, not even a kiss?'

'Maybe a kiss.'

'Bastard.'

'Well,' says he, pushing up on one elbow, 'at least it proves one thing, that you'll look after Nisha. I can trust you to keep her honour safe.'

'Don't joke, yaar. I am too ashamed.'

'Definitely, you are the right man.'

'I am not a man.'

'Well my brother,' says he, 'definitely the right animal.'

Someone suggests that I should not keep Zafar talking any more, but Zafar says not to worry. 'Old friends, it gladdens the heart to see them, and this bastard, with his impudence and his lopsided grin, he makes me laugh, and by god in whom I don't believe I feel better for it.'

So then it's time to give him the real news. Leaning right down to his ear, I whisper, 'Zafar, the thing I came to tell you, it's bad. I have proof that Elli doctress is working for the Kampani.' So I start telling him about what I saw at Jehannum, how I'd hidden under the table and caught Elli with the foreign lawyer, how he said she'd done a fine job and could go home, and then how he'd kissed her. Zafar listens to all this with no expression. When I've finished he says, 'Animal, you have done right to tell me, but I already know. Last night, Elli told Somraj. I'm afraid it will be bad for her. Try to see she too is okay.'

After these puzzling words he says, 'Brother, I'm burning up. Ask them to fetch ice. Crush it in a cloth and put it on my skin, please do the same for Farouq.'

'No deal! No deal!' The second demo in a week, here we are again, the paltaniyas of the Apokalis, the people's earth-shaking platoons. This day, which is the seventh of the Nautapa, it's the fiercest heat yet. Not yet ten in the morning but the steps outside the court house are like bars of hot metal. We've all arrived full of excitement because the Kampani's deal has not been signed and the hearing's about to begin. Zafar and Farouq are there, so weak that people must stand beside them and steady them. Zafar's staring out of eyes that already look dead. 'Sit, don't stand,' someone says. Zafar says he'll wait until they are inside. Then he will sit. Ten minutes are left before the court opens its doors and the hearing begins, but when the appointed hour comes, of the judge is no sign. We are used to their lateness, but people are saying the m'lord should have made an effort, he must know that some here are half dead with their fasting, and still refusing to touch water? After twenty minutes a court official comes out and mumbles a few words. People nearby exclaim in anger. 'What's happening? What's going on?' The news spreads like fire in dry grass. 'The hearing has been postponed. They've postponed the hearing.'

'NO DEAL! NO DEAL, NO DEAL!'

The chant begins again. People are furious. The judge, it seems, has been transferred, already he has left Khaufpur for some other court, they forgot to inform us.

Shouts someone, 'The Amrikans are coming.'

With an escort of armed police the four lawyers arrive at the courthouse.

Will they really feign surprise? What? the hearing's been postponed, well I never, who'd have thought it? The cops, knowing the mood and quality of the crowd, are not keen for the lawyers to leave their car, and once they're out are anxious to hustle them back in, but it's too late. They are surrounded by a gang of jarnaliss from the *Khaufpur Gazette, Doordrishti* etc, shouting questions. 'Why is the hearing postponed?' 'Has a deal been agreed?'

'We're here to offer generous humanitarian aid to the people of Khaufpur,' says the buffalo.

'Are charges against the Kampani being dropped?'

'NO DEAL! NO DEAL!' Sound of a crowd working itself into a rage.

'Will you clean the factory?'

'Where are your clients? Where are the accused executives?'

'We're confident that all outstanding issues will be resolved.'

'NO DEAL! NO DEAL! NO DEAL!'

'How much will the compensation be?' 'What is your agreement with the government?' 'Did you know the hearing would be cancelled?'

'NO DEAL! NO DEAL, NO DEAL!'

'Say again, quite a bit of noise going on here.'

Hear O paltaniyas, learn wisdom. You can shrill and cry as much as you want. You can scream in their fucking ears, still you will not be heard.

'When will the agreement be signed? Days? Weeks? Months?'

'Can't be too soon for me,' says the buffalo. 'I'm missing home. I have two Italian greyhounds. They sleep on my bed.'

 An old woman hobbles forward out of the crowd, it's Gargi, whose back is almost as bent as mine. 'Mr Lawyer, we lived in the shadow of your factory, you told us you were making medicine for the fields. You were making poisons to kill insects, but you killed us instead. I would like to ask, was there ever much difference, to you?'

So the buffalo asks what she is saying and a jarnalis standing nearby says, 'I don't know how to translate it.'

Then Gargi says that if the Kampani has any honour it must stand trial, and it should pay just and proper compensation for all the wrongs it has done.

'What's she saying now?' the lawyer asks.

'Sir,' says the jarnalis, 'she is asking for money.'

The buffalo reaches in his red-lined coat, gets out his wallet. 'Buy yourself something nice,' he says. Old Gargi's standing there with five hundred rupees in her hand.

'Mr Musisin, how do you justify what you do?' asks a voice that comes from a creature not of this world. It's Zafar, propped between two friends. His face is sunken, he has not taken a drop of water.

The lawyer knows who Zafar is. The smile on his face grows broad.

'Hey, Zafar,' he says. 'When you get to my age and you have two Italian greyhounds and you've read as many books as I have, and have as many friends among lawyers and judges, and have won as many cases, you don't have to spend time justifying yourself.'

'He won't let me see him. You must go, Animal. Tell him I love him, if he dies I will die too. Remind him of all the reasons there are for him to live.'

'He can't die.' Zafar is invincible, untouchable, immortal.

'Animal, I'm afraid. Elli says he's weak from his stomach upsets. He has forbidden her for her own safety to go to him.'

A huge stone slides in my bowels. I have done this, if he dies it'll be my fault. I'll go to him and say, Zafar stop this fucking nonsense, take some milk, take a little kheer. Meanwhile I'll pray, 'Gods of fate, or whatever, if you exist you know Zafar's a marked man, one day some Kampani hitman is sure to take his life. For love's sake I made one stupid mistake don't make me his fucking murderer.'

Bhoora Khan returns empty-handed from Huriya's place. Although Aliya's still burning up, the old people say they can no longer take her to Elli.

'Who says you can't?' Bhoora argued with them. 'Zafar brother would want Aliya to take treatment.'

'People say Zafar brother is dying. We cannot go.'

So then I know that this time the people will not come back. Elli's dream is finished and so is mine.

Seven days without water. Even Zafar knows it's over. He has to give up now or he will die. His body is failing, he is so weak, he can no longer stand. His eyesight is blurring. He whispers, 'Animal, is it you?'

I put my mouth right next to his ear, 'Speak brother, I am here.'

In that moment I love him utterly and know it will break my heart if he goes, plus I feel Nisha's love within me like a torrent.

'I'm okay,' he lies, his breath is rasping. 'Who wouldn't feel weak after a week without water? There's a stove in my chest. I'm burning inside. When I wash my face I feel tempted to take a sip. When I see someone drinking water my heart whispers let's have just a little drink. But then I think, if I drink what will happen to our struggle?'

'How is Farouq?' I ask, seeing my arch-enemy lying there on the rug. I feel pity even for him.

'Farouq has the Upstairs One,' he says. 'He gets strength from that. Me, I won't ask god to help, but I get strength from my friends. Like you, Animal, bastard.' He manages a faint smile. 'Such a bloody idiot you are, did you never realise that datura is an aphrodisiac?'

'What, you felt the urge?'

'What else?' says he. 'Am I not human?'

He lies back, someone places a cushion under his head. They are there waiting with frosted bottles, trying to tempt him with the cool water, heedless are they of the agony it causes him, they are trying to break his will and save his life, but still he will not drink. 'Animal, ask Somraj to come and see me. Take good care of yourself, mate. Best as you are able, look after Nisha.'

'We're going to win,' I tell him. Almost I am in tears. 'I'm confident we will win. Listen you bastard, listen, you darling cunt of a man, we are going to win.'

I am smiling at him through my tears, and trying to hold in my mind the vision of a world in which the power of nothing has swept away the Kampani and all the evil and cruel things are no more. Come, you power of nothing, if ever there was a time for you to show yourself it's now, it's now. Whatever he had, this man has given. Nothing more has he to give, except his life, and soon there will be nothing left of Zafar. Never has his power been greater than at this moment. The Nautapa is flaring out of his body, his breath is like flames. One breath from Zafar could set the world on fire.

How long do I sit there, beside the man who is going? An hour maybe, two, time has no meaning. My head is full of thoughts that circle like pigeons, always coming back to the same roost. On Zafar's face is an expression that is filled with peace, as if he has resolved all his struggles.

What is this thing called dying? Saying goodbye, letting go, one by one, of memories and sensations, the last time one ever thinks of cloves, or ginger, or green silk, or the white etawa bird. All the things that make up life, let them go one by one, until there is only now and here, the colours on the wall of the tent, that blur of light, voices . . . let all that too go.

'Zafar, my brother, I once heard you say something beautiful. You said, *jahaañ jaan hai, jahaan hai.*' We have the world, while we still have life.

'Fucking romantic.' These are the last words I hear him speak.

A great noise begins outside. 'The factory,' voices are shouting. 'They're beating people! We must all go there.'

At the factory gates there's a brawl going on. People from Jyotinagar, right across the road, are gathered there, demanding to be let inside. About forty cops have their backs to the gates. The rusting ironwork begins to rock. People have climbed over the wall and come up from behind. They're climbing on the gates, gripping the bars and shaking them, trying to pull them down. The gates are swaying. Guards come running from inside, but these are village oafs the Kampani has hired, the ones who sit drinking tea all day and night, they do not want to get involved. The police are screaming at them to attack the invaders, pull them off the gates, beat them, but the guards stand and watch. More and more pro-testers appear each minute, thin figures running out of alleys, shouting, waving their arms. I too push close, shouldering my way past knees and thighs, trying to avoid having my fingers stepped on. Rage I'm feeling, plus sorrow. I have just left Zafar, never will I forgive his death or the manner of it. I want to rend the bastard Kampani in bits, if I could attack that buffalo lawyer I would bite his cancerous tongue out and squeeze his throat till greyhounds pop out of his eyes and he feels maddened teeth tearing his heart. In this moment of anger I look up and there are placid clouds drifting across the sky. This shakes me. Outside of ourselves nothing cares.

Zafar and Farouq are far away in the old city, they have breathed their last, if this news should reach the crowd, god knows what the result will be. One of the women is shouting at the senior cop. He is afraid, I can see, though I cannot hear what is being said. She stoops, rises again with a slipper in her hand. She strikes him with it right across the face. The cop does nothing, his men are scared, now the fury of the people has been let loose who knows where it'll stop, it's a storm battering everything in its path, it's an avalanche pouring down a mountain, it's a flood that rises swiftly with no warning, it's a fire lit by lightning on a hillside where all is dry, awaiting the spark. These things I'm saying I did not believe before, now I do, the power of nothing is unleashed, as Zafar feared it is already out of control, it will destroy what it touches because it is fuelled not just by anger but despair. The cop who was struck's being harangued by others. The gates are rocking wildly, one's come away from its hinges and is hanging, the men clinging to it double their efforts, others are jumping on to add their weight. Still the guards stand watching, many of them have thrown down their sticks, it's not worth their lives to defend this place of horror, this land of cobras. The police are trying to get out from underneath, or they'll be crushed when the gates fall. Another hinge gives way and slowly, the barred portal to the factory sags, then dhoofs flat on the ground in a cloud of dust, the police have fled, some of them

310

too are sitting on the ground with their sticks laid down. The crowd surges into the wilderness beyond the gates, but now they're in they do not know what to do. There is an open space, to one side of the avenue of small mango trees that leads to the guardhouse and here the crowd gathers. Many sit down, there are no leaders to tell them what should happen next, this is something they've done themselves. Someone has to take charge, but there is no one. 'What shall we do now?' people are asking.

'Tear this place down,' someone cries. 'Burn it!' yells another, so I start shouting, 'Friends, do not burn anything here, or the chemicals will catch light, it'll be that night all over again.'

This word spreads in the crowd, who by now number hundreds, with more still arriving. 'Do not burn anything. Do not light matches.'

The ever-swelling crowd is full of energy, it wants to do something, but no one can agree what. The women, possessed by nothing's power, begin their chants, 'We are flames not flowers. With our brooms, we will beat the Kampani, we will sweep them out from Khaufpur. Out of India we will sweep them. Out of all existence.'

Of course it can't last. Dark vans are pulling up by the shattered gate, many vans, maybe twenty. Out jump police wearing helmets, carrying shields and long staves. They form up in ranks, then enter the factory. The crowd. which had gone quiet, watching, now resumes its chants of defiance, louder than before the whole crowd is singing. At such moments people get carried away and say things they otherwise never would utter. They're shouting, come on, do the Kampani's dirty work, beat us, take our lives, what do we care, who've lost everything anyway? The police advance, without halting or asking questions, their long staves begin to beat. Then there's uproar, cries of men and women being hurt, howls of anger from deeper in the crowd, which draws back, away from the zone of beating. A police general steps up, a loudhailer in his hand. His voice sounds twangy as he shouts. 'Go back to your homes, don't be led astray, the people who have organised this are Hindu extremists, they have come here from outside to sow hatred and divide your community.'

311

Despite the fear, there is a great shout of laughter. 'Go away,' voices shout. 'There are no Muslims or Hindus here, there are just humans.'

Plus one animal. I am lost in a thicket of legs, so I work my way to one side of the crowd, then I can see the fallen gates, police dragging people out, throwing them in the trucks.

'Leave us alone,' cry the voices. 'Go and lick the arse of your master the Chief Minister, who licks the hole of Peterson.'

'Get out! Go!' Then the chants begin again, flames not flowers, the chant of sweeping away with brooms, the song of the people's platoons.

Even now, the horror of that day has hardly begun. More police trucks are arriving. Out of one jumps my old enemy Fatlu Inspector, whom I caught with a stone at the CM demo, this fat bastard is entering the factory site with his gang of goons. They don't hesitate, but go straight into the crowd and then they are grabbing people, man, woman, doesn't matter, by any part they can reach, arm, hair, ear, and dragging them off kicking and protesting.

'Send for help,' people are yelling. 'Tell everyone to come!'

Fatlu, this putain, he is a bully, he takes pleasure in dealing out pain. He loves his power to hurt. At other times I have been afraid of him, I have run away, at the CM's demo I hid behind a tree, but today is the day Zafar died. I'm burning with a bloody rage. Fatlu has grabbed hold of a man from Jyotinagar, he is beating him with his fist. 'Bastard, where is your permission to enter this place?'

'Sir, I came with the others,' says this fellow, who's thin and weak, with all the woes of Khaufpur written in his face.

'Bastard,' says Fatlu, 'how dare you speak to me? Where . . . is . . . your . . . permission.' During each of these pauses, the fist falls on the man's head.

'We don't need your permission,' a woman shouts. It's Nisha. All in white is she, the colour a widow wears. The news is confirmed then, Zafar is dead. Fatlu continues to beat the man. Nisha grabs hold of his arm, tries to drag him off. Fatlu swings his elbow. She falls to the ground, holding her face. Blood is coming from her mouth. He has hurt Nisha, I will kill this bastard and eat his heart.

Fatlu never sees his death approach, I've come running up behind, he's missed me because I'm so low to the ground, I've grabbed the swine round the legs and hauled him down. With a shout, Fatlu falls. Struggling he's to get back on his feet, but I've got him pinned. In vain he strikes at my head, I am stronger, far stronger than he. My shoulders and arms are powerful, muscled like a wrestler's, I've told you this, and now they will end this bastard's life. My hands fasten round his throat. With what horror his eyes bulge. 'No more torture for you, sisterfucker,' I shout in his ear then take the ear in my teeth, I bite until blood is running between my lips, he is screaming. I will not stop, let the ear come off, that's just the beginning, I am going to tear out his throat and gouge his eyes, but rough hands are pulling me off, blows are falling, blows of heavy sticks, on my head, my back, my shoulders, nothing of me is there that is not being beaten. From far away, it seems, I hear Nisha's voice crying, 'Leave him alone, he was just trying to save me. Father, help him.' As the blows fall I'm thinking, Nisha darling, no use is it appealing to the father, nor to the mother, the son nor the holy ghost, for neither Christian am I nor Hindu nor Muslim, not Brahmin nor Sufi nor saint, neither man am I nor beast. I don't know what is being beaten here. If they kill me what will die?

The blows stop. I'm lying on the ground, my mouth is full of blood, which I hope is Fatlu's. Something slimy I've spat on the ground, then I see Somraj, who does not believe in direct or violent action, who trusts that law will flower into justice, walk forward and place himself in front of Fatlu inspector.

'You are a disgrace,' Somraj says, and slaps Fatlu across the face.

The sticks blur around Somraj, they come crashing from all directions. I see him fall, his white spotless kurta turning red, many of them are standing around him with the sticks flailing. In this way my dream comes true, the one where sticks descended on Somraj, and afterwards crows flew down upon his lifeless corpse. The thought comes to me, it's not his body that is dying, it's his heart. Lying hearing the thud of police sticks beating Somraj, I don't know what will happen to us. Maybe they'll kill us here and now, or drag us to their cells to finish us. So many die in the cells. What will it be like to die? Can it be worse than this horrible life? I am not afraid, just curious. Then a thing happens that no one could have predicted.

From nowhere a tide of ragged people surges over the police and sweeps them away. Thousands have come, they have heard of the fight at the factory and the plight of the Jyotinagar folk and they have come from the Nutcracker and Blue Moon and beyond, from Phuta Maqbara and Mira Colony, from Khabbarkhana and Qazi Camp, even from Chowk, the people have dropped what they were doing and run to our aid and the cursed police are gone. As they run for their trucks, they are forced to crouch behind their shields because the road is lined with crowds who want their blood, never have I seen such fury. One man, he's ragged, thin his ribs are like furrows ploughed in his flesh, no strength can he have for portering or load-lifting, but so filled with anger is his weak body that he has ripped a paving stone from out of the earth and flung it at the pandus. Now it's their turn to drop, it's their blood that stains the earth. Let them bleed, cunts, no stomach have they for this fight. One thing it's when people are unarmed, defenceless, but these newcomers are armed, the despair of twenty years has turned to rage, in some hands I see knives and swords gleaming. That's when I know that this will not end here. This day is not over yet.

People from the Claw find us and wipe the blood from us and bring us back to Somraj's house. How long were we in the factory, I don't know, it must have been hours, for the sun is setting, it is below the rooftops, the sky is streaked red like it too is wearing blood-soaked bandages. Somraj pandit is beaten sore, but refusing to go and lie down, his daughter is fretting over him, it's now I learn she's had no news from the old city.

'Animal,' she says. 'You were there. How is Zafar. Tell me is he alive? Tell me he's all right.'

I do not know what to tell her. The day is over, the time when they could have saved their lives is gone, the tent has become a shroud for Zafar and Farouq. Gone they are, right when most needed, for the power of nothing is unleashed and must be directed or it will achieve nothing but destruction and death. They are gone. I would rather she heard this news from anyone but me.

'You haven't been to see him?'

'Zafar forbade me,' she says simply. 'I have to respect his wish. Besides, I told him I wouldn't be there, that I could not bear to watch him die.'

Oh no, Nisha. I have the gift and I know the truth, you've been hoping that Zafar will hang on, will not let go until he has seen you. So you did not go and do not go, hoping to stretch out his life a little further.

'Go now,' I say. 'Quickly. Find an auto.' But it's too late and I am thinking that the streets are not safe. Distant uproars can be heard, police sirens too. Soon the army will be called, like they were on that night, when the politicians made them take thousands of bodies and throw them in the Chameli river.

'If Zafar dies, I will take care of you Nisha. I will marry you.'

'Please don't talk like that. He will not die.'

'I love you, Nisha. I always have. You are everything to me.'

'Poor loyal Animal, I can never marry you.' She starts sobbing and I go to put my arms round her. She accepts the hug, but then says, 'Animal, you must go to Ma. We don't know what may happen on this night.'

In the street outside her clinic I come across Elli, pale as a ghost she's. 'My god,' she says, 'what happened to you? Come inside.'

Well, I guess I am looking pretty bad, there are lumps all over my head, one eye is nearly closed plus my kakadus are stained with blood. The ache from these wounds is nothing compared to the ache in my heart. About Zafar and Farouq I don't want to think. In place of the anger there's a kind of numbness, a palace of desolation is my soul, not the kind of place I would choose to live, this world does not seem a good place to be, but I will go into Elli's clinic one last time because she should know what I think of her.

'Animal?' she asks, leading me towards her office, 'are you hurt bad?'

'It's nothing.'

'What happened?' she asks, again all caring concern.

This numbness I'm feeling, it's like volcanoes on the tele, outside they're black and dead, but inside red lakes are seething. I can't be polite to Elli.

'Don't you fucking know? Your friends cancelled the hearing.'

'So you've heard too.' She sighs. 'It's all over town that I'm a traitor. People think I've lied to them, Hanif and Huriya stopped Aliya coming to the clinic. Everything's just collapsed.'

'Elli,' says I, 'I don't know what game you are playing, nor why Somraj and Zafar want to protect you, but it's me, Animal, you're dealing with now. I saw you in the garden of Jehannum, kissing the Kampani lawyer and he's told you you've done a great job and can go home. So I guess you'll soon be off and forget us Khaufpuris and the promises you made about straightening my back and marrying pandit Somraj, all so many lies . . .'

'No,' she cries. 'No. Not lies.'

A this the red rage jolts up into my throat. 'Fishguts I'm, Elli, to believe I could ever walk upright, but to poison the hopes of a man like Somraj, how could you do that? I saw him today being beaten, all the life had gone from his eyes. No one else might say this to you, Elli doctress, so hear it from me. You say the world is made of promises, but you are no better than the politicians who lie with every word they speak, or your master the filthy Kampani itself, I curse the day I met you plus I can tell you this, no matter how sick people are here, we are better off without your sort, so hurry up, fuck off back to Amrika, the land where people like you belong.'

'Stop, please.' She's crying. 'How can you think such things of me?'

'What should I think? Zafar and Farouq are dead.'

316

'Dead? Oh god, oh no!' and she's relapsed into such grief, what acting, I wouldn't have believed it possible.

'For all of this we can thank your friends.'

She screams, 'They are not my friends! I hate that Kampani. I fucking hate them. I hate them worse than you do.'

'What? And will you also tell me that Amrikan lawyer man didn't kiss you, in the garden at Jehannum?'

'How could you know that?'

'You are married to this man,' I say, ignoring her question. 'Don't ask how I know, it's my gift, my voices tell me what's in your mind. You are married to this man yet you do everything to make Somraj fall in love with you. Don't you know how he has suffered? Torturing him, does it make you happy?'

'I've done nothing to be ashamed of.'

'Have you ever said a true or sincere word to any of us?'

Anger is catching and now it's in her voice too. 'Some friend you are, Animal. If the voices in your head know everything they should know that I am fucking divorced from that man. He tricked and cheated me as he has all the rest of us. I can never forgive him.'

'Oh, so how come you let him kiss you. Why did he say you'd done such a good job you could go home to Amrika? I was there wasn't I? Me, mister Jamispond. I was sent to Jehannum to keep an eye on the lawyers.'

'But you saw me, and immediately assumed the worst?' I can feel her eyes like hot lamps on my face.

'What else to assume?'

'What about the work I've done here? What about us being friends? Why didn't you come and ask me about it?'

'I felt sick.'

'Well hear this then,' says Elli. 'I don't work for the Kampani. My husband does. I fought with him about it, it's one of the reasons I divorced him and came here. But I was stupid. You can't right other people's wrongs. I am not going to apologise for anything, but get one thing

317

straight. Those four men are not my friends. I hate them like poison. To me, they're the worst people in the world. I was doing work I loved, I met a man I loved. They came here, they fucked all that up. God knows what I'll do now.'

'You'll go back to Amrika, like the Amrikan lawyer told you.'

'Like hell I will. I'm not giving up, I won't be beaten by those bastards. Animal, I don't blame you for thinking the worst, in your place I'd likely have done the same. But now you'll hear my side.'

So Elli tells me of the shock she had felt when the Amrikan lawyers came to the city. These were people who knew her, who could undo all her work. When Timecheck described the big guy with the red-lined coat, she knew exactly who it was. She'd been to his house, eaten pizza by his pool, shopped with his wife. Mel Musisin, he's a heartless bastard, but the biggest shock was when she saw the fourth lawyer on the local tele. It was her husband, Frank. For all the next day Elli lived in fear of the phone, sure enough that evening he called her, asked to see her. She refused, so he gave her the number of the hotel and his room number. On the night of the CM demo, Elli waved the others off feeling like a Judas. She stood on her roof and looked towards the hill where the CM's house was. Even across this distance, she could hear the crowd, the chanting. Then the rifle shots, hard flat cracks, echoing over the city. She rushed downstairs and turned on the tele, but there was nothing on but some old movie, *Badnaami Ka Dilaasa*. The solace of infamy. Elli hoped it was not an omen.

An anxious half hour passed before Somraj stepped from an auto, his kurta snowy in the moonlight. He took her arm and led her into the garden. On an impulse she grabbed his face in her hands and kissed him on the mouth.

'Shhh,' said Somraj.

'I didn't say anything.'

'Nisha? She's here? Zafar?'

'They're back.' She's touched her fingertips to his cheek, his lips.

'Please, not here,' says Somraj, removing her hands.

318

'Tell me what happened. Why did the police fire?'

'To frighten. Playing tough. The politicians want this deal.'

'But the court is ready to make an order against the Kampani.' Mentioning the Kampani made her feel sick.

'If they sign a deal, the case will be dead,' he says. 'Our only hope is they don't reach an agreement before the hearing. Once we have a ruling, it will be hard for them.'

That's why Musisin and the others are here, she realises, almost at once he echoes this thought. 'It's the first time they have sent lawyers.'

'Surely the government has people's interests at heart,' she tries, wishing to believe it. Somraj shakes his head. 'In this country decent people don't go into politics.'

'So what can we do?'

'Nothing.'

'Nothing? Like Zafar's power of nothing?'

'Zafar is Zafar and by nothing I mean nothing, but maybe he is right. There is a strength that comes from having nothing because you have nothing to lose. What is it? Maybe courage, or ingenuity, or desperation, it appears where there is no help and no hope. Look at how you came to us. Out of nowhere, and out of nothing came a clinic.'

And now Somraj tells her what at that time no one else knows, of Zafar's plan for a fast unto death.

Elli can no longer hide her unhappiness. Somraj, awkward and gentle as ever, reaches out his arms to her and draws her close to him. If ever's the time to share her secret it's now, but she does not have the courage.

What can I find to do? she's thinking. What can I do that might make even the smallest difference? Nothing presents itself. Elli closes her eyes and thinks about nothing.

It's past eleven when she leaves the clinic. She's wearing a burqa to disguise herself. Still she keeps to the dark side of the lane.

Elli walks up the wide road leading to the Chowk. It's late, but the place is still full of people. No one takes any notice. In a quiet place she removes the burqa and puts into a bag. Then hails an auto.

The Jehan-nabz Hotel is clean and softly lit. In the garden are dinner tables and waiters with turbans like roses clearing away dishes. Elli checks her reflection in a case of swords and guns that had belonged to the Chhoté Nawab. The few months in the Khaufpuri sun have browned her skin. The receptionist is discreet and efficient. 'Of course at once, madam,' he smiles, shortly afterwards reporting, 'The gentleman is coming right away.'

Nearly a year since she'd last met Frank. She wonders if he's changed, it would be odd to treat him like a stranger. But Frank looks as familiar as ever.

'Elli!' He catches up her hands. 'You look great.'

'So do you.' He looks elegant, completely relaxed. Never ruffled, always charming. She remembers how proud she had been when he used to sweep her into a room full of strangers, announcing, 'Hey everyone, this is my wife,' and how jealous she would get when the other women flirted with him.

'It's okay to kiss you? Just a chaste one?'

She offers her cheek, trying to hide the tumult inside. What can I offer him, she's wondering, to make him do what I want.

'Two Jack Daniels, long as the glass is tall,' he tells the hovering waiter.

'Frank, is there somewhere private we can talk?'

'There's my room,' he says, with a smile.

'Not that private. Perhaps we can walk in the garden.'

When they're outside and he takes her arm, she is not sure how to react. The hand steering her elbow is the old possessive Frank. He's still thinking of her as his wife.

If her ex-husband notices her awkwardness, he gives no sign. 'Back home it's late spring,' he says. 'You should see the flowers. They're out everywhere. Just before I came out here, I went walking in the woods with your folks. We saw all those things you used to tell me the names of. Let me see, Cow's tongue, that's yellow, right? Bloodroot, Indian pipe, that little thing that looks like a dog's tooth, Dutchman's bitches . . .'

'Britches,' she says, with a genuine laugh. 'How are my parents?'

'Martha's having a grand spell. Your dad's good. He said to tell you they are looking forward to your visit.'

'That's good, I'm looking forward to it too.'

Frank hesitates. 'Apparently you're bringing some friends.' Uh oh, she seeks escape in her glass, but the drink is going straight to her head. They have come to a group of wicker chairs in the middle of the hotel's wide lawn. Ahead is the blue glow of the swimming pool and near it a tree hung with coloured bulbs.

'Your dad says you're thinking of marrying an Indian guy. Is this true?'

'We've talked about it.'

'Are you serious?' Now his voice is a river of concern, as if she were a child about to do something stupid. Same old Frank, so reasonable, utterly lacking in imagination and adventure.

'He's a singer,' she says, as if this explains everything.

'A singer? What is he, in a band?'

'He sings classical music.' How can she begin to describe Somraj? 'Indian classical,' she adds, to stop him making a comment about opera or Pavarotti.

'Do you love him?'

This question pierces her. Don't ask me that, she thinks, or I'll cry. 'No more questions,' she says, trying to smile. 'I'm not on oath here.'

'The witness will answer,' he says in his light teasing manner.

'The answer is that you don't consider marrying someone if you don't love them. At least I don't.'

'Ouch,' he says, making a face. It was the way he always used to end their quarrels, make a funny face, make her laugh.

'You used to love me.' He's heading straight back into territory she wants to avoid. 'You know I want you back.'

'I'm sure you're better off without me.'

Frank begins to complain about his life in Pennsylvania, how it's work, all work these days, no time for fun.

He's stalling, she suddenly realises. He's wondering why I am here.

'Frank,' she says, 'I've come to talk to you about something important.'

She begins to tell him about the people she has met in Khaufpur. Of Hanif Ali, left blind for twenty years by the gases of that night, of the woman who poured her poisoned milk onto the ground. She tells him about me, the strange, half-mad boy who goes on all fours, and believes he's an animal. She describes the horrifying things she sees every day, and tells how the Kampani's refusal to share its knowledge of the poisons is hurting people.

'Elli, this is awful, but you know that people like me don't have control over those kind of decisions. All I can do is my own job.'

'Why do I have to be your conscience?' she cries. 'Make it your job. Can't you see that hiding behind trade secrets is totally wicked? There are people back home who know exactly what those gases do to the lungs, to the eyes, to the uterus. Frank, I see young girls who bleed three times a month and others who have one period in five months. No one knows how to treat them.'

'When I get back home I can knock on some doors.'

'If they withhold information that could save lives, that's murder.'

'Whoa Elli,' he says, 'now calm down, I would like to help you if I can. I'd do most things for you. But there's no point pretending I can do things I can't.'

'You can try,' she says. 'At least get the Kampani to clean the factory. Its poisons are in the wells, they're in people's blood, they're in mother's milk. Frank, if you came to my clinic I could show you. Specimens, I mean. Foetuses, babies that never made it. You wouldn't want to see such things, even in your nightmares.'

'You're right, I wouldn't.' He's silent a moment, then asks in what ways specifically is the water affecting people's health? What kind of illnesses are showing up? Has she seen the evidence with her own eyes? How can she be sure the chemicals in the factory are to blame?

Furiously, Elli cites names of chemicals, illnesses, people, her small hope is fading fast. Frank is here to do the Kampani's bidding. Then again at least he's listening and says he loves her. Suppose, just suppose, she can manage to touch Frank, to move him. All the Khaufpuris need is seven days.

'Elli I'm sorry,' Frank says. 'I honestly wish I could help you.' They are approaching the tree, beneath which is a long table loaded with food. 'You hungry? I can't eat any of this stuff. I live on omelettes and fries.'

She says, 'Frank I beg you. I'm pleading with you. You must stop this deal.' She clasps his arm. 'Please listen to me, if you had spent any time among these people, you'd understand.'

He stands appraising her. 'Elli, you are amazing,' he says. 'Full of passion, infuriating, adorable.' He reaches out, unhappily she endures the touch of his hands on her shoulders. 'I admire you,' he says. 'I always have. No, admire isn't a strong enough word. Elli, you know how I feel about you.'

'Then do this,' she says. 'Do this for me. Please do it.'

'Can't. It can't be stopped.'

'Then delay it. Give these people their chance of justice. Delay it till after the hearing.'

'You want this real bad, don't you?' he says. 'There's something I want every bit as bad. Can you guess what it is?' She shakes her head, not daring to think.

'It's to hear you say you're coming home.' He's facing her, now he puts his hands on her shoulders. 'Elli, you've done a great job here. Come home now. Hand over your work to local doctors and come home.'

'You know I can't do that,' she says. 'I couldn't even if I wanted to, and I don't want to.'

'Now you're sounding like me,' says Frank. 'There's no way you can do what I want, no way I can do what you want.' He bends his head and kisses her on the cheek. 'Sounds like we should make a deal.'

'What deal?'

He thinks for a while. 'What if I can find a way to delay the agreement, to put it off beyond the date you mentioned? Will you come home?'

'Can you really do it? How?' It's impossible, she thought, he can't mean it, he's a lawyer. If he did this, Zafar and Farouq needn't go on their fast, and the Khaufpuris would get their day before a sympathetic judge. 'You'd be doing such a good thing for the people of this town.'

'I'm not doing it for them. I'm doing it for you. And if I do it, you must come back to America. Promise.'

Sadness whelms up inside, as if the big lake under the hills has burst its bung and sent its waters rising swiftly and silently to drown her.

'I promise.'

There comes a banging at the clinic door. Outside is Bhoora's auto, light on, engine's ticking over. 'Come,' he cries when he sees Elli, 'there is no time, you must come right away.'

'What's going on?' I ask. He says he has come to bring Elli doctress to the Nutcracker. Aliya is bad, her fever is worse, the old ones fear for her life.

'Let me come too,' says I, afraid for Aliya but also for Ma Franci.

'Quickly, madam,' says Bhoora. 'Don't worry about your clinic. Somraj pandit has given orders it is not to be touched.'

Without another word she gets in and Bhoora guns the engine. Then we're jolting along through night-time Khaufpur, with the auto's narrow beam of light picking out a way. The road outside the factory is wrecked, it has been ripped to pieces, great stones and lumps of concrete lie in the middle, crowds are roaming around, inside and outside the factory, of police there is no sign, but a TV crew is outside the gates which are still lying flat, from the darkness inside the grounds come sounds of singing.

There's a small group of neighbours gathered outside Huriya's and Hanif's house, from within comes the noises of weeping.

We find the old man with his granddaughter lying in his lap. Aliya's face looks strange. She has rouge on her cheeks, her eyes are ringed with kohl, her mouth is smeared with lipstick. She is wearing a fancy new dress. Old Hanif's fingers are moving over her face, as if he is trying to memorise its details.

Huriya is sobbing. 'Save her doctress sahiba,' she says. 'God bless you, I don't believe what they are saying about you. Save this child. She is all we care for in this life.'

Elli gently lifts the old man's fingers from the child's face.

325

'Why have you dressed her like this?'

'The angel of death is here in this city. When he comes for Aliya, he will see her looking well, healthy. Death will believe he's made a mistake, he will not want to take her and he will go away.' He turns his eyes to the doctor he can't see. 'Won't he?'

The doctress on her knees, bent over the child, listening for her heart, stands, but does not reply.

'Non Elli, non!' I've cried in français so the old ones won't understand, may the anguish in my voice not give me away. 'Pas possible! Fais quelque chose, je t'implore!'

Eyes, I won't translate, there's not a language in this world can describe what's in my soul. Oh my poor friend, why did I never take you fishing? Come back and you shall ride daily on my back, my ribs you may kick as much as you like. Poor child, so sudden your going that your grandparents are still pleading with Elli to save your life. Oh dear old folk, a rupee's worth of rouge, a street-corner lipstick, the angel of death is not so cheaply bought.

Now the old bugger too is crying, I cannot watch. There is something so cruel about eyes which may not see, but may yet shed tears. My own breath is coming in sobs, in gluts like the lungs are refusing it, and why should I live? No longer is there love, nor hope, it's the death of everything good. Gone is Zafar, gone Farouq, hard enough is that grief to bear, plus I am aching from being beaten, but worse is the agony that now fills my body, wants to leak from my eyes, out of my mouth. O god if really you exist, how wicked you must be, how you must hate us folk to torture us so, while in the gardens of Jehannum the evil men are eating well and drinking wine, them you save while the poor go to the dogs, are you in heaven so starved of joy that you must take our best, our most precious, already you have my friends, call off your dark angel from this child, spare her life and I, Animal, who's servant to no one, will be your slave.

Says at last Elli doctress in the language of humans, 'C'est plus à moi.' It's no longer in my hands. The child I loved is gone.

A weird keening cry comes from beyond.

'God be merciful!' says the old lady, Huriya, and Hanif lifts his blind eyes to the sound.

'*Zafar bhai is dead!*'

Again that voice calls, others answer in the name of god in whom Zafar refused to believe. So at last the news has broken. Like dogs howling, first one, then another and another, voices from afar are wailing, the eerie sound floats up over the Nutcracker, from all sides it seems the echoes are arriving.

'*Farouq bhaiya is dead! God save us! Our Zafar bhai has died!*'

A voice from inside me says, 'Animal, this is the end of your carefree days.'

Another warns, 'Do not let them see you cry.'

I run outside, never has any Khaufpuri heard me howl. The heartless stars glitter like knives above the city.

'*Zafar bhai is dead! Farouq bhaiya is dead!*'

'Bhoora, quick, we must go to Ma, then you must take us back to Nisha.'

'Come,' he says, 'Ma is alone, let's go.'

I tell Elli ten minutes, we will be back, then it's the alley narrowing to a dirt track, the crossing over the rails, Bhoora knows the way well, so many times has he dropped me, finally we are bumping across rough ground with weeds glaring white in the auto's beam. There's light flickering inside the tower, outlining its opening. So she is there. The strange cries are still echoing over Khaufpur, drifting up into the night, where clouds are lit by a half moon. Like a tear, they said the moon was on that night, and is again on this night of tears. Poor Aliya, nobody shall miss her like I shall.

The dog comes running to meet me. She's jumped and licked my face. This alone, which has happened a thousand times before, makes me want to weep. Animals keep faith. Inside, I find Ma sitting by the oil lamp, in her hand is Sanjo's book, but she is not looking at the pages. By heart she knows this book. You could tear it to pieces, or burn it, and still she will remember every line, each word. She looks at me and says, 'It has come, Animal my dear, this is the night of Qayamat, the end of all things.'

'Ma, don't go out tonight. Tonight, you stay here, stay put. Keep the dog with you. Don't set foot outside tonight.'

She laughs at me, it's a horrible old woman's laugh that sucks and gurgles from lack of teeth, like a witch she looks, a haadal, a wild-eyed spirit of the night, her hair is tangled like the roots of a tree, incredibly old is her face, the lamp making shadows of its every line, of each wrinkle, as if indeed she's been hanging around since the dawn of time. 'Shouldn't I go out tonight? This is my night, it's the night for which I've waited so many years. Tonight Animal, it's me who's dangerous. Let the world beware.'

Well, I have no idea what she means by this, but I don't like the sound of it. 'Ma, Zafar bhai has died, the whole place will go mad. It's not safe for you outside.' I'm thinking that maybe in their fury people may turn on foreigners. Ma is well known in the Nutcracker, but who knows where her madness might take her?

'I don't want to be safe,' says she with that mad cackle. 'What do I care if I die? On this night of all nights, to die will be a blessing. Animal, the angels are here, thousands and thousands of them, they've come to make an end of this sinning, sorrowful world, tonight it will go up in flames, it will burn and shrivel into ashes and become dust. Who will mourn it? Will you? Tonight to this city, do you know who has come?'

'I don't know.' In my misery I am thinking that maybe some big politician has come from Delhi, or some fillum star. It couldn't be a nobody, could it?

'Tell me Ma, who has come? Is it the President of India?'

She lets out peals of laughter like the carillons rung by Jacotin of the nas supèrbe. 'You are so silly, Animal. Guess again.'

'Jacotin, avec son nas supèrbe,' I say, who feels like howling.

'Right you are to speak the language of the angels on this night,

Animal, they're coming for souls, mine maybe, and also yours.' It makes me shudder the way she has started saying this night, in the same way we always say that night.

'Isa has come,' says she, 'and Sanjo. I reckon they're here already. Long have I waited to see their faces, I must surely go to meet them. And do you know why they're here, mon pauvre petit? Because on this night the dead are going to come up out of the earth, like big mushrooms their skulls will push up out of the soil. Their bones will come up too, with a click-ety noise like a train on the level crossing, and then all the bones will join together and they will walk again. Tonight, mark my words, this city will be full of the dead.'

'What of those who were burned?'

'Rain will fall, their ashes will get glued together and then the people they came from will gradually reappear. God made Adam of dust, ashes will be no problem for Him. Animal, why do you think this is happening here in Khaufpur? It's because there are thousands upon thousands of dead here ready and waiting. God wants the Resurrection to get off to a good start.'

From outside Bhoora calls, 'Hurry Animal, I too must get home.'

'Ma,' I tell her. 'Ma, I love you dearly. Do not go out without me. Stay here, I will be back soon.'

'Where are you off to?' she says, her manner suddenly normal again. 'Such a child you are, nothing you've had to eat, already you're off again. Look at you, covered in bruises. And that black eye, you've been playing kabbadi again. Come, son, eat. There's a little rice, a little daal.'

'Stay here, Jara,' I command the dog, I swear if she could have nodded she would have done. Then I am back into Bhoora's auto and we are gone.

Elli looks exhausted, full of the despair of this terrible day. She climbs in beside me, closes her eyes and does not speak as we jolt out of the Nutcracker and back to Kali Parade. Another surprise. The streets are empty, the crowds of earlier have vanished, but still the weird howls are

329

still going up over Khaufpur, on this night something deep and dangerous is rumbling, the sound of people behind closed doors plotting
revenge. Twice in four hundred yards, on the road past the factory, we're
stopped by nervous soldiers with guns. Elli they eye with suspicion but
Bhoora tells them she's a doctor out on a mission of mercy. So then they
warn us there's a curfew, we must get off the streets right away. The
rumbling grows louder, and for the first time in my life I see a tank, a huge
gun sticks out of its head like the horn on a rhino beetle. When we get
to the Claw, Elli's gone without a word into her clinic. Almost before I can
dismount, Bhoora's turned his auto, headed for home. Me, I've headed
into Somraj's house for Nisha surely needs me.

Nisha does not cry, but neither does she say a word. She sits in the small
garden where the pond is now dry, the Nautapa has sucked up its water
and the fish are living in a plastic tub. On nothing her gaze is fixed. She
knows, of course. Must. She has heard the keening.

'Nisha, could I bring you something? Tea?'

'No thank you.'

'May I sit with you?'

'If you want,' she says.

'I would like.'

'Then come and sit.' So we sit, neither speaking, I don't know how she
is staying so calm. Maybe it is that screaming, praying, crying out for help,
these are things that people do when there's some hope left, but let go of
hope and and nothing is left but wind in the grass.

Our long silence is broken at last by the sound of singing. The words
I do not understand, but the meaning I catch is of such deep sadness,
maybe it is better not to understand.

Nisha stirs. 'Well,' she says, 'there's supper to prepare.'

'I will help you.'

In a small voice she says, 'It's just you and me now.' Then giving me
such a pitiful look, she cries, 'Oh Animal, why did Zafar leave me?'

330

'He was a hero,' I say, meaning it. 'He was too good for this horrible world.'

She shakes her head. 'They are wailing for Zafar, but I was the closest to him, and I cannot cry. Nearly, I was his bride. Look.' She shows me her wrists which are scratched and bruised.

'I broke my bangles like a wife should. I went to see him. I went with my father, but the tent was empty. Zafar and Farouq were gone. People said police and an ambulance had come, their bodies were taken to the hospital.'

'Did you go to the hospital?'

'Yes, but they were not there. The hospital denied they had come. So then we thought they've been taken to a military hospital, or maybe to prison, we began hoping they were still alive.'

'Did you ask the police?'

'There were disturbances. Dad said it wasn't safe to be out. We came back.'

'Your father, is he okay?'

She gives me a look. 'What is okay? It's like he's made of wood. Is that good? I don't think so. Dad is full of guilt. He says all of this could have been prevented if Elli'd had a chance to explain herself. She wanted to tell him, long ago, he says, but lacked courage. She went to Jehannum to plead with her ex, she was trying to save Zafar's and Farouq's lives.'

'But why do I still feel as if she has betrayed us?'

'I guess it's hard to trust someone,' she replies, 'if they have been keep-ing secrets from you. Some deep part of you always knows. You can never really get close to a person like that.'

I sit staring into the tub, in its green water the backs of rescued gold-fish can be glimpsed among whorls of weed. God forgive me, how many secrets have I kept from this girl?

'Nisha,' I say, taking her hand, 'Zafar asked me to look after you.'

'Thanks, but I don't want anyone to look after me.'

'You can't grieve alone.'

331

'You think I'm grieving? I was. For days I have been crying. Every tear that was in me I've cried. Of grief there's none left in me, but something worse.'

'I will help you. Let me be here with you.'

'What I feel is anger. So much anger it's going to blow my head off.'

'I too am angry. The whole city is angry.'

'But I want to rip things and tear and smash them,' says this most gentle of girls. 'I am so angry with Zafar that he did this, I'm so angry with myself that I did not stop him. Oh, I want to take a knife and carve out my womb and throw it in the street for the dogs to eat. Of what use is it now?'

'It's such feelings that are of no use, sister.'

'I'll tell you what's of no use,' she cries. 'My father's precious justice is of no use, our government's of no use, courts are of no use, appeals to humanity are no use, because these people are not human, they're animals.'

'Nish,' I say, ignoring her insult to animals, 'I will devote my whole life to making you happy.'

'How can you talk of happiness, at a time like this?'

I'm still holding her hand. 'Nisha, you yourself just now said there's only you and me. We can still go to Ratnagiri.'

'No!'

But the words are already blurting from my mouth, 'Marry me, Nisha, I'll never leave you. Babies, we'll have. I'll get educated, I'll find a job.'

'Stop it! Animal, stop! I've told you before, I will never marry you!' The rage of that day is rushing through both of us, I can feel her hand shaking. I should not say what is in my mind, I should bite it back, apologise, but already I'm gone too far, plus the hurt has been there a long time, it won't stay quiet.

'Because I am an animal, that's the real reason isn't it, that you can never marry me?'

She's wrenched her hand from mine. 'Have you gone mad? How dare you talk like this?'

'Because it's true. If I were human maybe I could be your lover. No chance of that now!'

'Animal, please!'

'I'll always be nothing but a fucking animal!'

She looks at me with crazy eyes. 'If you are an animal then fuck off and be one! Go and live in the jungle and see how much of an animal you are. Just leave me alone!'

So I'm gone, running out of that house, into the street and into this night. Behind me I can hear, or maybe I imagine, Nisha calling, 'Animal, I'm sorry, come back.' But I can't go back, not ever, for it's clear that she's revolted by the idea of marrying such a creature as me, who goes on fours and is first cousin to a hyena. How did you meet your husband? Well he was foraging in garbage bins in the old city. My head is full of screaming because I don't know what to do, I don't want to live any more. With great sobs, I find my way across the alley and sit with my back to the trunk of Elli's mango tree. What is the point of living? Everything I care about is gone, swept away in a day and a night. So fast does the world change. Zafar, Farouq, Aliya, all gone. Voices shrieking in my head are forecasting disaster. Ma, in the full ecstatic tide of madness, will be out on the streets somewhere seeking Isa. Maybe she's in the graveyards, trying to rouse the dead, telling them, come out it's time. Or maybe she's at the funeral ghat where the aghori sadhus sit with eyes like pools of blood, drinking from skull cups and eating the baked flesh of human beings, for tonight is this night the night of Qayamat which Ma calls Apokalis, a word in which is Kali's name, who's also called Ma. Yes, Ma is Kali Ma, why did I never think of this? Garlanded with bones she'll stalk the streets of Khaufpur crying the end of the world, with great strides she'll come to the factory to rouse the hungry and desperate spirits that live there, then the soldiers will shoot her. Fools, they cannot kill Ma. Ma is from the beginning of time. Ma will unstring their guts and hang their severed heads on her belt. She will drink their blood and her tongue will hang below her waist and when Isa comes she will greet him with bloody kisses and call up her beasts out of the abyss and they will let loose hell on the earth. So the voices rave at me. But I too am on the street. Maybe soldiers will shoot me. I get an idea. I will go and throw stones at the soldiers, I will defy their guns and stand in front of their tanks, and I will shout at them, come on you bastards, do your worst, I promise never to rise from the dead. I've had enough of this fucking world. Nay, if Isa came and begged me to rise up, if he promised to mend my bones personally with glue and reshape my body with his own hands, if he swore to make me straight and tall, still I would tell him to fuck off because this world is too cruel, it's too hard and no more of it do I want. Let them kill me. What do I care? Better I die, because torturing hope too will perish. How live, when Elli is going away and my back will never be straight and even Nisha who I loved above all things is gone from me? In a single day everything I care about is lost, I will throw away my worthless life. To whom shall I give my zippo? I reach into the side pocket of my kakadu shorts, my fingers encounter a hard shape, it's Faqri's box of golis. So I've slid it open and counted. Thirteen golis there are, like black goatshit pellets, it will be enough. One by one I crunch the golis, after each one I ask myself, do you want to die? Comes the reply, yes, eat one more. Another is crunched, and another. They taste bitter, yet not unpleasant. Thirteen golis I chew, my mouth like a dark cloud engulfing thirteen little black moons, a final swallow and it is done.

Four feet have I my brain is a hare my eyes are sacks of wool a gulf is where my palate was briny gutters are my cheeks a rushing and a roar is in my head from above and below voices are calling hell is burning in my guts why did I never notice before that the world is full of crazed beings? These demons running along the road carrying flaming firebrands, never have I set eyes on such creatures before. They have gathered outside the door of Elli's clinic and are calling with loud voices for Elli to come out.

'Kampani clinic, burn it down!'

How interesting. So the demons too are opposed to the Kampani. Who'd have thought they'd give a damn about our Khaufpuri affairs? Eyes glaring like eggs are oozing out of their faces. Now they've got a pickaxe and are hacking at the doors. 'Kindly exit and oblige,' calls a being who's mostly whiskered teeth. 'We wish to destroy this place.'

Of a sudden a door is gone, in its place is a dark rectangle that frames Elli, whose night clothes are shining in the moon's teary light. At the sight of her the demons become confused and whicker together in low voices.

Like the whole rest of the world, Elli doctress is angry. A fist of fire is she, and she yells at the demons to go away and leave her alone.

'Where should we go, madam?'

'Without burning this place we cannot leave.'

'Smash a window, put in fire.'

There's a sound like a lump of music shattering into shards, it is a whole raga in two seconds. Somraj comes flying out of the darkness like a giant white moth, such a fine sound he'll be wanting to catch and keep in a jar.

'Kill the bitch!'

'There will be no killing here,' says Somraj, placing himself between Elli and the demons.

'Stand aside panditji.'

'No. You shall not touch her.'

'Bhai sahib and bhaiya are dead because of her friends.'

'Those people are not her friends, bhaiya and bhai sahib were her friends.' The pandit's looking somewhat blurred, as if he's in two minds. He puts his arm around the shoulder of an equally blurry Elli and leads her across the way. The demons and their torches vanish into the door of the clinic.

I look up and see the half-moon perched in the mango tree, peering down at me through the leaves. 'I see you, Animal,' says the moon.

'I see you moon,' says the animal. 'Are you jamisponding me?'

'You are dreaming,' says the moon. 'You need to wake up.'

'I would rather dream.'

'There's a thing you must do.'

'What is this thing, O moon?'

'Wake up and find out,' it says and is disintegrated into shining pieces by moving mango leaves. The windows of the clinic are flickering orange. It comes to me that my little friend, the Khã-in-the-Jar, is inside and the thing I must do is save him.

Elli's office is alight. Flames are coiling like snakes in the corner, spitting fiery seeds at the walls.

'Oh don't hurry,' says the Khã-in-the-Jar. 'All the time in the world, me.'

'Where are you?' She must have shut him away.

'Over here you dozy cunt.'

'Where?'

'In the cupboard.'

I move towards it and suddenly I am sliding, there's liquid on the floor, it smells like rough daru, it's overpowering it makes my eyes water, I'm retching, my hands gash on something sharp, I'm slipping and sliding in pools that burn like raw hatred, I bump into something cold and slimy. It's the cyclops. His one eye stares at me. He smells like a rancid pickle.

'Leave him,' says the Khã-in-the-Jar. 'Eight we were, board members of the poisonwallah shares. Seven flasks were smashed and our friends are on the floor, any second this stuff will catch light and badoof!'

'I'll save them.'

'No no,' he says. 'By burning they'll be freed. My fear is that the flames won't reach this cupboard.'

'Then I'll save you.'

'Shabaash Animal, smash my jar too. Quick, there's no time.'

But I've disregarded the bugger's wishes. I've tucked his jar under my arm then it's out of there, fast as three feet can fly ignoring his yells I gain the street, apart from my mind spinning spiderwebs, the moon above constantly changing shape and the wolfshead gnawing my guts, things seem normal.

'Hey,' he's shouting. 'Where are you taking me?'

'You'll burn I swear but first we must have a chat.'

'Where's the time for chatting? Don't you know it's this night?'

'Shut up, or I'll be forced to do you no harm.'

This threat is very terrible to him, so his two heads glug fluid and seethe in silence. I'm out of the Claw in a flash, hiding in shadows. Various kinds of uproar can be heard, shouting coming from different parts, fires are burning, from the direction of the old city come loud bangs like gun shots. I need to avoid the main road so I'll take the short cut home. Many ways are there into the factory and I pick one on the Claw side where a small tree leans onto the wall. How to mount? Place Khã in fork of tree. Pull up. Move Khã higher. Climb. Place Khã on wall. Shift self onto wall. All the while I am muttering, 'Just a little while, we'll get home and have a talk then I am carrying my zippo I swear I'll burn you.'

'You'll regret this,' he snarls.

The clear light of the moon falls on the jar and I see with horror what it is I am carrying. The jar slips from my hands and falls, bursts, liquid gushes out. Lying on the ground inside the factory is the thing that was within, a half-rotted relic of that night.

Fleeing that cursed place through moon-licked grasses and bushes that bite, I am driven by a fear greater than snakes or dogs or men with sticks. The thing I am fleeing is more deadly than any of these and fouler than that poor creature rotting in his chemical womb. I am running from myself. I am running from the things I've done. I think of Zafar, whose death my poisons hastened, dry as a smoked fish he ended, yet right to the end how kind he was, the tears he could not shed are making my eyes watery lenses through which the world bends and bulges in unknown ways.

337

There are beings in the grass too, flitting beside me and mocking. The faces of the dead swim around me, jeering, is this that Animal who swore at us, insulted us, rebuked us for being powerless puffs of wind, mere gusset-gusts? Well, it is your turn, good it's to see you suffer, Animal, limping along with thorns in your paws and waking nightmares, look, here is the poison-khana, you didn't expect to see it, did you? You are lost in your own jungle. Come, climb it, do, and just try lording it over us this time, climb up to the top and go hang from the moon. Go on, leap off the top and grab hold of the moon. It will feel cool like ice. There, get your paws round the top of it, cling on. What, you are afraid of falling? That your back will break, that you'll die? What difference, son? Your back's already broken and you are dying. Feel the datura burning you up, the Nautapa is nothing compared to this heat which eats you from the inside.

I was right to eat the pills, I deserve to die, I should have done it sooner, made an end to myself, all of these things might have been avoided, yes it's good to be dying for at last I shall be free of myself, of grief, pain, horror, despair, self-loathing there will be an end, and whether there is resurrection or reincarnation, whatever plans angels, devils or gods may have in store, I am never coming back.

At last there is the wall again on the far side, and I'm through a hole in the bricks and ahead is the railway track and on the other side the low roofs of the Nutcracker, as I enter its alleys I sense something going on, the rumble of a crowd, voices raised in argument. What time is it? No using consulting the moon, it has slipped away to the other side of the sky. Hours must have passed. The fire in my guts is growing worse, but some clarity has returned. It will not last long for have I not swallowed thirteen of Faqri's golis? I am going to die, first I must say goodbye to Jara and to Ma.

'J'entends la voix d'une multitude d'anges et des autres êtres vivants, et leur nombre était des myriades de myriades et des milliers de milliers.' Thus is

338

the old woman shouting. She's hearing the voice of a horde of angels and other living beings, numbering millions and millions, they are crying out to god, and all the creatures of the air, on the earth and under it, in the sea, are crying. There is a tang in the air, my eyes begin to sting. Why is Ma cooking this late at night? Why is she frying chillies? Coming nearer to the tower, I begin to cough, the chillies are catching in my eyes, my throat, each breath feels like fire, matching the datura blaze in my guts. Still she shouts, 'Je regardai, et voici, parut un cheval blanc.' What are you doing you foolish old woman, yelling about white horses and crowns of victory? I know what comes next, it's the red horse whose rider has a sword to end men's gorging on one another's flesh, then a black horse, ridden by one who carries scales of justice. It is not just my eyes and guts which are on fire. There's a heat on my back, the ground around me is a mass of writhing shadows.

'Chants the voice of the madwoman, 'Parut un cheval d'une couleur pâle. Celui qui le montait se nommait la mort, et l'hadès le suivait, pour exterminer les hommes par l'épée, par la famine, par la peste, et par les bêtes sauvages de la terre.' It's a pale horse, on him's death with hell two-up behind, come they've so men may be extermined by war, famine and plagues, their bodies devoured by the wild beasts of the earth. My eyes are streaming, it is hard to keep them open, there seems to be smoke drifting, voices are shouting, 'Run, run for your lives! The factory is on fire!' I look behind, there's a glow in the sky, clouds of smoke are billowing upward. 'Run run,' the voices cry, 'the gas has come.' 'Run! Save yourselves!' 'That night has come again!' Now I know why the ground is heaving, the little light from the door of our tower shows the earth alive with snakes and other small creatures, rushing desperate to escape the flames.

Inside with the dog's Ma dressed in nun's get up, clutched to her chest is Sanjo's book, but she's not reading, who knows its every word by heart. Seeing me she cries in a loud voice, 'Come Animal, we've work to do.'

My eyes are burning so badly I can hardly see her. 'Ma, you must run.' Hardly can speak. 'Quick, to safety.'

'There's no safety,' says she. 'It's the Apokalis.' She moves to the door and stoops to go out. 'Come, the people need our help.'

Alas, knowing what must be happening in the lanes of the Nutcracker, I cannot move. Never will I forget this moment, filled with dread I'm, it's like my four feet have grown roots. Ma is standing in the doorway, waiting for me, curls of smoke are entering our tower.

'Come Animal.' Still I do not move. Ma smiles at me and says. 'Goodbye, my dear child. Always I have loved you and I always will, yes, until after the end of time itself. We'll meet in paradise.'

'Wait!' I cry, but she's turned and gone.

Jara gives me a reproachful look, then follows Ma, looking back over her shoulder as if to say, goodbye then, for never in this life shall we see each other again. And I, who am anyway doomed, who've already lost friends, love and hope, watch the last two beings I love go out into that cloud of death and have no courage to go with them. No courage have I, but I have shame. Shame drives me forward a few steps, then the poison smoke is in my face, I'm retching, tears are running down my cheeks, Ma and Jara are faint figures heading into the thickest haze, from which now fewer and fewer figures are emerging.

Then I'm jostling panic-stricken people in alleys where so thick is the fog that lamps are reduced to pinpricks. In my head is the nightmare of pandit Somraj who every night of his dreams sees Nafisubi Ali's child crying under a street light as in a brown light dying figures stumble past.

Running I'm, running, I don't know where, just to clutch onto one more hour, I do not want to let go even of these last burning moments, O lord how sweet it is, how tempting, is life.

Grey of morning comes jolting, my eyes can hardly open, there's a bad taste in my mouth, my lungs are painful, but the datura fire in my belly, that is now raging out of control, bending and warping the world, hard to accept what I am seeing, country scenes, trees, fields rushing past, amazed to be alive I'm on a truck full of people lying in huddles, their eyes raw and swollen, ahead a man is throwing up over the side, the rushing air sends drops flying back a foul spray comes blittering on my face, my own stomach's declared war on me, tearing itself apart it's, ripping me from the inside, air's gone purplish sun's risen in a ball of orange and purple light, violent, swollen and strange.

'Let me off, where are you taking me?'

'Lie still brother, they're taking you to hospital in Diwanabad.'

'No!' My gut's in hideous pain, but I am filled with revulsion for human life and human society, I want no more of it.

There is a line of forest on the hills.

'Let me down.'

'What will you do here? There's nothing here.'

'Fuck you let me down.'

The ground is weaving patterns under my feet, playing tricks on me's this earth, hot like burning coals, the hills are dancing, in the shimmer black birds with forked tails are darting. With some part of my mind I recall that this is the eighth day of Nautapa, then shame hits, plus despair. All whom I loved are gone, lost to me forever, distant is that city of disaster, its streets and alleys I knew so well, a far off and hopeless place, I will not go back, I won't, never will I return, if I am dying let me die here in the open like a beast, or else let me live here, far from people, never again do I want to look on a human face. I've kicked off my kakadus. I'll live as an animal, alone and free as an animal should, no master I'll have, no work, no duty but survival.

'Survive, will you?' The datura speaks, sitting coiled inside my gut, 'you have eaten thirteen of my dark golis, O Animal, now you shall see what you shall see.' The flames climb in my throat but can't exit, full of nothing I'm nothing full of flames, in my ear the datura sings a song:

> thou art an animal fierce and free
> in all the world is none like thee
> in fire's forge thy back did bend
> my bitter fire be thy end

'Vas te faire foutre!' Hopeless, friendless, alone, ill I may be, but I'll not be bullied. 'Fuck off!' I'm trying to speak, but my voice is a chirring cricket that hops from my tongue and is lost.

It is late afternoon when I enter the first trees, thorns, dry grasses, twigs snapping under my feet, howra hoora cries of birds, japing greenly go thus trees through, oh I'll discover my true state, die or live, animal returning to its truly home, four feet have I my eyes are stars my nose is snakes that lick their nostrils, dream lipless dreams, the sun above is like a mouth roaring out flames, the skin of my back is frying, a rod of fire is my throat, each breath is a fire-eater's gush of flame, Farouq you thought you were so great to walk across a bed of coals, try a stroll in my gut. Naked, I lie on my belly drink from a ditch and bite the sonofabitch sun, I feel like my own father whom I have never known.

Down inside me voices are speaking making no sense

seems the plant season so rare it floats, pimpish stuff in there, pimpish, leave where it's, ça fait un peu boui-boui, this is our kingdom

Shady is the forest but under its trees is no relief. I am searching for other living things, none do I see, coloured like the back of a shrike's the forest, browns and fawns, grasses dry, dry thorns, dry trunks, its leaves are

342

suffering in the heat's fierce fetch, not just in me's this agony but world. Where are you, animals, let me introduce myself? I stop and nothing's there but stirring of leaves. This ground is strange to me, gone beedi wrappers, orange peels, plastic, here are bent grasses, twigs in patterns and piles mixed with old leaves on the forest floor, shapes that curl and spiral like twists of a stair are seeds. Here's one beetle-winged, I am looking for signs left by hoof, paw, belly of snake, nothing can I find. My nose discerns only the scent of parched earth, my only fellow beings are these silent sufferers rooted in dust waiting for rain.

'Silent, say you?' sniggers the datura, 'then wait for night O Animal. Let night come, you shall hear what you shall hear.'

'What, are you still here?' The sickness is squirming in my guts like a snake. 'I do not think that you will kill me. I am stronger than you, I will defeat you.' The datura gives such a buffet of pain I go staggering my legs and arms give way I am biting the bitter soil.

'I've not yet begun,' says the datura.

Comes night plus a falling moon, caught in tangles of branches above my head. 'Should we show him?' asks a familiar voice. 'Yes, show,' says another.

'It will be wasted,' says the first. 'A great fool, he's.'

A tear drips from the moon's eye and lands on a branch. Lines of light spread in all directions, racing from tree to tree, till all the trees of the forest have silver edges, their voices are nothing I've ever heard, like deep flutes filled with water. 'Show the animal, show him what he really is.'

A light appears on the forest floor, glow's spread till it's all around me.

'Ha ha ha, so much for kidnapping, what would you like to chat about?' whispers he ex-of-the-jar. 'Datura and moonlight, not a good cocktail, and this is just the beginning. Can you imagine what's coming?'

'My own death.' Waves of sickness are pushing up inside gut heaves throat yawns jaws gape, up comes nothing.

'So Khã,' says he, 'let's talk. What shall we discuss? Death and life? This and that?'

343

The nausea is bucketing through me horrors and griefs in my belly are rioting up comes nothing. 'Don't torment me, Khã, thirteen dark moons have I swallowed and I am going to die.'

'Are you going to die, my dear?'

'I think so, Khã.'

My mouth opens a cobra slides up out of my throat its body fills my guts its tail dangles out of my arsehole every muscle in my body strives to expel it, up comes nothing.

'Just so, it's time for the zippo,' says my mate, his first head. 'Click whirr whoosh, do the needful kindly.'

Adds the second, 'And oblige.'

A datura is growing in my gut pushes forth leaves and flowers out of my mouth and out my nose. 'I don't have my zippo, Khã, I have lost it.' My tongue wags furry as a dog's tail.

'Then snap your fingers,' says he. 'It makes no difference.'

A flick of the thumb, a whooouf of blue flame, a violet flash. My little two-headed friend is no more.

'You are handsome bastards,' I tell the two tall angels that shimmer there in the moonlight.

'Don't we know it?' they laugh, and give me friendly glances. 'Free, at last, thanks to you, Animal.'

Trees are writhing in the darkness I call out are you in pain, it's me who's dying. We are not in pain we are dancing. What, dancing with joy? We have no need of joy cry the deep flutes of the trees, we are in need of water and so are you O animal. Find water if you want to live. Where can I find water on this dry hill? Go down, go up, your choice. My feet are raw with blisters, I can go no further. Then lie here and we shall wrap our roots around your bones. I need my bones, friends. Lie here, die here, we are no friends of yours, soon you will have no need of your bones.

You are an animal fierce and free
you shall see what you shall see
que ta chair devienne sèche
we shall feast upon your flesh

Above my head a monkey sits on a branch, eating a fruit it's, spitting seeds onto the earth, the fur slides from its face, revealing the skull beneath, its flesh drips in furry glowing blobs, all bones is the monkey, one by one the bones fall and lie shining in the moonlight, earth opens a brown mouth sends out a green tongue it becomes a tree gobbles the monkey's bones, tree grows tall, shining fruits appear among its leaves, a monkey sits on a branch eating the moon.

Now it's fury, I've jumped up and yelled at the trees, 'Keep your cut-price visions I'm not impressed putain con, who do you think you're dealing with I'm not just any animal I'm THE ANIMAL have some fuck-ing respect or I'll climb up and wank on you, you don't scare me.'

'Plus you don't scare us,' say the trees, joining branch to branch they're, dancing in a ring, each tree leaping to the next quicker than eye can follow, ugly selfish demonic beings they have become, they reach down and rake me with thorny claws. All the night I cannot sleep for fear of the trees which will devour me if I sleep, grasses push sharp needles into my hands and feet, coiled in my gut the datura is rolling on its back laughing,

The sun rushes up in hot smokes of red and green, gargling in my throat's a new fire of thirst, tongue's thuggish, bitter as a pheasant's heart. Mouth agape, I climb in the forest, turning in circles, from waterless agony is no escape, to it is no end. I think of Zafar whom I poisoned, strange dreams I gave him, plus pain, yet even while dying he forgave, if I meet his ghost it may not be so kind, spirit of Zafar I'll say, I too chose this death. The ache in my guts has a familiar edge, burnt in sharp blues and oranges, I know this beast that stalks within, it's my old enemy hunger, gradually its shape clears, thirsty I'm plus so hungry I could eat anything, I tear grass, chew bark, berries, dig up roots plus mushy things and gnaw them all earthy. I've ripped the petals off flowers and munched them.

Starving hunter creeps on all fours across the forest floor, dry twigs avoid, make no sound, I have spotted food, a lizard sunning on a rock, its little legs pump its fat body up and down, it has plump cheeks, a fine and meaty tail, I find a stone, fling, thud, lizard's off rock flying, I've only caught it in the ribs, it's lying panting its mouth open, a dent in its side, mine now, but the lizard's skittered away in damaged panic, me on it like Jara on a rabbit, it's wriggling under my hand. How to kill it? I can feel its heart jump, lizard eye's glaring, just bite its head off bloody, you were not made for roots, think like a tiger, let red lust close your eyes, unhinge your jaw prepare to kill.

'Don't eat me,' cries the lizard, 'I'll tell you something most important.'

'Sorry, I am too hungry to spare your life.'

'I won't taste good, If you think datura's bad wait till you taste my venoms, boy you will wish you'd never been born.'

'Already I wish that.'

'Nothing it's compared to the wishing you'll do if you eat me,' says the creature with a sad look in its eye, like it's lost hope of saving itself.

'Go then,' I say, releasing it. 'I am sorry I hurt you.'

'A broken rib may mend,' says the lizard. 'but your nature you can never change. You are human, if you were an animal you would have eaten me.'

Night comes, no food nor water have I found, moon's thinner as if it too is starving, it's a night of still air in which a chouette is calling, hoo hoo, I rest my cheek against the hairy bark of a tree and hear its slow thoughts, climb, hand over hand, into the branches and sit there, Animal alone in his kingdom. Grief comes to me, all my rage and fear empty in dry coughing sobs. I call to my fellow creatures, 'Brothers and sisters, the lizard's wrong, I am one of you, come to live with you. Show yourselves.' None come, but there's a rustling, it's the lizard whose life I spared, she

346

says, 'Hey Animal, soon you'll be a shrivelled old sack, I will creep into your dry carcase and lay my eggs around your heart.'

The voice takes you where it wants, not where you want to go. It tells you there is no deceiving, what you see you shall see, you have chosen. The voice tells me things I couldn't know, shows me stuff I don't want to see. If I could open a window and run I would but no escape there's, the window opens inward, to the visions and uncapturable beauty. The trees are tusked in Siva, I vomit rainbows, when I dung I make the earth. The voice inside me says, to enter a temple you must bring only yourself, this is why, Animal it's right that you should starve.

'Where shall I go, where shall I look?'

The voice inside me says, whichever way you turn, this is the way.

A ball of fire is rising between my eyes, whose twin's spitting flame in my gut, it's the heat of coming death, voices in my head are chattering, arguing, beyond is that other voice, which sounds deep inside, yet seems to come from outside and everywhere. I am climbing through a forest which grows greener the higher I go. Of water is no sign yet I sense it all around, I can hear the trees suckling through greedy tubes plus gurglings in the guts of unseen creatures. Why do they avoid me? 'Come out,' I cry. 'Come out and tell me, am I a man?'

'WHAT IS A MAN?' The voice roars right in my ear like a thunderclap, it flattens me. Torn in pieces I'm, parts of me break off and float away. My misty thoughts go spinning and become the moon. The glare in my eye's my eye turning into the sun, my breath's a hot wind, riding it is a tiny god drunk with his own power whose body is covered with sores, from my middle parts come gusts of air, out of my head slides the universe.

'Who are you?' I've asked, who's lying head pressed to the earth hearing a million things, stamping of ants, worms chewing grit, millipede legs whirring like drums in a parade, my stomach heaves, up comes nothing.

Now if I open my eyes there are trees and dry grasses and thirsty plants and sun, but if I close my eyes creatures of all shapes and colours are floating and drifting. The dream animals come near, one by one they approach, they don't look friendly, but even before my open eyes the world is changing, never till now have I seen trees clothed in feathers, why is grass growing from the backs of my hands? Under my four feet as I walk the earth comes into being. I do not know which way to go, do not need to know, for by turning my head from side to side the seven directions come into existence and whichever way I turn it is the way and I walk into it.

'Fuck you then!' I shout, 'I'll live alone!'

Now all of this happens in the first hour of the third day, I mean the first hour of daylight, while I'm yelling like this the sun is trying to rise. After this I've lost every trace of time, voices and creatures are gone, all I remember is being alone, naked, looking for water in that burning jungle. Weak I'm, hardly can I drag myself forward. 'Stop moving and you'll die,' drawls a new voice in my head, like it doesn't give a fuck. Hard it's to keep moving, one moment the world's on fire, the next I've begun shivering, frozen in the blaze of sun.

'Not the world, it's you who're burning,' this voice informs me. Then, as the world spins in a wreck of colours and shapes, they've all joined in, all my voices, old, familiar and new, in a chorus full of hate.

> your torment never can be eased
> for your soul it's that's diseased
> tu n'est pas animal mais bête
> your crimes we never shall forget
> and all the friends that you betrayed
> will come to curse your sorry shade

A man and a woman dressed in Khaufpuri fashion appear among the trees, they approach me, smile kindly and say, 'Poor child, you have had a horrible life. Curse the day that Kampani left us dead in the road drowned in our own blood, we are your parents, we have come to take you home.'

I find Nisha sitting on a rock weeping and she says, 'Animal, I have been looking for you all over, it's you I love after all not Zafar dead and gone, you shall have your desire for it's mine too, so do whatever you want, go ahead Animal, fuck me, stick your big cock in me.'

Elli comes to me and says, 'Animal climb up in one of these trees and I will undress so you can see my cunt and watch me touch myself and when you come down I'll straighten your back and make you into a human.'

Farouq appears before me bringing a suit and tie, says he, 'I'm sorry for all the bad things I did mate next year I'll lie down flat on the hot coals so you can walk over my body and save your four paws from burning.'

Zafar's there beside me, walking among the trees, carrying the world on his back, he smiles at me and says, 'Let me carry you too, Animal, your feet are sore, by the way I forgive all you did, because you did it out of love.'

The buffalo says, 'Here I am far from my two Italian greyhounds to offer you a big important job with the Kampani with plenty of salary plus you can ride in my car.'

Evening brings Pandit Somraj walking towards me through the trees. He's holding two birds, one per hand, squeezing them to make them sing, says he, 'No music in this world you cannot learn.'

With night comes Ma, carrying a corpse, its head she has bitten off, is stuffing its guts in her mouth, 'Are you hungry Animal, are you thirsty?'

'Fuck off! All of you! Leave me alone! '

The moon rises. By its light I reject all gods including god, all deities, avatars, godlings, I spit in the mother's milk of holy men, babas, sadhus, gurus, rishis, sufis, seers, priests, rulers of heaven and earth, I shit in the mouths of presidents, prime ministers, chief ministers, politicians, governors, magistrates, generals, colonels, policemen, kampanis, lawyers, jarnaliss, fat-wallet bastards, owners of cocks bigger than mine if any, also smaller, I curse all merchants, chai-wallahs, sellers of cloth, fruit and vegetables, pill-peddlers, magicians, pimps, doctors, sleight-of-hand conmen, beggars, keepers of dancing-bears, hunger-strikers, Khaufpuris, non-Khaufpuris, the living, the dead.

I am a small burning, freezing creature, naked and alone in a vast world, in a wilderness where is neither food nor water and not a single friendly soul. But I'll not be bullied. If this self of mine doesn't belong in this world, I'll be my own world, I'll be a world complete in myself. My back shall be ice-capped mountains, my arse mount Meru, my eyes shall be the sun and moon, the gusts of my bowels the four winds, my body shall be the earth, lice its living things, but why stop there? I'll be my own milky way, comets shall whizz from my nose, when I shake myself pearls of sweat shall fly off and become galaxies, what am I but a complete miniature universe stumbling around inside this larger one, little does this tree realise that the small thing bumbling at its roots, scraping at its bark, clawing a way into its branches, is a fully fledged cosmos.

I, the universe that was once called Animal, sit in the tree and survey the moonlit jungles of my kingdom.

'Now I am truly alone.'

Oh how strange this thing feels, so curious to touch, I'd forgotten how it grows in the hand, swells to fill my fist. Close the fingers round its stem, aim it at the stars, pump it like a shotgun to blast the night with living galaxies.

That night I died. I crawled down from that tree to find somewhere to finish. Fever was crackling in me, I was dry as a sucked-out, shrivelled orange, the lizard was waiting.

here is the sun
lewd irish nun

Of death I remember nothing.

My first knowledge of the afterlife is light sliding in between huge rocks. I am in a place where giant slabs rear from the earth and lean one on another. Fever's gone, hunger and thirst are no more, body feels light as a stalk. I know what's happened. I've died and am now a ghost. Is this heaven or is it hell? No fire's here, in the shade of the rocks it's cool. High, far above my head swallows are nesting. So weak I'm, newly born into this new life, hardly can I crawl to the entrance.

The outside world has changed. Gone is the burning heat of the Nautapa. A cool air's leaning up through the forest, each leaf on every tree is clear and sharp in a green cloud light. Across the valley trees on another hillside are churning in an invisible storm. I'm lying on my side, looking up into the sky, which is dark, above me large birds are circling. Not all the potatoes did I eat, this is what comes into my mind, together with the thought that the birds are coming down, soon their wings will cancel the light. Zafar's voice says, 'What an ingenious equation.' I look for Zafar but everything's dark. Later I become aware that I am still lying in the entrance to the cave, my face is wet. There's a sound of roaring and rushing. It's water. Rain is falling out there in the world softening the shapes of the forest, the lines of trees on the hillsides, all are misted in grey rain blowing across and water is dripping down from the rocks and pouring in white chutes down the slopes, the water is in my hands and my face and in my eyes, washing them clean, it's in my mouth, tasting like no mere miracle. Again Zafar's voice speaks to me, 'If there is heaven on earth, it is this.' So that's how I know I am in paradise. I drink and drink and drink till my stomach's hard as a melon.

Towards the end of my first day in paradise the rain clears, a red sun hangs in the west, sending long shadows into the cave. With newly wakened eyes I see what before I'd not noticed, there are scratches on the rocks, and daubs of colour that are not natural marks but like paintings done by a child's finger. There are animals of every kind, leopards and deer and horses and elephants, there's a tiger and a rhino, among them are small figures on two legs, except some have horns some have tails they are neither men nor animals, or else they are both, then I know that I have found my kind, plus this place will be my everlasting home, I have found it at last, this is the deep time when there was no difference between anything when separation did not exist when all things were together, one and whole before humans set themselves apart and became clever and made cities and kampanis and factories.

Time in paradise is like in the Nutcracker, it ceases to have meaning, suns and moons migrate into the sky and tumble into the west. Days pass, or maybe it's just one, or years, or thousands of years, I am immortal. There is nothing of me that will die. The memories of what happened to me in the forest when I was still alive are like pale forms glimmering in darkness and it comes to me what I thought was life was nothing but darkness. The time before the forest is a fading nightmare of a city of stinks and misery, I think of thousands and thousands dead in the last moments of Khaufpur. Our whole lives were lived in the dark. Those who were there with me are now in paradise, where's no Khaufpur, no India, no trace of flames, hell is not visible from here. These hills, these forests go on forever. Such thoughts are like dreams that attach themselves to this or that, to a bird flying past, or a grass stalk bent under water drops. All things speak to me. From a tiny place inside the curl of a fern comes a voice, that old voice I love, 'Now Animal, you are safe, you and all the people of the Apokalis, because *he* will shelter them, no more shall they suffer hunger or thirst, nor have to do heavy work, never again will they be tormented by the sun nor by burning winds, for he will care for them and lead them to the sources of living water, he will heal their sores and their coughs and fevers and he will wipe the tears from their eyes.'

Thud. Something's fallen near my head. High above in the arch of this jungle temple, with swallows darting round it, a beehive is hanging. On the ground is a lump of waxy bee-comb. I've grabbed it, bitten into it, honey's running between my lips down my chin, never has anything tasted so good.

Much comforted by this food and by Ma's words I sleep, in my dreams blind bearded men weep over I don't know what. Next thing sun's streaming into the cavern. I've eaten more of the honeycomb, then crawled to drink from a pool that has filled among the rocks. In this pool for the first time I see my heavenly self. My new face is skin stretched around a skull, huge and dark are my eyes, my strong chest is a rack of ribs, plus here's a great disappointment, in paradise I thought I would be upright, didn't Ma promise it? but stretch as I might I'm still bent. Plus I soon learn that in heaven just as in the earthly world is no escape from crapping, my bowels are weak and watery.

I get to wondering what has happened to all the others who died, not one of them have I seen. Somewhere in these endless jungles must be the city of god and there the poor will be gathered. Singing with joy they'll be, like it says in Sanjo's book. I eat more honey, drink water and try to sing, but although in my head I can hear music from my mouth comes nothing but croaking, like one of Somraj's frogs.

At some point I've heard leaves rustling, may be a boar, or a deer. Then such joy. It's Jara. Thrilled I'm to see her, I give a great shout, which stumbles out croaking. So she did die in that cloud of poison, surely Ma's with her, they've come to join me in heaven. Jara comes whining to the foot of the rocks. She's a loud ghost of a dog, because then she's barking, attracting other ghosts. Soon they too appear before me. Climbing up the hillside through the trees is the shade of Farouq and behind him comes a ghostly Zafar, thin and slow on his spirit feet. Of course, these two were the first to die. I am outside my rock fastness at the top of the slope, they've not yet seen me, but Jara raises her head and sniffs. Then she's leaping forward, up the hill.

'With all my strength I call, 'Farouq, you were wrong! There are bees in paradise!'

'Zafar,' comes the distant voice of Farouq. 'We have found him.'

Both of them begin to run. Behind them, other figures are appearing out of the trees. Looks like Chunaram, so he too's dead, plus Bhoora, following after these come Ali Faqri plus some lads from the Nutcracker. So Ma was right, the whole city must have perished.

Then Jara's on me, licking and whining, tail's a blur. 'Welcome to paradise,' says I as the dog jumps at me, licking my face, whining, placing her paws on my shoulders. 'What took you so long?'

Zafar's ghost comes up and stands smiling down at me and Jara. He kneels and puts his arms around me. 'By god in whom I refuse to believe, we have found you.'

'Welcome to Paradise,' says I, 'there's honey and water for all. The Apokalis and the bad times are over.'

'Fucker,' says the ghost of Farouq, all grin he's. 'So you are alive.'

I have to be honest, at the sound of his rough tongue, great gladness fills my heart. 'This is heaven,' I say happily, 'and we are all dead.'

'Cobbler's arse, do I look dead to you?' He's given me a tight hug till my bones are cracking.

'Who are you calling cobbler's arse? Bordel de merde!'

'Heap! Dungpile!'

'Type of a fart!'

Ha ha ha, we're rolling on the grass with our arms round one another, then he looks at me and says 'In the name of god in whom Zafar refuses to

354

believe, get dressed, or we'll all die of fright.' He holds out something, it's my kakadus. 'Found in a ditch. The truck driver who dropped you, he showed us the place. Eight days we've been combing these jungles.' He lifts me up and says, with a tenderness I've never before heard, 'You fucking cunt.'

'You who're the cunt,' I says. 'Don't need kakadus here. We are in paradise, where there's clean water and honey, delicious to eat, every and all things in the forest talk to you, just listen, you too will hear.'

By now they've all come up, this speech of mine they've heard in silence, then one after the other my friends kneel down and embrace me and whisper their fond greetings in my ear.

'Why Bhoora,' says Zafar, as the good auto-wallah with arms around my neck's kissed me with tears rolling, 'I am thinking this too is a chicken day.'

'What chicken?' It's Chunaram. 'Today is a kebab day. At my place. All are invited.' He takes a great breath. 'Today, kebabs are free!'

Says Farouq to me with a wink, 'See how he loves you?'

Ali Faqri says, 'Praise god you are alive. Abdul Saliq sends wishes plus safe return to Khaufpur.'

'Don't you understand?' I say to them. 'Khaufpur's gone. No more of that misery, here we are all free in paradise.'

'Animal, you just take it easy,' says one of my Nutcracker chums. 'We'll soon have you down from here.' To Zafar he remarks, 'He must have a fever.'

'Pity Elli doctress has left,' says another.

'We'll take him to my place,' says Zafar. 'He shall stay with me.'

'What? Where are you taking me? I don't want to go anywhere.'

But already they are lifting me up. 'So light he's. Hardly weighs at all.' Then we're all moving down to the trees. I weep, I struggle, I say, 'Do not take me away from here, not unless it's to the city of god.'

'Animal brother,' says Zafar kindly. He has me by a shoulder and I can see his face. 'Try to understand. You did not die. By a miracle you are alive and we are taking you home.'

'This is my home now, it's my place.'

'Then we shall come back again when you're better. You have a fever, you are starving. One more day up here you would have died.'

But still I don't get the message. For a while I've raved on about how dying was no big deal, that living in darkness and poverty was the real problem. 'Zafar, it's paradise for us. we've left behind the world of suffering.'

'Alas,' he says, 'I fear not.'

Halfway down the mountain they stop for a rest. 'Animal, are you hungry?' asks Bhoora. 'We have food.' From a bag he produces a small tiffin of rice, daal soup, pickle.

'Did Ma send it? Where is she? I thought she'd be with you.'

A look passes between them. 'Eat sparingly,' says Zafar. 'First take a little soup. We learned this following our own fast.'

Zafar says that when news of the factory riot reached him and Farouq they decided to stop their fast. 'Police came, they took us to a private clinic where the CM was waiting. He told us that rumours were flying round that we had died, he asked us to help stop the trouble.' Zafar and Farouq agreed to the CM's request on condition that the CM swore by his temple gods to listen to what they had to say, and not to do anything or make any deal without their consent. This the CM promised. They were taken by a jeep to the places where the trouble was worst, to show themselves, that they were not dead, they calmed the people and sent them back to their homes.

'What about Nisha?' says I, beginning at last to doubt. 'She knew you were dead.'

'The first place we went was the Chicken Claw, to show ourselves to Nisha and Somraj-ji. That's when we heard you had run off. Nisha begged us to find you.'

'Now I know you're lying. Nisha hates me.'

'She does not, she likes you more than me I think for she told me, "Zafar, you bring him back or don't come back yourself."'

356

'She really said that?'

'Yes, plus she told me when we found you to give you this.'

My heart fails. He hands me a cap embroidered in blue and scarlet silks.

By this gift, I lost my immortality, I knew then that Zafar really was alive and so was I. Life dropped like a heavy mantle about my shoulders and I began to weep for pity that I was to return to the city of sorrows.

When it's time to move on, they go to lift me up again.

'Don't carry me. On my own feet I'll come.'

'I've been meaning to ask,' says Farouq. 'Why did you run away and come all the way up here?' But this I don't wish to tell.

With the dog jumping round all, we move slowly down through the forest where I'd done my dying, by daylight in company of friends it seems harmless. The animals that were absent before now choose to show themselves. Farouq exclaims when he sees branches dipping beneath a troop of monkeys. Birds we see, deer in the distance, something like a giant squirrel's tail hanging out of a tree. Soft clouds of rain come drifting between the trees, by a place where water is running's laid a long white snake skin, perfect from nostrils to tip of tail. Says Zafar softly, 'hameen ast-o hameen ast-o hameen ast.'

Down by the road's waiting Bhoora's auto, he lifts me in. 'Come,' says he. 'Now we'll go home.'

Zafar and Farouq squeeze in either side of me.

'Wait! What about Jara?'

'The dog is okay,' says Farouq with a grin. 'Just look behind to see what a popular bugger you are.'

Right behind us is a bhutt-bhutt-pig full of people plus, I guess, Jara too.

'Bhoora brother,' says Zafar. 'Let's go. Back to my place.'

'No, no,' says I. 'Just take me back home. Ma must be worrying.'

There's a silence, then Zafar says, 'You need a doctor, and Elli has gone back to Amrika. We'll go to my place.'

Eyes, someone had mentioned Elli leaving, but not until now do I know that she has gone back home. 'She's not returning then.' Eyes, I'm not even thinking of my back, just sad it's that things had to end this way. 'I would have liked to say goodbye.'

'No need.' It's Zafar. Something not right about the way he says this.

'Why are you smiling, you bastard?'

'They're repairing Elli's clinic. Your mate Dayanand is there, the blue-lungi foreman's there chain-smoking beedis. It will be ready by the time she returns.'

'She's coming back?'

'See, we bring good news.'

'Zafar brother, what does this glee mean?'

Says Farouq, 'Elli went back to Amrika, but she took Pandit-ji and Nisha with her.'

'But,' says I, 'she promised her husband, the lawyer, that she would go back to him. She told me this herself.'

Says Zafar, 'She promised to go back to Amrika. She did not promise to go back to him. What it means . . .'

But I know what it means. It means the music of Elli's promise will be heard loud and joyful at her wedding. So then I'm clapping.

'Congratulations, Farouq brother. Zafar brother, to you double congrats!'

'Why double?' Grinning like he knows the answer.

'Because there'll be not one wedding but two. You will marry Nisha and I'll be there cheering. I love the pair of you. I swear, my brother, may god in whom you don't believe, be my witness.' With these words, which I had no idea would fly out of my mouth, a great peace enters my heart. 'Zafar brother, this gift which you gave me, please wear it at your wedding.'

I've given him back the precious embroidered cap.

'So after all, we won. The power of nothing rose up and destroyed our enemies.'

Says Zafar, 'When is anything ever as simple as that?'

The auto's bumping along the road that leads south to Khaufpur, behind us the hills are dwindling. The countryside is green from recent rain.

After some time Farouq asks again why I'd run away. The way he asks this, it's like there is another question hidden behind the first.

'After the factory went up, poison smoke came. Ma said it would be like that night all over again.'

'It was not,' replies Farouq. 'This time people knew what to do, they got out. Even so, three died.'

'Three? I thought it must be thousands. That fire was hell itself. It was burning my back as I ran away from the factory.'

'Three is three too many,' says Zafar. 'So you were in the factory. We thought as much.' They share a silence whose meaning I can't fathom.

As we rattle along, Zafar and Farouq tell the story of what happened in the days following the fire.

Seems that after they had extracted their promise from the CM the city returned to a peaceful state. Right away the politicians got it into their heads that since things were back to normal they should after all quietly proceed with the deal. It would have to be done in secret. They reckoned that if they did the double-cross quietly plus delayed announcing it, it would be too late to stop. Zafar and Farouq were no longer in danger of dying, it would be difficult to make another demo, plus this time police and army were ready. So a meeting was set up, it would take place not in a government building, where all kinds of eyes would see, but right in the place where the Amrikan lawyers were, in other words, Jehannum.

The morning of the meeting came. Up and down the road from the old city to the hill above the lake, police were out in numbers. Jeeps were going back and forth. Unless they were guests, people were being turned away from Jehannum. The police would stop them at the gate. Nobody could get in. If people asked why this was happening, they were told it

359

was because there'd been threats to the Amrikans. 'We are taking no chances,' the police said.

Early on that morning, a woman was seen making her way up the hill. A poor woman she was, clad from head to toe in a black burqa. No one could see her face, she must have been young, for she was tall and stepped swiftly. In her hand she carried a jhadoo, a simple broom, used for sweeping floors. When challenged at the gate, she said she was going to her work as a cleaner. Little mind they gave her because soon messages were coming to prepare for the reception of some big shots, who'd be arriving shortly at Jehannum. Sure enough, the cars soon showed up. Not government cars, mark you, the CM, Zahreel Khan and others, they all came in plain white Ambassadors, one by one they disappeared inside.

What all happened next, the world learned from these folk themselves. The shameful meeting began in a room with a big table, the four Amrikans were on one side, the politicians on the other. They had begun their arguing and haggling when without warning their eyes began to sting. An evil burning sensation began in their noses and throats, a little like the smoke of burning chillies, it caught nastily in the throat, it seared the lungs, they were coughing, but coughing made it ten times worse. Something was in the room, something uninvited, an invisible fire, by the time they had realised this it was already too late. These big shot politicians and lawyers, they got up in a panic, they reeled around, retching, everything they did just made the pain and burning worse. Tears streamed from their eyes, hardly could they see. One of the lawyers was trying to vomit, the rest of them ran in panic. They rushed from the room, jostling in the doorway each man for himself, the buffalo it seems being too bulky to rush, was left behind while the others scrambled to save their skins. These Kampani heroes, these politicians, they were shitting themselves, they thought they were dying, they thought they'd been attacked with the same gas that leaked on that night, and every man there knew exactly how horrible were the deaths of those who breathed the Kampani's poisons.

Says I, 'It's poetic justice of a fully rhyming kind.'

But Zafar says that poetic justice, rhyming or not is not the same as real justice, but being the only kind available to the Khaufpuris was at least better than nothing. So that person must have thought, who had entered the hotel and carefully emptied a bottle of stink bomb juice into the air conditioner.

'Was this your doing?' I ask Zafar.

'It was not,' he says. 'We knew nothing of it until afterwards. We were busy searching for you.'

What made the whole thing fully grand was that someone had tipped off the press, they were waiting with their cameras when these goons stumbled out into the lobby. Once the secret was out, the deal was dead. The Kampani was saying that it was the victim of terrorism, the culprit should be prosecuted and locked up for years, but the jarnaliss took a different view. They said that one stink bomb, however disgusting, could not compare to the terror the Kampani had brought on the people of Khaufpur, plus how could the Kampani bosses demand that anyone should be prosecuted while they were themselves refusing to appear before the Khaufpur court?

Not a soul knew who had done it. At last police remembered the woman in the burqa. The hotel staff were questioned, but none of them knew who she was. One or two had seen her with her broom. She spoke to no one. Soon after the start of the meeting this same woman left the place and went away down the hill. Nobody paid her any attention, all that witnesses could say of her was that she was tall, plus carried herself like one who knew what she was about. p. 67

This mystery woman who had killed off the Kampani's deal, this heroine, for so she was in the kingdom of the poor, how did she so completely vanish? All the city wanted to know, plus many beyond in Amrika. Intelligence wallahs were crawling all over the bastis.

'Never will they find her,' I cry. 'See the Nutcracker, how the houses lean together, open in and out of one another, where better to hide

361

something than in a labyrinth with no doors? Cops enter here, she's gone that way, secret police arrive there, she's back here, and which police-wallah, secret, or dead secret, will dare to twitch aside the veil of a respectable Hindu lady or ask a Muslim woman to remove her burqa? Never are they going to find her, not if they search a thousand years.' I've begun laughing. 'In just this way did Ma escape from Père Bernard.'

'It was not Ma,' says Zafar sharply. 'Animal, whatever other name may come to your mind, don't say it.'

Farouq says, 'Animal, there's another thing you must not mention. Police are asking how the fire in the factory started. Don't ever say you were in there.' From his pocket he gets something and hands it to me. 'We found this inside the factory.'

It's my old zippo, charred black, twisted by fire.

I'm staring at my zippo, wondering how it could have dropped inside the factory, then it dawns. 'But are you thinking that I started the fire? I could not have, I had lost my zippo, I did not have it with me, I swear. I know this for sure, because when I was in the forest, when I burned the Kha . . .' And that's when doubt struck, plus horror, for I could recall the datura playing tricks, laughing at me.

'We've told no one. If you have any sense, neither will you.'

'You thought that's why I ran away.' I'm remembering that little silence, after they'd asked me this.

'We don't think anything,' says Zafar. 'You lost it, it wasn't you, that's that.'

As the auto approaches the edge of the city there is a way off to the right which leads to the Nutcracker. This is where I've assumed we will go first, but when we reach the place the auto carries on past.

'Why this way? Are you not taking me back to my place? I have to see Ma.'

'Tonight at least,' says Zafar, 'you will stay with me.'

'But why? Ma will be worrying.'

'I'll explain everything when we get back. You need a bath, sleep, when you wake up tomorrow, then we'll talk.'

Then it strikes me that whenever I mention Ma there's this little pause, and they change the subject.

'Zafar! Please tell me! Where is Ma? What's happened to her?'

So at last comes out the tale which I myself could have supplied had I not willed myself to blindness.

'Animal, Ma did not leave the basti. She was in there till the end, help-ing other people get out, cover up their eyes. She did not protect herself against the gas, plus people who saw her said she was singing, she took the gas deep in her lungs.'

'But she is okay?' I cry in a voice to my own ears like a child's.

Farouq shakes his head. 'Sorry, mate.'

Zafar says, 'People are saying she and Huriya Bi were heroines, saints, some are talking of erecting a statue to them. Where did they find such courage, I'll never know.'

'So Huriya makes two,' says I, with tears arriving. 'Who's the third?'

But already I know what they are going to tell me. When Ma went into the basti she headed straight to the house of Huriya to warn them that if they stayed they would die. Already the air smelt of burning chillies, people were coughing. Huriya refused to let Ma go alone, she took a loving leave of her husband Hanif and their little Aliya, then she went with Ma. Many people witnessed this, dozens told how Ma and Huriya moved ahead of the cloud, warning people to get out. They were last seen heading towards the factory. Those who heard reported that Ma was calling out in loud, clear and perfect Khaufpuri.

'The third is old Hanif, isn't it? He stayed with Aliya, he would not have left her.' Then's left only to wonder how all the grief and pity in the world can force their way out of two eyes.

'Farouq,' I say at last, 'you asked why I went to the jungle and I would not tell you, but I will now though it'll enable you to tease me forever.'

Then between the double disgrace of sobs and snot out it all comes, how I had tried to comfort Nisha and made that clumsy offer of marriage, which she scorned, how I had said it was because I was an animal, how she got angry with me. 'Better it would have been, friends, had you not found me, for I don't think I can bear to go on being an animal in a world of human beings.'

Whatever reply I might have expected, it wasn't what I got, which was two pairs of arms about me, while Farouq's in one ear whispered, 'Animal, I swear I will never be rotten to you again,' and in the other Zafar's saying, 'Animal, my brother, you are a human being. A full and true human being.'

'Why are you saying this?' I've snivelled.

Says Zafar, 'Fool.' With that he's pressed his lips to my head and all three of us are in tears.

It's now we arrive at the level crossing near the start of the Nutcracker, the one where the railway line runs past the factory, where I carried Aliya on my back. Our auto's waiting at the closed barrier. We are on the left side of the road. On our right a big truck comes and blocks the other side. The long train goes through, 2652, Sampark Kranti Express. When it has passed we see that behind the further barrier a crush of autos, bhutt bhutt pigs, buses etcetera is also fully blocking the road. The two barriers lift, both sides stare at each other, then all rush forward at once until we are firmly stuck in a muddle of horns and curses.

Says Zafar, 'Welcome home.'

So I got it back, my familiar life, I have it back. Everything the same, yet everything changed. After staying three days with Zafar I returned to the tower where I'd lived with Ma. Time passed, the travellers returned from Amrika, in due course I danced at their weddings. All live together now in Pandit-ji's house, I still have my lunch there every day.

Eyes, what else can I tell you? Life goes on. It will take time, so we're told, to appoint a new judge in the case, the hearing's again been postponed, the Kampani's still trying to find ways to avoid appearing, but

Zafar is confident we'll get them in the end. There is still sickness all over Khaufpur, hundreds come daily to Elli doctress's clinic. Abdul Saliq stands at the Pir Gate telling the low-souled to fuck off and die, Farouq's still a pain in the arse, Chunaram has various new scams, Faqri's doing good business, the factory is still there, blackened by fire it's, but the grass is growing again, and the charred jungle is pushing out green shoots. Moons play hide and seek in the pipework of the poison khana, still the foreign jarnaliss come.

Three weeks ago, a fat package arrived, covered in blue and red Amrikan stamps it was, and addressed to Animal, Esquire c/o Elli at the clinic. Inside were many forms, plus a letter with good news for me, money has been found, my operation is booked. Elli was delighted, a huge hug she gave me and said that soon I won't know myself. Zafar says he'll help me to get a passport, in a couple of months I'll leave for Amrika. Elli and Nisha will accompany me. All I have to do is sign a paper.

Long have I sat with this paper under the old tamarind tree that was Ma's parlour. Thought and thought I've, asked aloud for advice, my voices had none to offer, but began their crazy hissing, khekhe fishguts noises. It's then I've remembered the tape mashin in the wall. I will tell this story, I thought, and that way I'll find out what the end should be. I'll know what to do. When I started speaking, when I heard dead Aliya's voice calling, it was like she and the others who are no more came back to be with me. My dear ones, heroes of my heart. Eyes, I can't tell you how I miss them, until I die this wound will never heal. They've been here through every minute of this telling. Ma's here with me now, sitting smiling she's, calling me son. Let me clear my eyes of dust and rainbows. Yes, I can see her. 'We'll meet in paradise,' she says. I know that one day I will meet her there.

Eyes, here's what I'm thinking, and this I'm speaking to the mashin, I've told to no one but you. Of the cash I earned from Zafar and Co, which was four hundred bucks a month, each day I spent only four. In a tin

365

inside the scorpion wall is more than ten thousand rupees. Eyes, it was for my operation, but now that cash, plus a little persuasion from Farouq's friends, will go to buy Anjali free and she will come to live with me. See Eyes, I reckon that if I have this operation, I will be upright, true, but to walk I will need the help of sticks. I might have a wheelchair, but how far will that get me in the gullis of Khaufpur? Right now I can run and hop and carry kids on my back, I can climb hard trees, I've gone up mountains, roamed in jungles. Is life so bad? If I'm an upright human, I would be one of millions, not even a healthy one at that. Stay four-foot, I'm the one and only Animal. What reply would you give Elli?

I am Animal fierce and free
in all the world is none like me

Eyes, I'm done. Khuda hafez. Go well. Remember me. All things pass, but the poor remain. We are the people of the Apokalis. Tomorrow there will be more of us.

(Some common Hindi words listed here have a specifically Khaufpuri twist, and have different meanings in other parts of India. *ñ* signifies a nasal twang, as in French *noñ*)

aaj kahaañ chalogé? – Where are you off to today?

alaap – slow opening exploration of a raga's scale

Aawaaz-e-Khaufpur – the Voice of Khaufpur

abba – father

achchha – okay

aghori – ascetic devotee of Siva, typically naked, whose meditation is death

Ambassador – Morris Oxford car, made in India under licence

Amrika -America

anaar – pomegranate

arré – an exclamation, like 'hey!'

Ashara Mubarak – the eve of the 10th of Muharram

asteen ka saamp – literally the snake up your sleeve, traitor

baar sau chees -Animal's nonsense inversion of chaar sau bees (q.v.)

bada batola – a braggart, big mouth

badmaash – rascal

baingan – aubergine

baingan bharta – aubergine baked on coals, peeled, mashed and spiced

bakra banaana – to scapegoat

bakwaas – nonsense

barfi – milky sweets, of a fudge-like texture

basti – literally village, but in Khaufpur means a poor community

battameez kutté, main tumhe nasht kar doonga – shameless dog, I'll destroy you *beedi* – leaf-rolled cigarette

behanchod – sisterfucker

bhai, bhaiya – brother, often used as a term of affection as in Zafar bhai

bhang – intoxicating drink made from cannabis leaves

bhatt-bhatt sooar – 'bhutt-bhutt' pig, a large three wheel vehicle, it can carry thirty people and gets its name from the noise it makes and its ugly upturned snout above the front wheel

bhayaanak rasa – the emotion of dread, terror

bhel-puri – a popular street snack

Bhimpalashri – afternoon raga, Bb->C Eb E G Bb C, C Bb A G F Eb D C

bhonsdi-ka – fart-born

Bilaval – raga, whose scale is almost identical with western C major scale

biryani – a dish of meat in rice

Brahma – in Hinduism the Creator god

burkha – the black head to toe robe with eyegrill of some Muslim women

chaar sau bees – 420, refers to section 420 of the Indian Penal Code which deals with cheating

chuna lagaana – to deceive someone, to make an idiot of them

cha-hussain – a gullible fool, someone who's taken for a ride

chai – tea

chai chappa chai – a song from the film *HuTuTu*, 1998

chakra – circle

channa – chickpeas

chapaat-zapaat – nonsense phrase made up by Animal to signify excitement

chapaati – flat bread, roti

chataka – a kind of swallow, said to drink only raindrops

daal – lentils

dada – godfather, criminal ganglord

dadi – grandmother

daru – crudely distilled liquor

datura – Datura strammonium (Jimson Weed), a highly poisonous plant

Deshkar – raga of scale C D G->E G G->A C, C Bb->A Bb->A G->E C

dhaap – as the sound suggests, a heavy slap

dhaivat – sixth note of the Indian scale, equivalent of 'la'

dha pa ga – notes of the Indian system, sa re ga ma pa dha ni sa

dholak – double ended drum slung round the drummer's neck

dikhlot – good looking

elaichi – betel nut, see *supari*

enteena ko strain karo – strain your antenna, ie think harder

fataak – bang! crack!

fillim khatam – lit. film over, you've missed it

frangipani – Plumeria rubra (indica), fragrant white or pink whorled flowers

galla mandi – vegetable market

gandhara – third note of the Indian scale, equivalent of 'mi'

garooli – Animal's nonsense word for a cigarette

gaya zamaana – past age

ghurr-ghurr – to stare

ghusspuss – usually whispering, but here means the beast with two backs

goonda – thug, heavy, muscle

government-waali – of the government

guftagoo – conversation

gulli – narrow alley

gup, gupshup – shooting the breeze

gutka – perfumed and sweetened chewing tobacco, a speciality of Khaufpur

guttu ghumana – to charm, or cast a spell on someone

guzz – one of Elli's rare mistakes, she meant *ghuss*, or squeeze

haathi – elephant

369

hashish – cannabis resin

hindi mein samjhaun? – should I tell you in Hindi? ie do I have to spell it out?

holi – Spring festival of colours

imli – tamarind

Inglis – English

Isa – Jesus

isayi – Christian

ishtoo – stew

itraana – to be a bit too clever, protest too much

jaan – life

jaanvar – animal

jahā jaan hai, jahaan hai – while we have life, we have the world

jahaan – the world

jarnail – corruption of English 'general'

jhadoo – household broom, made of a bundle of long grass stems

jugaad – a great idea, a jugaadu, a genius of good ideas

juloos – demonstration march

jungli – wild

kaané – cross-eyed

kabbadi – a rough game, involving wrestling opponents to the ground

kachambar – cucumber chunks with pepper and lime juice

Kali – Hindu mother goddess, dark goddess of death and destruction

kameez – long loose shirt, usually worn over *shalwar*

kankana – ever youthful, full of energy

karnail – corruption of English 'colonel'

khañ – Khaufpuri term of familiarity like 'mate'. See *yaar*.

khaañsi – a cough

kheer – a milky pudding

khuda hafez – lit. God protect you, in Farsi. Used as a farewell.

KLPD, khade lund pe dhoka – betrayal of the erect dick, used of disappointments *kismiss* — what English sounds like to non-English speakers

kulcha — flat breads, thicker than a chapatti, not as thick as a naan

kurta — fine embroidered muslin shirt worn by men and women

kushti — wrestling

kutiya ki aulad — son of a bitch

kya main Hindi mein samjhaun — See *Hindi mein samjhaun?*

kyō khā? — So, friend?

laal imli ka gataagat — tamarind pieces in salt and spices, sold as a chew

laat sahib — a big shot, corruption of English 'Lord sahib'

langur — long-tailed monkey

lassi — a yoghurt drink

latkan — a helpmeet, a benefactor, a close mate

look london talk tokyo — a case of a bad squint

Lukhnawi — from Lucknow, a city renowned for its courteous speech

lund — schlong, dick, penis

lund latkayé — with dick dangling

lund pasanda — the dick's favourite

madhyam — fourth note of the Indian scale, equivalent of 'fa'

Mala Sinha — film actress

Malkauns — serious raga of the night,

marsiya — a Muharram song about the martyrdom of Imam Hussein

masjid — mosque

maut pade — lit. may you die, means to hell with you, can be a greeting

mazaaq — fun, a fun jape

mehboobi — beloved

mela — fair

miyañ — polite word meaning gentleman, a cultured person

muharram — Shi'a festival of mourning for the death of Imam Hussein

munsipal — municipal

murgi-ka-panja — Chicken claw

musaafir — traveller

naala — an open drainage canal

naan — flat unleavened loaf

namaaz — a Muslim's five times daily prayers

naqsheen katora — one whose face is scarred by smallpox

nasha — intoxication

Naya Adalat — the new courthouse, which is two hundred years old

neem — Azadirachta indica tree, bitter and astringent, used in herbal remedies

nishada — seventh note of the Indian scale, equivalent of 'ti'

õ — nasal o, identical to the last syllable of French Proudhon

oot pataang — nonsense

ous raat — that night

pancham — fifth note of the Indian scale, equivalent to 'so'

pandu — contemptuous name for a policeman

qasam Khuda ki — by god

raakhee — a token tied by a girl on the wrist of a boy she regards as a brother

raal tapkana — to drool, but in Khaufpur to stare, casting the evil eye

raat-ki-rani — lit. Queen of the Night, night jessamine, cestrum nocturnum

Rajshree — film actress

Rampuri knife — switchblade with serrated edge, synonymous with gangsters

Reshma — film actress

risabha — second note of the Indian scale, equivalent of 're'

romanchik — literally hair-raising, causing tiny hairs to stand on end

roti — flat bread, chappati

sa re ga — equivalent of do re mi in the Indian scale

saala, saalé — used like English 'bloody', (literally brother in law)

sadak chhaap — street-stamped, used of street kids, hardened by that life

Sadda Miyā ki tond — the belly of Sadda Miyā, a self-important person

sadhu — a Hindu ascetic, one who has renounced the world

sahib — title of respect, signifying a chief or boss

santoor — large zither

Saraswati — Hindu goddess of music and literature

sarauta — Nutcracker

sardarji — a Sikh man

sargam — the Indian solfage, sa re ga ma pa dha ni sa

shabaash — Well done

shadja — First note of the Indian scale, equivalent of 'do'

shalwar — a pair of light loose trousers fitting closely round the ankles

shalwar kameez — long loose shirt worn over a pyjama, with a scarf

shamiana — a marquee tent, usually bright and heavily decorated

Shammi Kapoor — film actor

Shatrugan -Shatrugan Sinha, well known film villain

shayiri — poetry, typically in a recital or contest

sherwani — a fancy embroidered tunic

Siva — Hindu god of dance, music, etc, he is also the great destroyer

supari — small pieces of betel nut, sweetened, used to freshen the breath

taal — lake

talaiyya — pond

tamaasha — hoohah, spectacle

tapori — a loafer, a spiv

tauba tauba tauba — prayer to Allah meaning 'forgive'

thook — a spit

topi pehnana — to make a dickhead of someone

utar dena — to make someone else pay

Vilayat — Europe

vintage car — an older person who likes hanging around with the young

wah wah — wow, bravo, bravissimo

wali saheb — used of one who is simple-minded

Waqar and Wasim — Waqar Younis & Wasim Akram, Pakistani swing bowlers

x-ray — skeletal, how Zafar and Farouq looked during the hunger strike

yaar — friend, chum, used like the English 'mate'

Yavanapuri — morning raga

yoga sutras — classical treatises on yoga, the most famous is Patanjali's

zabri — prick, Lebanese slang Animal picked up who knows where

zapaat — long and thin, like Zafar's nose, a kingsize conk

zari-work — intricate embroidery with gold and silver thread